Forge Books by
Carole Bellacera

BORDER CROSSINGS
SPOTLIGHT
EAST OF THE SUN, WEST OF THE MOON

East of the Sun,
West of the Moon

Carole Bellacera

TOR®

A TOM DOHERTY ASSOCIATES BOOK
NEW YORK

This is a work of fiction. All the characters and events portrayed in this book are either products of the author's imagination or are used fictitiously.

EAST OF THE SUN, WEST OF THE MOON

A Tor Book
Published by Tom Doherty Associates, LLC
175 Fifth Avenue
New York, NY 10010

www.tor.com

Tor® is a registered trademark of Tom Doherty Associates, LLC.

ISBN: 0-765-34029-1
Library of Congress Catalog Card Number: 20011023253

First edition: August 2001
First mass market edition: July 2002

Printed in the United States of America

0 9 8 7 6 5 4 3 2 1

To My Friend, Lana Kay Quinn

YOU'RE ALWAYS WITH ME

Acknowledgments

To Tammy Stuart and Hope Tarr for reading
this manuscript and giving me insightful feedback.
To Jill Grosjean for championing it.
To my editor, Stephanie Lane, who is always
such a delight to work with.
And, of course, to my family, Frank, Leah and Stephen
for the endless support.

Prologue

January 1990

A light snow had begun to fall in midmorning, but it wasn't the weather that made Leigh change her plans to meet Ellen for lunch in Georgetown. In fact, she had every intention of keeping her appointment. After showering and slipping into a satin kimono, she'd opened the medicine cabinet and grabbed the plastic bottle of contact lens disinfecting solution only to find it empty. Later, she would look back on that moment with a sense of irony. Incredible that an empty bottle of ReNu would be the start of a chain of events that would irrevocably change her life.

She knew Bob kept an emergency bag packed and ready for his frequent impromptu trips back to Ohio. This time, however, he hadn't come home to get it. He'd flown directly to Cleveland from National Airport along with his administrative aide, Rebecca D'Andrade. A two-day trip, he'd told Leigh during a hurried phone call from his office on Capitol Hill. No eyebrows raised at home. Leigh, after twenty years of marriage to a politician, had grown quite used to his chaotic schedule.

But now, as she searched through his emergency bag for his bottle of ReNu, she found something that *did* raise her eyebrows.

She turned the box over in her hand, squinting to compensate for her nearsightedness. The photo of a leather-clad buxom blond beauty pouted out at her. It took her a moment to register the label: Rough Rider brand condoms. For a full minute, Leigh stared at the box, perplexed. What was wrong with this picture?

A condom package in her husband's travel bag.

It was like a mathematic formula that didn't compute. Or when it *did* compute it still seemed completely illogical, at least for a few seconds. Then it hit her full force with the impact of a punch in the stomach.

Condom package + her tubal ligation ten years ago = Betrayal.

It wasn't just the realization that Bob and his Rough Riders must've been on an extremely friendly basis with Rebecca, a fertile young redhead whose typing speed was considerably lower than her bra size. It was much more than that. Bob hadn't touched Leigh sexually in months. It had started with occasional instances of impotence. A combination of hard work and stress, he'd claimed. There was no need to see a doctor; it would work itself out. Months passed, and Leigh eventually gave up trying to interest her husband in sex. She was forty years old, and a celibate wife.

Now, with the discovery of the box of condoms, she had stumbled upon her husband's ultimate betrayal. Apparently, he was impotent only with her.

Leigh dropped the Rough Riders back into Bob's travel bag. Her fingers felt dirty from contact with the box. *What does a wife do in this situation?* she wondered. She heard a sound at the open doorway of her bedroom. Felt his eyes upon her. She looked up, and there he stood.

Erik.

Her heart pounded as she recognized the brooding expression on his lean handsome face. Even without her contacts, she could see the way his blue eyes centered on the rise and fall of her breasts under the thin fabric of her kimono. For months, she'd fought off a consuming attraction to the Norwegian. Telling herself it was wrong; she was a married woman. A *good* woman who'd always been faithful to her husband. Yes, even after he'd stopped being a real husband to her. She was a good mother who always put her children first.

And Erik? He was too young. He was a guest in their home, a friend of her college-age son. But he wanted her; he'd made that much clear. And *God!* She could no longer deny that she wanted him just as much.

Studying him, she asked herself again. *What does a wronged wife do now?*

Part One

East of the Sun

1

July 1989

"Mark, you have truly lost your mind."

Leigh tossed the flyer back to her nineteen-year-old son. "You don't think I have enough to do? I'm working on deadline to get these illustrations to Ellen. Aaron's scout troop sees me so much they're considering me for membership, and Mel has me running a chauffeur service between here and the mall. And now, you want me to host a Scandinavian exchange student for an entire year?"

Mark gave her his famous pleading puppy-dog look, one he knew she was susceptible to. "It would be great for my sociology class. Think of what it could teach me to have a foreign student living with us."

Leigh sighed and turned back to her drawing table. "That argument might wash if we were talking about a student from Zimbabwe." She darkened the outline of a plump rabbit with her charcoal. "But Scandinavia isn't much different from America in culture."

Mark ran an exasperated hand through his thick, dark brown hair. "Will you at least think about it? You've always talked about how much you want to go to Europe. Having a European in the house would be almost as good as going there."

"But, Mark, a *year*. That's a long time to have a stranger living with us."

"He wouldn't be a stranger for long. And if you're worried about his character, you've got to know what it takes to be a graduate exchange student. We're not talking about a slacker here."

"That's not what I'm worried about." A wry smile flickered on her lips. "You keep saying *he*? Isn't it possible our houseguest could be a girl?"

"That thought *did* occur to me." A teasing light sparkled in Mark's brown eyes. "I've read about those hot Swedish ladies."

Leigh leaned back and stretched her aching muscles. "Don't believe it. I'm sure all the girls in Sweden aren't blue-eyed blondes with lush bodies."

"Does this mean you'll think about it?" Mark wore a smug look on his face as if he knew he'd already won.

It screamed to be wiped away.

"Your father probably won't go for it. You know how busy he is."

It worked. The smug look disappeared and frustration replaced it. "That's just the point. He's never here. He's either on the Hill or away on some business trip. He probably wouldn't notice if you moved in a whole *army* of exchange students."

"Don't get smart. Anyway, we'll still have to discuss it with him." Leigh dismissed him, turning back to her sketch. "As soon as I get a chance, I'll mention it."

His dark eyebrows lowered. "You'll probably have to make an appointment with him."

"I *said* I'll talk to him. That's all I can do."

"Thanks, Mom." He gave her an endearing smile.

Leigh felt her heart melt. Mark's smile always did that to her—and he knew it. With an affectionate ruffle of her ash-blond hair, he left the room. She sat for a moment staring at her unfinished illustration. It was for a new children's book due out at Christmas. In another week or two she'd be ready to drop it off to Ellen. The illustrations would appear in Hydra Kouripoulous's picture book, the last six of which Leigh had been commissioned to illustrate. With the publication of each one, her sense of satisfaction had grown, and even Bob's patronizing attitude toward her "hobby" didn't diminish the accomplishment she felt. Her art was a career to her, but somehow, her husband had never quite accepted that.

Leigh stood and walked over to the window seat overlooking the gently rolling hills and knolls of Northern Virginia. In the distance among the tall oak trees, she could see one of the attractions of the three acres of land they owned, a flowing brook that meandered through the property and ended with a small cascading waterfall into a rock-carved pond. It was one of her favorite places to sit and read or sketch . . . when she had the elusive spare moment.

With a sigh, she turned from the window. No use putting it off any longer. It was time to put down her pencils and charcoal and go downstairs to start dinner. With one last glance at her unfinished sketch, she descended the winding stairs from the loft studio into the bedroom and jogged downstairs to the kitchen. It was a room that, most of the time, filled her with delight. A spacious country kitchen with an island cooktop and sink. Plenty of cabinet space including a corner lazy Susan and counters of slate blue Mexican tile to match the flooring. But today, her beautiful and functional kitchen gave her no pleasure. Somehow, Washington's hot humid summers were not conducive to gourmet cooking, even to the most adventurous of chefs.

But hungry kids were hungry kids, and Leigh was determined they wouldn't live off McDonald's hamburgers all summer. As she browned the chopped sirloin for lasagna, the back door swung open.

"Hi, Mom."

Her ten-year-old son, Aaron, stepped into the kitchen, followed closely by Ivan, the family golden retriever.

"Hi, babe. Close the door. You're letting the hot air in."

Aaron acknowledged her command by slamming the door fiercely, sending a shaft of pain through her skull. "What's for dinner?"

Leigh glanced at her son. "What've you been doing?"

Aaron's normally shiny blond hair was dark with sweat and

black grime. His face and clothing appeared to be covered with the same gruesome substance.

"Nathan and me were playing war games down by the creek," he said, scratching the back of his filthy neck. "We were killing Arabs."

Leigh grimaced. Amazing how much he sounded like his father. "Aaron, I don't like hearing things like that from you. It's vulgar and racist, and I won't have it."

"But Dad says it," he protested.

Leigh gritted her teeth. "Like I said, it's vulgar and racist." *I may not be able to stop Bob from spouting off his firebrand politics, but I'll be damned if I have listen to my ten-year-old mimicking him.* Aaron shrugged and reached for the cookie canister. Leigh lunged for it, grabbing it first. "No, you don't. It's too close to dinner."

"Jeez, Mom. I'm starved."

"Tough. Dinner will be ready in an hour. Why don't you and Nathan go swimming? He can stay for dinner."

Aaron's face brightened. "Okay." He ran for the back door.

"Get cleaned up first." Leigh called after him, but he was already gone. With a sharp bark, Ivan leaped up against the screen door and watched him go.

After Leigh popped the lasagna into the oven, she stepped outside to water the peonies planted along the back of the house. *Like walking into a sauna,* she thought, as the sticky humid air enveloped her. At that moment, Melissa appeared with her best friend, Andrea. With shining blond hair, the fifteen-year-old girls were almost carbon copies of each other, especially since their wardrobes apparently were interchangeable. Andrea was wearing a sleeveless red-plaid shirt—the same one Leigh had bought for Melissa only a few days ago.

"Hi." Melissa wore the terminal expression of boredom she'd acquired since turning thirteen. "We'll be up in my room till dinner's ready. Oh, it *is* okay if Andi eats with us, isn't it?"

Leigh smiled. "Sure. What have—?" The girls turned to go into the house. "Hey, not so fast. I haven't seen you all day. What've you two been up to?"

Andrea grinned sheepishly. "Oh, you know . . . hanging out . . ." Her reply was drowned out by a shriek that blasted through the air. Two wiry bodies bolted from around the corner of the house and jumped into the swimming pool with a loud splash.

Melissa shrieked as pellets of chlorinated water saturated her neat miniskirt. She turned furiously to her mother. "Mom. Did you see what that little monster did?"

Leigh laughed. "What are you, a witch? Think you're going to melt?" She twisted her fingers into claws and grimaced. *"I'm mellltting . . ."*

Melissa rolled her eyes. "Mom, please." She looked over at her friend. "She's *so* lame!"

Leigh grinned and turned back to the flowers. "Why don't you two go for a swim?"

"With those two little brats in the pool? Forget it. Come on, Andi, let's go listen to *Guns N' Roses*. Have you seen their new video? It's so cool. . . ." Her voice trailed away as she led Andrea into the house.

Leigh turned off the hose, stood back, and glanced at her watch. Surely Bob would be home any minute. But then, just as she stepped into the house, the phone rang, and she knew that they'd be eating without him once again.

2

Leigh watched the lightning bugs flicker in the darkness. The summery smell of charcoal lingered in the humid night air. The neighbors had cooked out again. From Melissa's room on the second floor, rock music throbbed through the closed windows. Aaron had disappeared with Nathan shortly after dinner, and Mark was out with his girlfriend, Vicki. Bob still wasn't home.

Working late again. She should've known better than to expect him home for dinner . . . just because it was Friday.

Something had come up, he'd said. Something always did on Capitol Hill.

"Mom?"

Aaron stood just outside the back door.

Leigh brought the lounge chair to a sitting position. "Hi, hon. I thought you were off with Nathan."

"He had to go home."

His voice sounded strange. She peered at him closely. "Aaron, what's wrong?"

"Nathan's dad is taking him camping to Big Mother for the weekend. And he said it was okay if me and Dad go with them. But he's still not home, is he?"

Leigh felt the urge to take the boy in her arms, but she knew better than to try it. These days, whenever she so much as gave him an affectionate smile, he'd protest, "Mom, you're *embarrassing* me." Still, she wished there were a way she could wipe that look of disappointment from his face.

"He was held up at a meeting," she said lightly. "You know how it is with him, Aaron. He's explained what his work is like."

"Yeah, I know. He's an important congressman, and he helps make the laws for our country."

"Right. Why don't you come here and sit with me?"

She was surprised when he did. He sat on the edge of her lounge chair and stared down at his beat-up sneakers. Leigh reached out and ruffled his dark blond hair.

"But you know what I don't understand?" He gazed up at her, confusion shimmering in his blue eyes. "Nathan's dad is a surgeon. He takes people's hearts out and fixes 'em. How come *he* has time to take Nathan camping, but Dad doesn't?"

Leigh knew Aaron expected a reply. Trouble was, she couldn't think of one. *Why, indeed?* It was a question she'd often asked herself. Lately, more than ever. "Well, being a congressman is different from a doctor. They have a lot of complicated work to do. And it's not a nine-to-five job. Not that a being a doctor is either, of course . . ." Her explanation trailed off. Lame. Very, very lame. And Aaron wasn't buying any of it.

Resignation had settled on his young face. "Even if he does come home any minute, it'll be too late, won't it? About going camping tomorrow?"

Leigh wished she could disagree, but it would be unfair to get his hopes up. "Yeah, I think so." At his disheartened silence, she went on, "But next time, maybe. If you give him some notice, I'm sure he'll arrange to take some time off to go camping."

Aaron stood up. "I'm tired. I think I'll go to bed now."

His unusual desire for an early bedtime told Leigh just how very disappointed he was. Her heart ached as she watched him walk away with slumped shoulders. "Aaron," she spoke softly. "Dad works very hard to give us a nice life. This house, the pool . . . everything else. You have to remember that when you feel bad because he isn't around as much as you'd like."

I have to remember that, too, she thought. *Remember how well he takes care of us.*

Aaron hesitated outside the back door and turned to look at her. "I just wish Dad was a doctor. Then we'd have a nice house *and* a father who does things with us. Like Nathan's dad." He turned and went into the house.

Leigh gazed at the blue lights shining at the bottom of the pool. The exchange with Aaron troubled her. He was at an age when a father-figure took on great importance. Perhaps she could get Mark to spend more time with him. A big brother would be better than nothing.

The pool looked inviting. She wished she had the energy to change into her suit and go for a swim. But a heavy lethargy had swept over her. Just as she decided to go to bed, she heard the car pull into the driveway, and a few seconds later, footsteps sounded on the flagged path leading to the patio.

"Hi." Bob's voice was soft with weariness. He bent and placed a brief kiss on Leigh's cheek, then deposited his athletic frame into a lounge chair near her. He ran a hand through his rumpled black hair and closed his eyes. Despite the lines of fatigue on his face, he still looked youthful and handsome, more like thirty-five than knocking at the door of forty-three.

"I made lasagna," she said. "I'll go heat yours up."

He shook his head. "I called out for Chinese from the office."

"Oh. Well, you can have it for lunch tomorrow." Leigh glanced at him. He seemed to be in a fairly good mood. Maybe if she felt him out and the time seemed right, she could ask him about the exchange student. "How was work today?"

"The usual. Won a verbal match with Kipper Lightfoot, that liberal from California. He's pushing for the ban on assault weapons." He gave a short laugh. "I told him, sure, let's take arms out of the hands of law-abiding citizens and see how quick the thugs and street punks take over. As if crime isn't bad enough already. Goddamn Democrats."

Leigh held her tongue while he went on to talk about the battle lines drawn on Capitol Hill between the "anything goes" Democrats and the Republican "Contract with America" good guys. He wasn't usually so effusive, and Leigh took it as a good sign. She listened quietly, occasionally asking questions she hoped wouldn't ruin his mood. Finally, Bob lapsed into silence and drowsily gazed into the pool lights. She decided to go for it.

"Mark came home from the university with a flyer about exchange students. He's hoping maybe we can take one in for the next school year." She paused, but when there was no response, went on. "I told him I'd ask you."

Bob yawned and loosened his tie. "I don't care, as long as it doesn't interfere with our routine." He looked at her sharply. "I don't want to be eating any Indonesian food or trying to speak some silly foreign gibberish."

"Mark says they'll be fluent in English. And it'll be one of the Scandinavian countries."

"Jesus. That's all we need." In the near darkness, Leigh sensed the smile in his voice. "Some fisherman with herring breath saying, '*Fjerna, snurkel, bjorna . . .*'"

Leigh laughed. That was one thing; Bob still had the power to make her laugh. "You're such a bigot. Just last week you met with a Swedish delegation—what was it?—for Leif Ericson Day? And now, here you're making fun of them."

"They were Danes," Bob said. "And I'm not making fun of them. They *do* talk like that."

"I'm sure." Leigh felt her heart lighten. If only he could be like this all the time. This was the man her father had brought into her life. The handsome, witty young attorney destined for Capitol Hill stardom. "So, it's okay if I tell Mark we can do it? Take in the exchange student?"

"Sure, if that's what he wants. Just remember, if it backfires, it was your idea." He closed his eyes.

"You're such a pussycat when you're tired." Smiling, Leigh reached over and ran a finger along his thigh, hoping to keep him in his good mood. "I was just thinking about taking a swim. How about a skinny-dip?"

Bob yawned again and swept a hand through his ruffled black hair. "No, I think I'll take a shower and go to bed."

It was early for bed. Perhaps if she put on that sexy new nightgown she'd bought at Victoria's Secret the other day, they could do something besides sleep. When *was* the last time they'd made love? More than a couple of months ago, that was for sure. The last time they'd tried, he hadn't been able to get an erection. And since then, he hadn't touched her. Maybe it was time *she* initiated it. "I have an idea. Let's shower together."

"Not tonight, Leigh, okay?" Bob stood up and headed for the door. "I need to get some sleep."

Leigh stared after her husband as he disappeared into the house. She felt as though a sudden frigid wind had swept down out of the humid night, surrounding her with its winter chill. Slowly, she turned her head and gazed into the inviting waters of the pool, trying to fight off an overwhelming sense of loneliness.

"Girl, you'd better sit down, because I've got some news that's going to put goose pimples on your toenails."

"Ellen?" Leigh smiled at the sound of her agent's voice on the line. She cradled the phone on her shoulder and added a bit of charcoal to the rabbit's tail. "I *am* sitting down. What's up?"

Ellen paused dramatically. Then in an excited rush, she said, "Honey, you've won the Smyth-Huxbury Award for the illustrations in Hydra's last book."

Leigh dropped the phone. She scrambled to catch it before it clattered onto the floor, but wasn't quick enough. She reached down and snatched it up. "*Omigod, Ellen! Are you serious?* I won? I *won*? Oh, God, you're kidding. I didn't even know it was entered."

"I entered it for you, girl. But then I forgot about it. Anyway, they're presenting the awards at the Watergate on August tenth." Ellen took a deep breath and went on, "It's going to be a formal dinner, and I've already held a gun to Joey's head and got him to agree to go. All you have to do is work on Bob. Maybe afterwards, the four of us can go hit the Washington night life."

Leigh's smile dimmed. *Not going to happen.* She could never imagine Bob spending an evening with Ellen, a fiery black woman who'd marched to the White House with Martin Luther King, Jr. Not to mention her Italian husband who taught Soviet history at the University of Maryland and made no apologies for his leftist political leanings. God, would the sparks fly if they got on *that* subject. "Well, we'll see," she said noncommittally.

When she shared the news with the kids, they swarmed around her, all talking at once. Mark gave her a warm hug. "I always knew you'd be a prize-winner, Mom. Someday, we'll probably see your paintings in the National Gallery."

"Right." Leigh grinned. "Next to the van Goghs and Rembrandts."

"That's *bad*, Mom!" Mel bestowed upon her the first genuine smile in what seemed like months. "*I* knew you were good, but isn't it great someone else thinks so?"

Yes. Yes, it was. Not that the work alone didn't give her joy, but it was thrilling to have it validated by others. Especially people as illustrious as the Smyth-Huxbury judges.

"Mom, can I take the book into school?" Aaron asked. "Nathan thinks we're going to get Mrs. Pritchert for fifth grade, and she's really mean. But if I show her my mom is an artist who wins prizes, maybe she'll go easy on me."

Leigh smiled at him. He looked so cute she couldn't resist stealing a kiss from his dimpled cheek. "Yes, you can take in the book. But Mrs. Pritchert might not be so easily impressed."

Hours later, Leigh discovered that Mrs. Pritchert wasn't the only one who wouldn't be easily impressed. She was in bed reading when Bob came in at a quarter past eleven. She waited until he'd showered and climbed in next to her before telling him the news.

"Ellen called today. Bob . . . I won the Smyth-Huxbury Award."

Silence. Then, "The *what*?"

"It's an award for illustration in children's picture books. There usually are over fifteen hundred entries. Can you believe it? I *won* it, Bob. *Me*! I still can't believe it."

"Hey, babe. That's great." He leaned over and gave her a light kiss on the lips. "Really nice. You deserve it." Stifling a yawn, he turned over on his side. "Jesus, I'm beat."

Hey, babe. That's great. Really nice. Slowly, Leigh switched off the bedside lamp. She stared up at the dark ceiling, feeling as if a giant glacier was inching its way through her very soul. *No, damn it.* She wouldn't let him do this to her.

"They're giving me the award on August tenth at the Watergate. Ellen and her husband will be there, and . . . you'll come, won't you?"

His only response was a low "Mmmm?"

"This is the most exciting thing that's ever happened to me, Bob. Please tell me you'll come."

He was quiet for so long she thought he'd fallen asleep. But finally, he groaned and turned over onto his stomach. "Yeah, sure, honey. I'll be there."

The night before the awards banquet, Bob received a phone call from a lobbyist in Atlanta asking him to speak at a National Rifle Association convention in place of a senator who'd fallen ill. He'd accepted without even hesitating—and that was what hurt the most. Leigh had tried to swallow her disappointment. After all, she was a congressman's wife, a person whose needs had always come second to those of Bob's constituents. And it wasn't as if the award were really a big deal. As Bob had so diplomatically put it, "Let's face it, Leigh. It's not the Pulitzer, is it?"

An obviously furious Mark volunteered to take Leigh to the awards banquet. When they arrived at the Watergate together, Ellen didn't even raise an eyebrow. But why *should* she? When had Bob ever showed up for one of *Leigh's* functions?

Because her feelings were so bruised by Bob's lack of interest, Leigh had taken extra care with her appearance, choosing a sleek black dress with capped sleeves, elegant but understated. She drew her layered shoulder-length hair into a sophisticated French braid, allowing a few tendrils to escape around her face.

Mark, looking handsome in a black tux, had been openly appreciative. He gave a low wolf whistle as she descended the stairs. "Wow, Mom! You're a fox!"

Leigh gave an embarrassed laugh. "Not too bad for almost forty, I guess."

He shook his head, grinning in admiration. "Whatever. I'm not kidding. You look *hot*, Mom."

Would Bob think so? She shook her head. Who was she kidding? When was the last time he'd even noticed her appearance, much less complimented her on it?

As she settled into her chair at their reserved table, Leigh resolved to forget about Bob and whatever he was doing in Atlanta. This was her evening, and nothing was going to mar it.

For most of the night, she did just that. Until Ellen and Joey got up to dance. Leigh sat at the table, running a finger absentmindedly over the elegant plaque engraved with her name, unaware that Mark's eyes were upon her.

"He should've been here," he said, his brows lowered.

Their eyes met. It was almost as if he could read her mind and glimpse the naked pain she felt at Bob's neglect. But it was only for a moment. Leigh looked away. She wouldn't allow her son to know how much she hurt.

"God, he infuriates me," Mark said in a low, angry voice. "Doesn't he realize what this meant to you?"

"It couldn't be helped. You heard him. Business comes first."

"Oh, yeah, I heard him. It's the same old story every time, isn't it? We all know it by heart."

"Mark, this isn't the time to discuss this."

"Well, *when*, Mom? When are you going to stop making excuses for him? He doesn't give a shit about any of us, does he?"

"Mark, please." Leigh glanced around warily. Bob had trained her well. A congressman's wife didn't make scenes—under any circumstances. "Ellen and Joey will be back any minute. Why do you choose a time like this to start something?"

But there was no stopping him now. "He never made it to my senior play, remember? I had the starring role, but did that matter to him? No. A business dinner was more important. *Jesus!* I'm amazed he made it to my graduation. Of course, he left as soon as it was over. Had to meet a constituent. Sometimes I feel like we should make an appointment with him at his office. Maybe write a letter to him or something."

Leigh grabbed his hand and squeezed. "Here they come. Can we please drop this?"

He did, but it was obvious to Ellen and Joey that something had happened. Conversation became strained, and after a while, Leigh decided the only thing to do was go home.

As Mark drove across Memorial Bridge, Leigh stared out at the illuminated beauty of the Jefferson Memorial. Yet, she wasn't really seeing it. They were both silent. Leigh didn't know what to say, and it seemed that Mark's explosion of words had blown itself out.

But in that, she was wrong. He pulled into the driveway of their English Tudor home in Great Falls, but after switching off the ignition, made no move to get out. He stared moodily at the elegant house: the picture of American affluence.

"I loved that house we had in Alexandria." He turned to look at her. "You didn't want to leave it either, did you?"

"I didn't know you were so attached to it. You were only seven."

"I remember it was small, but it had great places to hide. All kinds of nooks and crannies. And I also remember you trying to talk Dad out of moving. I wanted to stay, too, but we didn't count, did we? Dad wanted a big house, and that was that."

Leigh's hand moved to the door handle. "Yes, but it worked out. I love this place now." She opened the door and climbed out.

"I hate this fucking house," Mark muttered.

Leigh's first impulse was to reprimand him for his language, but she just couldn't do it. Because along with the fury she heard in his voice, the pain came through even more clearly.

On August 22, Erik Haukeland arrived from Norway at Dulles Airport. The day fell on a Friday, and as usual, Leigh had a million things to do. She'd barely returned home from the art supply store when it was time to leave for the airport. Mark and Melissa rode along with her, and she was grateful for that. She wouldn't be solely responsible for conversation with someone who probably had a limited knowledge of English.

Mark was hoping for a close friendship with the Norwegian, and Mel couldn't wait to meet an exciting male college student who just might be interested in blond teenage girls.

"I hope you won't be disappointed, Mel," Leigh said as she took the exit to Dulles. "Like I told Mark, not all Norwegians are blond and beautiful. Besides, he's too old for you."

"Mom." Melissa rolled her eyes. "Twenty-seven is not too old."

"Like hell it's *not*."

"Not only that," Mark spoke up from the passenger seat. "He won't be interested in a skinny teenager like you when he sees all those hot babes on campus."

Melissa threw him a murderous look. "Oh, shut up."

"All right, you two, I know it's a stretch, but try to pretend you're adults." A sticky, stifling heat swept into the Volvo as

Leigh lowered the window to accept the parking ticket at the airport lot.

A few minutes later, they waited in the USAir lounge as passengers from the New York shuttle disembarked. Melissa clutched a large, hand-painted sign that read: *Velkommen til Amerika, Erik.* Leigh had a feeling Mel regretted bringing it. It had drawn lots of stares, and if there was anything Melissa hated, it was being the center of attention.

"Maybe I should get rid of the sign, Mom," she said.

"Don't you dare . . . after all the work you put in on it." Leigh threw her an encouraging smile. "Besides, I think it's a good idea. How else will he know us?"

Leigh's eyes focused on an approaching blond giant wearing a backpack and carrying a tennis racket. Brilliant blue eyes connected with hers for an instant and then moved on to the sign. His straight white teeth flashed in a delighted smile, and the stranger spoke to Melissa.

"God aften. Jeg er meget takk nemlig. Snakker de norsk?"

Melissa stared up at the tall Norwegian, her blue-green eyes sparkling with sudden interest. "I . . . I'm sorry . . . ," she stammered. "But I don't understand Norwegian."

"Oh. My apologies," he said in perfect English. "When I saw the sign, I thought perhaps you could speak Norwegian. Still, thank you for the greeting. It is very thoughtful." He held out his hand. "I am Erik Haukeland."

Dreamily, Melissa shook his hand and murmured, "I'm Melissa Fallon. And this is my brother, Mark."

Mark stepped forward and heartily grabbed Erik's offered hand. "Hi. Glad to have you here." His eyes paused on the racket in Erik's other hand. "Hey, you play tennis? We'll have to hit the courts some evening." He remembered his mother. "Oh, Erik, this is my mom, Leigh."

Leigh had been studying the newcomer as he exchanged greetings with Melissa and Mark. He was casually dressed in faded jeans and a blue-and-gold-striped polo shirt. Although he stood over six feet, and was rather lanky, his arms were corded as if he lifted weights. He wore his wavy blond hair long on the back of his neck, but cut short around his face.

High cheekbones and an aquiline nose testified to his Nordic heritage along with arresting blue eyes banded by dark blond lashes. When he looked down, smiling at a shy Melissa, Leigh noticed dark blond eyebrows arched in a way that gave him a slightly quizzical expression.

Erik turned to her, a surprised smile on his attractive face, and spoke in an accented voice with a low musical timbre. "Mrs. Fallon? I thought perhaps you were Melissa's sister."

Leigh's heart gave a sudden bump. His gaze drilled into her, as if he were peeling her apart, layer by layer. Under his scrutiny, she felt the color rise in her face. In consternation, she glanced away. "Well, let's go get your luggage."

"No need," he said lightly. "I have everything right here. The rest of it has been shipped."

Leigh felt as if she'd recovered enough composure to look at him again. "Okay. I guess we'll head home then."

He gave her a slow smile. "I'm looking forward to that, Mrs. Fallon."

"Call me Leigh." She turned to lead the way to the exit.

As they headed to the parking lot, Leigh felt Erik's gaze burning into her back, and although the temperature hovered in the nineties, a sudden chill of anticipation quivered through her.

3

At dinner, conversation flowed easily between the Fallons and their Norwegian guest. It was as though they'd all known Erik Haukeland for years. Even Bob appeared to be enjoying the Norwegian's lively manner and friendly smile.

At Melissa's request to hear about his family, Erik took a sip of coffee and grinned. "Remember, you asked for this. I have *quite* a family. Two brothers . . . and a sister, as well. Let's see, Bjørn is thirty. I'm next, followed by my sister, Dordei, who is twenty. Then there's my brother, Magnus, who is sixteen."

Aaron grinned. "Did you say your sister's name is Dorky?"

"Dordei," Erik corrected.

"Do they call her Dorky Dordy?"

"*Aaron.*" Leigh and Melissa both glared at the boy.

"Don't mind him, Erik," Melissa said quickly, her face flushed with embarrassment. "He can't help it if he's brain-damaged. Besides, I think Dordei is sort of a nice name."

Leigh gave her a who-are-you-trying-to-kid look. This was her daughter speaking, the one who usually had nothing good to say about anyone unless he had waist-length blond hair and wore chains and leather.

"You probably think a lot of our American names are weird, don't you?" Mel asked.

"What could be weirder than Dordy?" Aaron mumbled as he shoveled a huge bite of apple pie into his mouth.

Leigh frowned at him. "Aaron Michael, if you can't be polite to our guest, you can go to your room."

"Ah, but I don't wish to be treated like a guest for a whole year," Erik said with a wry smile. "I hope you will think of me as part of your family."

He really *was* very nice, Leigh thought. She smiled at him. "I'm sure when you leave next summer, it will feel like we're losing one of the family."

"Besides," Aaron said, obviously hoping to correct his gaffe. "Mom's real name is Kayleigh. How's that for weird?"

"Kayleigh," Erik tested the word on his tongue and smiled. "I like it. Sounds Irish."

Leigh nodded. "Yes. Like the Irish dance, but it's spelled differently. It was my great-grandmother's name. She never stepped foot out of Ireland as far as I know."

"Why don't you go by it?" Erik asked. "It really is quite beautiful."

She shrugged. "I tried it for a while in college, but it always got shortened to Kay or Leigh. So, I gave up."

"*Leigh* is more American, anyway," Bob said, reaching for his coffee cup. "It's a good, solid name for a politician's wife. *Kayleigh* sounds like she grew up in Limerick or Cork, for God's sake. And I'd just as soon not emphasize our Irish heritage. Last thing I need is for the voters to connect me with the Kennedys and their bleeding heart liberal politics."

"God knows we wouldn't want that," Leigh said, voice heavy with sarcasm. She gave an inward grimace. What had come over her? She usually had more restraint.

Bob glowered at her. And Mark looked like he wanted to applaud. Ignoring them both, Leigh glanced back at Erik and smiled. "Anyway, I use Kayleigh for my art. It's a name people seem to remember."

Erik returned her smile. "Oh, *ja*. While you were preparing dinner, Aaron showed me the picture books you illustrated. I found them exquisite."

His blue eyes locked with hers, and she felt flushed by the warmth in their depths. "Thanks." What would be his reaction if she told him how she'd kept her first book on display in the living room until she found Bob using it as a coaster?

"I will be glad to call you Kayleigh," Erik said. "That is, if you do not mind. I think it fits you perfectly."

Aaron chose that moment to ask for more pie, and Leigh didn't get a chance to respond to Erik's request. Later, she wondered what she would've said. She couldn't get the image of his expression out of her mind. It was as if he were looking past her eyes, almost as though he knew her better than she knew herself.

Classes started a few days after Erik arrived, and both he and Mark were gone for the better part of each day. In the afternoons, the house came to life as everyone arrived home around the same time. By then, Leigh was ready for companionship and even a little noise.

Erik had adapted to life at the Fallons with ease; it was as if he'd always been there. In fact, he was almost too popular. Mark, Melissa, and Aaron were falling over themselves competing for his attention, and not wanting to slight them, he tried to divide his time equally among them. Of course, being nearer in age to Mark and spending so much time with him at George Mason University, they became friends quickly. Mark introduced Erik to Vicki, who immediately offered to fix him up with a coed from the university. Leigh had walked into the rec room just in time to hear Vicki's offer and was amazed when Erik politely turned her down.

"Thank you, but I'm afraid I'm not quite ready for American women." He gave an embarrassed grin. "I don't mean that to be an insult, you understand. It's just that American women are different from European ones. I think it would be best if I sort them out on my own."

Vicki, an attractive brunette with a wry sense of humor, contemplated him for a moment and then said, "You may not be ready for American girls, Erik, but you can bet they'll be ready for you. Especially if you play hard to get like that."

Yet, Leigh was sure he wasn't "playing." There had been something in his eyes as he spoke. Like a flash of lightning, it came to her. Of course. There was a girl back home. In fact, come to think of it, it was a miracle he wasn't married. A man with his looks. Question was, how had the girl ever let him get away without a fight?

Whenever the opportunity arose, Mel tried to monopolize Erik's free time. Leigh discovered he had the gift of making each of her children feel like the most important person in the world. And it wasn't contrived. He truly seemed interested in all of them.

But it was Aaron who drew his special attention, much to Leigh's delight. With Bob's work schedule and Mark's social life, her youngest son was starved for male companionship. Somehow, Erik had picked up on that. He made sure he spent plenty of time with the ten-year-old, playing basketball, bicycling, or swimming in the pool until the autumn weather set in. On a crisp Saturday near the end of September, Aaron breathlessly ran into the sewing room where Leigh was finishing his pirate costume for Halloween.

"Mom!"

Leigh's heart lurched at the urgency in his voice. *"What?"*

"You'll never guess what."

Her hand dropped onto her pounding chest. She wondered how long it would be before she'd regain her normal color. "What, Aaron?"

"Erik is taking me camping next weekend to Hungry Mother." The dimples deepened in his cheeks as he danced around the room in delight.

Erik appeared in the doorway. "I meant to ask you first, Kayleigh. Mark has agreed to go, too. May we have your permission?"

Leigh looked doubtfully from one face to the other. "This time of the year? Won't it be kind of . . . cold?"

"The forecast is calling for a week or two of . . . what is it you call it? Indian summer? But even if they are wrong, I've already spoken with Mark about your camping gear. You have nice thermal sleeping bags and a Coleman heater." Erik dropped a hand onto Aaron's shining blond head. "Aaron tells me this Hungry Mother State Park is quite nice. And it's only a few hours away."

"Please, Mom?" Aaron pleaded, eyes yearning. "It'll be so much fun."

When Leigh still hesitated, Erik added, "We'll drive down on Saturday morning and come back Sunday afternoon. I'll take good care of Aaron. Believe me, I've had much experience camping in cold weather."

"I guess you have . . . ," Leigh said slowly.

The tone of her voice told Aaron all he needed to know. "Then, we can go?"

His blue eyes sparkled and his freckles fairly glowed in excitement. How could she say no? She nodded, and Aaron threw himself into her arms. He gave her a big wet kiss on the cheek right in front of Erik and then scrambled away. Leigh smiled and wiped the saliva from her face. "Wow. How did you get him to do *that*?"

Erik looked as if he wanted to plant a big kiss on her, too, but instead, he put his lips to the tips of his fingers and blew one in her direction. "Thanks, Kayleigh. You made that little boy very happy."

"Not me," Leigh said. "It wasn't me, at all."

His answer was a smile that warmed her all over.

*　　*　　*

"Yes!" Leigh pumped a fist into the air, her eyes glued to the small television set on the kitchen counter. "Way to go, Redskins!" The band struck up "Hail to the Redskins" and Leigh sang along with it gustily while searching the refrigerator for a bottle of Coors to celebrate the victory. Too bad Bob had fallen asleep in the rec room before the fourth quarter.

The back door slammed, and Aaron ran into the kitchen, grasping a grimy metal bucket. "Look, Mom." He reached into the bucket and pulled out a dripping fish.

Leigh tried to hold back a shudder. She was not a fish-type person. "Wonderful, Aaron," she said, trying to look enthusiastic. "You caught it yourself?"

"All by himself," Mark spoke from the doorway of the utility room.

Erik appeared behind Mark. Leigh's eyes flicked over their mud-stained jeans and filthy skin. She'd never seen two sorrier-looking young men in her life. She sniffed and wrinkled her nose. They didn't smell too pleasant either.

Aaron dropped the fish back into the water. "Hungry Mother was great, Mom. Erik taught me how to make a fire with sticks, and I showed him how to make s'mores."

With a wry grin, Erik stepped into the kitchen, his lean jaw covered with blond stubble. Mark followed, also in need of a shave. Leigh shook her head and smiled. "You guys look like you haven't seen civilization in weeks. And you were only gone one night."

"Speaking of being civilized . . . ," Mark said with a grin. "What was that you were doing when we walked in?"

Leigh lifted the Coors bottle. "Celebrating, what do you think? Majewski kicked the winning field goal with only four seconds on the clock."

Erik grinned. "How did you get so crazy about this game? I always heard it's the American men who like sports while the women complain about being widows during football season."

"Not in *this* family," Mark said. "It's Grandpa Jim's fault. Since there were no boys in the family, he turned Mom and Aunt Barb into football fanatics."

"*Redskins* fanatics," Leigh corrected.

Erik's hand clamped down on her shoulder. "I like that. A lover of sports. Just like a Norwegian woman."

Uneasy at his spontaneous touch, Leigh shifted away. "You want a beer, Erik?" At Mark's "Me, too," she shook her head. "You want me arrested for contributing to the delinquency of a minor?" She grabbed another beer from the refrigerator and two Cokes.

Aaron placed his bucket on the kitchen table and sifted through its contents, his brow puckered. "Here's a rainbow trout, and a couple of little catfish. Oh, this is a sunfish, but I don't think they taste good. . . ." He pursed his lips and a little dimple flickered in his cheek.

Leigh rested her hands on his shoulders and gazed into the smelly bucket. "Wow. You caught all those, Aaron?" She wondered if there was a spot on his dirty little neck where she could steal a kiss.

"Most of 'em. Mark and Erik helped, though." He looked up at her, his blue eyes shining. "We had so much fun, Mom. Last night, we sat up almost until the sun came up and told ghost stories. Erik had some *really* scary ones, didn't you, Erik? Tell her the one about the Bominal Snowman that lives in the mountains and eats campers for dinner."

Erik took a long swallow of his beer, avoiding Leigh's eyes. "Later, Aaron. Why don't we take the fish outside and clean them. Then I'll fry them up for dinner, Norwegian-style." He looked back at her. "Unless, of course, you have something else planned, Kayleigh."

"Are you kidding? Erik, you can take over my kitchen any time."

"Great." He gave her a warm smile and turned back to Aaron. "Come on, *liten bror*, let's get started." With a hand on Aaron's shoulder, he followed the boy out the back door.

"I'll be out to help in a minute, guys," Mark called after them. "Have to report in with Vicki first."

Leigh stared at the back door. "Mark, what does *liten bror* mean?"

Mark grinned. "Little brother. He's been calling Aaron that

all weekend. You should've seen them, Mom. They were, like, *glued* together. If Erik told Aaron diamonds grew in trees, he'd be out shaking the branches." Mark gave a rueful laugh. "I felt like the invisible man this weekend. Erik just has a way about him."

After Mark left to make his phone call, Leigh stood at the kitchen sink, gazing out at the lengthening shadows. It had been a long time since she'd seen such a sparkle in Aaron's eyes.

That night Leigh dreamed of Erik. It was a hazy dream, but very, very sensual. She and Erik . . . making love. Even after she awoke, aroused and heated, she still felt the impression of Erik's tongue tasting her lips, and his hands . . . God . . . his hands moving over her, touching her breasts, skimming her stomach . . . his artistic fingers gently parting her thighs, stoking the fires of her comatose libido.

The dreams had started after his arrival, but lately, they'd become more frequent. Fantasies, she told herself. Just fantasies. And what was wrong with that? They'd never be anything more.

Besides, these days, fantasies were all that was left of her sex life.

"This is the last time you'll get me out to that stadium in weather like this," Bob growled, hands clenched on the steering wheel.

Leigh gazed out the window at the U.S. Capitol, gray-washed and dingy in the rain. Bob had started in as soon as they'd reached the car in the stadium parking lot. It was a story she'd heard before. Next, he'd complain about the season tickets.

"As if I could give a shit about the goddamned Redskins. If it weren't for having to keep up appearances . . ." A BMW cut in front of him, and he slammed on the brakes, glaring at the driver. "Asshole." Then, it was back to the matter at hand. "*Three hours.* Three fucking hours in the rain. And then those wimps fumble the ball and the Cowboys run it back for a touchdown. *This* is what I'm paying for?"

In the backseat of the Mercedes, Mark, Aaron, and Melissa were ominously silent. Like Leigh, they knew there was no reasoning with Bob when he was in one of his black moods. Best thing to do was just grin and bear it.

"I'd love to go up to Jack Kent Cooke and tell him exactly what I think of his stinking little team. . . ."

Oh, stuff it. It was all Leigh could do not to speak aloud, but she restrained herself. No sense in subjecting the kids to the shouting match it would bring on.

It was with a great sense of relief that she saw their exit coming up. She couldn't wait to get into a hot shower; the drizzling rain had chilled her to the bone. Fifteen minutes later, she stood under the hot spray of water and wondered what Erik had done with himself while they were at the game. She'd felt uncomfortable about leaving him at home, but there was nothing else to do. Except for scalpers selling at three hundred dollars a shot, Redskins tickets were impossible to get at the gate. Anyway, she'd offered him her seat, but he'd turned it down, insisting he didn't really know much about American football.

Wrapped in her warmest, oldest fleece robe, Leigh descended the stairs to prepare dinner. Just sandwiches and soup tonight. She hadn't the energy to do anything else. As she passed by the rec room, she noticed a light on and went in. A blazing fire burned cozily in the grate. Nearby, Erik sat comfortably in the big La-Z-Boy recliner, reading. That wasn't what caused her to stop short. It was the book in his hands. *The Taming of the Troll* by Hydra Kouripoulous. Illustrations by Kayleigh Fallon.

He looked up and smiled. "This is a great story. But the illustrations are truly brilliant."

So incongruous, thought Leigh. *The big blond man sitting there reading a children's picture book.* "Thank you," she managed to say.

"I hope you don't mind," he went on. "I mentioned to Aaron that I'd like to look at your illustrations, so this morning, he brought me your books. I've enjoyed reading them."

Leigh's mouth dropped open. "You're *reading* the picture books? All of them?"

"Of course." His eyebrow lifted at her obvious surprise. "*You* had to read them to do the illustrations, didn't you?"

"Yes, but I don't see why you'd want to."

He closed the book on his lap and lovingly ran a hand over the cover. Leigh found herself almost hypnotized by his hand. It was big yet artistic, with long slender fingers and neatly squared nails. A burnished down of blond hair matted the surface up to his finely chiseled wrist to disappear under the cuff of his woolen sweater. *Sensitive hands,* Leigh thought. How would they feel upon her body?

She shook her head to tear her mind away from that dangerous thought and realized he was answering her question.

"I'm working toward my Ph.D. in psychology, remember?" He winked and gave a wry grin. "I thought if I read your books, I could learn more about you."

Why would you want to, Leigh wanted to ask, but for some reason, felt it better to veer away from that, too. She smiled, trying to keep her tone light. "Well, that would make sense if I wrote the books. But I only draw the pictures."

"Only?" Erik opened the book again and stared down at it. "Why do you belittle yourself, Kayleigh? Illustrating a book is a great accomplishment. As for me learning about you through your illustrations, you would be surprised what can be determined about psyche through one's art. Why do you think Edvard Munch painted works like *Ghosts* and *Chamber of Death?* He was preoccupied with death, of course."

Yes, Munch. Leigh was familiar with his work. Especially *The Cry.* Every time she'd seen that painting, she'd felt an empathy for the horrified-looking subject, identifying with the need to let it all out with a healthy scream.

She sat down on the other chair near the fireplace and curled her legs under her. "I can certainly see that. But you're looking at illustrations I was commissioned to do. All of that stuff came out of Hydra's head, not mine."

Erik looked at her, and Leigh had the uncanny feeling that

his eyes were burning into her soul. "After I first arrived, Mark took me on a tour of the house and showed me your studio. Forgive me, but I took the liberty of glancing through your sketchbooks and the unframed canvases against the wall. Mark said you wouldn't mind."

"I don't. I'm not shy about my work."

"You shouldn't be. You are very good."

Leigh gave a slight smile. "So, Erik, what did you learn about me from my paintings?"

He was silent for a long moment. When he finally spoke, his face was serious. "Forgive me for my honesty, Kayleigh. I believe you go through life pretending to be content, trying to be everything to everyone. The perfect wife, the perfect mother. But in doing that, you're neglecting yourself. Kayleigh, you are living in a vacuum, anesthetizing yourself to life." He stared at her for a moment and then spoke again softly, almost as if he were talking to himself. "What will it take to wake you up?"

She felt the blood draining from her face. Then anger sledgehammered through her, sending her heart racing. What gave him the right to psychoanalyze her? Who the *hell* did she think he was? She drew her legs out from under her and stood. Erik stared at her, and in his eyes, she saw a flicker of uncertainty, chagrin, perhaps.

He opened his mouth to speak, but she cut him off. "You don't even know me, Erik." She was trembling, her hands clenched into fists at her sides. "Not enough to judge me, anyway. Excuse me. I have to go start dinner."

She turned and walked out of the rec room, holding her head high. It was only when she reached the kitchen that she took a deep breath and released it in one tremulous sigh. *Oh, God . . . How had he known?*

Still trembling, she squatted down next to the lazy Susan and gave it a twirl. She was supposed to be searching for something, but *what*, for God's sake? Her brain was spinning like the lazy Susan. She heard a footfall at the door and stiffened.

"Kayleigh, I apologize," Erik said quietly. "I have a tendency to tread where I'm not welcome. It drives my family mad. Please, can you forgive me?"

Slowly, she turned. He stood just inside the kitchen, his face sober, eyes sincere. She wilted, the anger inside her melting away. But she couldn't let him know how close to the truth he'd come. Besides, she wasn't ready to concede that. Yet. She forced herself to look away from him, her eyes scanning the rows of cans. *Oh, yes. Soup!*

"Let's just forget it, Erik," she said. "No harm done."

"Thank you," he said quietly.

Leigh reached for a can of tomato rice soup. "What about tomato rice?" she asked. "Or would you rather have bean with bacon?"

No response. She turned and looked over her shoulder. Erik was gone.

On Saturday—a bright, cool October day—Leigh stopped outside Erik's door with a basket of his folded clothes. She knocked, knowing he was inside because she could hear the stereo playing. As he opened the door, she heard her name, but it hadn't come from him. A male voice was belting it out from the compact disc player near Erik's bed. Leigh gaped in surprise. Erik put a finger to his lip and motioned her inside.

"Listen . . ."

She walked in hesitantly, checking to make sure the door remained open behind her. Then she heard her name again.

Kayleigh, remember dancing in the rain,
On the smoky cliffs of the land's end?
Laughter blending with the wild winds of Inishmore.

During a long instrumental bridge, Leigh spoke, "Who is this?"

"A rock group from Ireland. Banshee."

Leigh grinned. As a teenager, she'd been jealous of all the Sherrys, Carols, Kathys, and Sheilas who got sung about. Now, finally, someone had used *Kayleigh* in a song. As the next verse began, Erik motioned her to a chair near the stereo and handed her the lyrics sheet so she could follow along.

> *Kayleigh, remember making love in the storm,*
> *Lost in the mist, consumed by fire?*
> *You made the world stop . . .*

Leigh felt the heat rise and spread across her face at the line "making love in the storm." In her mind, she saw herself with Erik and had to force herself to banish the thought. What was *with* her lately? Sure, she and Bob hadn't had sex for months, but why, suddenly, was it all she could think about?

Through her eyelashes, she stole a glance at Erik. Dressed in faded jeans and a red-plaid flannel shirt, he relaxed on the bed, his head propped up by an elbow. His flaxen hair was attractively disheveled and his unnerving blue eyes glittered with excitement. At that moment, Leigh was struck by how young he really was. Only twenty-seven. A mere baby. How could she possibly have such lascivious thoughts about him?

The song ended, and Erik sat up. "Well, what did you think?"

"Where on earth did you find that song?" Her eyes fell on a Tower Records bag lying on the bed. "Did you just buy it?"

Erik laughed. "*Ja.* The song was popular a few years ago in Europe. As soon as I heard your name, I was determined to find it. Did you really like it?"

Leigh stood up. "I loved it. But it must've been a lot of trouble to go through just so you could play it for me."

Erik jumped up from the bed and stopped the compact disc player in the middle of the next track. The sudden silence in the room made Leigh uneasy, especially when he turned and she saw the penetrating look in his eyes.

"I've always liked the song," he said quietly. "But now that I've met you, it means more to me."

Seconds ticked by as Leigh stood there, searching for something to say. Erik stared at her, unsmiling. Her heart accelerated as he took a step toward her.

A door opened downstairs and a moment later, a voice called up. "*Mom!* Can I have a snack?"

Leigh felt a surge of relief. She moved toward the door. "Go ahead, Aaron," she called, a tremor in her voice. She looked back at Erik. "I've got to get back to work." She nodded toward the basket of clothes on the floor. "More laundry to fold, you know." She left his room, almost stumbling in her haste.

Instead of going downstairs to the laundry room, she hurried to her studio. Her heart was still pounding when she sat down at the window seat and stared out at the golden-russet colors of autumn.

He knows. . . . He knows I'm attracted to him. . . . I haven't been able to hide it. . . . He knows and he's going to try to take advantage of it.

Leigh had no idea what to do. How had it happened? Had she somehow given off signals to him? If she had, it had been unconscious. What if he made a stronger advance? Would she be able to summon enough common sense and willpower to resist him? She *had* to. From now on, she would be as formal as possible with him. She had to remind herself that Erik was her son's friend and treat him accordingly—like a son.

Above all, she had to forget she was a woman around Erik. That would be the most difficult of all, because when he looked at her with those wonderful blue eyes, she felt more womanly than she ever had before.

4

Leigh awoke to rain beating a tattoo upon the roof. She reached for the alarm clock and then relaxed, realizing it was Sunday morning. She closed her eyes again, enjoying the warmth of the electric blanket and the music of the rain. A remnant of a dream lingered in the edges of her mind, yet when she tried to focus upon it, it remained elusive and finally disappeared.

It had been about Erik, of course. Since yesterday in his room, she'd forced herself not to think about him . . . not in that way, but this morning, perhaps because of the early hour, or the rain, her unguarded mind reached for him. She imagined him in the guest room, sleeping nude under the satin comforter. How cozy his room would be with the rain beating against the window. The thought of his naked chest glistening with golden hairs brought a warm flush to her body. She looked over at her sleeping husband. He was turned away from her, clad only in pajama bottoms. It had been such a long time since they'd had sex. She tried to remember the last time. *Oh, God!* Had it really been over six months since their last failed attempt? She'd tried to get him to go to a doctor to see if the impotence was physical, but he'd flat-out refused. His solution was to ignore the problem and hope it would go away on its own. Typical male bury-head-in-the-sand attitude.

God, she wanted to be loved. Badly. She reached out a hand and gently traced the line of a scar on his right shoulder. It was from a college football injury, he'd told her. Leigh slid toward him, hugging her body against his back and sliding her arms around him to caress his hard flat stomach.

"Bobby . . . ," she whispered, kissing his shoulder.

He groaned and turned over on his back. Leigh slid halfway up on him and nuzzled his chest. Bob's eyes fluttered and the rate of his breathing quickened. Her hand crept down to the waistband of his pajama bottoms. Deftly, she popped open the snaps and slid her hand inside, pleased to find he was erect. He moaned as she began to arouse him. Quickly, changing position, she took him into her mouth. She was wet and ready for him, but first she wanted to taste him, to make both of them want it more. Maybe this is what she should've been doing all along. Taking control.

"Oh . . . baby . . . yeah . . . ," he moaned. Suddenly he wrenched himself away from her and rolled her onto her back. Pulling her nightgown up around her waist, he greedily parted her legs and plunged deep inside her. Leigh, shocked at the abruptness of his entry, felt all desire drain away. In a moment, it was over. Bob collapsed on top of her, his chest thundering wildly. A few seconds later, he withdrew and dropped back onto his side of the bed. Leigh tugged her nightgown down, feeling the cold stickiness of semen against her legs. She sat up and pulled the electric blanket around her.

Beside her, Bob spoke, a satisfied grin on his face. "Maybe you should wake me up like that more often."

Leigh remained silent. She'd never felt more alone.

Everyone except Bob had gathered at the kitchen table for breakfast when he walked in, a dark scowl on his face. He stared out the window at the rain. "I'm not sitting out in that stadium again in this fucking weather."

"Do you *have* to talk like that in front of the kids?" Leigh said. "Besides, it's not the end of the world if it rains during a Redskins game."

"Well, you can be a lunatic if you want to, but I told you last time I wouldn't sit in that stadium in the rain again." Bob sat down and helped himself to a large serving of scrambled eggs. "I don't know why I let you talk me into buying those damn season tickets anyway."

"You were the one who said it looked good for a congressman to support the capital's team." Leigh's tone was mildly sarcastic. "I wanted the tickets because I actually *like* the Redskins."

"Well, I'm not going today. Maybe Erik will be crazy enough to use my ticket." Bob looked over at him, a sour expression on his face. "But I guess you Norwegians don't know anything about football, do you?"

Mark spoke up, "Yeah, Erik. You can't live here in Redskins territory without becoming a fan. What do you say? Want to go to the game?"

Erik shrugged. "Why not? A little rain doesn't bother me."

Leigh could have sworn she saw him throw Bob a challenging glance.

Bob glowered and unfolded the morning paper. An uneasy silence fell, but it didn't last long. He scowled at the front page. "You'll have a hell of a time getting downtown today. The idiot liberals are marching on the White House again."

"Why?" Leigh asked.

"Oh, they're pissed off about the Crouch Bill, the one about the homeless. The president vetoed it, you know. And well he *should* have. Stupidest thing I've ever heard. Raising our tax dollars to build more shelters. Like that's going to make a bit of difference. Damn *right* of him not to sign."

Erik stared at Bob, an incredulous look in his eyes. Slowly, he put down his fork. "Am I to understand you don't have any empathy at all for the street people I see every time I go into D.C.?"

Bob looked at him. "Ninety-eight percent of those people are certifiably wacko. The other two percent are addicts or alcoholics. Why should the average taxpayer have to foot the bill for people like that?" He shook his head. "And even if we *do* build more shelters, it won't change a thing. Half those people don't even want to use them. They'd rather sleep on subway grates. We might as well take the taxpayers' money and flush it down the toilet for all the good this bill would do."

"More coffee, anyone?" Leigh stood and headed for the kitchen. She knew from experience it was impossible to argue with Bob about his right-wing politics. Poor Erik didn't know what he was getting himself into. When she returned with the coffeepot, the two men were glaring across the table like gladiators in the Colosseum.

Blue fire sparked from Erik's eyes. "I can't believe you're really serious. Or are you just trying to convince yourself it's true to lessen your guilt?"

"I don't feel guilty," Bob retorted. "I've worked hard for what I have."

"*Ja,*" Erik said. "But because you're a public servant, you have a responsibility to help out those less fortunate."

"My only responsibility is to my constituents, and let me tell you, the majority of them are hardworking taxpayers. Blue-collar workers who know the value of a day's work. The little guys who work in the mills and the factories. Who bring home a paycheck every week to feed their families. Those are the kind of people that made this country strong, certainly not the foreigners ... most of them illegal aliens who come here and take jobs from good hardworking Americans."

Erik's eyes grew appraising. "Oh, so now we are talking about the foreigners, not the homeless. What are you trying to say, Bob? That America should be only for hardworking native-born people like you? That some people are more equal than others? Is that what you are saying?"

"You're twisting my words," Bob snarled, eyes crackling with anger.

It was getting way too hot in here. Leigh decided it was time to intervene. "Why don't we talk about something else?"

Bob threw her a disgruntled look. "No. I want to find out why all these Europeans feel the need to be so self-righteous." He glared back at Erik. "I suppose Norway has all the answers, right?"

"No country has all the answers," Erik said flatly. "But we do not have a homeless problem."

"And you know why? Exorbitant taxes, that's why. Thank you very much, but I'll choose the good old U.S. of A. any day. A place where I get to keep what's mine."

For a long moment, Erik stared at him silently, eyes hard. "How very noble of you." He pushed his plate away. "Excuse me. I'm afraid I've lost my appetite." He turned and left the room. With a disdainful look at his father, Mark stood and followed him out.

"Arrogant bastard, isn't he?" Bob muttered, reaching for his coffee cup.

Leigh's fork clattered to her plate. She stared at her husband. "You know something? Sometimes you can be a real jerk."

Without waiting for a response, she stood and left the room. Damn Bob. She wouldn't allow him to ruin her day. She'd get dressed for the game, and they'd all go without him. And have a better time, at that.

At the door of her bedroom, she paused, and on impulse, turned and headed in the other direction toward the guest room. Through a round window cut high in the wall at the end of the hallway, she could see the rain sluicing down from a slate-gray sky. The blazing leaves of autumn glistened wetly on the trees, some of them falling to the ground in death throes as she watched. An inexplicable shiver ran through her. She shook her head, trying to rid herself of the depression settling upon her, and turned from the window to rap firmly on Erik's door.

"Come in."

She found him at his desk, a textbook opened in front of him. He looked up and ran his fingers through his tousled hair. "Kayleigh?"

"Erik, I just want to apologize for Bob's behavior this morning. I don't think he believes half of what he says."

"If he does, I pity the American people," Erik said, a faint edge of bitterness in his voice. "Your husband . . . he's . . ." His eyes stormy, he searched for the right word, ". . . *hard-nakkethet* . . . obstinate. I can't believe an intelligent person would think like that."

"His parents weren't rich, you know," Leigh tried to explain. "He went to college on a full scholarship and worked his way through law school. That's why he thinks the way he does. He feels that if *he* could make it, why can't everyone else?"

Not that he didn't have a lot of good luck along the way. A savvy stockbroker and some opportune investments had paved the way for a good portion of Bob's financial success.

"*Ja*, but his reasoning borders along the thinking of Hitler's. Kayleigh, I've worked with the mentally ill. They do not choose their illness any more than you or I would choose to have cancer. Can your husband really believe that they, and the others, don't deserve all the help we can give them?"

Leigh shook her head. "I honestly don't know what he thinks anymore. Anyway, I'm sure he didn't mean to insult you."

A slight smile appeared on Erik's lips. "I'm sure he did. But it doesn't matter. The thing I can't understand is . . . forgive me, Kayleigh, but you are so different from him. What made you—?" He stopped, a chagrined look on his face. "I'm sorry. I almost did it again, didn't I? I'm—how do you say?—off boundary?"

Leigh smiled. "Out of bounds. But it's okay. You want to know what made me fall for him?" She turned away to stare out the window at the rain. Her voice was soft when she spoke. "He was different back then. Softer. Ambition did something to him. Changed him." She turned to face him. "Mark is very much like Bob used to be. I fell in love with him because he made me laugh. No man had ever really done that before."

Erik gazed at her pensively. "Does he still make you laugh?"

Not for a long, long time. But she couldn't tell him that. It would be disloyal. She pointedly glanced at her watch. "We need to leave soon. The game starts at one. Can you be ready in about fifteen minutes?" At his nod, she turned to go, but his voice stopped her.

"Kayleigh." He watched her closely. "Do you always apologize for your husband?"

Leigh shrugged, embarrassed. "Bob rarely feels the need to apologize for anything."

Erik shook his head and muttered, *"Slov Amerikansk."*

She started to ask him for a translation, but the expression on his face changed her mind.

The table reserved for Bob was a choice one, nestled in the back of the restaurant near the fireplace. Leigh took a sip of Earl Grey tea and glanced at her watch. Two o'clock. She'd been waiting almost an hour for him to finish with an impromptu meeting so they could celebrate their twentieth anniversary with lunch. But Aaron would be home from school soon. If Bob had been able to get away at half past twelve as they'd planned, she would've been home in plenty of time. She decided to call and leave a message for Aaron on the answering machine.

But instead of the machine picking up, Erik answered the phone.

"Hi, Erik," Leigh said, surprised. "Why aren't you in class?"

"They canceled for something called a pep rally. It has to

do with this big game against Notre Dame tomorrow."

"And you went home instead?"

"Yes, well . . ." Leigh could hear the smile in his voice. "It's not the Redskins, is it? You've spoiled me for other teams."

Leigh laughed softly. "Now, how did I do that? Listen, Erik, can you give Aaron a message for me? I'm at Antoine's on the Hill. Bob and I were supposed to meet for lunch, but he's been held up. Tell Aaron to go play at Nathan's until I get home. I'm not going to wait past three, so I'll be there at least by four o'clock if Bob doesn't show."

"Of course, I'll tell him. And Kayleigh, enjoy yourself, *ja?*"

"Yeah, thanks. Talk to you later."

That taken care of, Leigh returned to her table and ordered another cup of tea. She'd told Erik she'd wait until three o'clock, but by that time, it would be too late for lunch. Maybe she should just go home. Obviously, Bob wasn't going to make it. Either something else had come up or, more likely, he'd simply forgotten.

She sipped her tea and stared glassily into the burning fire. Twenty years. And each year that passed seemed to mean less to Bob than the last. The first few anniversaries, it had been elaborate nights out, dancing and dining at the best restaurants. Even during the lean years when Bob had been a junior congressman in the Ohio state legislature, they'd managed to have some kind of romantic evening together. Now, they couldn't even get together for a quick lunch.

Leigh glanced at her watch. Five to three. "That's it," she whispered, reaching for her purse. As she moved to get up, she heard a murmur of excitement from the table to her left. She turned and gasped at the sight of a cloud of multicolored balloons coming toward her, each of them printed with HAPPY ANNIVERSARY.

A delighted laugh escaped her lips. Unbelievable—that Bob would do such a crazy romantic thing! The balloons hovered in front of her, swaying and bobbing with the air currents. Slowly, they rose toward the high ceiling, and Leigh found herself staring into Erik's dancing blue eyes.

She was stunned, speechless.

"I had a feeling he would not be able to make it," he said, tying the balloon ribbons to the back of her chair. "I thought these would cheer you up." He took a seat opposite her.

The waiter appeared, and Erik ordered coffee. When the man had gone, Leigh finally found her voice. "What would you have done if Bob had been here?"

He looked surprised. "Why, I would've brought you the balloons and left. Would he have found that odd, do you suppose?"

"Yes, probably."

"Ah, well. I *am* a foreigner. You cannot expect me to know these things."

The waiter arrived with the coffee. Erik waited until they were alone before speaking again. "So, how many years is it?"

"Twenty. How did you know it was our anniversary?"

"Mark and I stopped by the bakery this morning to order you a cake. We're going to present it after dinner tonight. Please be surprised. I wasn't supposed to tell."

Leigh felt very close to tears. When she'd first seen the balloons, she'd thought Bob had finally done something wildly spontaneous, and she'd been filled with hope that things would change. That they could be in love again. She looked down into her near empty teacup and blinked quickly.

Erik's hand covered hers. "Cry if you want to, Kayleigh. It will help."

She felt his steady gaze but couldn't look at him. His hand was warm on hers, warm and strong. His strength seemed to flow into her, and suddenly the hurt wasn't so bad. She shook her head and stared at the fire.

"Thanks for the balloons, Erik," she said quietly.

He stared at her for a long moment, not speaking. Then, he squeezed her hand and sat back in his chair to finish his coffee.

Bob still wasn't home by the time Leigh went to bed that night. There had been no phone call. No card or flowers. Nothing. As Erik had warned her, the kids presented her with the anniversary cake, carefully avoiding the painfully obvious absence of the other half of the marital team. Leigh had done her best to pretend nothing was wrong.

The tears she'd held back at Antoine's came as she buried her face into her pillow. For the first time in months, she cried until her chest ached before falling into a restless sleep.

It was after two o'clock when she heard Bob come into the room. She knew the time because she lifted her arm and peered at the illuminated face of her wristwatch. He undressed in the darkness and crawled into bed next to her. She didn't move, just continued to lie stiffly on her right side, facing away from him. He didn't touch her. In fact, he seemed to take extra care to stay as far away from her as possible.

"I waited for you at the restaurant," she said, trying hard to keep her voice neutral. She felt him stiffen. After a moment, he turned over and draped an arm across her breasts.

He released a drawn-out sigh. "Oh, Christ, Leigh. I'm sorry. All hell was breaking loose on the Floor. I just couldn't get away. I'm sorry I didn't have Becca call you." He propped himself on an elbow and leaned over to peck at her cheek. "I'll make it up to you next year, okay?"

Without waiting for an answer, he turned over on his side, muttering, "Good night."

Leigh gazed up at the ceiling, dry-eyed. *Happy Anniversary to you, too.* She supposed she should consider herself lucky for that grudging little kiss on the cheek.

There hadn't been any physical intimacy between them since that October morning she had initiated sex while he was still sleeping. Over a month ago. She didn't want to believe it, but she was beginning to think that the only reason he'd been able to perform then was because he *had* been asleep. Could he only make love to her when he wasn't really aware of what he was doing—or whom he was doing it to?

Leigh stared into the darkness, her heart leaden. *What has happened to our marriage?* When had he stopped loving her? And dear God, when had she stopped *caring* that he'd stopped loving her? But that wasn't really true, was it? She *did* care. She just didn't know how to change it.

But something had to be done. They couldn't go on living

this sham of a marriage. Existing in the same house, but living separate lives. Tomorrow she'd go to the library and check out some books on rejuvenating a lackluster relationship. If she could get Bob to read them, discuss them with her, maybe then they could get their marriage back on track.

Making that decision made her feel better. And with the sound of Bob's soft, rhythmical breathing beside her, she finally fell back to sleep.

It wasn't until the weekend that she got the chance to corner Bob about the books she'd checked out. One of them, *Celibate Wives,* seemed especially appropriate to their situation. In the three days since their anniversary, she'd read it from cover to cover, earmarking one particular chapter, which seemed especially relevant to them. The more she read, the more excited she got. It wasn't a hopeless cause. There *were* some things that could be done to get their marriage back on track. As long as they both agreed there was enough of a marriage left to *get* back on track. Leigh had to believe there was. Deep down, she thought Bob still loved her. On some level. And she? She loved the Bob he used to be. Not the bad-tempered, tight-assed workaholic he'd become in the years since they'd moved from Ohio to Washington. But was there any way of finding that old Bob again?

On Sunday afternoon she found him in his study, poring over a new bill he wanted to propose. It wasn't a good time. She knew that. But when *was* a good time for Bob? And she'd resolved that the weekend wouldn't get away without them talking about this. Holding the book in her hands, she sat down in the chair opposite his desk and waited for him to look up. It took a few moments, but finally he did. He frowned, his mind obviously still on his work.

"Well?"

Leigh didn't know how to begin. Bob stared at her. She knew he was perplexed. He wasn't used to her invading his space. Especially when he was working.

"What is it?" His voice was impatient.

She took a deep breath. "We need to talk about us. Our problem."

He released a frustrated sigh and looked down at his legal pad. "Not now, Leigh. I'm busy."

"You're *always* busy. But, Bob . . . we can't go on like this."

He leaned back in his chair, folded his arms across his chest, and assumed a maddeningly patient expression. Like an overworked father forced to take a moment out to listen to his whining child.

"Okay. So, what's 'our problem' this time?"

Leigh stared at him. Was he playing dumb? Or was he really so clueless that he didn't realize they had a problem? His condescension made her want to slap him. Cut to the quick. *Our problem? Oh, nothing, really. Just that you can't get it up with me, you ass!* But of course, she would never, ever say anything so cruel.

No, she couldn't be cruel, but she could be blunt. "Your impotence," she said flatly.

His face reddened. He looked away from her as if he couldn't bear to meet her eyes. "That's just a temporary problem. Things will get better when Congress recesses."

"But that won't be for another month. I don't think this can wait. I think you should see a doctor, Bob."

His mouth thinned. "No way. I'm not going to let some psychiatrist dig around in my mind and start asking me asinine questions like if I hated my mother. No fucking way!"

"I'm not talking about a psychiatrist," Leigh said calmly. "A medical doctor. First, you need to find out if the impotence is physical."

"Would you stop using that word? I'm not impotent! I've got a lot on my mind these days, and I'm just not that interested in sex. So, *sue* me!" He scowled across the table at her. "Besides, didn't we screw a few weeks ago? You didn't seem to think we had a problem *that* morning, did you? In fact, if I remember correctly, you didn't have any reason to complain about my performance then, did you?"

It was Leigh's turn to blush. "Yes, I remember that morning

very clearly." *Wham, bam, thank you, ma'am.* "But, Bob, we still have a problem, and you know it. Here." She leaned forward and placed the book on his desk. "Can you take the time to read this book? You don't even have to read it all. I've book-marked one particular chapter that describes our situation. Please, Bob, will you just promise me you'll read it?"

He sighed and shook his head. "Whatever, Leigh. I'll try and get to it."

"You have to do more than try. If you care at all about me . . . about getting back anything *close* to what we used to have with each other, you've got to promise me you'll read that chapter."

"For Christ's sake!" Bob reached for the book, his face glowering. "*All right!* I *promise* I'll read the goddamn book. Now, will you let me get back to work?"

"Of course," Leigh said quietly, and stood up. Holding her head high, she left his study.

The book was due back at the library on the twentieth. He had almost three weeks to read it. Every Saturday, Leigh checked his progress when she went into his study to dust. The book-mark remained at the beginning of the chapter, where she'd inserted it.

On the Saturday before the twentieth, she picked up the book, looked once more to see if the bookmark had moved. It hadn't. She sank to the sofa, clenching the book in her hands. Her heart hammered as the truth hit her. *He doesn't care. He really doesn't care at all.* She bit down on her lower lip, her eyes swimming with sudden tears. And if he didn't care, how on earth could she *make* him care? Here, in her hands, she held the proof that her marriage was in shambles.

It dropped from her limp hands, hitting the carpeted floor. Leigh stood as a spasm of fury coursed through her. *No!* She couldn't let this go! She'd confront him, demand that he read the book. Threaten to leave him if he wouldn't.

From the back of the house, a door slammed. *"Mom!"* Aaron bellowed from the kitchen. "I'm hungry! What's for lunch?"

Her anger drained away. She bent, picked up the book, and took out the bookmark. Then she left Bob's study and headed for the kitchen.

The book was never mentioned again.

5

As Leigh turned to the stove to check on the beef stew, she heard the back door open and the stamp of boots on the doormat. Erik. She knew it was him because of the subtle scent of his sandalwood aftershave.

"God aften," he said, coming up behind her to peer into the stew-pot. "Mmmm . . . smells delicious. I'm famished."

Leigh stiffened at his nearness. Her heart gave a sudden lurch as his large hands clamped down on her shoulders. He leaned over her, so close she could smell the fresh scent of his flaxen hair. She closed her eyes, fighting an overwhelming desire to turn and rub her face against his bristly jaw. Instead, she forced herself to move away from him to open a cabinet, her eyes searching for something she didn't need.

"Reminds me of aromas from my mother's kitchen. Have you heard of *rommegraut*? It's a porridge flavored with sour cream and cinnamon, a Norwegian specialty." His eyes wore a faraway look as he gazed out the kitchen window. "It's especially good on a cold afternoon like this."

"It sounds delicious." Leigh moved to the refrigerator and opened it. "You wouldn't be homesick by any chance, Erik?"

He shrugged. "Perhaps a bit. Especially with the holidays coming up next month."

"Well, you're going home for Christmas."

"True. But you know, I think when I am at home, I will be homesick for America. I guess you just cannot win."

Leigh brought out tomatoes, lettuce, and cucumbers for salad and dumped them on the counter. "I guess not. Anyway, you'll be here for Thanksgiving. You know about that holiday, don't you?"

"Of course. It's your Turkey Day. And if I remember my American history correctly, it is about Pilgrims and Indians, *ja*?"

"You forgot pumpkin pie."

"Oh, *ja*, pumpkin pie. I am looking forward to my first Thanksgiving."

"I think you'll enjoy it. My family is driving out from Ohio. They're really anxious to meet you. By the way, where's Mark?"

"Studying at the library for midterms." Arms folded, Erik leaned against the counter, gazing at her. "Tell me about your family, Kayleigh. What are they like?"

"There's not much to tell. They're just ordinary people." She pulled open the cutlery drawer to search for a serrated knife. "Down-to-earth Midwesterners. I think you'll like Dad. He was a senator on the Hill for several terms, you know. We moved to Washington when I was fourteen. That's how I became such a big Redskins fan. Dad is a gruff old bear sometimes, but if you get him talking about something that interests him, you'll be his friend for life. Just to prepare yourself, he's suffered a hearing loss in the last few years. The TV will be on full blast while he's here. I think Mark told you what a football nut he is."

"Like his daughter." He grinned. "And your mother? Is she like you?"

Leigh cored the lettuce and rinsed it under the faucet. "In some ways. She's quiet, rather reserved. A bit old-fashioned, I think. She's never had a career. I don't know what she'd do if she didn't have Dad to take care of."

"May I slice the tomato for you?" He reached across her and grabbed one of the ripe fruits. Expertly, he cut it into wedges. "What about your sister? Barbara, isn't that her name?" He popped a piece of tomato into his mouth and grinned. "Ulterior motive, *ja*?"

"Just for that, you'll have to slice the cucumbers, too." She placed two cucumbers on the cutting board. "Oh, Barbara is as different from me and my mom as you can get. She's outgoing and vivacious. A real extrovert. It wasn't easy growing up in her shadow. Following her in school. All the teachers expected me to be just like her. Instead, I was painfully shy."

"Well, it appears you've come out of her shadow now. A successful artist, a good mother. Are you ready for these?" When she nodded, he scraped the cucumbers into a bowl.

Leigh began to toss the salad. "Yeah, but every time I get together with Barb, I always start to feel like that same shy little girl. I don't know, Erik, it's as if she were born under a lucky star or something. Everything has always worked out for her. You should see her with her husband. They've been married longer than Bob and me, yet . . . oh, I don't know. You'll see what I mean. They have such a special relationship. . . ."

"You deserve better," Erik said quietly.

Leigh looked at him. His eyes met hers steadily. A long silence fell, yet it was as if something unspoken passed between them. Her pulse raced. Abruptly, she grabbed the salad bowl and turned away.

Behind her, Erik spoke, "I'm sorry. That was inappropriate."

With one hand, Leigh made some adjustments in the refrigerator to squeeze in the salad bowl. The cool air fanned her hot cheeks as she struggled to regain her composure. She cleared her throat. "You're just too easy to talk to, Erik. It must be the psychoanalyst in you."

It was the perfect thing to say. The tension between them eased at once.

Erik laughed. "Perhaps I should look into writing an advice column. But actually, I want to ask *you* for some advice. Do you mind if I have a cup?" He nodded his head toward the coffeemaker.

"Help yourself. I'll have one, too."

Erik poured the coffee into mugs and brought them to the kitchen table. "There's this girl in my Abnormal Psychology class," he said, taking a seat. "She is, to use an American phrase, coming on to me."

Immediately Leigh had a vision of the girl . . . tall, blond, pert breasts, shapely ass, seductive smile. A tide of unreasonable jealousy ripped through her. She bit her bottom lip and sat down opposite Erik. "So, what's the problem? You don't like her?"

"Oh, she's hot, as Mark would say. But to put it bluntly, I'm not interested in going to bed with her. And she isn't easily discouraged." Erik scratched his head, his brows knitted in thought. "The thing is, Kayleigh, I like her. She's intelligent and easy to talk to. Fun, as well."

"I'm not sure I know what the problem is, then," Leigh said. "Keep it on a friendly basis."

Erik grinned ruefully. "That's easier said than done. Like I said, this girl is hot."

Leigh shook her head. "Erik, I'm afraid I'm still confused. Are you worried she's going to seduce you?" She felt the blush spreading across her cheekbones. "You can't tell me you've never been in this situation before. A good-looking guy like you . . ."

Erik's eyes drilled into hers. "No. But I'm at a period in my life where I prefer to remain celibate." He paused, his gaze dropping to his coffee mug. His index finger circled the rim restlessly. "Personal reasons. Let's just say my philosophy has changed in the last couple of years."

"Oh." Leigh didn't know what to say.

"I guess I just wanted to feel you out on this. Should I tell her up front that I want our relationship to remain platonic, or should I wait until the situation actually comes up? I don't want to be rude, you see."

Leigh shrugged. "I guess it depends on the girl. But if it were me—if I were interested in someone, I'd want to know right away if there was no chance of it going any further than friendship."

Erik smiled. "*Ja*, you would. You're forthright. That's why I like you." His hand reached out and covered hers. "You're so easy to talk to. My sister, Dordei, is there for me at home when I need advice. Perhaps you can fill in for her here."

With a feigned casualness, Leigh withdrew her hand from under his, yet even afterwards, she could still feel his touch. "Sure, Erik. Any time."

He stood up. "Thanks, Kayleigh. As Mark would say, I guess I'd better go beat the books. See you at dinner."

Leigh smiled at his mistake, but as soon as he left, her expression sobered. She sat at the table a moment longer. He'd compared her to his sister. She should feel relieved. She tried to tell herself she was. But inside, she knew the truth. It wasn't relief she felt; it was disappointment.

Leigh dipped a sponge into the bucket nearby and attacked the charred mess in the oven again. Cleaning the oven was one of her least favorite household chores, which was why she always procrastinated about doing it. She was the only congressman's wife she knew who refused to have live-in help. It was something to do with her upbringing, she supposed. Her father had served seven terms in the Senate, and Mom had always done her own housekeeping. That's just the way it was on the Connelly side of the family. And ordinarily Leigh enjoyed the housecleaning. She took a great deal of pride in her home and loved the way it felt to finish the weekly cleaning, to have the whole house looking sparkling and new— even though it never stayed that way for long.

But cleaning the oven was one job she wouldn't mind farming out to a maid. It didn't make sense, anyway, having an oven in this state-of-the-art kitchen that you still had to clean by hand. What were the previous owners thinking? The stove was one of the first things she'd planned on replacing as soon as it died a timely death. But that didn't appear as if it would happen anytime soon.

She sighed and continued scrubbing. Burned-on cherry pie filling, she guessed. This was what she got for being an avid baker. But she'd finally run out of excuses for putting it off. Especially with Bob's Christmas party coming up next week. He'd sprung it on her just a few days ago.

"I invited a few people over for a little get-together on the nineteenth," he'd said offhandedly.

Trouble was, Bob's "little get-togethers" usually meant a Capitol Hill crowd of forty to fifty. Of course, she'd have it catered, but even so, there were a thousand details that would have to be taken care of by—guess who?

"Worthless goddamn cleaner," Leigh muttered, scrubbing at the burned-on crud.

"Talking to yourself, Kayleigh?"

Startled, Leigh craned her head back to see Erik standing in the kitchen next to a slender girl who looked as if she'd just stepped out of the pages of *Glamour* magazine. She had silky light-brown hair that just grazed her shoulders in a sweeping bob, deep blue eyes, and a smile that would beguile a Tibetan monk.

"Kayleigh, I'd like you to meet Dawn. She's in my Psych class."

Dawn thrust out a slender hand and then withdrew it self-consciously when she saw Leigh's soiled rubber gloves. "Hi, there, Mrs. Fallon. I'm happy to meet you." Her southern accent was thick and syrupy. "Erik is always talking about his American family. He's just crazy about you all."

"Where are you from, Dawn? That's certainly not a Virginia accent you have." Leigh hoped her smile was pleasant, yet the slight edge in her voice couldn't be disguised.

"You're right, ma'am. I come from a little town in Tennessee. I'm sure you've never heard of it. Three Pines? It's at the foot of the Smoky Mountains."

Leigh's eyebrows rose. Her mother's side of the family came from Bristol, Virginia, a few miles from the Tennessee state line, and Leigh was well attuned to the nuances of the southern accent. Tennessee was one thing, but this Miss Cornbread and Grits accent was straight out of *Gone with the Wind.*

"Dawn, we'd better go hit the books," Erik said. He looked back at Leigh. "We're going to study for our Psych midterm in my room." He hesitated. "That's not a problem, is it?"

Leigh almost choked on the words. "It's your room, Erik. You don't have to ask permission to have friends over." She didn't miss the flirtatious smile Dawn threw at Erik when she said *friends.* Her hand tightened on the sponge.

Erik smiled back at Dawn. "Shall we?"

"Good-bye, Mrs. Fallon. It sure was nice meeting you. Erik

told me you're like a second mother to him, and now I can see why." Dawn tucked her hand into Erik's, and they left the room.

Viciously, Leigh threw the sponge into the bucket, not caring that the filthy water splashed her jeans. With a harsh snap, she stripped off the gloves and hurled them into the sink. Wheeling around, she marched into the bathroom and flicked on the light. She groaned as her eyes met her reflection in the mirror. God, she looked awful. Her skin was lifeless, her hazel eyes dull. She wasn't wearing even a hint of makeup. A black streak of oven gunk smudged one cheekbone. As if that weren't bad enough, her hair was hidden under an old cotton scarf, and she was wearing her oldest pair of jeans with one of Bob's oversize jerseys from his college football days.

What a way to meet Erik's prom queen. After seeing that picture of young perfection, Leigh felt like she was ready for a wheelchair and a ten-year supply of Geritol.

What were they doing in his room anyway? Hardly studying. How could Erik *possibly* study with a girl like that around? She should march up there right now and put a stop to whatever was going on. A vivid image of glamorous Dawn in Erik's arms caused her to cringe with envy. If only she were Dawn's age and free and single, able to be with Erik without guilt. Why couldn't she have met him twenty years ago, before Bob?

Because, she thought grimly, twenty years ago, Erik had been only seven. "I've got to stop this . . . insanity . . . ," she muttered. She knew she had no choice but to control this ridiculous obsession. Yet, she couldn't stop her mind from imagining the scene upstairs in his room. Erik and Dawn . . .

She gave a frustrated groan and stalked out of the bathroom. She still had the damn oven to finish.

Leigh glanced over at Erik's profile as the tenor onstage at the Kennedy Center sang "Every Valley Shall Be Exalted" from Handel's *Messiah.* His face wore an expression of rapt enjoyment. A rush of pleasure swept through Leigh, and for the thousandth time that evening, she realized how glad she was that he'd come along with her, Mark, and Vicki. Mark had acquired the tickets to the *Messiah*-Sing-Along from Vicki's brother, a trumpet player in the National Symphony Orchestra. She'd been able to get only four tickets, which meant two unhappy kids were left at home. Aaron, because he wanted to go, and Mel because she was stuck baby-sitting on a Friday night.

The chorus joined in, and hastily, Leigh glanced down at her music sheet and began to sing along. She felt Erik's eyes upon her and looked up. He gave her a warm smile as he sang in a rich baritone. She felt herself blush and quickly looked away.

Moments later, at the overture to the "Hallelujah Chorus," she stood with the rest of the audience. She bit her lip, determined to sing through the chorus tonight without choking up, something she'd never been able to do. The piece always caused an uncontrollable emotional reaction in her. Invariably her throat closed up with emotion and her eyes grew misty. It was so embarrassing. This year, she'd get through it.

It didn't work. By the last *hallelujah,* tears were streaming down her face. She turned away from Erik. She didn't want him to see her emotion. The concert ended. When the applause died out, the murmur of conversation filled the auditorium as the audience prepared to leave. Leigh continued to face away from Erik as she fumbled for her purse on the floor. His warm hand pressed upon her shoulder.

"Kayleigh, thank you for inviting me."

Quickly, Leigh brushed away her tears and turned to him, plastering a smile on her face. In astonishment, she saw that his blue eyes were watery and his face pink-tinged.

With a chagrined smile, he shrugged. "Handel always does this to me."

Leigh was glad Bob had refused to go with them. He would never have understood.

When they arrived home, Leigh wasn't at all surprised to find the Mercedes gone although it was after ten o'clock. Erik and Mark headed to their rooms to study. Leigh felt restless, too keyed up to watch TV or sleep. Handel's music still played in her mind, joyous and uplifting. She decided to make herself a cup of hot chocolate and go for a walk out by the brook.

The December night was clear, but not terribly cold. There was no wind, just the lulling sound of the waterfall as it tumbled over the smooth rocks. Leigh sat on an antique park bench she'd found at a yard sale in Occoquan a few years back. The hot chocolate was at just the right temperature. Warm and velvety smooth. But even after she'd finished it, she didn't feel like going in.

As a child growing up in a rural area of Ohio, she'd had many hours to spend alone. Barb, at five years older, had had her own friends and was always off with them. Leigh hadn't minded. She'd liked being alone, spending hours drawing, writing, or making up songs to sing. One summer, her dad had hung a swing from the branches of a big old oak in the backyard, and there, Leigh had spent many hours, just swinging and singing softly to herself. Those had been some of the happiest hours of her childhood.

"For unto us a child is born . . ." The anthem wouldn't leave her mind. Under her breath, she began to sing it. At the points where she didn't know the words, she hummed. It had always been her dream to sing Handel's *Messiah* in a choir, but at Bowling Green State, she'd been too involved with art and the piano to try out for choir. Tonight had been the closest she'd ever come. It had been a wonderful evening.

She reached the part where the males voices joined in. Her voice lowered an octave, "For unto us a child is born . . ."

"Unto us, a son is given . . ."

Her head whipped around. A few feet away stood Erik, hands in his jacket pockets. Even in the darkness, she saw the flash of his smile.

"Don't stop," he said. "Come on, sing with me. 'And the government shall be upon His shoulder . . .' "

Softly, Leigh joined in. "And His name shall be called Wonderful . . ."

"Councillor, the Mighty God." He came forward and sat down next to her.

"The Everlasting Father, the Prince of Peace," they finished together. It *should've* felt corny, but it didn't. Only right.

"I think we need a few more voices," Leigh said with a self-conscious laugh.

He smiled. "I think we sounded grand. You have a truly lovely voice, Kayleigh. I meant to tell you that tonight."

On the pretense of making herself more comfortable, Leigh moved a few inches away. He was sitting too close for her peace of mind. "Oh, thanks. I've always enjoyed singing. To myself, anyway."

He reached out and touched her gloved hand. "Music is in your soul, I can tell. Have I told you my mother is a musician? She was a violinist for the Oslo Philharmonic before she married my father. I believe the love of music is in our blood." His hand tightened on hers. "Let me see your hand. Here, lose the glove for a moment. I'll keep it warm."

He's flirting with me! Warning voices inside her brain told her to put a stop to it immediately. But tiny shivers were coursing through her as he stripped the leather glove from her hand. She could no more pull her hand out of his grasp than she could stop breathing. Besides, what was the harm in a little flirtation? It would never go further than this. She would never allow it to.

He held her bare hand between his soft gloved ones, peering at it. Slowly he turned it over and touched her palm, tracing her life line with his index finger. Leigh held her breath, almost light-headed by the thrill of his touch. Even through the leather of his gloves, she could feel the heat of him. It was as if a fire raged inside his hands, burning through bone, skin, and leather to scorch her.

He didn't seem to notice her agitation. A flicker of a smile appeared on his lips. "Ah . . . piano. You play it, do you not?"

"Not for a long time," she said, a soft catch in her voice. "It was my major in college. I had planned to make it a career, but then . . . well, other things got in the way, and I decided to switch to art."

"Bob?" A cool look came into his eyes. "That's where you met, isn't it? In college?"

Leigh looked away, concentrating on the waterfall's pale shimmer. "Well, actually, I met him here in Washington during the summer between my junior and senior year. He was an aide to my father during his last term in the Senate." She gave a short laugh. "I took him to a couple of concerts at the Kennedy Center, but it was obvious he was bored to death. Eventually, I decided to give up the piano. The rehearsals and concerts were taking too much of my time."

"And you've regretted it ever since, haven't you?"

She felt his gaze but refused to meet his eyes. "I regret a lot of things," she said, and then was horrified by her candor.

"Is Bob one of them?"

The question hung in the air between them. His hand tightened on hers. Until that moment, she'd forgotten he still held it between his. Was it because it had seemed so *right* there?

"Kayleigh . . ."

Leigh drew her hand away and stood up. Things were getting too dangerous. Spinning out of control. She hurriedly pulled on her glove. "I'm freezing, aren't you? Tired, too." She stifled a yawn. "I have a breakfast meeting with Ellen tomorrow. Guess I'd better get to bed."

Erik stood up. "*Ja*. I should, too. Come on, let's go in." He didn't speak again until they were inside the utility room. He helped her out of her parka and hung it on the nearby hook, then shrugged out of his own. Leigh turned to the kitchen.

"Good night, Kayleigh," he said. "Sleep well."

6

"Excuse me, Senator. There's someone over there I have to speak to." With a polite smile, Leigh extricated herself from Senator Isaac Winston's much-too-friendly grip and casually moved away to join a group of women standing near the Christmas tree.

"I saw her at Mel Krupin's the other day . . . and I swear, she looks fifteen years younger." Belinda Winston paused and crammed an hors d'oeuvre into her fleshy mouth. "I have *got* to find the name of her plastic surgeon."

"Speaking of plastic surgery," Janine Hudson chimed in. "Did you hear Cissy Heywood had breast implants? Jim says all the men at the club have trouble looking her in the eye now."

"Yeah, we know where they're looking," said Sharon Reynolds. "That's Cissy for you. Has to have the biggest house, the biggest car, and now, the biggest breasts."

The outspoken Carla Emmett, the wife of a congressman from Texas, gave a short, brittle laugh. She was one of the few congressional wives Leigh genuinely liked. Perhaps it was because she wasn't afraid to be more than her husband's shadow.

"Speaking of boobs, check out Rebecca kissing up to your husband, Leigh. Hot Damn! If my Ted looked like that hunk of yours, he'd have to kill me before I'd let him hire an AA like her!"

"Oh, Carla!" Leigh smiled. "As if you have to worry. Ted is nuts about you. Anyway, don't you think you're exaggerating? I wouldn't exactly call a conversation *kissing up.*"

One thin black eyebrow lifted. "I don't care what you call it. I'd just watch that little cupcake if I were you, Leigh. I've been on the Hill long enough to recognize her type. She's ambitious. And ambitious women in Washington know the best way to get to the top is through the bedroom doors.".

"Well, I'll keep my eyes open," Leigh said lightly. How could she explain to Carla that Bob wasn't interested in Rebecca or any other women? His ambition to get ahead took precedence over everything else. Besides, when would he possibly have time to have an affair?

The conversation swirled around her, repetitive and trivial, topics she'd heard discussed hundreds of times before. Finally, she decided she couldn't take another second of it and excused herself. No one noticed as she moved away, glancing around the room to make sure everyone had a drink and no one was left alone. For a moment, her eyes lingered on Bob and Rebecca standing in a corner, involved in an apparently absorbing conversation. Could Carla possibly be right? Was there more to their relationship than boss and employee? She just couldn't believe it. Not Bob. He was too staid, too fearful of scandal. And sex had never been a high priority for him.

The party appeared to be a success. *Well, it should be,* she thought. The cost of the buffet had set them back a small fortune, especially since Bob had insisted on the best. Pearly white beluga caviar filled two huge Waterford crystal bowls on a sideboard and was surrounded by finger foods from around the world. A rented silver fountain spurted Bob's favorite champagne, Taitlinger Rose, 1976. The drinks were flowing, the food was disappearing faster than the hired servers could keep it on the buffet table, and everyone seemed to be having a good time. Bob would have no cause for complaint.

She found Mark in the middle of a deep conversation with the Coe boy, the son of the Republican congressman from Idaho. Over by the Christmas tree, Erik stood surrounded by several teenage girls, including Mel. In spite of his sisterly treatment of her, Mel apparently still harbored a girlish infatuation with their Norwegian houseguest. And why not? Leigh was only too aware of his heady effect upon women.

She had just joined a group of the younger wives when she saw Bob take the glass from Rebecca's hand and stride over to the bar. A moment later, he appeared at her side. "The bartender is overwhelmed, and he's almost out of ice. Isn't there somebody else who's supposed to be helping him out?"

"I'll see what I can find out." She gave Lois Judd an apologetic smile. "I'll be right back."

The kitchen was deserted. She supposed the bartender's assistant had stepped outside for a smoke or something, and she didn't intend to hunt him down. Instead, she went to the freezer to get the bag of ice herself. As she closed the freezer door, she heard a footstep behind her, followed by a slurred voice. "So, this is where you wandered off to!"

Leigh sighed and turned around. "Do you need another drink, Congressman?"

Isaac Winston, the congressman from Georgia who'd been

on the Hill for years, was drunk—as usual. It happened at every party he attended. She wondered how he managed to stay in office with such an obvious drinking problem. He wasn't a bad-looking man—in fact, was relatively handsome—but his oily smile and cold brown eyes gave Leigh the creeps. Briskly, she emptied half the bag into the ice bucket, anxious to return to the family room.

Winston gave her a greasy smile and lurched toward her on unsteady feet. "It's not a drink I want, Leigh. You know that."

Leigh edged along the counter, moving closer to the door. "Congressman, maybe you've had enough."

"Maybe you *haven't* had enough." He grinned.

"Excuse me," Leigh said coldly. "I have to get back to my guests."

"Oh, come on, baby." He took a step closer. "I've seen the way you've looked at me tonight. You want it and you want it bad. And I'm the man to give it to you."

With a lightning movement, he was upon her, one hand fumbling her breasts while the other slid under her short velvet dress and moved up her thigh. Leigh reacted automatically, grabbing the nearest weapon, a liquor glass on the counter filled with half-melted ice cubes. Winston gasped and sputtered as the icy water hit the back of his neck.

"For God's sake, Leigh!"

She turned to see Bob in the doorway, his face white with shock. "What the *hell* is wrong with you?" He strode into the kitchen, grabbed a napkin from the table, and turned to Winston. "Isaac! I'm so sorry! I don't know what to say. . . ." He dabbed at the man's sodden neck. Leigh stared incredulously. Had Bob *any* idea how ridiculous he looked?

The cold water appeared to have sobered Isaac Winston for the moment. He gave a short, garbled laugh. "Don't worry, Bob. It was just a little joke between me and your lovely wife. Good thing I have a sense of humor." He continued to chuckle, but his eyes had hardened into dark brittle stones. "Guess I'll go scare up another drink."

After he made his way out of the room, Bob whipped around to Leigh. "Are you crazy?" he snarled. "Do you know what kind of power that man has? What are you trying to do? Ruin me?"

Stunned, Leigh stared at him, her body still trembling. Fury washed over her. "That man just attacked me! He practically raped me right here on the floor! Or in addition to giving your parties, do you expect me to also spread my legs for your fellow congressmen?"

Bob drew close to her, his anger matching hers. "You know something?" he said. "You're a very neurotic woman. The man has had a little too much to drink. So *what* if he flirts with you? That's no reason to dump a goddamn drink down his back! Now, are you going to bring out the ice or not?"

She turned, grabbed the bag of ice on the counter and thrust it into his gut. *"Get your own fucking ice!"*

For just a second, she thought he was going to hit her. His face had grown deathly white, his brown eyes as cold as the ice bag he cradled. But he didn't say a word. Just turned and marched out of the kitchen. Leigh stood still for a moment, her heart pounding. She looked down and realized she was still holding the liquor glass. *Flirting?* Her hands tightened on the liquor glass as blind rage engulfed her. She hurled the glass to the floor, releasing a cry of frustration.

She stared down at the tiny shards glittering atop the blue ceramic tiles, and the dam burst. Tears rolled down her face in a steady stream as she bent, sobbing, to pick up the pieces. Suddenly Erik was there at her side.

"Let me help." He knelt down beside her.

A shard of glass sliced her finger. *"Damn!"* she yelped. Her finger began to throb, and she cried harder. Through her tears, she watched the blood ooze out of the wound and was unable to move.

"Fordomme!" Erik exclaimed. He stood up and grabbed a dish towel from the counter and quickly wound it around her finger. "You're white as a ghost. Come sit down." He pulled her to her feet and nudged her into a chair at the kitchen table. Leigh tried to stop the flood of tears, but her throbbing finger only made it harder to gain control. She felt ashamed to have Erik see her like this, but something in her had snapped, and

there was nothing she could do about it. As she wept, he sat near her, silently cradling her injured hand tightly between his. He didn't try to console her with words—didn't attempt to stop her from crying. It was almost as if he knew how much she needed to release the pain. After a moment, when her weeping softened, he drew away the bloody towel and inspected the cut. "It doesn't look too frightful," he said. "Is there some antiseptic and bandages in the lavatory?"

Leigh nodded. "In the medicine cabinet."

While Erik stepped into the bathroom near the utility room, Leigh made an effort to regain her composure. By the time he returned with bandages and first-aid cream, her tears had stopped, and she sat staring blankly at a plaque on the wall. LEIGH'S KITCHEN. TONIGHT'S MENU, 2 CHOICES. TAKE IT OR LEAVE IT. Erik sat down opposite her and gently dabbed ointment onto the cut.

"Why don't you tell me what happened?" he asked quietly.

Leigh shrugged, making an effort to underplay it. "Oh, nothing. Not to hear Bob tell it, anyway. He walked in and caught the Honorable Congressman Winston groping me, and then had the nerve to say he was just *flirting* with me." She shuddered, remembering Winston's beefy hand moving under her dress. "I guess we have different ideas of flirting. I call it sexual assault. But then again, I'm neurotic, so what do *I* know?"

Erik's eyes sparkled dangerously. "He called you neurotic? *Kristus!*" He placed a bandage onto her finger, and afterwards, didn't release her hand but held it between his. "That drunken sot deserves a good throttling."

"The man is a disgusting pervert," Leigh said. "He always comes on to me, but never like that before."

Erik muttered something in Norwegian. Leigh couldn't be sure, but judging by his tone, she felt certain it was a curse.

"But don't worry. I took care of him this time. I dumped a drink down the back of the bastard's neck. Of course, Bob took *that* moment to walk in."

Erik smiled wryly. "Good for you. I wish you'd dumped

one down your husband's neck, as well. I detest the way he treats you, Kayleigh."

Leigh rubbed her temples with a trembling hand. "It's hot in here." She tried to get to her feet. "I've got to get out of this house and get some fresh air."

Erik's hand clamped down on her shoulder. "Don't move. I'll get our coats. You're not going anywhere by yourself."

She managed to smile. "What do you think I'll do? Throw myself into the brook?"

But he'd already left the room. He was back in a moment, two coats hanging over his arm. "I brought your down coat. It's really getting cold out there."

Leigh stood up, fighting dizziness as he helped her into her coat. He pulled on his heavy fur-lined flight jacket and together, they stepped out the back door. Leigh caught her breath as the icy wind hit her. Almost immediately she felt the disoriented, dizzy feeling begin to disappear. She sniffed the cold night air. Snow? Was it possible they would have a white Christmas? Erik would love that. But then, Erik wouldn't be here; he was going home tomorrow. The thought saddened her.

Without speaking, but as if they were on the same wavelength, they headed toward the grove of trees surrounding the pond and waterfall. The rush of water was loud in the frigid stillness of the night. Near the trees, they found they were sheltered from the wind, and the cold was bearable. A glimmer of moonlight beamed from the black sky, playing on the sharp angles and planes of Erik's face. They stood silently for a few moments, staring at the white cascade of water spilling into the pond.

"The waterfall is called a *foss* in Norway," Erik said finally, his voice musical over the sound of the tumbling water. "There is one special waterfall in Norway I would like you to see. Reiardsfossen in Ose. There is a rather romantic legend about the place. Shall I tell you?"

"Please! I love legends!"

"Me, too. In this one, there was a man named Reiard who was very much in love with Ann, the daughter of the richest man in the province. Reiard asked for her hand in marriage, but her father told him he would have to prove his love by riding his horse over the brink of the falls. He did it successfully, but on his triumphant return, the horse slipped. They plunged to their deaths before the horrified eyes of Ann and her father. The girl was so distraught she flung herself in after him."

"Oh, how awful!" His words had painted a vivid picture in her mind.

Erik's teeth flashed in a crooked grin. "Awful, *ja*, but romantic. Norse lore is filled with romantic tragedy. Kayleigh, I wish you could come to my country. I know you would love it. There is a little town in the south called Nisserdal. It's the home of *Yulnissen*, Father Christmas. When I was a young boy, we would visit there on holiday. I was always hoping we would see Father Christmas, but, of course, we never did. I think if we had seen someone who resembled him, it would have ruined our fun."

"You sound homesick. But earlier tonight you told me you didn't want to go home."

He was quiet for so long she thought he wasn't going to respond. But finally, he did. "*Ja*, I did say that."

"Is it because of Dawn?" Leigh asked. "You know, you won't be separated for long."

He turned to look at her, his face astonished. "*Kristus!* Is *that* what you think?"

"What else?" Leigh said. A shiver swept through her, but she wasn't sure if it was caused by the cold or the blazing heat in Erik's eyes.

He drew close to her and pulled his hands out of his pockets to grasp hers. In the moonlight, his eyes drilled into hers. "It's *you* I don't want to leave. Kayleigh, I'm falling in love with you."

Leigh gazed at him, astounded by his admission. She hadn't lost *that* much blood. Was this another of her bizarre fantasies? But Erik's impaling gaze was too real to be imagined. She felt paralyzed by his nearness. His hand softly touched her cheek, brushing her wind-tousled hair away with tenderness. Slowly, he bent his head and touched his lips to hers. They were warm, so very warm. He drew away as if to gauge her reaction. Leigh stared at him, her mouth half-open, her breathing shallow. Her hands had somehow crept up to the shoulders of his jacket. They tightened convulsively against the material in a silent protest at his withdrawal. Sensing her need, his mouth descended again, his tongue tentatively exploring between her lips. When she didn't pull away, his mouth hardened on hers, and the kiss became urgent with need and longing. For an exquisite moment, Leigh gave herself up to it, encouraging the heat inside her to erupt into a blaze.

Finally, from somewhere, she found the strength to pull away, to let the cold air of the December night bring her back to reality. She stepped away from him, still feeling the rapid pounding of his heart against her chest. Or was that hers? She found it difficult to meet his gaze, but when she did, his expression was almost too much to bear. He looked so young, so vulnerable. What in the world was she doing out here with him? She must be crazy! God, she'd sworn she'd never let this happen. But it had, and now she had to try to fix things before it was too late.

She drew a deep breath before speaking. "I'm sorry. I don't know why I let you kiss me. I guess I've had too much to drink tonight."

"That's not so," Erik said bluntly. "You know what is happening here, and it has nothing to do with how much you had to drink tonight."

"I'm going back to the house now." Leigh's eyes evaded his. "Let's forget this happened, Erik. It was just a weak moment for both of us. That's all."

"Do you really believe that?"

When she didn't answer, he eyed her silently, and then shrugged. "If that's the way you want it. Merry Christmas, Kayleigh."

After Erik's return from Norway, Leigh couldn't help but notice his change in attitude toward her. No longer did he linger in the kitchen at night as she loaded the dishwasher, chatting about his classes and the idiosyncrasies of his professors. Instead, he avoided being near her. She tried to convince herself she was relieved, but her emotions knew differently. Every time she heard a footfall, her heart lifted, thinking it was him, but it would turn out to be Mark or Bob, and she'd have to disguise her disappointment. On the few occasions she found herself alone with Erik, he never brought up the incident by the waterfall. It was almost as if it had never happened, except they both knew it had.

Kayleigh, I'm falling in love with you. His words had been hoarse with intensity. She knew he'd believed it at the time. But now, with his coolness, she wondered if while he was home, he'd realized it was nothing more than a schoolboy crush. That possibility bothered her more than she wanted to admit.

But worse than Erik's new attitude toward her was the realization that his relationship with Dawn had turned serious. He spent almost every night with her. On at least two Saturday nights, he hadn't returned home at all. Leigh tried to pretend it was no big deal. But she hated the thought of Erik being with Dawn.

"Damn it," she said, crumpling another drawing. She simply couldn't concentrate today. With a grunt of exasperation, she slid back her chair and stood up. She'd go downstairs for another cup of coffee. At least it gave her an excuse to get away from the drawing table. The phone at her desk rang just as she reached the stairs.

It was Ellen. "Girl, have I got some good news for you."

"Well, I can use some," Leigh said glumly.

"Deanna Harper is coming to town tomorrow, and she's very interested in meeting you. She thinks you might be the perfect artist to do the cover of her new book. Are you free for lunch?"

Leigh's heart raced. Deanna Harper was a celebrated author of young adult books. It would be a great career boost to do the art for one of her covers.

"Of course I'm free," Leigh said. This could be just the motivation she needed to pull her from the doldrums.

"Great. Why don't you meet us at Clyde's in Georgetown about one o'clock? And bring your portfolio."

"I'll be there." Leigh smiled. "See you tomorrow." She hung up with a renewed sense of anticipation. Perhaps this year, spring would come early.

As Leigh crossed the Chain Bridge on her way into Georgetown, she wondered what Deanna Harper would be like. She knew the divorced Harper lived well in New York from the income of her controversial books for teenagers, books about first sexual experiences, drugs, peer pressure, even masturbation. Although many parents disapproved of Harper's candidness, Leigh felt she handled those touchy subjects with taste and sensitivity, and she'd had no qualms in allowing Melissa to read every book.

In a few moments, Leigh would be meeting the famous author. Possibly, she would be working with her soon. A pleasant tingle went through her as she miraculously found a parking place along the street in Georgetown. That was a good omen if she'd ever seen one.

Inside the entrance of Clyde's, the hostess ushered her to a corner table where her agent and a dark-haired woman waited. "Well, here she is. Finally!" exclaimed Ellen. "Where have you been?"

"Am I late?" Leigh apologized. "I lost some time because of construction on the bridge." She turned her attention to Ellen's companion.

"Two minutes, but we'll forgive you this time. Leigh, meet Deanna Harper. Dee, this is Leigh Fallon."

Deanna Harper looked nothing at all like Leigh had imagined. Wearing snug black leggings and an oversize bulky sweater that went past her hips, Deanna had shoulder-length ebony hair that fell in a mass of unruly curls. She wore absolutely no makeup on her flawless face, and her eyes were huge and brown behind a pair of big, round, tortoiseshell glasses. The only thing that saved her from being a classical beauty was her Streisand-like nose. Leigh had never before seen such a striking woman except on television and at the movies. Could this really be the woman who wrote those sensitive teenage novels?

Deanna clasped her hand in a warm greeting. "Leigh, I'm thrilled to meet you." She spoke with a strong Brooklyn accent. "I've admired your illustrations for years. My daughter, Carrie, is fifteen, and she *still* hasn't outgrown your animal books."

"Thank you," Leigh said, unable to digest such praise from a writer of Harper's caliber. "And my daughter, Melissa, is crazy about *your* books. So am I, I might add."

"Well, that's reassuring." Deanna turned to Ellen and smiled. "I like her already."

". . . and we got up to my apartment and were lying on the bed, kissing the hell out of each other . . ." Deanna swallowed the dregs in her wineglass and leaned across the table toward Leigh. "Well, I casually reached down to unzip his pants and he shrieked and jumped away from me as if he'd been stung by a killer bee." She paused to light a cigarette while Leigh waited in anticipation. "Turns out this guy was a raving queen. He'd been going to a psychotherapist who'd convinced him to give women another chance. And he picked *me* to experiment on. Leigh, this guy was gorgeous. I was totally *blown away* when he told me he was gay. Anyway, I made some coffee, we smoked a few joints and ended up talking till morning. I talked him into getting a new therapist, and now he's out of the closet and as happy as a pig in shit."

Leigh laughed at Deanna's bawdy language. For the past hour, and over a bottle of Chablis, the writer had been regaling Leigh with stories of her colorful life. Ellen had left for another meeting shortly after lunch, leaving Leigh to fend for herself with the charismatic Deanna Harper. *Not that I was able to get a word in edgewise,* Leigh thought in amusement. *What a talker!* Still, it hadn't taken Deanna long to offer Leigh the cover assignment. And she'd accepted it immediately, knowing she would love working with her.

Deanna ordered another bottle of wine and began to tell Leigh about her present lover. "He's a twenty-three-year-old

CPA who does strip-o-grams on the side. We have a really good relationship. Based completely on sex, of course. Sometimes, I think that's the way it should be. What about you?"

"What *about* me?"

Deanna's brown eyes assessed her. "Do you have a lover?"

"Of course not." Leigh laughed. "I'm married."

"I know that," Deanna said. "But you're a real attractive lady. Kind of a toned-down Sharon Stone. You must have guys coming on to you all the time. Aren't you ever tempted? Don't look so shocked, Leigh. I'm a writer. People are my business. We've been sitting here for almost two hours, and we've talked about everything under the sun. Except your husband. You've barely mentioned him. I've heard about Melissa, Mark, and Aaron. And that Norwegian student staying with you. But the only thing I've heard about Bob is that he's a congressman and spends most of his time on the Hill." She shook her head. "Something tells me your marriage is lacking. Am I right?"

Leigh felt the color rise on her cheeks. Deanna stubbed out her cigarette in the ashtray and laughed. "Oh, Leigh. I'm a stupid bitch and should mind my own business. Problem is, I can't. I'm too nosy. But you'll get used to me."

Leigh glanced at her watch through somewhat bleary eyes and gasped. It was after four o'clock. And rush-hour traffic into Virginia was going to be *murder*. "I've got to get home." She signaled for the check.

"I'm not about to let you drive after drinking all that wine," Deanna said sharply. "I'll take you home."

"Well, you drank as much as me," Leigh said, and then bit her lip. Of course, a woman like Deanna Harper wouldn't be driving herself. "Oh, God. What *a faux pas*."

Deanna's eyes twinkled. "Yeah, you really blew it, kid. Forgetting I'm one of the rich and famous. It just proves you can take the girl out of Brooklyn, but not Brooklyn out of the girl, huh?"

After the check was settled, Deanna stood, somewhat unsteady on her feet. She giggled. "This is one reason I love being rich. I can drink as much as I want and never have to worry about driving drunk. Not bad for a snotty little Jewish girl, right?"

"Deanna, I can't let you drive me home. What about my car?"

Deanna shrugged. "When Gabriel gets back to the city, he can drive your car home to you. Just give me the keys."

Leigh hesitated, wondering what Bob would say.

"Come on." Deanna insisted. "You obviously are too ineb-innev-inebriated to drive."

"I guess you're right." Leigh laughed, giddiness sweeping over her. Besides, she was having so much fun she welcomed the long ride back with Deanna. And it wasn't as if she got to ride in a limo every day.

Together, the two women stepped out into the dark January afternoon. Usually, the early darkness of winter depressed Leigh, but not tonight. The liquor and Deanna's vibrant personality had warmed her thoroughly. She felt as if a whole new world had opened up to her.

Leigh stepped out of the shower and wrapped a thick bath towel around her. Shivering, she dried off and quickly slipped on a white satin kimono. As she opened the medicine cabinet to look for the ReNu disinfecting solution, she wondered about the condition of the roads. She really needed to meet with Ellen in Georgetown to discuss the Harper contract, but she hated driving if the roads were slick. Snow in the D.C. area seemed to bring out the maniacs in force.

"Damn!" She shook the plastic bottle of ReNu, but heard no slosh of liquid inside. "Who put this empty bottle back in here?" Frowning, she tossed it into the trash. "Now, what do I do?"

Then she remembered Bob's emergency bag. He always kept a bottle of disinfecting solution in it. Luckily, when he'd called yesterday to tell her he had to make a quick trip to Cleveland, he hadn't had time to come home for his bag.

She found the travel bag on the floor of his closet and brought it over to the bed. As soon as she opened it, she saw the box of condoms right on top. Rough Riders. Without her contacts, the picture of the buxom blonde was blurry, but there was no doubt in her mind about the contents.

She sat down on the bed, her stomach queasy. Her fingers trembled as she turned the box over in her hand, her mind whirling with the significance of her discovery. Condoms. Bob hadn't had a need for these in the last ten years. Unless he was sleeping with someone other than his sterilized wife.

Rebecca. Of course.

So, Carla Emmett had been right all along. Leigh dropped the box back into the bag, her fingers icy, her mind numb. Suddenly her skin prickled.

She looked up. Erik stood in the threshold. He stared at her, his blue eyes dark with an unmistakable emotion. Longing. Outside, the falling snow hissed softly as it hit the ground, adding a provocative aura to the knifelike tension in the room.

Finally, Erik spoke, his voice husky. "I'm sorry. I didn't realize . . ."

Leigh stood and tightened the belt of her kimono. "Erik. What are you doing home from class?"

His face had taken on a pink glow. "Class was canceled because the professor's wife died of her illness last night. I don't have another class until two."

"I'm sorry to hear that. I mean, about your professor's wife . . ." She trailed off.

His face had changed, gained composure. "I'll let you get back to . . ." He gave a slight shrug, but instead of moving, gazed at her a moment longer.

Leigh shivered. Stoic as he was, he couldn't hide the fire in his blue eyes. She stared at him, thankful that her nearsightedness veiled the intensity of his gaze. Even so, she felt weak and breathless. For just a second, she considered asking him to stay. But sanity won out.

"Yes," she said. "I've got a lunch meeting in town." Leigh turned to her dressing table, running her fingers through her drying curls. When she looked back at the doorway, he was gone.

7

Leigh stood at the latticed window staring out at the snow drifting lazily to the ground. In her mind, she saw Erik's face again. His strained longing expression had driven all thought of Bob and Rebecca.

"He wants me . . . ," Leigh whispered. What a concept. It had been *so* long since she'd felt desired. A moment ago, when he'd stood in the threshold of her bedroom, Erik had looked different, much older than he had when he'd first arrived. From the beginning, Leigh had berated herself for having lustful thoughts about a man only nine years older than her son. Now, for the first time, she began to think of Erik *as* a man, one who could make his own decisions. It no longer mattered that he was young, that he was a friend of her son's, that he was a guest in her home. None of it mattered anymore.

He wanted her.

Slowly, Leigh turned from the window and moved toward the door. From Erik's room, she heard the haunting first movement of Vivaldi's "Winter" from *The Four Seasons*. At the small round window at the end of the hall, she stopped and gazed through the pie-wedged panes of leaded glass, dreamily watching the snow. The flakes were larger now. She hoped school wouldn't be dismissed early. But even with that threat, she turned away from the window and moved to the threshold of Erik's door.

It was ajar. Her heart thundered. With a dry mouth and clammy hands, she stopped in the doorway and watched him. He stood at the window staring out. Her eyes centered on his slim buttocks in the snug-fitting jeans and then moved up to where his blond hair curled over the back of his collar. How strong and broad his shoulders were in his blue-plaid flannel shirt. She longed to run her hand under his silky curls, her fingertips caressing his strong neck, touching the pulse quivering there below his ear.

Out of nowhere, the realization hit her. She couldn't go through with it. She wasn't a seductress. She'd been raised in a devout Presbyterian household. *She couldn't do this*!

She backed away from the threshold. But at that moment, Erik turned and saw her. A light flared in his brilliant blue eyes. "Kayleigh," he said in a half-whisper.

In the heavy silence between them, the music of Vivaldi played, achingly sweet. The moment was fragile. Leigh knew any abrupt intrusion from the outside would break the spell forever. *I should be praying for a phone call.* Instead, she found herself praying nothing would interfere with what she knew was about to happen.

He moved toward her, his face like carved stone, his eyes smoldering. Escape was out of the question now; no longer was it desired or needed. Turning back now would be tantamount to stopping a tidal wave. She could only stare up at him, her breathing shallow, waiting for his touch. He reached out, clasped her hands, and drew her into the room. Releasing her, he closed the door. And it was as if he were locking out the other world.

He turned to her. For a long moment, they faced each other, close but not touching. Finally, he reached for her. His hand gently skimmed her neck, trailing down over the curve of her breast and then hesitating at the belt of her robe. He untied the knot, his eyes locked with hers. She felt the fleeting touch of his fingertips at her shoulders and the robe dropped from her limp arms onto the floor. His eyes roved over her, savoring, just before his strong hands moved across her collarbone and slid up her neck under her damp hair.

"Kayleigh," he whispered. His mouth closed over hers. With a soft moan, Leigh opened to him, allowing him to explore the tender inner flesh of her lips with his tongue. After a long moment, he drew away, his fingers skimming her shoulders. Immediately, his lips branded her, traveling from her shoulder down to the swell of her breast. Leigh closed her eyes, her fingernails digging into the flannel of his shirt. At the touch of his lips against her skin, her blood had become electric rivers of fire, coursing through her vessels, igniting her body. She felt mindlessly possessed. The world beyond this room no longer mattered. The past, the future. Nothing was real but this moment.

"Erik . . . ," she whispered. "I want you."

He drew his mouth away from the hollow of her throat and straightened. His eyes held hers. "I know. I've wanted you since the day we met. Why did we take so long?"

Her gaze dropped to his chest. Slowly, she unbuttoned his shirt and tugged it out of his jeans. A second later, the flannel lay discarded on the floor. She slid her hands beneath his T-shirt to touch him, to feel the crisp hairs under her fingertips, to explore the masculine circles of his nipples. With a soft groan, Erik drew away, pulled the T-shirt up and over his head, whipping it onto the carpet. In a second, she was back in his arms, his mouth plundering hers. Just as she was certain her legs would no longer support her, Erik swept her into his arms and deposited her on the bed. Through half-closed eyes, she watched as he unbuckled the belt on his jeans, his golden-haired chest rising and falling with restrained excitement. His jeans fell to the floor, followed immediately by his Jockey shorts.

"*Kjareste* . . . ," he whispered, sliding onto the bed next to her, wrapping his arms and legs around her, warming her blood as if he were a protective winter cloak. Between Norwegian words of endearment, he nuzzled her neck while his hands roamed freely over her willing body. As if reliving one of her erotic fantasies, Leigh gave herself up to the sensation of Erik's hands and mouth as they explored unhindered every inch of her body. Half-crazed with the need to feel him inside her, she sighed in relief when he, after long moments of exquisite torture, rolled onto his back, pulling her on top of him. With tenderness, he eased into her. Eyes closed, savoring the delicious feeling of his fullness, Leigh was still, barely breathing.

"Sit up . . . ," Erik whispered. ". . . *ja . . . det god.*" His thumbs gently circled her kiss-swollen nipples. "Open your eyes, Kayleigh. I want to watch your face while we make love."

Leigh gave a soft moan. Her eyes fluttered open to look into the deep blueness of his. Slowly, he began to move beneath her. Leigh caught her breath. How could she have lived this long without ever experiencing anything like this? A moment later, she was beyond thinking. There was nothing else in the world but this encompassing plane of physical sensation. The two of them moved together in an ancient primal ballet . . . but for Leigh, a new world of love had opened up, and she realized that until today, she'd been an emotional virgin. Today, this moment, she was making love for the first time.

It seemed to go on forever. Leigh, in the back of her drugged mind, hoped the loving would never end. They moved together in perfect unity, as if they were programmed for each other by a higher authority. Imperceptibly, the tempo quickened. Erik's eyes darkened, the slight lines around his lips tightened with tension. Finally, with a groan, he arched his back, his eyes closing in astonished exhilaration, and at the same moment, Leigh felt as if a sudden earthquake had erupted deep inside her. A strangled moan escaped her dry throat as exquisite spasms rocked through her, carrying her to a peak of sensation she'd never dreamed possible.

Gasping, disoriented, she fell against Erik's sweat-dampened body. "Oh, God . . . ," she murmured against his damp neck. "Oh, God . . . Erik . . ."

Still inside her, he caressed her back and buttocks, covering her face with tiny kisses, murmuring in Norwegian. Finally, after a long moment, he rolled her onto her side and withdrew from her, his hands curled tightly in her hair. He searched her face tenderly and then smiled. *"Vilter pike . . . ,"* he said. "Wild girl . . ."

Leigh blushed.

"No, don't be embarrassed. There is nothing wrong with being uninhibited."

Leigh heard the soft thud of snow against the window and

realized that the music of Vivaldi had ended sometime during their lovemaking. She couldn't speak. No words would come. Instead, she kissed the salty hollow of Erik's throat as her fingers played with the hair of his chest. She wished she could stay here like this forever. Many thoughts meandered through her mind as she lay against his warm, sated body. Without a doubt, this had been no inexperienced schoolboy that had just lifted her to the heights of passion. How many other women had he been with? she wondered. Dawn, for sure. Leigh felt a wave of jealousy sweep through her.

Uncannily, Erik read her thoughts. "Do not think of her, *kjareste*," he murmured, one hand lightly caressing the swell of her left breast. "She meant nothing to me. All I ever wanted from the beginning was you."

"Those nights you didn't come home . . . ," Leigh said.

"I was like a child. I wanted to make you jealous. After the night we kissed down by the lake, I knew you felt as I did. But you were determined that we stay away from each other. When I went home for Christmas, I talked to my sister, Dordei, about the situation."

"You told her about me?"

Erik chuckled and squeezed her tightly. "No, *kjareste*, I told her about a woman I had fallen in love with who wanted nothing to do with me. So, she suggested that I—how would Mark say it? Give her the cold shoulder? I followed her advice. And . . . well, you know now that it worked."

Embarrassed again, Leigh buried her face in his shoulder. "Yes, I was easy for you."

Erik's finger tipped her chin up so their eyes could meet. "Kayleigh, I was determined to make love to you. I knew you felt the same and I also knew you couldn't deny it forever. But let me tell you about Dawn. I never had sex with her. On those nights I stayed away, I spent the night in the dorm room of a friend. It was you I wanted. *Only* you." One hand slid down the curve of her buttock, sending shivers through her hypersensitive skin.

The fires inside her hadn't really had a chance to die, and now they flared again. Erik moved down her body, his tongue circling her nipple. Her blood stirred. She felt his erection against her thigh, and couldn't wait to feel him inside her again.

The phone shrilled into the empty silence of the house, paralyzing them. Erik drew his lips away from her breast to look up at her.

"We're no longer alone," he said.

She knew what he meant. The outside world had encroached. "It's Ellen." Leigh scrambled up from the bed, grabbing Erik's flannel shirt from the floor. She ran down the hall toward her bedroom, pulling on the shirt. The phone was on its fifth ring when she reached it.

"Where the hell are you?" It was Ellen, and she was angry. "We were supposed to meet for lunch a half hour ago."

Leigh had the phone propped onto her shoulder as she fumbled to button up Erik's shirt, somehow feeling as if that would make her feel less guilty. "Ellen! God, I'm sorry. But this snow! I . . . couldn't get the car started." Amazed that she could lie so easily, she went on, "I tried to call, but I couldn't get through. There must be a problem with the lines because of the snow."

Nude, Erik walked into the bedroom.

"My agent . . . ," Leigh mouthed to him as she listened.

"There doesn't seem to be a problem with the lines now," Ellen said dryly. "Look, I have the Harper contract ready for signature. We need to get it back to her."

"Can you send it by courier?"

Erik had slipped behind her and was now sliding a hand under her shirt, his fingers searching for the sensitive center between her legs. Leaning against him, she felt the thrusting hardness of him against her lower back. Her breathing quickened. She spoke hastily into the phone, "Look, I can't talk now. Okay. I'll be watching for it." She waited just long enough for Ellen's disgruntled agreement and slammed down the phone, then turned in Erik's arms.

Their lips met in a fierce, hungry kiss. After a moment, Erik pulled away and slowly unbuttoned the shirt she'd so painstakingly fastened a moment before. Gently, he slipped it off her shoulders.

"Forgive me if I'm too rough," he whispered. "You do strange things to me." Her answer was to draw his blond head down to her for another long, drugging kiss. Then, she was lost and could only moan incoherently as he eased her down onto the carpeted floor.

This time, their lovemaking was tumultuous, almost violent in its intensity. It was over in a few short moments. Incredibly, her orgasm surpassed the one before. Afterwards, Erik got to his feet and drew her up with him. Without speaking, he walked to the bed and drew back the satin comforter. His eyes implored her. Her limbs felt weak as she moved to the bed and slid in. A second later, he was with her, his warm body holding her against him as he gathered the covers around them. Neither spoke for a long time, but finally, in a solemn voice, Erik said, "You know, we can never go back to the way it was before."

"I know," Leigh whispered. "Why do you affect me the way you do? I've never felt like this before."

He kissed her damp neck. "I don't ever want you to feel like this with anyone else."

Leigh's eyes grew heavy. "No, never."

"Kayleigh," he said. "Look at me." His blue eyes were serious. "Do you feel guilty?"

Leigh searched his face, her fingers lightly caressing the invisible whiskers on his jaw. "I suppose so," she whispered. "But I don't want to think about it now."

"Don't *ever* feel guilty about us," he said quietly. "Promise me."

Somewhat bewildered, Leigh gazed into his beseeching eyes. "I promise."

Sighing, Erik allowed his eyes to close, although his arms didn't loosen his grip on her. "I will never forget this day," he said. "When I am back in Norway on a winter day like this, I will look out at the snow and remember you and our lovemaking."

With his words, Leigh felt a vague chill creep over her, and even the warmth of his long body next to hers couldn't make it go away.

A feeling of alarm woke her. Carefully, Leigh eased away from the heavy weight of Erik's arm to look at the digital clock on the bedside table. She gasped in disbelief. Almost two o'clock! Mel and Aaron were due home from school at two-thirty.

"Erik!" Leigh shook his shoulder gently. "Wake up, Erik."

He groaned and tightened his hold on her. For a moment, she relaxed against him, burrowing her face into the hollow of his neck. Had she ever before felt this warm? With every shallow breath she took, she inhaled his musky fragrance. It was heady, delicious. She pulled away to look at his sleeping face. A wave of emotion washed over her, a feeling that couldn't be attributed to just good sex. But it was so impossible she fought against it. Remembering the time, she leaned down to kiss his bristly jaw. "Erik, love, you have to wake up. The kids will be home from school soon."

This brought a response. One hand moved slowly over the swell of her breast and turning, he planted a succulent kiss against the side of her throat. "See? I want you again," he whispered, his hand guiding hers onto his stiff penis.

The telltale heat suffused throughout her eager body, but this time she knew she had to quench it. She drew away from him and threw back the covers.

"You missed your class," she said as she walked naked to her closet.

His head propped upon a pillow, Erik's amused eyes followed her every movement. "I would miss a thousand classes for the opportunity to make love to you."

Leigh pulled on an old robe and turned back to him, her eyes soft. "Thank you," she said. "I'd almost forgotten what it felt like to be desirable."

Erik's face hardened. He threw the satin comforter back and swung his long legs over the side of the bed. As he stood up, Leigh suppressed a gasp at the beauty of his nude body. He stopped in front of her, his blue eyes icy. "Why don't you leave him?" he asked. "He doesn't deserve you. And you know you don't love him."

Leigh stared up at him. "I can't do that to the kids. And I'm not strong enough to make it on my own."

His hand caressed her face, and his expression softened. "You are, you know. And someday, you will realize that." He bent down to kiss her lips lightly. "God, Kayleigh, I can't get enough of you."

Leigh found his lips again; she clung to him longingly, not wanting to let him go. After a long moment, he pulled away with a sigh. "I've got to get to my room and get dressed."

"What will you say to Mark when he asks why you weren't at classes this afternoon?"

Erik shrugged. "I'll tell him I developed one of my migraine headaches." He grabbed his discarded shirt from the floor and smiled at her. "Tonight, *kjaereste*? After everyone is asleep?"

A thrill of excitement shivered through her. "I'll come to you," she said.

He flashed his beguiling grin and disappeared through the door. Leigh walked to the window and stared out pensively. The snow had stopped and a weak sun struggled to break through the clouds.

The deception had begun.

8

"You're awfully quiet tonight, Leigh. Have a rough day?"

Leigh's eyes darted up from her untouched plate. Bob stared at her, a disquietingly curious look on his face. Her cheeks grew warm. "No. I'm just kind of tired." She felt Erik's eyes upon her, but didn't dare look in his direction.

It had been almost two weeks since she'd spent the afternoon in his arms. Every nerve in her body screamed with tension. Since Bob's return from Ohio, she found it hard to look at Erik because she knew her desire was written upon

her face. She could see it on his, too. How was it be possible
no one else saw it?

At night, as Leigh lay next to Bob's prone body, she had
to fight the impulse to get up and make her way to Erik's
room. She knew she was flirting with catastrophe. Carrying
on an affair right here in her home under the nose of her
husband. It was insane! Even so, she was consumed with when
she could be with Erik again. And she knew he felt the same
way. She could see it in his eyes when she dared look at him.

"I thought maybe Deanna Harper was giving you a hard
time," Bob said, popping a slice of chicken breast in his
mouth.

"Oh. She's coming by tomorrow. Maybe I'm just a bit nervous about her looking at my work. What if she doesn't like
it?"

Bob shrugged. "Then you'll do it over."

Another long silence fell at the table. Finally, Mark looked
up from his food and said, "Mom, Vicki's brother gave me a
couple of tickets for the concert at the Kennedy Center tomorrow night, but we already have plans to see the Capitals
game. He said to give them to you and Dad."

"Really? What's the program?" Leigh asked.

"Just a minute. I've got the tickets here in my pocket." Mark
rummaged in his jeans and pulled out two tickets. "Oh, you'll
like it, Mom. Hugh Wolff is conducting and Rostropovich is
the guest cellist. Let's see, they're doing Schumann's Cello
Concerto, Bloch's *Schelomo*, and Dvořák's Cello Concerto."

"Sounds wonderful," Leigh said.

Bob shook his head. "I can't go. I have a late meeting tomorrow. And even if I didn't, I can think of more exciting
things to do than sit at the Kennedy Center and fall asleep to
that depressing music."

Leigh shrugged. Maybe she could get Deanna to go.

"I would love to go to the Kennedy Center," Erik said.

Aghast, Leigh stared at him; he gazed back calmly.

"Good idea," Bob said. "Why don't you take that little hot-
tie that was over here studying with you a while back?"

Mel's face pinkened, although with embarrassment or jealousy, Leigh couldn't guess. Aaron snickered. Leigh sat still in her seat, wondering how Erik would respond.

"I would prefer to take Kayleigh."

Everyone stared at him. Leigh felt the blood rush to her face. A knot of panic curled in her stomach. Erik had lost his mind! Why else would he risk arousing suspicion like this?

He shrugged, his face bland. "Dawn doesn't like classical music. And I like to share it with someone who appreciates it as well as I do. So, why not?" Pointedly, he looked at Bob. Only Leigh caught the ice in his eyes. "You don't mind, do you, Bob?"

Bob eyed Erik morosely. "I don't tell *Leigh* what she can or cannot do." His tone was mildly sarcastic. "She's a grown woman. Ask *her* if she wants to go."

"I will." With a smile that was almost a smirk, his eyes went to Leigh. "*Kayleigh*, would you care to go to the Kennedy Center with me tomorrow night?"

Leigh couldn't believe his audacity. Obviously, there was a streak of defiance in him that made him enjoy flirting with disaster. Still, she couldn't help but admire his nerve. Deep down, she felt like laughing. It was Erik's polite way of showing his contempt for Bob.

It was on the tip of her tongue to decline his invitation, but a warning light in Erik's eyes made her stop and think. If their relationship had been innocent, what would be wrong with her going out to the Kennedy Center with him? In fact, wouldn't it look rather odd if she refused to go with him after only a moment ago expressing a desire to hear the program? And what excuse could she give for not going? Besides, wouldn't it be wonderful to have a legitimate night out with her lover? She imagined sitting in the dark concert hall with him, holding hands, giving themselves up to the caressing, vibrant sound of the cello.

She took a sip of her iced tea and smiled at Erik. "Sure, Erik. That sounds like fun. I always enjoy a night out at the Kennedy Center, but it's like pulling teeth to get Bob to go with me."

"How can anybody stand that old people's music?" Mel

pouted. "Erik, I'm surprised at you. I thought you liked rock."

"I do." He smiled at her. "But I've told you before, a well-rounded person can enjoy many different things. I was brought up on classical music." His eyes returned to Leigh. "My favorite is Vivaldi's *The Four Seasons*. Especially the 'Winter' section. It's so . . . passionate."

Leigh felt the blood drain from her face as she remembered the significance of that piece. It had been playing the first time they made love. She swallowed a piece of chicken that suddenly tasted like rubber. What had gotten into Erik? He was going too far with his taunting. She stood up. "I'll get dessert."

When she returned to the dining room with the cake, Mel and Mark were arguing about classical music. Finally, Bob exploded. "Shut up! Can't we have some goddamn peace while we eat?"

An uncomfortable silence fell as Leigh cut the cake. In an attempt to lighten the mood, she said, "Why don't we get out the Trivial Pursuit game tonight? Or do you guys have too much studying to do?"

"I suppose I could take time out from studying for a while tonight," Mark said. "It shouldn't take me too long to beat everyone."

"No, thanks," Mel said. "I don't feel up to competing with Mr. Genius there . . . unless Erik will agree to be my partner," she added hopefully.

"I'm afraid I can't make it tonight." Erik looked straight at Leigh. "I have a date with Dawn."

Leigh placed her iced-tea glass down on the table and made an effort to relax the tightened muscles in her face. So stupid of her to believe he'd actually given up the prom queen! Had he also lied to her about not sleeping with her? Avoiding his eyes, she pushed away the remainder of her uneaten cake, got to her feet and began clearing the table.

In the kitchen, she vented her rage upon the cabinet doors and the dishwasher. What a fool she was! Of course Erik hadn't given up that southern tart. After all, he was a virile young man and his gorgeous classmate had the hots for him. The thought of Erik with that little bitch made her crazy.

"Bastard!" she muttered as she gave the dishwasher door a final slam.

On the pretense of an insomnia attack, Leigh waited up for Erik. She sat in the family room, her eyes glued to *The Tonight Show,* but her mind was elsewhere. Her anger had cooled since her earlier abuse of the pots and pans, but insecurity had taken its place. Erik had been gone for over three hours. It drove her nuts to think that he was spending those hours with Dawn—maybe in her arms. How could she, a forty-year-old woman of average good looks, compete with a nubile coed who could model for *Cosmopolitan*?

She heard the sound of the back door opening. A moment later, Erik appeared at the entrance to the family room, as if he knew she'd be waiting. He paused a moment, then walked over to the love seat and sat down.

"Hi," he said with a slight smile.

Leigh glared at him, the anger bubbling up all over again. "How's Dawn?"

"She's fine. She said to tell you hello."

"Tell her I said to *go to hell!*" She jumped to her feet. Erik rose and grabbed her arm as she started for the door. She tried to wrench away. *"Leave me alone!"*

Erik tightened his hold, pulling her to him, his lips very close to her ear. "I told you once before you had no reason to be jealous of Dawn."

"Then *why* are you still seeing her?"

Erik's mouth quirked in amusement. "Think about it. Didn't you tell me we were supposed to carry on as usual, so we aroused no suspicion? Wouldn't it look rather odd if I suddenly quit seeing Dawn? She's our cover, *kjaereste.*" His lips brushed hers. "But I must tell you I am very flattered." His face sobered. "Kayleigh, you know, sometimes I have doubts about you, too. I wonder if you're using me to make up for the neglect you feel from your husband. I sometimes think you still love him, that I am just a diversion. But then I remember how we are together, and I realize I'm wrong to have such doubts. And I feel ashamed for thinking like that."

"I know," Leigh whispered, on the verge of tears. "I do feel ashamed. It's just that I get crazy when I think of you with that little mealy-mouthed Scarlett O'Hara."

Erik drew her close. She rested her head against his warm chest. "What do you think it's like for me? I lie awake at night and think of you sharing a bed with *him*. That's when I get crazy, love. I want to go in there and snatch you away from him."

Slowly, Leigh pulled away from him. She'd never told him that Bob hadn't touched her in months. In fact, she'd told him nothing about her relationship with her husband. "I'm sorry." She walked over to turn off the television. "We really shouldn't be in here like this. Sometimes the kids come down for a glass of milk or something."

He gazed at her solemnly. "So many restrictions. If you would come to Norway with me, we would never have to hide our love from anyone. Europeans are more open-minded."

"Oh, Erik, don't talk fantasies to me. You know that's impossible!"

"I will go home in June. That's only four months away." His eyes were very dark. "What then? Will that be the end of us?"

Leigh's hand massaged her temples where a headache had begun to throb. "What else can it be? I can't deal with this now. I'm going to bed."

Erik moved toward her. "Kiss me good night . . . properly."

She didn't protest when he took her into his arms. His mouth closed over hers, warm, searching. As she returned his kiss, she felt a heavy sadness settle over her. How empty her life would be once he was gone. But she'd known when she got herself into this situation it couldn't last forever. Still, she hadn't counted on falling in love with him.

The rich sound of the cello swelled out into the dark concert hall and faded away. A moment of silence lingered in the auditorium before giving way to enthusiastic applause from the Kennedy Center patrons. As the lights brightened, Erik turned to Leigh and smiled, his hand tightening on hers.

"Ah, Kayleigh . . . this night is going too fast. Intermission, already?"

"It's too good to be true, isn't it? You and me together here." She gave him a sad smile. "It can't last forever."

A shadow flickered in his blue eyes, and for a moment, Leigh knew her words carried a heavier meaning. She stood up. "Why don't we go out on the terrace? The Tidal Basin and Jefferson Memorial are gorgeous at night."

"But you'll freeze in that thin dress!" he protested.

"Only for a moment," Leigh pulled him to his feet. "Come on, it won't kill us. I promise."

The terrace was almost empty; very few others had braved the cold February night. As they walked over to the wall facing the Jefferson Memorial, Erik grabbed Leigh's hand and gave her a smile that made her heart skip a beat. She knew she should pull her hand away. After all, she wasn't a celebrity congressman's wife, but there could well be someone here at the Kennedy Center who could recognize her. But her hand felt so good in his, she just couldn't make herself do it. Besides, there was no one out here. The last couple had already gone back inside. They leaned on the wall and gazed at the lighted Jefferson Memorial. To their left, headlights from Maine Avenue beamed brightly as heavy traffic passed under the terrace below them, yet the noise from the passing vehicles was so muffled they could talk easily.

"You're right," Erik said. "It is beautiful. Washington is such an impressive city. I wish we could go up in the Washington Monument at night. But I guess it would be too late when we leave here, wouldn't it?"

"Probably. I'm not even sure if they take tourists up after dark this time of the year." She sipped her wine, beginning to wish she had her coat.

With his uncanny intuition, Erik shrugged out of his tweed jacket and wrapped it around her shoulders.

"Oh, no, Erik! We can go back in now."

"No, I'm used to the cold. It doesn't bother me." Erik smiled. "Besides, you look so lovely out here with the Jefferson Memorial as a backdrop." His long fingers slid beneath her hairline at the back of her neck as he leaned down to kiss her. His mouth was warm. She clung to him greedily, her nails gripping his firm biceps through his sweater. Then she remembered where she was and pulled away from him, her body trembling.

"God, you make me stop thinking . . . ," she said. After a deep breath, she remembered what she wanted to discuss with him. "I wanted to talk to you about Mel. You do realize she has a crush on you, don't you? I'm really beginning to worry about it."

Erik looked puzzled. "I'm sure I haven't done anything to encourage her."

"Oh, I'm not saying that," Leigh said. "But I just wish you could think of a way to *discourage* her. She wanted you to take her to a Valentine's dance at school. When I told her it was out of the question, she refused to go at all."

"Do you think it would help if I had a talk with her?" He hesitated a second, then added, "I could tell her I'm seriously involved with Dawn."

Leigh shrugged, trying to control the familiar rush of jealousy she felt at Dawn's name. "Yeah, maybe you should. It may be the only way to discourage Mel. But I don't have to like it," she added, half-mockingly.

Erik's arm tightened about her shoulders. "Come on, let's go in. You're turning as blue as your dress."

They'd just walked back in through the doors when Leigh heard her name.

"Leigh Fallon! You didn't tell me you were coming here tonight."

Standing directly in front of them, dressed in leather pants and a knee-length satin tunic, was Deanna Harper. A burly, black-haired young man with arresting brown eyes stood next to her, sipping a glass of champagne.

"Hello, Dee." Leigh tried to put warmth in her voice, but she was so startled, it came out brittle. Her cheeks grew hot. "Wonderful concert, isn't it?"

Deanna scanned Leigh and Erik, her eyes frankly assessing. She smiled warmly. "I'd like you to meet a special friend of mine." One hand slid sensuously up the arm of the man beside her. "This is Dominic Boccelliano. And who might this be?"

"Erik Haukeland." Leigh had regained her composure. "He's our boarder from Norway. Bob couldn't make it to the concert tonight, so Erik got elected."

With a dazzling smile, Erik returned Deanna's handshake. She began telling him about a trip she took to Sweden the year before, asking him about the similarities to his country. With his usual good humor, Erik joked about the general Norwegian superiority over their Swedish neighbors. Leigh and Dominic stood listening, he, indifferent, she with a plastic smile glued to her face. *She knows,* Leigh thought. She could tell by the speculative look in Deanna's eyes. *God, is it so apparent?*

The lights in the sumptuous lobby flickered, signaling the end of intermission. Gradually the crowd moved back toward the concert hall.

"Well, we'd better get going," Leigh said. "I'll talk to you soon, Dee."

Deanna smiled and waited a second until Erik turned away, then tapped Leigh on the shoulder. "You damn well *better* talk to me soon," she whispered, eyes dancing.

Back in the concert hall, Leigh tried to recapture the tranquil mood she'd enjoyed before the intermission. It was impossible. She kept seeing Deanna's knowing expression. And if, as she suspected, Deanna had guessed their true relationship, what would it mean to their future?

9

The next morning, Leigh found she'd been right to be worried. Deanna called at nine o'clock sharp.

"Hey, girl. Now, *that's* what I'd call a hunk. How come you didn't tell me he was so gorgeous? And level with me— how long has it been going on between you two?"

Speechless, Leigh stared down at the drawing she was working on.

"Man," Deanna went on. "I wish I could find a guy who'd look at me the way he looked at you. How did you do it, Leigh? It's always lust with my men. Not that I *want* more, you understand. But how the hell did you make him fall in love with you?"

Leigh finally found her voice. "Deanna, I don't know what you're talking about."

There was a short silence on the other end of the line; then Deanna laughed. "You can't bullshit a bullshitter, Leigh, but hey, if you don't want to talk about it, that's cool. Anyway, I forgot to tell you something last night. You know that conference coming up next month? The one for writers and illustrators of children's books?"

"Yeah, I haven't decided if I'm going or not."

"Well, you damn well better. I'm going to be in the Caribbean that week, and I want you to stay in my penthouse. That way, you won't be stuck in some midtown hotel being bored to death. And . . ." She paused, and Leigh could almost see the wicked smile on her lips. "You can bring Erik. Just think . . . you'll be away from prying eyes . . . all alone in my apartment. I have a water bed . . . and a sauna. Can you imagine it, Leigh?"

Leigh was already imagining it. Her face flamed hot. "He won't be able to get away from school." Immediately, she realized her mistake.

Deanna laughed triumphantly. "Hon, I've been out of college for more years than I care to remember, but I'm damn sure there's still such a thing as spring break. And isn't it usually around the end of March?"

Leigh didn't answer. She was too busy wondering whether to confide in Deanna or not. Finally she plunged in, "I don't know if we could manage it, Dee. What will everyone think if we both disappear at the same time?"

"Talk to Erik. I'm sure he'll come up with something. Look, I'll have a key to the apartment made and drop it off with you before I go home. Oh, man, this is so juicy. And to think, I thought you were such a wholesome little thing."

"I *am* wholesome," Leigh said. "But Erik makes me forget that. I've never met anyone like him, Dee."

"Sounds like love," Deanna said. "Gotta go. I'll stop by tomorrow."

Leigh hung up the phone, her brow furrowed. That word again. *Love.* Impossible, totally futile love.

An omen, Leigh thought. It had been a good omen that Erik's spring break coincided exactly with the week of the conference in New York. Together, they'd prepared his cover story. He would be spending spring break with a classmate in North Carolina.

In reality, he'd caught the shuttle flight to New York the day after Leigh left for the conference. They'd had two days together before the conference started on Friday.

Hand-in-hand, they'd traversed Central Park, feeding the ducks and watching the motorized sailboats at the pond, lingering at the Alice-in-Wonderland statue, nibbling on ice cream, and watching the people go by. They'd taken the ferry to Liberty Island where Erik had insisted they climb all 354 steps to Lady Liberty's crown. With Erik, she'd looked at New York with new eyes, and it had been beautiful.

But the magic really happened after they'd returned to Deanna's penthouse in the evening. What bliss it had been to make love without fear of discovery. And to wake in the morning in his arms.

On Thursday afternoon, they'd returned to the apartment earlier than usual, knowing that once Leigh's conference began the next day, their time together would be limited. Erik made love to her slowly and sweetly, and afterwards, Leigh summoned the courage to ask him a question that had been lingering in her mind for the last few weeks.

"Will you stay through the summer, Erik?" she whispered. "We spend July and August at our beach house in Delaware. Bob will be in Washington most of the time. We can find time to be alone there."

One eyebrow rose, and his mouth quirked in amusement. "So, the summer is all you're offering me?"

Her hand slid up his sweat-dampened chest. "What more do you want?" she asked lightly.

His eyes burned into hers, all trace of laughter gone. "I want you to leave your husband and come to Norway with me."

When she realized he was serious, she looked away. "Erik . . ."

"I know. You don't have to say it." He snuggled her closer to him, his lips brushing the top of her head. "I'll stay with you, Kayleigh. As long as I can."

When Leigh awoke, it was to see Deanna's bedroom aglow with the golden light of the setting sun. She stretched languidly, wondering how long she'd been asleep. Yawning, she sat up. After a moment, she swung her legs over the bed and stood up, pulling on a robe to cover her nudity. She moved quietly through the apartment, searching for Erik.

He wasn't there. Out on the balcony, she found his opened book on the wicker table. Apparently, he'd awakened earlier and read for a while. Had he gone for a walk? A ripple of apprehension swept through her at the thought. But immediately, she pushed it away. It was stupid to worry about a six-foot-four-inch man in peak physical condition. He would be back soon. Maybe he'd just gone out to get them some dinner.

Leigh decided to sit in the sauna for a few minutes. Her muscles still ached from the climb at the Statue of Liberty. Wrapped in one of Deanna's luxurious bath towels, she settled herself on the redwood bench and poured a small amount of water onto the hot rocks. The steam billowed around her. She took a deep breath, closed her eyes, and smiled. The Finns were right about the saunas. There was something almost mystical about it.

She'd lost track of the time when the door to the sauna opened and a cool blast of air swept into the small room. Naked, Erik walked in. Her relief at seeing him, intact and uninjured, was so great she stood up to meet him, clutching the towel around her. The door closed behind him, and they were enclosed in a cocoon of heat and mist.

Erik's hand reached for hers, and without speaking he led

her back to the bench. He turned to ladle more water onto the rocks. The steam surrounded them so he all but disappeared from sight, but she knew he was there for his warm hands were upon her shoulders as he knelt down between her legs and slowly unwrapped her towel. He leaned forward and took her nipple into his mouth, tonguing it until it grew hard and stiff. Then, he moved to the other one. Leigh's fingers entwined in his damp, flaxen hair as her mouth parted to draw in the misty, hot air in tiny gasps. A lovely heat radiated out from the cleft between her legs as his mouth left her breasts and trailed wetly down her midsection to her navel where his tongue delved in hungry ardor. But the journey wasn't over. He drew away from her and gently pushed her back onto the bench. His blue eyes burned into her hungrily as he parted her legs and then bent his head to taste her.

She felt his tongue, warm and wet between her thighs. Electric shock waves burned from her lower belly. She moaned and opened her eyes, but all she could see were white walls and mist. The delicious torment of Erik's tongue was almost too much to bear. She moved languidly, arching her back, her hands clenched upon taut wet breasts. The hard bench beneath her body cut uncomfortably into her shoulder blades and buttocks, but she was beyond caring. She murmured incoherently, then finally gasped out, "Erik. Please, now, now, now . . ."

In one smooth movement, Erik scooped her into his brawny arms and moved toward the door of the sauna.

"*Ja,*" he whispered. "But not in here."

A blast of cool air hit them as they passed through the doors. Leigh shivered against his naked chest, burrowing her face against him. But the chill passed quickly after he placed her upon the water bed and gently rolled her over onto her stomach. The warmth of his body covered hers from behind as he urged her up on her knees. His long slender fingers slid down the soft skin of her belly to the sensitive button between her legs. A voltaic thrill shot through her. She felt his erection throbbing against her buttocks, and she whispered deliriously, "Yesyesyesyes . . ."

"Soon . . . ," he murmured. ". . . We have so much time, *kja-*

reste." His hands moved to her nipples, teasing them mercilessly as Leigh rocked back and forth, wanting him more than ever before. She burned for him, craved him.

"Hurry." Leigh gasped. "I'm on fire for you."

"Ja." One hand moved back to the throbbing center between her legs and at the same moment, he eased into her from behind.

"Oh, God!" Leigh cried out, awed by the enraptured storm of sensation she was experiencing. As his strokes intensified, it was as if he were touching a place that had never been explored before. The adventurer had uncovered a reservoir of unbridled emotion that had lain dormant for years. Erik had discovered her soul.

They reached the peak together with a blinding explosion of fireworks. Leigh gasped and slumped to the bed, inexplicable tears streaming down her face. Erik withdrew from her and rolled over at her side, his shaking hands still clutching her to him. She buried her face into his neck, unable to stop weeping. He held her tightly, and as she moved her hand up to caress his jaw, she felt the wetness there and knew she was not alone in her sweet anguish.

Deanna called a few days after their return from New York. "Do you know The Wayfarers in Alexandria? Can you meet me there at one o'clock for lunch?"

Leigh arrived at the quaint little restaurant in Old Town and followed the maître 'd to the front parlor overlooking the quiet cobblestone street. Deeply tanned from her trip to the Caribbean, Deanna grinned up at her.

"Am I late?" Leigh asked, looking at the half-eaten wedge of pie on Deanna's plate.

"No," Deanna mumbled before swallowing another huge bite. "I just couldn't wait. I have a passion for their chocolate mousse pie. Don't worry. I'm still having lunch."

The waiter appeared to take their order. Both of them decided on the restaurant's specialty, steak and mushroom pie, English-style. Deanna grinned. "What the hell? Let's have a bottle of wine, too. There's nothing like chocolate mousse washed down by a nice glass of burgundy, right?" She waited until the waiter had gone before she smiled slyly and leaned forward. "Well, am I going to have to drag it out of you? How was your week in New York? Did Erik enjoy the water bed?"

Leigh felt her cheeks pinken. "It was very nice."

"It was very nice," Deanna mimicked. "God, Leigh. You're not talking to UPI! I promise I'll keep mum."

"It's just that I feel uncomfortable talking about Erik and me."

Deanna's face grew serious. "Hey, look, I know it's none of my business. But we *are* confidantes in this. I thought maybe you might like to talk about it. It's hard to hold in a secret like that. Leigh, you're positively glowing! Don't you want to talk about him?"

"Yes, of course I do," Leigh said. "But I don't want you to think it's just a sordid affair. Erik wants me to leave Bob and go to Norway with him."

Deanna's mouth gaped. "Are you serious? Jesus!"

"Of course, the whole idea is preposterous! I told him it was out of the question. I think he's accepted it, but he's not happy."

"What did you expect?" Deanna lit up a cigarette. "The man is in love with you."

"He *thinks* he's in love with me. When he's back in Norway, he'll think of me with affection and then marry a beautiful blonde." Avoiding Deanna's eyes, Leigh fiddled with her crystal water glass, moving it around on the rose linen tablecloth. "A *young* beautiful blonde," she added.

"I think I hear that old green-eyed monster in your voice," Deanna said. "Are you in love with him?"

"How can I be in love with him?" Leigh asked, pushing the water glass decisively away. "I'm too old for him!"

"What has age got to do with love?"

The waiter arrived with their lunch. They were silent for a few minutes, each lost in her own thoughts. Then after taking a sip of wine, Deanna looked at Leigh sharply. "How do you feel about your husband since you've been with Erik?"

"Most of the time, I hate him," Leigh said. Then, a second

later, "No, it's not hate. Just strong dislike. I wonder what I ever saw in him. He's so insensitive, so sterile." She leaned forward. "Deanna, when Bob made love to me—we're talking ages ago, by the way—he refused to do oral sex. Thought it was unsanitary, I guess. Yet, it was fine if I did it to him. The hypocrite!" She paused and then muttered, "I wonder if he goes down on Rebecca?"

"Who's that?"

Leigh grimaced. "His administrative aide. I believe they've been having an affair for the last year."

Deanna shrugged. "That's typical. He's a leader of this great country, isn't he?" Then she grinned. "I take it there's no problem in the sexual department with Erik?"

"Just one." Leigh smiled. "We can't get enough of each other."

Deanna laughed. "A problem like that, I can deal with." She paused to take a sip of wine and then asked, "Why don't you leave Bob? It's obvious you don't love him anymore."

"You're beginning to sound like Erik. Dee, I haven't loved Bob for years now. But what kind of woman would I be if I threw my marriage down the drain and went off to Norway with Erik? What about the kids? How can I tear their lives apart like that? Besides, it's not a bad life. I have my work, and the kids and . . ." Her voice trailed away.

Deanna pushed her steak pie away and smiled. "And when you get lonely, there'll always be another young stud around to seduce, right?"

"Is that how you think of me?" Leigh asked, hurt at her sharp words. "A middle-aged slut, right?"

"No, Leigh, you're not a middle-aged slut. That term might describe me, but not you. I think you're trying to convince yourself you're having a casual affair with Erik. Okay, so maybe it *is* more than sex. Maybe it *is* a beautiful relationship. Still, you know it will end. Even though Erik has made it clear he wants it more permanent, you're determined to keep it a casual affair in your mind. Do you know what I think, Leigh? I think you're in love with him, too. And when he leaves, you're going to be crushed."

"Okay. I love him." Leigh pushed away her plate. "But I'm being realistic. Our age difference makes it impossible for us to share a life together. Besides, sooner or later, he'll tire of me. A younger woman will catch his eye, and I'll be history."

"Haven't you ever heard of living in the present? If that happens in the future, you'll deal with it. As far as the age difference is concerned, remember, Norway is a more liberal country than the U.S. Probably no one would bat an eye at it there. Leigh, you're in love with each other. Don't let him go back to Norway without you."

Leigh stared at Deanna for a long moment. Then slowly, she shook her head. "No. It's impossible. A life with Erik is a fantasy. I have to stay here in the real world. Not for Bob, but for the kids. I can't run out on them."

Deanna gazed at Leigh solemnly. "Okay. I can understand that, but remember one thing, Leigh. The kids won't be around forever." She stabbed her cigarette butt into the ashtray and added, "And neither will Erik."

10

The house at Rehoboth Beach never changed from one year to the next. Leigh stepped into the foyer and gazed up the narrow flight of stairs leading to the bedrooms on the second floor. The same old blue-flowered wallpaper stretched the length of the stairwell. Every year when she entered the house, she saw the wallpaper and vowed this year would be its last. Yet, she never got around to doing anything about it. This year would probably be no exception.

She sighed and looked into the two downstairs bedrooms on her left. She'd decided that Erik and Mark could take those. To the right was the living room and combination dining room. The furnishings were simple, a wicker rocker, a casual sofa, a Shaker-inspired wood dinette set and woven rugs on the Wedgwood-blue painted floors. Overlooking the ocean, a huge screened-in porch led off from the living room.

On the other end of the dining room, a step down led into the large country kitchen, a room Leigh didn't intend to spend much time in this summer. To the left of the kitchen there was a small bathroom that connected to one of the downstairs bedrooms.

Leigh stood in the kitchen, gazing in dismay at all the unpacking to be done. The back door banged, and Aaron ran in with Ivan at his heels. The towheaded boy grabbed a dart from the dartboard hanging on the utility closet door and took careful aim.

"Mom, when are we going down to the beach?"

"As soon as we get settled in." Leigh began to unpack the groceries. "And no, you can't go down now. Go upstairs and start putting sheets on the beds. Where's Mel?"

Aaron shrugged. "Probably up in her room, listening to records. Just like at home."

Bob stepped into the kitchen, carrying two more bags of groceries. "What are you making for dinner, Leigh?"

"Surprise! I'm not making anything," she announced. "I thought we'd go out to that great seafood place in Dewey Beach. The one where I had the swordfish last summer."

A frown crossed Bob's face. "I hope you're not planning on eating out all the time we're here."

"I'm not planning on cooking all the time we're here. I'm on vacation, too. Remember?"

Bob grumbled under his breath as he deposited the bags on the table. Amused, Leigh ignored him and continued with her work.

Better get used to it, Bob. Your docile little wife is gone forever.

Midnight had come and gone, and still, Leigh lay in bed, wide awake. A typical first night at the beach. Beside her, Bob snored contentedly. Leigh tried to convince her active brain she was exhausted, but it refused to cooperate. It didn't help that there was so much noise outside from partying college students at the house next door. A few minutes ago, someone had been blaring a trombone—someone with very little musical ability. It hadn't gone on long, thank God. Someone had had the good sense to take it away from the hapless musician, and, Leigh hoped, buried it where it wouldn't be unearthed for a couple of centuries.

Still, she knew it wasn't just the noise outside that was keeping her awake. Her body was calling out for Erik. It had been over a month since they'd been together. Early in June, Bob had returned to Ohio for a few days, giving her the opportunity to visit Erik's room every night he was away. But since then, there hadn't been a chance for them to meet. It was starting to get to her. His physical proximity was torture. The expression in his eyes told her it was the same for him. Yet, what choice did they have? In spite of everything, Leigh was glad he was here and not in Norway.

The harsh eruption of a motorcycle careering down the street forced Leigh to give up the pretense of sleeping. She threw back the light blanket and groped for her robe in the darkness of the bedroom. Quietly, she made her way down the carpeted stairs, thinking perhaps a glass of wine out on the porch would help relax her. A few minutes later, with a goblet in hand, she carefully opened the door to the porch and made her way to a lounge chair.

"Where's mine?"

She gasped, and wine spilled over her hand. "Erik. You startled me."

He was sitting in her favorite chair. She placed the goblet down on a table between them. "You want some?"

"Oh, yeah," he said dryly.

Leigh moved toward the door. He placed a restraining hand on her arm. At his touch, a delicious tingle swept through her body. "Never mind. I'll share yours." He released her arm and picked up the goblet from the table. She sat down, feeling his eyes upon her in the near darkness. "Cannot sleep? I'm having the same problem. What do you suppose can be wrong with us?"

As Leigh's eyes adjusted to the darkness, she could just make out his cynical grin. She took the goblet from him, shivering at the electric touch of his fingers against hers. "First night at the beach always gives me insomnia. It takes a while to get used to the noise." She took a sip of wine.

"Right. The noise." Erik threw his head back against the lounge chair and closed his eyes. "*Kristus!* What am I doing here? I'm such a fool to have agreed to stay the summer with you."

Leigh felt a rush of fear. Was he about to tell her he was leaving? She couldn't bear it right now; she wasn't ready to give him up. "Don't talk like that. At least we're together. There isn't an ocean separating us."

"You call this being together?" Erik said, a bleak chill in his voice.

Leigh was silent. What was there to say? She took another sip of wine, but it now tasted bitter. Silence stretched between them. Outside the screened porch, she was aware of the many sounds that filled the night . . . the breakers pounding the shore, the melancholy cry of a whippoorwill. The night wind was alive, whispering through the long grass of the dunes nearby.

"I want to fuck you."

He said it so casually that Leigh didn't react at first. When the mocking words sank into her consciousness, her face flamed with humiliation and anger. His tone had been so cutting, almost cruel. She stood abruptly and would have breezed past him, but he was too fast for her. Like a flash, he stood and locked his hands on to her arms. His mouth plundered hers, and for the first time in the ten months she'd known him, she struggled against his embrace. Pushing her hands against his hard chest, Leigh tore her mouth from his. "Erik. You've been drinking!"

He threw back his head and laughed softly. "*Pokker!* I've only had a six-pack of beer." His hands moved sensuously down the back of her robe to caress her bottom.

"I said, I want to fuck you." His mouth nuzzled at her neck.

Leigh pushed him away. "Is that all it is to you? Just another fuck?"

Erik stared at her, his chest heaving, and Leigh could see the anger creeping across his face. Finally, he spoke very quietly. "You know that's not true, Kayleigh. But what about you? Isn't that all I am to you? Just another fuck?"

He turned and walked somewhat unsteadily into the house, leaving her standing alone, trembling.

An oppressive heat wave had descended upon the Delmarva Peninsula. Leigh found it difficult to spend more than an hour on the beach at one time. Even with frequent splashes in the cool surf, almost as soon as she returned to their quilt on the sand, her pores oozed sweat from the merciless fury of the sun beating down from a cloudless sky.

She glanced at the watch in her beach bag. Instead of roasting here in the sun, why not go shopping? It would be a perfect opportunity to check out the bargains at Gershman's or the Factory Outlet. She stood up and brushed the sand from her turquoise one-piece swimsuit, her eyes searching for Aaron in the surf. There he was on the raft, and Bob was nearby. She turned to Mel, who was lying on her stomach reading *Lady Chatterley's Lover*. She frowned. Although she believed Mel was mature enough to read whatever she wanted, she still had misgivings about this one. Was it because the book hit a little too close to home? Leigh didn't like the comparison between herself and Constance Chatterley. After all, the story didn't end happily.

After telling Mel she was going shopping and getting no response, Leigh made her way up to the boardwalk. She passed a place that sold fresh-squeezed lemonade and on impulse, bought a glass. She found an empty bench facing the boardwalk and sat down to sip the drink. A young, good-looking lifeguard passed and gave her a dazzling smile. Leigh blushed and smiled back.

"I'm going to tell Dad you're flirting with that lifeguard."

Leigh turned to see Mark and Erik walking up to the bench.

"Does he know you come out here to ogle the beach boys?" Mark teased.

"I can look, can't I?" Leigh laughed, avoiding Erik's brooding eyes. "What have you guys been up to?"

Mark grinned. "Just walking up and down the boardwalk,

checking out the foxes. How about a sip of that lemonade you've got there?"

Leigh handed her drink over, and Mark took a big gulp. "Mmmm . . . good stuff. You coming back to the beach, Mom?"

A large-breasted bikinied woman walked by, and Leigh couldn't help but gape. Tiny pasties of cloth covered an area slightly larger than her nipples and there was little more on her bottom. Mark and Erik turned to see the object of her stare, and their mouths dropped open. Mark completely forgot what he'd been saying. All three watched until she'd disappeared in the crowd.

Leigh cleared her throat. "I'm sorry, Mark . . . what did you say?"

His eyes reluctantly returned to her. "Uh . . . oh, are you going back to the beach?"

"No, I think I'll head back to the house and take a shower after I finish my lemonade. It probably wouldn't hurt the two of you to get out of the sun for a while. Erik, your shoulders are getting red."

Erik didn't answer. Mark shrugged. "I'm not worried. I think I'll go for a swim. What about you, Erik?"

"Not now. I'm going to go look around in that T-shirt shop over there." He studiously avoided Leigh's eyes.

Mark was already walking away. "Okay, catch you later."

Leigh watched as Erik turned away from her and headed toward the shop across the boardwalk. A heavy ache settled in the pit of her stomach. She didn't know how much longer she could take this coldness from him. It was so unlike him. Two days had passed since that appalling scene with him on the porch. Yes, she'd been shocked and hurt by his callous attitude toward her, but since then, she'd realized it hadn't been only his drinking that had caused him to lash out at her. It was their situation.

It couldn't be easy for him to have to deceive people he genuinely liked. And then, there was their forced celibacy. The electricity had been building up in them for weeks, and out on the porch that night when they'd been so close, yet couldn't be together, his frustration had exploded into a shower of ugly, vengeful words. Leigh understood that. She'd felt much the same way. Still, she'd hoped his cold attitude toward her wouldn't last. She missed his caressing smile, the warm look in his eyes. Watching him disappear into the crowd, Leigh blinked away sudden tears. *God, what an impossible situation!*

She caught her breath. He had stopped and was turning back. The tears blurred her eyes, but still, she could see him coming back to her. He was so incredibly breathtaking, dressed only in brilliantly patterned surfer shorts, his blond hair shining in the sun. Two bikini-clad girls watched him appreciatively as he passed, but he didn't notice them. His piercing blue eyes were pinned on Leigh. Elation swept through her as he approached.

He dropped down onto the bench beside her. "Forgive me." His hands were clenched, and she could see he was struggling not to touch her.

She understood that feeling because she was fighting it herself. Instead of reaching out and stroking his jaw as she wanted to do, she had to settle for gazing directly into his eyes. "Oh, Erik. It's been so awful without you. . . ."

"I know. For me, too. I've been acting like a child. I knew what I was getting into long before you came to my room that morning. My eyes were wide open. When I went home for Christmas, I made a decision to make you mine. No matter what the consequences."

Leigh's eyes dropped to his long slender fingers resting on his knees. "It's my fault," she said. "I should've been strong enough to resist you. We would both be better off if I had."

"No. Don't ever say that, Kayleigh. No matter what happens in the future, we must never regret what we had." His eyes searched her face. "Can you honestly tell me you regret anything we've done?"

Leigh drank in the look in his eyes and whispered her unhesitant answer. "No."

Leigh stepped into the outdoor shower stall, threw her towel over the top, and then shrugged out of her kimono. With a quick twist, she turned on the taps and stood under the cool spray. She sighed, relishing the heat of the sun baking down on her as the relieving balm of water flowed over her parched skin. Everything about this outdoor shower felt sensuous to her. The contrast of the sun and the cool water, the smooth wooden platform beneath her feet, the lush green cascade of ivy that grew wildly over and around the floor. She loved the scent of the shampoo as it slid from her head and down her body, leaving her with a sense of freshness that could never be duplicated in an ordinary shower.

When she showered here, she always took her time, carefully soaping her body, shampooing her hair and rinsing it over and over. Everyone else in the family always complained that she took too long. Of course, no one wanted to use the shower in the upstairs bathroom. But at least today, Leigh knew she could take as long as she wanted. Everyone was still at the beach. It was early, only two o'clock. With any luck, she'd have the place to herself for at least an hour, maybe two.

Just as she worked up a lather in her hair, an unmistakable knock came at the shower door. "Damn," Leigh muttered. So, it was too good to be true. "What is it? I just got in!"

"Kayleigh, let me in."

Leigh caught her breath; then her fingers fumbled at the latch. A second later, Erik stepped inside, grinning wickedly. His hands reached for her.

"Are you crazy?" Leigh sputtered. "Erik! Someone might come by. They can see our feet under the stall!"

"Shhh." His amused blue eyes met hers as his hands massaged the shampoo through her hair. "Don't worry. Everyone is still at the beach."

"But they might come ba—" Her protest was muffled by the pressure of his warm mouth against hers.

"Time to rinse." He guided her back into the spray of the showerhead, and the suds slid from her sleeked hair, down onto her shoulders and breasts. His supple fingers threaded through her wet blond tresses, pushing the strands up to meet the cascade of water, guiding her head back and forth to rinse it clean. "It squeaks," he said softly. "Must be clean."

An inevitable lassitude had crept over her as she felt his strong fingers in her hair. She no longer cared if they were discovered. The palms of her hands rested on Erik's glistening chest.

She smiled lazily. "What now?"

He drew away. "Now, it's my turn." Her eyes dropped to his hands as he untied the drawstring of his surfer shorts. In one quick movement, he slid them down his hips and stepped out of them. He was already erect.

"Shampoo, please." Leigh poured the rich shampoo into her palm and leaning against his wet body, she reached up and began to work a lather into his thick hair. The tips of her breasts pressed against the golden hairs of his chest as his hands traced down the curves of her side to rest lingeringly on her hips. His erection pressed against her belly, urgent and promising. Leigh caught her breath.

"Okay . . . ," she whispered. "That's enough."

Erik held his head under the shower, and the water sluiced down his back. She leaned forward and playfully nipped at the wet skin near his armpit.

"Sweet . . . ," she said. "You're the flavor of suntan lotion and salt." She reached for a bar of soap in a dish behind her and began to work up a lather between her hands. Then slowly, sensuously, she soaped his body. She started with the strong cords of his sunburned neck and then traveled down his broad chest. She gave special attention to the area under his arms, softly stroking the tufts of soapy hair. Next, she washed his hard flat stomach, following the line of hair that narrowed down to his pubic bone. Eyes closed, Erik gasped when she finally took his stiff penis in hand. She slid her soapy hands back and forth, smoothing her fingertips over his rounded knob, deliberately torturing.

"*Kristus!*" he growled. "You're killing me. . . ."

Suddenly his teeth bit gently on her lower lip as his eager hands clutched her buttocks. He lifted her up to where his penis could find the opening it sought.

"Oh . . . ," Leigh breathed as the delicious fullness of him ripened inside her. Her legs wrapped around him in a fervent embrace.

Their lovemaking was slow, silky, wet, entirely different than ever before. The water sprayed over them as they climaxed together silently. Leigh held on to him tightly, her hands clutching the wet hair at his nape, her face burrowed into his neck.

"Erik! Are you in there?"

It was Bob's voice outside the door of the shower.

Still gripped by the last undulating shocks of pleasure, Leigh and Erik froze, their hearts hammering, eyes locked in alarm. Erik recovered first.

"*Ja.* What is it?"

Leigh marveled that his voice sounded so unconcerned.

"You have a phone call." There was a lascivious chuckle. "It sounds like your girl, Dawn. Better hurry. She's very anxious to talk to you."

"Can you tell her I'll be right there?"

"Sure thing."

They waited silently until they heard the back door slam. Then slowly, Erik withdrew from her. He eased her down to where her feet were once again on the wooden platform.

"God, Erik. That was too close," Leigh whispered. "If he had come out a minute later—"

"Or earlier," Erik said wryly. "He would have heard us."

"Hurry!" Leigh grabbed his sodden shorts from the platform and handed them to him. "Get out of here and get your phone call before he comes back out."

He pulled on the shorts and gave her a quick kiss on her shoulder. "It still would've been worth it if we'd been caught."

"Get out of here or we *still* might get caught!" Leigh unlatched the door. She pushed him out and then stood under the cooling jets of water. It was the first time she'd ever felt hot under a cold shower.

11

Leigh walked into the kitchen just as Erik was winding down his conversation with Dawn. She went to the refrigerator to get a soft drink, telling herself she wasn't interested in what he was saying, but she knew she wasn't fooling herself. She popped the soda can, took a sip, and listened.

"That's great, Dawn. I look forward to seeing you." His eyes met Leigh's across the room. "*Ja*, I'll do that. The Atlantic Sands is nearby. You'll be arriving sometime on Saturday? Okay. I miss you, too. Good-bye." He hung up the phone and turned to Leigh with an embarrassed grin. "Dawn is coming down on Saturday."

Leigh knew her simmering anger showed plainly on her face. "And the question is, why did you tell her she could?"

Bob walked into the kitchen, freshly showered and changed. "So, how's your girl doing, Erik?"

"Great," he answered. "In fact, she's coming down for a visit this weekend."

Bob smirked. "Lucky you! Most guys would kill for a weekend with a honey like her."

The phone shrilled out. Leigh glared at Erik. "I'll get it." She hoped it was Dawn calling back so she could have the pleasure of hanging up on her. But it was Rebecca calling for Bob. Ever since she first suspected Rebecca's relationship with Bob, Leigh had found it difficult to be other than curt with the woman. Without acknowledging Rebecca's "How are you, Leigh?" she held out the phone to Bob. "It's your AA." When he took it, she went back to the counter where she'd left her soda. Erik moved over to her.

"Can I have a sip?"

She banged the can down on the counter and watched as the liquid fizzed up through the opening. "Help yourself!"

He took a long draw from the soda can. "Ah! That's good. There's something about an outdoor shower that really makes one thirsty." He grinned, a devilish look in his eyes. Leigh glared back silently. His face grew serious. "Why are you angry at me?"

Before she could answer, Bob hung up the phone and turned to them. "Leigh, bad news. I have to drive back to Washington tomorrow for a couple of days. A problem has come up that can't wait until next week."

Although Congress wasn't in session, Bob had insisted that two weeks was all he could spare away from Washington because of social obligations and various other "pressing engagements," most of them having to do with a certain sexy redhead, Leigh was sure. As usual, she and the kids would be staying at the beach house for the rest of the summer and Bob would make weekend visits. Now, at the news of Bob having to return to Washington even earlier than planned, Leigh couldn't help glancing at Erik. His expression told her that he, too, was aware of what this meant to them.

She looked back at her husband. "Well, you'd better get packed."

Bob grinned, obviously relieved. "What? No tantrums? Don't you remember last summer when you hit the roof because I had to go back to Washington a week early?"

Leigh shrugged. "Maybe I'm not the same person I was last summer."

She turned and walked out of the kitchen.

In the cool shade of the bedroom, Leigh stretched languorously and turned on her side toward Erik. He was sleeping on his stomach, his legs splayed across the bed. Leigh gazed at him, a tiny smile playing across her lips. Dead to the world. And why not? After they'd finished an encore of yesterday's shower scene, he'd promptly led her up to her bedroom, where he'd proceeded to make love to her again, this time more slowly, savoring every inch of her body. With Bob back in Washington and the kids off for an afternoon at the arcade and miniature golf course, they had plenty of time.

In the quiet after the storm of passion, she found herself whispering words that had been playing in her mind lately.

"How can I let you go?" If Erik heard her, he made no comment. They fell into an exhausted sleep in each other's arms.

In the dim light of the room, Leigh checked her wristwatch. Almost three o'clock. It would probably be a good idea to get Erik out of the bedroom. Just in case the kids decided to return from the amusement arcade early. She moved her foot along his hairy calf while one hand traveled up his naked buttock and rested at the small of his back. He moaned softly and turned his head away from her. Leigh laughed. It wasn't going to be easy to wake him. Quickly, she rolled over on top of him, sitting astride his firm buttocks. Her hands slid up the sides of his chest to stop just under his armpits as she leaned down to plant a kiss on the middle of his perfect back. Erik groaned loudly and then muttered, "*Kristus!* You still haven't had enough? I've turned the woman into a sex maniac. . . ."

"What makes you think I wasn't already a sex maniac before I met you?" Leigh asked, laughing. "Now, wake up before I tickle you to death." Her fingers teased at his armpits, and he squirmed. "Besides, I didn't wake you up for more sex. It's getting late."

"Why not?" He murmured into the pillow. "I'm ready. And so are you, judging by your wet pussy on my ass."

Frowning, Leigh rolled off him. "You're sounding more American every day. I must say I like the Norwegian side of you better. It's not so vulgar."

"Oh, don't be such a hypocrite, Kayleigh," Erik said mildly as he turned over and sat up. "You know you love it when I talk dirty."

Leigh wasn't in the mood for his wry sense of humor. She tried not to notice how disarmingly attractive he looked, sitting naked in the middle of the rumpled bed, his blond hair curly and still damp from the shower. She leaned over and swept his briefs from the floor. "Here! Put these on. You look cold."

Erik grinned as he caught them. "Yes, Mother."

Leigh froze as she drew on her silk kimono; a hot flush traveled over her face. She turned to him and said quietly, "Don't *ever* call me *mother* again, Erik Haukeland."

Erik's carefree grin disappeared. "You are a real enigma,"

he said. "One moment, you're laughing, warm, sexy. And the next, you draw on this cold mask and become untouchable. I can't get used to how quickly you change."

Leigh bent over to sweep up a damp towel from the floor. "Well, you don't need to get used to it, do you?" she said. "After all, we won't be seeing each other after next month." She hurled the towel at him. "Why don't you just get out of here and go get dressed!"

Erik caught the towel and dropped it to the floor near the bed. His eyes had darkened ominously. "I don't really like you too much when you're like this. I guess you could say I feel like I'm being used. When we're in bed together, we're equals. But the minute the sex is over, you suddenly become an authority figure. Kayleigh, why can't you accept the fact that we *are* equals. A man and a woman. No more basic than that. It doesn't matter that you're older. You're too defensive about your age."

Trembling, she moved to the mirror and tried to comb the tangles out of her hair. "Erik, I know you're into psychology, but I don't appreciate being analyzed. And don't tell me I'm defensive about my age. I never was before I met you. Oh, God, why *can't* you be older?"

Erik stared at her, a look of near pity in his eyes. "Why can't you be happy with what we have together? If I were older, would it make a difference? Would you come to Norway with me . . . leave your husband and children?"

Leigh slammed down the comb. "No! I could never leave them!"

A stony mask settled over his face. "I didn't think so. I am such a fool to be in love with you. You're a very selfish woman, Kayleigh."

"Is that so? Then perhaps you should be spending your time with Dawn instead of me."

Erik stood up and began to pull on his clothes. "Well, at least I know where I stand with her."

"And I know where I stand with you! After all, you invited her down here for the weekend."

Erik stared at her, his blue eyes stormy. "I did not invite

her down. She called and told me she was coming. What could I say? 'Sorry, Dawn, but I'm sleeping with Kayleigh, and I don't think she'd like it.' Anyway, we agreed I was to pretend to have a relationship with her."

Fresh fury flowed through her. "Is it a pretense? I find it very hard to believe you don't want anything to do with a girl who looks like Brooke Shields. And the entire world knows she's hot for you. Why don't you just admit you're glad she's coming up?"

A maddeningly cool look had stolen into Erik's eyes. His answer was not one she was prepared for. "*Ja*, I *am* glad she is coming up. It will be a nice change to have a woman around who will be giving me all of her time and attention. Not just a snatched moment in a fucking shower with her boy-toy!"

Unable to believe what she'd heard, Leigh stared at him. An agonizing pain stabbed up from her stomach into her chest, rendering her speechless for the moment. Erik stared back, his face expressionless. Oh, how she detested that smug Scandinavian stoicism! When her words finally came, they were the result of her desire to hurt him, to make him feel the same pain blistering inside her.

"I bet you just can't wait to fuck her, right, Erik? Maybe you can keep a scoreboard, and see how she measures up to me."

His face didn't change. "You're right. I can't wait to fuck her. How about this? Maybe *you* could join us. We could do a three-way in the shower. Hell! Dawn is so horny for me, I'll bet she'll go for it. Who knows?" He gave her a cold grin. "Maybe it'll open up a complete new world for you!"

Leigh felt the blood drain from her face. "You're disgusting. . . ."

"Perhaps I am," Erik went on. "But there's one thing you're wrong about. I won't be comparing her to you. I already know the difference. Dawn is warm all the way through, but you . . . You're hot on the outside, but underneath it all, Kayleigh, you're just a cold bitch."

"Get out," Leigh said, very quietly.

And he did.

*   *   *

The wave crashed on the dark beach with unusual force. Too late, Leigh tried to move out of its path. The cold sea foamed around her legs, soaking her jeans and depositing great globs of sand into the folded cuffs. She gasped at the icy temperature and waited until the wave receded before moving on. Even the sand was cold beneath her bare feet. It had to be after ten o'clock, yet, she had no desire to go back to the beach house. She knew she couldn't face anyone and pretend everything was okay . . . that her world hadn't fallen apart. Even worse than facing her children, she dreaded the inevitable meeting with Erik. She simply couldn't bear letting him know how the ugly words he'd hurled at her this afternoon had ripped her heart out.

She moved on, away from the lights of a volleyball game and toward a darkened section of the beach. She needed darkness right now. A place where she didn't have to look at anyone or have them stare at her. She dropped to the ground, huddling against the stiff night breeze. Her fingers traced letters in the sand and angrily, she brushed them away, knowing she'd written his name. How she wished she could obliterate the pain from her heart as easily. Far away in the west, thunder rumbled and the breeze quickened. Her head dropped to her knees. If only she could cry, maybe then she could put it all behind her, start to rebuild her life.

She lifted her head to stare out at the lights of a ship on the black sea. A cold drop of rain splashed onto her cheek. Maybe it was all for the best. Perhaps now was the time to try to repair her damaged marriage . . . if it *could* be repaired. Thank God, Bob had never found out about them. There was that, at least. Erik would soon return to Norway, and she would only have to contend with his memory. Finally, a tear tracked down her face. Erik wouldn't be an easy man to forget.

Lightning veined the southwest sky and thunder rumbled again. The rain fell harder. Leigh reluctantly got to her feet and trudged back toward the volleyball game. Two young men were scrambling to take down the nets while children gathered up balls. Leigh passed them and made her way up the steps leading to the boardwalk. Rain soaked through her light jacket, and she shivered. A hot bath and a cup of spiced tea would make her feel better. That had been Great-grandmother Kayleigh's remedy for everything. She wondered if it would work for a broken heart.

If only she could get through the house without encountering anyone. Little chance of that. She stepped onto the porch of the beach house and went to the front door. Inside the foyer, she slipped out of her wet jacket and hung it on the doorknob. First, the tea. She'd make a pot and take it upstairs with her. As she went into the living room, she heard voices in the kitchen and stopped. That couldn't be Bob's voice. He was in Washington.

But it *was* him. He stood with his back to her, talking to someone on the phone.

"Mom!" Aaron jumped up from the kitchen table.

Mel, a coffeepot in hand, rushed to the door of the kitchen to stare in surprised relief. Bob ended his conversation, hung up the phone, and turned to Leigh, his face a mask of anxiety.

"Leigh, are you all right?" he asked tersely. "It's almost midnight. Where've you been?"

Leigh ignored the edge of anger his voice carried. She saw the concern on his face and suddenly, he was the old Bob . . . the one who had so infatuated her that first summer in Washington. He stood before her, tall, reassuring and protective. For the moment, it was exactly what she needed. Tears welled in her eyes. She went to him and wrapped her arms around him.

"I'm so glad you're home," she murmured against his shirt.

A violent clap of thunder woke Leigh early. Rain drummed on the roof of the beach house. She lay still, listening to it, dreading the thought of running into Erik downstairs. But she couldn't hide from him forever. Might as well face him and get it over with. Her stomach growled. When had she last eaten? Wearily, she drew herself out of bed and pulled on her robe. She reached for her glasses on the bedside table. Why bother with putting in her contacts? Who cared how she looked?

At the bottom of the stairs, she paused. Erik's door was closed. He'd had a late night, probably, and wouldn't be getting up for a long time. She went into the kitchen and headed straight for the coffeepot. As the coffee perked, she stood at the kitchen window, staring out past the blue gingham curtains at the rainy morning. The weather suited her mood. With grim satisfaction, she thought of Dawn starting out her long drive to the beach in the pouring rain. Maybe it would rain all weekend. But then she thought of the girl lying in Erik's arms, oblivious to the weather outside. She whirled away from the window and reached for an iron skillet from the shelf on the wall. With a noisy clang, she dropped it on the burner and turned to the refrigerator for the bacon and eggs.

A sleepy Aaron entered the room just as she was scraping the scrambled eggs into a plate. "I'm hungry."

She gave him her breakfast and fried more bacon. As she sat down to eat, Erik walked into the room. She pushed away her plate, her appetite vanishing. She knew he'd never seen her look so awful. The remnants of yesterday's makeup streaked her face, and her eyes were red-rimmed and smudged with mascara. Her hair had been damp when she'd gone to bed and now it was flattened and unruly, probably sticking up in all the wrong places. Feeling his stare, she raised her chin defiantly and gazed back at him. Let him see the real Leigh Fallon for once.

He glanced quickly at Aaron and then back at her. "We have to talk."

Leigh shook her head. "Not now."

"When?"

Leigh glanced at Aaron, who was engrossed in the morning paper's comics. "I think you said it all yesterday."

"*When,* Kayleigh?" he demanded, his voice rough with emotion.

Leigh turned to Aaron. "Sweetheart, could you go wake up your father? Tell him I'm making breakfast for him."

She waited until Aaron left the room before turning back to

Erik. He looked haggard, his face unshaved and his eyes bloodshot from last night's drinking.

Leigh took a deep breath. "I've decided I have to try to make a go of this marriage with Bob. We both knew it would end between us, Erik. The only thing you can do now is accept it . . . and go back to Norway as soon as possible." She felt tears come to her eyes. Quickly, she stood up and turned away from him, hoping he hadn't seen them.

"I can never accept it." His hands grasped her shoulders and whirled her to face him. He stared at her, his eyes like blue ice chips. "I *know* you love me."

Leigh tore away from him. "I was *infatuated* with you. Nothing more. We had some good times, that's all." Her eyes refused to meet his.

"You are the world's worst liar, Kayleigh," he said softly, his face twisted in a bitter smile. "But let me tell you this. I'm sorry for hurting you yesterday. I feel *nothing* for Dawn. I lashed out at you because your attitude hurt me. Kayleigh," His hand fastened on her chin as he forced her to look at him. "I love you. You will remember that." Softly, his fingers caressed her jaw.

The warm look on his face was too much for her to take. A tear tracked down her cheek, falling wetly onto his finger. "Go away," she said, shakily.

His hand slid down her neck onto her shoulder as he continued to stare at her. Finally, he drew away. "*Ja* . . . if that is what you want." He turned and went out the screen door. Leigh dropped to the chair, her breakfast forgotten. The pain she felt was worse than anything she'd ever experienced. It was even too deep for tears.

12

It was after four o'clock in the afternoon when Leigh came downstairs, dressed in her silk kimono. Her resolve to make her marriage work had led to a humiliating and ultimately unsuccessful attempt to arouse Bob, and it had ended with him pulling away from her and declaring he wasn't in the mood. As if that hadn't been painfully obvious. Leigh had silently gotten out of bed and filled the bathtub with hot water and bubble bath, trying to soak away her depression. It hadn't worked.

The rain had finally stopped, but the clouds hung low in the sky, gray and sullen. She found Aaron fast asleep on the sofa and the TV blaring. She switched it off and went into the kitchen. A note from Mel lay on the table amidst the remains of someone's half-eaten lunch. *Gone for a walk. M.* Gone to see if she could find the lifeguard she'd been mooning over, Leigh translated. She had no idea where Mark was . . . or Erik. . . .

A knock came at the front door.

"Hi there, Leigh." Dawn stood on the porch, smiling brightly and looking ravishing in tight jeans and a slinky lavender top. "I didn't think I was *ever* gonna get here. Do you know it rained on me almost all the way from Washington?"

"No kidding?" Leigh said. "Well, come on in."

"I guess I'll just leave my stuff in the car," Dawn said. "Erik said something about gettin' me a room at the Atlantic Sands."

And will he share it with you? Immediately, Leigh felt guilty as she thought of Erik's earnest expression that morning. Deep inside, she'd known he couldn't mean what he'd said. The only reason she hadn't returned to his arms was because he'd hurt her so intentionally, aiming his barbs at a place where he knew she was vulnerable. Her age—and her shaky self-confidence where Dawn was concerned. Besides, their relationship had had to end sooner or later. She'd done the right thing by ending it now.

"Where's Erik?" Dawn asked, glancing around the living room. Her shiny golden-brown bob cradled her perfect oval face. *Looks like a model for a Pantene commercial,* thought Leigh, gritting her teeth. Could the woman *ever* look less than perfect?

"I don't know." Leigh led her out to the porch. "I haven't

seen him since this morning. Have a seat. I'll get us a couple of Cokes."

When Leigh stepped out onto the porch with their drinks, she saw that Dawn had made herself comfortable in a lounge chair. Her eyes were closed, but they opened the minute she heard Leigh's footsteps.

She reached for the soda. "Oh, thanks. I'm dyin' of thirst." Dawn finished a long draw of the soda and sighed deeply. "Oh, yeah, that's good. You say you don't know where Erik is? But I know he's expectin' me. He should be here. I told him I'd get in about four or five."

Leigh shrugged. "Maybe he forgot."

A peal of laughter greeted this suggestion. "Oh, come on, Leigh. He for*got*!" More laughter. "What a sense of humor you have. Seriously, I hope he gets here soon. This is the big weekend, you know. A room at the Atlantic Sands. Once I get him to stay with me, he'll forget all about that little Norwegian girl who's kept him so chaste."

Leigh felt an immediate sense of relief. So, he'd been telling her the truth all along. He *hadn't* slept with Dawn. Yet. Leigh looked at the girl's pretty face, hating her smugness.

"Why don't you leave Erik alone?" Her words were barely audible.

But Dawn heard them. "What on earth do you mean?"

"Leave him alone." Her eyes met Dawn's shocked ones. "Please . . . he's in love with the girl in Norway. He . . . he's very vulnerable right now. He doesn't need you to confuse him."

With a scornful laugh, Dawn placed her empty glass on a table nearby. "You talk as if he's your son. Leigh, Erik is a grown man. I think he's intelligent enough to make his own decisions. I doubt very much if he'd welcome your concern. Besides, if he's so in love with some girl in Norway, why didn't he go home at the end of the college term?" Her eyes suddenly grew hard. "Why did he come here to the beach with you?" Her carefully cultivated southern accent had disappeared.

Leigh recognized the trap and struggled for a logical explanation. "Maybe he needed time to think out his feelings."

With a catlike smile, Dawn said, "Why don't we quit playing these silly games, Leigh. I guessed the truth about you and Erik a long time ago." Her eyes grew frosty, but the smile remained on her pouty lips. "How long has it been going on?"

Leigh felt the blood drain from her face. It took her a moment to catch her breath so she could speak. "What are you talking about?"

Dawn didn't answer. She just smiled. The silence was broken by the slam of the screen door.

"Dawn! How you doing?"

Leigh looked up to see Mark standing in the doorway.

"Hey, there, Mark," Dawn said. The accent was back and in fine form. "You're nice and tanned, I see. Have you seen any gorgeous Norwegians runnin' around lately?"

A tremor had invaded Leigh's body. She felt nauseated. God, the bitch knew, but what was she going to do about it? Dawn was like a patient cat batting a defenseless mouse back and forth, careful not to dig in her claws too viciously, but savoring the moment of the kill. Leigh stood up abruptly.

"I'll go down to Louie's for pizza," she said to Mark. Before he could reply, she whirled around and hurried upstairs to get dressed.

Five minutes later, she raced out of the house, a rising tide of panic threatening to erupt inside her. She struggled against it; her only hope now was to remain calm. But no matter how she tried, she couldn't escape the dark feeling of foreboding descending upon her.

Leigh walked into the front door of the house. The trip to the pizza parlor had calmed her. What could Dawn do with her suspicions? She had no proof, and Leigh hadn't admitted anything. Besides, the affair was over. Past tense.

Aaron jumped up from the TV, his eyes on the pizza box. "It's about time! I'm starving!"

"Did you remember to get mushrooms on half of it?" Bob asked, glancing up from papers he was studying at the dining room table.

Leigh nodded. "Isn't Mel home yet? And where are Mark and Dawn?"

"Mel has a date with that lifeguard, and Mark and Dawn went out to look for Erik. How about something to drink with the pizza?"

A half hour later, Mark and Dawn returned.

"I just can't understand where he is," Dawn said plaintively as she came into the room. "It isn't like him to disappear, especially when he knew I was comin' today."

"I saw Erik," Aaron mumbled through a big bite of pizza.

Leigh, Dawn, and Mark looked at him. They all spoke at once. "When?"

"After lunch. He came in, looking awful. Like a drowned rat. He asked for you, Mom, and I told him you and Dad were upstairs taking *a nap*." He gave a sly snicker. "He went back out into the rain. Didn't say where he was going."

Alarm bells clanged in Leigh's brain. Once again, she saw Erik's face as she told him to leave her alone. He'd seemed resigned, as if he'd finally accepted there was no future for them. Could he have left for Norway? But surely not. Most of his belongings were still back at the house in Virginia. But maybe he'd gone back there to get everything? Maybe he was hitchhiking—how else could he get back to Virginia? No! She wouldn't believe he could leave without saying good-bye. He had to be around Rehoboth somewhere.

"I'm sure you just missed him," she said. "Did you check all the shops . . . or what about the arcade? I know he likes to play that shooting game."

"We checked everywhere, Mom," said Mark. "This is weird. It's not like Erik at all. We'd made plans to take the girls out to that seafood place in Dewey Beach tonight."

An hour later, after a second search of the beach town brought no results, Leigh pleaded with Bob to call the police. He vetoed that idea.

"Jesus!" Bob slammed his briefcase shut with a black scowl. "What *is* it with you women? He's a grown man! Maybe he wants to be off on his own for a while."

Dawn glared at him. "He *knew* I was coming today. Something has happened to him, *or he would be here!*" Again, her Scarlett O'Hara accent was gone.

Bob gave her a cynical grin. "He's probably shacked up with some blonde beach bunny."

Dawn threw him a murderous look and opened her mouth to reply. The telephone rang. Leigh reached for it, an ominous feeling rising in her, but Bob was closer. He picked it up and barked, "Fallon residence." He listened for a moment and murmured a few words. Leigh drew closer. Was it Erik?

"Yes. Thank you for calling. Someone will be right there."

"What is it?" she asked as soon as he hung up. "Where is he?"

He turned to her. "That was the Bethany Beach Emergency Service. Erik was found unconscious behind the Atlantic Sands Hotel. Appears to have a head injury."

"Oh, my God!" Dawn gasped.

Leigh felt her body turn to ice. She grabbed her purse from the kitchen table, fumbling for her car keys. When she found them, she raced to the hallway closet for her raincoat.

"I'm going with you," Dawn said. She'd already pulled on a weatherproof jacket.

Leigh stopped at the front door and turned to face Dawn. "No, you're not." And without giving her a chance to argue, Leigh strode out the door, closing it decisively in Dawn's face.

Leigh ran up the steps to the entrance of the Bethany Beach Emergency Service. In her haste to leave the house, she'd forgotten her umbrella, and her hair and coat were drenched by the driving rain that had started to fall again.

The electronic double doors whooshed open. She rushed up to a counter, where a large uniformed nurse stood, a telephone to her ear. Leigh waited for her to get off the phone, nervously chewing on the nail of her little finger. She shoved her hand into the pocket of her raincoat and leaned onto the counter, her eyes pleading with the receptionist to acknowledge her. Finally, the woman hung up. "Yes?"

"I received a call about Erik Haukeland. He was brought in with a head injury."

"Oh, you'll want to talk to Dr. Leighton. Just have a seat, ma'am, and the doctor will be with you in a moment."

"But can't I see Erik? What is it? God, he isn't—" Her heart lurched at the awful thought.

"Oh, here's Dr. Leighton now. This lady is here to see the young man with the head injury."

Leigh turned to a tall young woman dressed in green scrubs. It had to be the doctor because she wore a stethoscope around her neck, but she looked like a teenager.

"Are you a relative of Mr. Haukeland?" the doctor asked.

Leigh was almost frantic. "We're his host family. He's a Norwegian national going to school here in the states. Doctor, is he all right?"

"He's going to be fine," she said. "He's conscious now and asking for someone called Kayleigh. Is that you?"

"Yes. Please, can I see him?"

"Of course. But I do want to transfer him to a hospital in Ocean City for the night. He's suffered a concussion from a blow to the head, and I'd just feel better if he's kept in overnight for observation. But I don't expect any problems. It's more than likely he can go home tomorrow."

"I don't understand—a blow to the head? But how—you mean he was attacked?"

"According to the police, a wallet with his identification was found near him, but there was no money in it. It looks like a mugging. Also, he was found in the parking lot behind a hotel. Not a real safe place to be at night. He was probably jumped by a couple of punks. Out-of-towners, of course." Dr. Leighton shook her head. "It happens every summer. People think because they're in a small beach town there's no such thing as crime. Come on, I'll take you to him."

Erik was lying on a cot in a tiny room off the corridor, his face turned toward the wall. Leigh's eyes fastened upon the bandage wrapped around his head. Was his injury worse than the doctor had admitted? But when he heard her footsteps, he turned toward her, his blue eyes alert.

"Kayleigh . . ." He smiled. "*Kristus!* I'm so glad to see you."

Leigh couldn't speak because of the lump in her throat. She walked toward him and sat gingerly on the edge of the cot. "Oh, Erik . . ." She leaned against him gently, her cheek resting on his shoulder.

His hands caressed her back. "Promise me one thing," he whispered, a wry smile on his lips. "If you ever meet my family, don't tell them I was jumped by two little punks and didn't manage to get one punch in."

"How can you joke about it?" Leigh felt very close to tears. "You could have been killed . . . and it would've been my fault. I've treated you so terribly . . . said so many awful things to you . . ."

"Look at me, Kayleigh. . . ."

Leigh lifted her head so she could look into his eyes. His face was solemn. "I'm the one who should be begging *your* forgiveness. And that is the only thing I want before I go home. I've accepted that you cannot give up your family for me. I was wrong to ask you to do it. I was being selfish, as usual. You see, Kayleigh, I've rarely had to accept defeat in my life. Things have always come too easily for me." His hand tightened on hers. "You are the one thing I want that I cannot have."

Her eyes blurred. "I love you, Erik. You've got to believe that. But it's better for both of us if you go home and pick up your life. We'll never forget what we had together."

An orderly entered the room and announced they would be taking him out to the waiting ambulance in a few moments.

Leigh stood up. "I want to go with him."

"Against the rules, ma'am. But there's nothing to stop you from following behind in your car."

Suppressing an exasperated sigh, Leigh turned back to Erik. "I'll meet you at the hospital, darling." She leaned down to him. Their lips clung together for a long moment.

She straightened, turned to leave the room—and froze. Bob stood in the doorway, staring at her. She felt herself blanch. His face was gray with shock, his mouth agape in silent disbelief. For an endless moment, they stared at each other, locked in the mocking embrace of truth. Finally, Bob turned away, his broad shoulders slumped. Even after he was gone, Leigh stared at the empty doorway, unable to comprehend that finally, the entire world she knew was crumbling around her. Slowly, she turned back to Erik and saw he'd also seen Bob. Their eyes met in silent communication.

"Okay, let's get you on this gurney," said the burly ambulance attendant. A moment later, the gurney rolled past her.

"It will be okay," Erik called out to her. "We'll face him together tomorrow."

But Leigh knew it wasn't going to be that easy. She walked out of the room, her feet leaden, and moved mechanically down the short corridor leading to the lobby. As she'd known he would, Bob was waiting for her, pacing back and forth, his hands thrust into the pockets of his raincoat. He saw her approaching and stopped. The look in his eyes hurt the most. So betrayed. Leigh had never guessed her husband could look so vulnerable. Rebecca, she reminded herself. *Remember Rebecca. Remember all the nights you wanted him to make love to you, and he turned away.* But still, she felt like a piece of shit. She stopped in front of him and waited for him to speak. Oh, God . . . surely he wasn't going to cry. She simply could not bear that.

He blinked and cleared his throat. "I just couldn't accept what Dawn told us . . . I couldn't believe it of you." His voice was low and husky. "*Why,* Leigh?"

Leigh shook her head, unable to speak. The lump in her throat threatened to choke her. Her eyes burned from all the tears she'd shed in the last two days. Finally, she knew she couldn't bear another moment of looking at Bob's bereft face. Without a word, she turned and walked away.

"Leigh."

She stopped, but didn't turn around.

"Don't go to him. I'll arrange for him to go back to Norway. Don't see him again, and I'll try and forget what you did to me. We'll go on as if it didn't happen."

Leigh stood stock-still. She could feel his eyes boring into her back, and she knew he was willing her to turn around. It would be so easy to do the right thing. To turn to him and say "Okay. I'm sorry I hurt you. I promise I'll be a good girl from now on." With those simple words, life would go on as it had for the last twenty-one years.

She stared through the double doors ahead of her. It was dark and rainy outside. Nothing waited out there but insecurity and question marks. And possibly, somewhere in the future . . . Erik. She took a deep breath and began to walk. The electronic doors opened for her. She went through and stepped out into the rainy night.

13

Erik was released from the hospital the next morning. The night had been a long one for Leigh. They'd refused to let her stay with him in his room, so she'd chosen to sit it out in the third-floor lounge. There was no way she could go home. Not after that moment with Bob in the emergency room lobby. She'd made her choice, and for once in her life, it hadn't been the easy way out. Now, she'd have to live with the consequences of that decision. But what would be the next step?

Throughout the endless night, her mind had run a frantic rat race, accepting one wild idea and rejecting another. The coffee she drank from a machine in the room only exacerbated the situation. Of course, there would be a divorce. If Bob didn't file, she would. But what then? Go to Norway with Erik? For a crazy moment, she'd made up her mind to do just that. But then reality set in. She knew she couldn't rush into such a decision. It wouldn't be fair to Erik to leave with him now just because her marriage had ended. Better to let him go home alone. Then perhaps in a few months, after she'd pieced her life back together, if she still felt the same about him, if he felt the same about her . . . maybe then, Norway.

Oh, God! It was all so crazy, so complicated. Had she really done it? Had she really walked out on Bob? Oh, yes. No confusion about that. She'd done exactly that, and there was no going back now.

Early in the morning as the first pinkish light rose in the east, Leigh reached her decision. She would call Deanna, explain the situation. Perhaps she could stay at her penthouse while she looked for an apartment in New York. She had the money in her account from the cover fee of Diana's book. It hadn't been touched. Of course, she'd still have to look for a job, but there again, Deanna could be of help. Her connections in New York were unlimited. What about the children? Aaron and Mel. Would they even *want* to live with her? She'd just have to wait and see.

At nine o'clock, Erik was examined and discharged. Moving gingerly, he walked with Leigh to the Volvo. Grimacing, he slid into the passenger front seat and touched a hand to the white gauze bandage on his head.

Leigh noticed. "Still hurts, doesn't it?"

"*Ja*, a bit. Nothing I cannot handle."

She covered his hand with her own. "I'm so glad you're okay." She leaned toward him to kiss him. His hands tightened on her shoulders as their lips clung for a long moment. Reluctantly, she pulled away and switched on the ignition. "You ready? This isn't going to be easy."

He nodded. "I know. We'll get through it."

On the short drive back to Rehoboth, he spoke only once more. "Does this change anything with us? I mean, Bob finding out? Will it make you change your mind about Norway?"

She pulled her eyes from the oceanfront road to glance at his solemn profile. "No," she said softly. It was better not to give him any false hope.

He stared out at the silvery blue ocean on his right. "I did not think so."

Bob sat at the kitchen table, staring down at his hands folded in front of him. A crumpled pack of Marlboro Lights lay near an ashtray brimming over with butts. Leigh hadn't seen him smoke for over two years. They walked into the room, Leigh in front of Erik.

"I was wondering when you'd show up," Bob spoke in an oddly flat voice, still staring down. Finally, he looked up. His eyes were bloodshot as if he hadn't slept at all . . . or had been crying. It didn't matter. Either way, Leigh felt racked with guilt. Desperately, she tried to think of something to say, but she knew it would be meaningless. There was nothing to do but wait for him to make the first move.

He stood up abruptly and strode to the counter to pour himself a cup of coffee. Leigh could've used a cup herself, but she didn't dare ask, and he didn't offer. Funny, how she suddenly felt like an interloper in her own house. He turned around and leaned against the counter, his eyes glued to her, not veering once toward Erik, who waited silently behind her. He took a sip of coffee.

"I realize you were upset last night," he said quietly. "Not in your right mind. That's why I'm giving you a second chance." He flicked a baleful glance at Erik. "*He* goes back to Norway immediately." His eyes returned to her. "You come home with me, and we'll forget this ever happened."

Leigh was so astonished, she couldn't speak. He was willing to forgive and forget? Just like that?

His face was implacable. "A divorce wouldn't be in my best interests. You know that. Just think what the liberal press would do to me if your shoddy little affair with this . . . *foreigner* . . . gets out?"

Of course. How stupid she was to have thought, for even a moment, his motives could be anything but selfish. And what a hypocrite! Throwing her "shoddy little affair" in her face, and yet, he'd been screwing Rebecca for God knew how long. For a moment, she wanted to hurl the accusation right back at him. But no. There was only one thing she intended to say to him right now.

She took a deep breath and lifted her chin. Until this moment, she hadn't been sure what she'd really do, but now, looking into Bob's smug brown eyes, she knew she'd reached a fork in the road. And only one of the paths led to freedom.

"I want a divorce, Bob." Her voice was quiet but firm.

Astonishment flickered in his eyes. There was complete silence in the room. Just the rattle of the dilapidated clock over the stove and the gentle hum of the refrigerator.

"And if you won't file for it, I will," Leigh added.

Bob tossed the remains of his coffee down the sink. "Well, it sounds like you've made up your mind. I don't suppose you've given a thought to the kids, have you?" He gave a short harsh laugh. "Of course not. Too preoccupied with yourself and your lover. But just so you know, Melissa and Aaron don't want to see you. I don't know about Mark. He's pretty upset."

Leigh's heart constricted; she felt nauseated. Her voice rose. "You told them?"

"Your concern is touching. As a matter of fact, I didn't *have* to tell Aaron and Mark. They were here when Dawn dropped her little bombshell last night. And when Mel got in from her date, she could see something had happened, so Mark told her. Okay, Leigh, you want a divorce? You've got it. I'm not stupid enough to fight it and bring more publicity down on me. I'll give you a *quiet* divorce so you can be with your lover. But don't think for a minute you'll get the kids. I won't have them living with someone like you."

Erik made a sudden move behind her and Leigh turned to place a restraining hand on his arm. Imploringly, she looked up at him, mentally begging him to be cool. She turned back to her husband. "Mark is old enough to choose—"

"But he won't choose you," Bob went on quietly. "None of them will. They don't want anything to do with you."

"I don't believe you."

"Believe it." He moved toward her, stopping a foot away. His brown eyes studied her. The hurt look was gone, replaced by disgust. "You know, I always thought you were a little boring . . . but I never dreamed you'd turn out to be a common whore."

This time, she couldn't stop Erik. He stepped around her and grabbed Bob by the shirt front. His upper lip curled, revealing straight white teeth as he snarled, "You son of a bitch, you'd better mind your mouth or I will cram your teeth down your sanctimonious throat! It is something I've been wanting to do for a long time now."

Bob sneered, defiantly glaring up at the taller man. "Take

your hands off my shirt, you fucking communist. She's still my goddamn wife and I'll say whatever the *fuck* I want to her."

"Go ahead—but I promise you will pay for it."

Leigh touched his arm. "Erik, please let him go. It's not worth it."

Erik's eyes blazed into Bob's for an endless moment. Finally, he released him and pushed him away with a grunt of contempt. "You're right, Kayleigh. He's *not* worth it." His voice lowered, his eyes skewering Bob. "How she put up with you for so many years, I'll *never* understand."

Bob smoothed out his shirt and without a backward glance at Leigh, walked out of the kitchen. Too late, Leigh remembered Rebecca. Why hadn't she thrown his cheap little affair in his face during his attack on her? But she knew why. This wasn't about Bob. The truth was, even if he *had* been true to her, she still might have turned to Erik. The knowledge of Bob's affair had only made it easier for her. Leigh felt Erik's hands on her shoulders, and she turned in his arms, resting her head against his solid chest.

The screen door creaked. Leigh drew away from Erik and turned to see Mark stepping into the kitchen. Like his father, he looked only at Leigh, his face sober. "Tell me it's not true, Mom."

Her vision blurred. "I can't do that, Mark."

A closed expression settled over his face. His eyes moved to Erik, anger glimmering in their depths. "You were my friend," he said. "And all the time you were screwing my mother."

Leigh winced. Erik stood calmly beside her. He tightened a hand on her shoulder, eyeing Mark stoically.

"It's a good thing you got that bump on your head last night," Mark growled. "Because if you hadn't, I'd beat the shit out of you right now."

Tears flowed down Leigh's face. She took a step toward her son. "Mark, please don't hate me."

"I don't hate you," Mark said, his face a mask of indifference. "But I sure as hell can never respect you."

"No wonder you were always pushing me away from Erik!" Mel's caustic voice came from the doorway. She stood there, her blue-green eyes glittering with unshed tears. "You wanted him for yourself, didn't you, Mom? Or were you already sleeping with him?"

"Oh, Mel, please . . . ," Leigh said, her throat thick with tears. God, this was a nightmare. Would she ever awaken? "Try and understand—"

"Understand? I only understand that my mother is a middle-aged woman who seduces younger men. *You make me want to puke!*"

She twisted on her heel and ran out, her long blond hair flowing behind her. Mark gave Leigh one last cold glare and followed his sister.

Leigh collapsed against Erik's chest. "God, what have I done?"

Erik turned into the driveway and switched off the ignition. For a moment, he and Leigh sat silently, staring at the lovely Tudor home. Even now, it was hard for her to digest the fact that she would no longer be living here.

"Kayleigh," Erik said. "Do you want me to stay or go? I will do whatever is best for you."

Leigh bit her lip. Of *course* she wanted him to stay. How could she not? But was that fair to him? When she couldn't promise him anything? Besides, she had the kids to think about. Bob had offered her a quiet divorce. If Erik stayed, the press would surely discover the truth, and the resulting scandal would destroy the kids. She couldn't risk that.

"I think it would be best if you went home, Erik."

He nodded. "I'll go make my reservation." His hand reached out to lightly caress her hair; then abruptly, he opened the car door and got out. She followed him. As they stepped into the cool dimness of the living room, the musty smell of an unlived-in house assaulted her nostrils.

"Let's open some windows," she said. "I've always hated walking into this closed house after vacation." A sob caught in her throat as she remembered this was the last time she'd ever have to do it.

Erik disappeared down the hall toward the kitchen. Leigh assumed he was wasting no time in getting to the phone. An irrational anger washed over her. How like a man to cut out just when everything fell apart! Immediately, she felt ashamed of her thoughts. She'd told him that was what she wanted. How she wished she could tell him to stay, or that she would come with him. But they both knew it was impossible. No matter that the kids didn't want to see her right now, she still couldn't go off to a foreign country and leave them.

She wandered around the living room, lovingly caressing the Hummel figurines on the cherry wood hutch. She'd bought one for every birthday she'd been married, a personal gift to herself. There were twenty now scattered throughout the house. She looked around the immaculate living room. So many memories. Good and bad. How could it have ended so suddenly? She shook her head. She'd asked for it, hadn't she? Now, there was only one thing to do. As soon as Erik was off the phone, she'd call Deanna.

He walked into the living room, his face grim. "Well, it's done. I leave tomorrow afternoon."

Leigh turned away; she couldn't bear to see the pain in his eyes. An overwhelming weariness swept over her. All she wanted to do was crawl into bed and give herself up to the tranquil world of sleep. She went into the kitchen, thinking if she put on a pot of coffee, it might help to motivate her. But first, the phone call.

A few minutes later, she walked into Erik's room, two mugs of steaming coffee in her hands. He was on his knees on the floor, placing books and compact discs into a large cardboard box.

"Want some coffee?"

He looked up. "*Ja, takk.*" Settling back against the side of the bed, he took a sip and placed the coffee mug on the floor. "Did you get Deanna?"

Leigh nodded. "She wants me to fly right up. I guess I'll leave the day after tomorrow."

Erik reached over and drew a compact disc from the pile near him. "I want you to keep this."

Leigh took the disc from him. Banshee—the CD with the song, "Kayleigh."

"Oh, Erik . . . ," she whispered. "How can I listen to this after you're gone?"

He stood up and came to her, taking the hot mug of coffee out of her hands. After placing it on top of his desk, he took her into his arms and kissed her hungrily. He drew away, leaving her trembling.

"Let's make love one more time," he said. His hand stroked her rumpled hair as she buried her face into his chest. A muffled sob escaped her throat.

She looked up at him. "I can't," she said. "Erik, I just can't bear . . . knowing it's the last time."

"Then just sleep with me. Sleep in my arms tonight, Kayleigh. I just want to hold you."

She would never have dreamed it was possible. But on Erik's last night in America, they slept in each other's arms without making love.

The morning came too quickly.

Outside the huge windows overlooking the skating rink in Central Park, slate-gray clouds hovered low. Far below on the sidewalks, New Yorkers strode briskly, hunched over, faces down as they braved the frigid wind. Glitzy Christmas decorations danced forlornly from light poles, in an attempt to bring gaiety to the dismal December day.

A false impression of warmth and happiness dwelled inside Deanna's luxurious penthouse. At least, it seemed that way to Leigh. A glowing gas fire crackled cheerfully in the huge stone fireplace at the end of the spacious living room while music of Tchaikovsky's *Nutcracker Suite* flowed from hidden speakers throughout the apartment. In the corner, an elaborately decorated Christmas tree reigned, surrounded by countless professionally wrapped gifts from Cartier, Bloomingdale's, and Saks Fifth Avenue.

Leigh couldn't help but compare the artificial scene with

visions of past Christmases back home in Virginia. She loved Deanna dearly, but they were poles apart in the way they celebrated the holidays. Maybe it was because Deanna, having grown up in an orthodox Jewish household, hadn't celebrated Christmas until she was an adult. Or maybe it was simply because she was a city person whereas Leigh was born and bred in the cornfields of the Midwest. It was the little things that Leigh couldn't get used to.

Like the way she relished baking delicate butter cookies and chocolate frosted yule logs—and Deanna preferred to visit the gourmet bakery on Madison Avenue. Or how Leigh enjoyed taking the time to wrap each Christmas gift, sometimes more than once if it didn't look absolutely perfect by the time she was finished. Deanna, on the other hand, wouldn't dream of wrapping her own gifts.

"Are you kidding?" She'd laughed when Leigh suggested an evening of gift-wrapping. "They'd look like they were done by drunk chimpanzees!"

Leigh loved quiet gatherings with close friends, drinking hot chocolate or buttered rum and listening to Christmas carols. Deanna felt it wasn't Christmas if she wasn't jockeying from party to party, dressed in her wildest holiday clothing and dangling reindeer earrings of eighteen-karat gold. Because of these small but significant differences, Leigh found herself alone for many evenings this December. Tonight promised more long lonely hours to herself.

With a sigh, Leigh turned from her contemplation of the bleak afternoon. It had been a long day, the first of a three-day break from her part-time job. Deanna, who just happened to be friends with the owner of an art gallery in SoHo, had helped her secure a position as salesclerk. Now, Leigh wondered how she could possibly get through two more days alone in the apartment. With Deanna's heavy social calendar, she'd be popping in and out just for a change of clothing.

It was December 11, and she still hadn't heard a word from her children. Bob's hand at work, of course. Hard to believe he was being so vindictive. But she should've known he would be. He hadn't wasted any time in getting the divorce. A quick trip to Mexico had taken care of all the details. Funny, how easy it was to dissolve a marriage. And what had she gotten out of it? The Volvo, the beach house, and her freedom. She'd immediately sold the Volvo. There was no need for it in her new life in New York. After thinking it over, she'd decided to hold on to the beach house. It would be an excellent source of income during the summer months. Washingtonians would pay big bucks for an oceanfront cottage, and since Bob had paid it off years ago, her only fees would be to the realty company to handle the rentals.

Because it was a no-fault divorce, Leigh was sharing joint custody of the children with Bob. Only on paper, though, because they were living with Bob—Mark and Melissa because they'd chosen to live with him, and Aaron because Leigh felt it would be unfair to uproot him from the place he'd called home all his life. She'd taken the Amtrak down to spend the weekend with him three times, but each time she'd returned to New York, her heart broken all over again at leaving him behind. And she wasn't sure the visits were doing him any good, either.

Almost five months had passed since the day Erik had left. A few days afterward, she'd received a telegram from him. "I miss you. E." She'd wept when she read it. Two weeks later, a letter arrived from Norway. Since then, there had been one every week. As she read the long letters, she could almost see him, feel him next to her. It was uncanny. She would read his words slowly, savoring them. Then carefully, she'd fold them up and put them away. She'd forced herself not to write back.

To what end? What purpose? In these months in New York, she'd taken a long look at herself, and she couldn't help wondering what Erik had possibly seen in her. Oh, sure. She was decent-looking for a forty-year-old, and her body hadn't yet given way to middle-age flab. But that was just it. She was middle-aged. *What had she been thinking*? That a great-looking young guy like Erik could really be in love with her? Oh, she didn't deny that he *thought* that. But that would change once he settled down at home and found someone closer to his own age. It had been a fairy tale to think she could actually go to Norway and make a life with Erik. Completely unrealistic to think she could leave her children—even if they weren't speaking to her—and live halfway across the world. No, the whole idea was insane! So, she hadn't answered Erik's letters, knowing that sooner or later, he'd give up, quit writing . . . and then, he would truly be in the past. She believed that point was near. His last letter had been furious. "Why are you such a fool? You are the most stubborn, impossible woman I've ever met! I *know* you are reading this. So *answer, dammit!*"

He'd called twice. Once, Deanna had taken the call when Leigh had been at work. She'd dutifully written down his phone number and message. "Call me, Kayleigh. We need to talk." With near boneless fingers, Leigh had taken the Post-it note and tucked it into the bottom of her lingerie drawer. She couldn't bring herself to throw it away; she wasn't sure why.

The last call had come early one morning in October. Deanna was still in bed, and Jackson, her butler, had taken the day off. The phone rang, shattering the silence. Leigh, sitting at the table, reading the newspaper, and drinking her morning coffee, ignored it and allowed the answering machine to pick up.

Her hand clenched on her coffee cup as she recognized Erik's velvet-smooth voice. Her heart began to drum. "Deanna, this is Erik Haukeland, calling from Oslo. Could you please get a message to Kayleigh for me? I haven't heard from her, so I do not know if she is still living with you or not, but please, tell her she must call me. I've *got* to talk to her. Something has happened here and—well—I cannot go into it. Just tell her I need to—oh, *Kristus!* Tell her it's *imperative* that I talk to her. My number is 011-47-2217—"

Leigh almost toppled her chair as she jumped up and lunged for the phone on the wall. "Erik? Hello?" Her palm flattened over her pounding heart.

It was too late. He'd hung up.

With a trembling hand, she replaced the phone in its cradle. *It's for the best,* she told herself. Talking to him would only open old wounds. Moving stiffly, she walked to the answering machine and pressed the message button. Listened to his voice again. And then one more time. She swallowed hard, her finger resting on the erase button. Then, biting her lower lip, she pushed it. "Message erased," announced the monotone voice. How she wished she could erase it from her mind so easily. He'd sounded so . . . sad. Almost desperate.

Thinking about it now, her eyes blurred with tears. From the foyer, she heard the front door slam. Quickly, she blinked the tears back and tried to compose herself before Deanna came in.

"I wasn't expecting you home so early," Leigh said, forcing a smile as Deanna walked into the room.

Something was wrong. Deanna's brown eyes lacked their usual sparkle, but they were still sharp enough not to be fooled by Leigh's forced expression of well-being. "For God's sake, Leigh, why don't you quit feeling sorry for yourself and *do* something about it!"

In astonishment, Leigh watched her turn and stomp into her bedroom, slamming the door behind her. She sat still, wondering what on earth was wrong. She'd seen Deanna through many moods since she'd moved in with her, but this was the first time she'd seemed so angry, so impatient with her. Still, she knew she deserved it. Deanna had put up with a lot from her lately. Maybe it was time to start seriously searching for an apartment. But every time she'd mentioned it, Deanna begged her to stay.

Darkness fell, and Deanna stepped out of her room to put on a pot of tea. Leigh followed her to the kitchen, murmuring an apology. Yet, Deanna remained aloof. "Forget it," she said curtly, refusing to meet her eyes.

Leigh knew for sure something was terribly wrong when Deanna didn't go out to one of her parties that night. Instead, she retired to her room with her pot of tea. Leigh watched TV for a while and then, at eleven o'clock, got up to go to the bathroom. As she made her way down the hallway, she passed Deanna's room and saw that her door was ajar. A sound inside made her hesitate. Was Deanna . . . *crying*?

Knowing she was risking a rebuff, Leigh tapped lightly on

the door and pushed it open. "Dee? What's wrong?"

Deanna was curled on her bed in a fetal position, sobbing into the pillow she hugged tightly to her midsection. Leigh stood still, not knowing what to say or do. It was as if Deanna hadn't heard her.

"Dee?" she said again, and this time, she saw Deanna's face move toward her. Gradually, Leigh's eyes adjusted to the darkness; she could just make out the novelist's features.

Tears glistened on Deanna's high cheekbones, and her tangled black hair fell around her shoulders in an unruly mass. Her brown eyes were huge as she gazed into Leigh's face. "I'm so scared," she whispered.

Leigh sat on the edge of the king-size water bed. "Why?"

Deanna didn't answer. She buried her face into the pillow. Leigh waited, intuitively knowing Dee wanted to talk but that for some reason, she couldn't get the words out. When she finally spoke, Leigh wasn't prepared for what she had to say.

"They want to cut my breasts off."

Stunned, Leigh stared at her. Through her tears, Deanna attempted a smile, but it was more of a grimace. "Yes. Can you believe it? I had a biopsy today. Cancer. They say that a double radical mastectomy is my only hope. Shit! I can see it now . . . introducing the great novelist, the boobless Deanna Harper! God, maybe I should give up writing and join a circus. . . ." Her voice trailed away into sobs.

Leigh tried to swallow her cold fear. *Cancer. Oh, Jesus.* She took Deanna into her arms, wishing she could come up with the right words of comfort. But her mind remained a horrible blank. *Cancer,* it shrieked. On and off like a neon sign. Finally, Deanna's sobs subsided and she was quiet. When she spoke again, she sounded almost like the old Deanna.

"Hell, some of the best of 'em have had it. Ingrid Bergman, Eva Perón, Betty Ford. And Betty Ford is still alive! If she can lick the big C, I can. . . ."

"When did you find the lump?" Leigh asked.

"A few months ago. I tried to ignore it, but I could tell it was getting bigger. So I went in two weeks ago. The doctor seemed pretty concerned and ordered a mammogram. The results were suspicious, so I had the biopsy today. It's in both breasts. Typical, isn't it? I can't do anything halfway."

"Dee, why didn't you tell me?"

Tears welled again in Deanna's eyes. She hugged her knees to her chest, shivering slightly. "God, I'm so fucking cold! What's the thermostat on?"

"Come on." Leigh stood up and grabbed Deanna's velvet robe. "Put this on. Come in the kitchen with me while I make some coffee."

A few minutes later, they sat across from each other at the kitchen table. Listlessly, Deanna stirred her coffee and stared down into its murky depths. Her voice was uncharacteristically soft. "I didn't tell you because I kept hoping it would turn out to be nothing. Besides, you have enough problems. Your kids are giving you a hard time and . . ." She looked up and met Leigh's gaze, and for a moment, she looked like her old self. "You've been walking around like a goddamn ghost since that Viking left. Hell! You remind me of me fifteen years ago. So fucking stubborn."

She fell silent, stirring her coffee, her eyes faraway. Leigh waited without speaking.

"I never told you about my ex-husband, Carrie's old man," Deanna went on softly. "Caught the son of a bitch with our neighbor, a twenty-one-year-old tartlet. Didn't give him a chance to explain . . . didn't want to hear it. I divorced his ass, even though Carrie was on the way. But I never stopped loving him. For years, he begged me to take him back. And I was tempted, but I always stopped myself. My pride, I guess." She paused and took a sip of her coffee, then looked up at Leigh, her eyes bright with unshed tears. "Billy was killed in that plane crash in Washington, D.C. The one that hit the bridge. He was on his way to Florida to join a law firm down there. A few days before he left, I almost called him to tell him not to go. In fact, I'd dialed the number and let it ring twice before I hung up." Deanna stopped and stared at the wall, a bleak expression on her face. "If I hadn't hung up that phone . . . he might still be alive today."

Leigh sat quietly, instinctively knowing what her friend was getting at. Deanna looked straight into her eyes. "Leigh, if you love him, go to Norway. You'll never forgive yourself for barring him from your life. I know about the letters. You always cry when you read one. It's obvious he's in love with you. Why don't you give yourself a wonderful Christmas present and go to Norway to be with Erik?"

Leigh felt a wave of panic wash over her. "But what if I go there, and it doesn't work out? What if he's changed? Or *me*? What if I go to Norway and find out it wasn't love at all?"

"At least you won't always be wondering what might have been. And what the hell? You'll have a nice Christmas holiday in Scandinavia. I wish I could go with you."

Leigh chewed her bottom lip. "What about the kids? I mean . . . *if* things work out with Erik. How can I live in another country and never see my kids?"

"You don't have to make any major decisions now, Leigh. Just go to Norway for a few weeks. See what happens. Who knows? Maybe Erik will come back to the States with you. Besides . . . your kids aren't going to be young forever. They'll grow up and move away. Start their own families. Should you sacrifice your chance at happiness just so you're within a few hours' drive from kids who—face it—aren't even talking to you!"

Leigh shook her head. "I don't know. Bob tells me I'm an awful mother. And if I go to Norway, maybe I am. Anyway, how can I leave you? What about your surgery?"

"It's scheduled for Monday morning. I'll be fine by Tuesday, and you can leave on Wednesday. That will give you enough time to get your shit together, telegraph Erik, and tell him you're coming." Deanna leaned forward and clutched Leigh's hand. "Leigh, this is not rocket science! Just go to Norway. See Erik. See how things are between you. That's all I'm suggesting. Hon, if you go to Norway, that will be the best Christmas present you could give me." Her lips quirked in a tremulous smile, and she added ironically, "Unless of course, you're giving out nice plump breasts this year."

"Dee! How can you joke like that?" Deanna's attempt at

humor struck tiny darts of pain into Leigh's heart. It was somehow more pitiful than her tears.

Deanna's face grew hard with determination. "Shit! What else can I do? Cry some more? I can tell you right now, Leigh Fallon, that was the first and last time you'll ever see Deanna Harper cry. I just hope those suckers get all the fucking cancer out. If they don't, I'm going to sue their asses off and then I'll will all my millions to you, so you and Erik can have homes all over the world." She squeezed her hand. "Thanks, sweetie, for letting me get this off my chest. Ha! I just can't stop making puns, can I?" Her eyes sparkled with tears. "Now, why don't you get the hell out of here and go call SAS. It's not going to be easy to book a flight for anywhere this time of year."

Leigh got up and went to Deanna. She leaned down and hugged her tightly. From the living room, she could hear the roar of laughter coming from the TV and then the familiar rumble of David Letterman's flat Midwestern accent. She didn't think she'd ever be able to watch him again without thinking of Deanna.

14

"*Velkommen til Norsk!* I am ecstatic. E."

Again, Leigh read the telegram. It was worn and tattered from the constant perusal she'd subjected it to since receiving it three days ago. She'd been half-afraid he'd be lukewarm about her arrival, but the telegram had put her mind at rest. Glancing out the window of the 747, she could see only darkness, but from her calculations, she guessed Oslo was about an hour away. At the thought of actually coming face-to-face with Erik again, she felt a flutter of butterflies in the pit of her stomach. Was she being foolish, racing halfway around the world to be with a man thirteen years younger than she?

Deanna had come through her surgery in excellent condition. The night before, her daughter had arrived from Switzerland to be with her. Her prognosis was good the oncologists declared. They were confident they'd removed the malignancies, but Deanna would have to undergo a round of chemo with a radiation followup. She'd been alert and upbeat when Leigh saw her before leaving, joking about finding a Dolly Parton wig to compensate for her "lack of boobies." What a courageous woman she was. Leigh had never admired her friend more. She could only hope *she* could be so brave if anything that horrible ever happened to her.

A flight attendant moved toward her down the aisle, and Leigh stopped her to ask for a drink, hoping it would relax her keyed-up nerves. After the attendant passed on, a well-dressed man with thinning light brown hair and dark-rimmed glasses smiled warmly at Leigh from across the aisle.

"Do you have relatives in Norway?" he asked with an accent that immediately brought Erik to mind.

"No." Leigh smiled back. "I'm visiting a friend."

"Oh." The man looked interested. "I thought you might have Norwegian blood. Because of your fair skin and blond hair, I just assumed you were visiting your homeland."

"If I were, I'd be on my way to Ireland," Leigh said, enjoying his warm open manner.

"Aha. Then you may have Norwegian blood, after all. The Vikings invaded Ireland, you know, and I'm sure there were quite a few that found themselves enchanted by a beautiful Irish girl and settled there." He thrust out a well-shaped manicured hand. "I'm Knut Aabel. I work for the Norwegian Embassy in Washington, D.C."

Leigh leaned over and shook his hand. "I'm Leigh Fallon. I used to live in the Washington area, but I recently moved to New York. So, you're going home to Norway for Christmas?"

Knut smiled, and Leigh was amazed at how it transformed his rather ordinary face. He was really quite attractive. "Yes, I'm going home to Tromsø. It's up north. After we arrive in Oslo, I'll have another hour's flight to go."

"Oh, you're from the land of the midnight sun."

He smiled, his blue eyes amused. "*Ja*, but right now, we are in the period of darkness."

"Of course. It's winter," Leigh said. "I've often wondered what that must be like . . . living in total darkness."

The flight attendant arrived with Leigh's drink. "Thanks," Leigh said, and took a sip, hoping the man would keep talking. It would make the time go by faster.

Knut winked at her. "Well, except for the high suicide rate, it's no problem. Seriously, though, I would think one who wasn't used to it would find it maddening. But I rather missed it in America. I'm afraid I still suffer from homesickness." He smiled again, adding, "I can hardly wait to see my daughter, Kristin. She will be fifteen next week."

"My daughter is sixteen," Leigh said softly. She felt a pang in her heart as she thought of Melissa and their last meeting.

Knut's blue eyes widened behind his glasses. "You're joking. You don't look old enough to be the mother of a sixteen-year-old."

"Thank you." Leigh wondered what he'd say if she told him she had a son who was twenty. She glanced at him. Where was his wife, the mother of his teenage daughter?

It wasn't long before she found out. He told her he'd been a professor of literature at the University of Tromsø before he went to America. A discussion of Henrik Ibsen and O. E. Rölvaag followed. After a while, the conversation shifted to his personal life. Leigh noticed he became more gregarious with each tiny glass of aquavit he consumed. She'd never tried the Norwegian "water of life" made from distilled potatoes and caraway seeds, but Erik had told her about it, and she was sure she would sample it at some point during her stay in Norway. Watching Knut's grimace after he'd tossed the contents of the shot glass down his throat, Leigh wasn't sure she wanted to try it. Knut followed the shot of aquavit with a quick sip of beer and then began to tell her about his ex-wife.

"Sigurd just couldn't get used to America. I should say she *refused* to let herself get used to it. She just wasn't happy there. I, on the other hand, loved it. It was so adventurous, so challenging. But Sigurd wanted to come home. After two years, she took Kristin and returned to Tromsø. As soon as she got home, she filed for divorce."

"Sounds like Beret in Rölvaag's *Giants in the Earth*."

"That's it." Knut gestured with his beer glass. "*Ja!* She was *just* like Beret. Always finding fault with everything. Not allowing herself to see the good side of life in America. But at least she won't drive me to my death like Beret did to poor Per Hansa." His friendly blue eyes roved over her and stopped on her left hand, where her wedding ring was conspicuously absent. "And you? You're not married?"

"Not anymore," Leigh said. "Divorced."

"And what brings you to Norway? Just a holiday? Oh, but you said you were visiting a friend. A man, of course."

Leigh felt a blush creep up from her neck.

"*Ja*, I thought so."

At that moment, their discussion was interrupted by an announcement from the pilot: they would soon be making their descent into Oslo. Knut reached into his coat and pulled out a small white card.

"I'll be getting back to Washington on the fourth of January. Perhaps if you ever come down, we can meet for coffee. I have to tell you it's been very pleasant talking to you."

"Thank you. I've enjoyed it, too." She took his business card and tucked it into the side pocket of her purse; then she checked her seat belt to make sure it was secure. Very soon now, she would be seeing Erik again. A quiver ran through her body at the thought. How different would he be here on his home ground? Her mind darted to the night ahead. She was sure they would be staying at his apartment near the university. What would it be like to make love without the fear of discovery? Five months had passed since the afternoon they'd last made love before that final explosive argument. Her body quivered in anticipation as she thought about his touch. Soon, now. Very soon.

She glanced out the window two seats away. There was nothing to see, just darkness. Her hands gripped the armrests of her seat as the huge jet descended. Knut looked over and smiled reassuringly.

"I'm not crazy about landings myself. That is why I drink so much aquavit."

"Maybe I should have tried some," Leigh said with a nervous grin. But her anxiety had nothing to do with the landing of the aircraft.

They landed at Oslo's Fornebu Airport with a gentle bump and taxied toward the terminal. It wouldn't be long now before she would be with Erik.

With a friendly smile, Knut wished her a happy holiday and headed for the customs line for Norwegian nationals. Leigh was grateful to find the Norwegian customs officials courteous and efficient, and in a mere fifteen minutes, she was through. She entered the giant terminal lounge, her heart bumping. Anxiously, she glanced around, searching for Erik's tall, blond form. How she needed the comfort of his warm blue eyes upon her at this very moment. But she didn't see him anywhere.

She dropped her carry-on at her feet and stood there uncertainly, wondering if she should wait or go for her luggage. From the intercom, a female voice announced in Norwegian a departing flight for Copenhagen, and a moment later, it was repeated in English. She thought of how similar the announcer's accent was to Erik's, and then, through the crowd, she saw him.

He hadn't caught sight of her yet; his eyes still searched the crowd. Her heart drummed at the sight of him. He wore the same fur-lined flight jacket he'd worn last Christmas in their climactic walk by the lake, and in his blond hair, tiny crystals of ice glittered like diamonds under the lights of the terminal. Leigh grabbed her bag and made her way toward him.

His eyes fell upon her. An expression of relief swept over his face as he lunged for her.

"Kristus!" His arms wrapped around her in a bone-clenching grasp. "I thought you'd changed your mind."

Leigh dropped her bag. Her hands slid into his opened coat as she hugged him, her face nestling against the scratchy warmth of his wool sweater. How good it felt to be here with him. She knew she'd made the right decision.

He drew away slightly so he could lift her chin and gaze into her eyes. "Kayleigh," he whispered. "I can't believe you are really here."

"I can't believe it either," she said shakily. Her fingers hesitantly touched his blond stubble.

"Sorry," he murmured. "I forgot to shave. All I could think about was your arrival. Kayleigh . . ." He gave a soft groan, holding her against him as if afraid she'd disappear. Slowly, his mouth closed upon hers. The holiday crowd, along with the bright lights and noise, slipped away. Leigh was lost in the fantasy world where Erik's kisses had always taken her, the world where nothing mattered but the present.

In Erik's small but neat flat, Leigh stood at a wood-paned window, gazing out onto a quiet side street near the University of Oslo. Huge snowflakes fell furiously from the dark sky, but disappeared almost immediately on contact with the pavement and sidewalks. Behind her, she heard Erik's rustling movements as he built a fire in the brick hearth on the other side of the room.

She turned away from the window and glanced around his flat again. It was so like Erik. The furniture was scant and functional, clearly Scandinavian in design. The walls were paneled in a warm pine, reminding her of a mountain chalet in Colorado where she and Bob had once spent a week. In the corner of the room there was a day bed that also served as a sofa and opposite that, near a tiny kitchenette, stood a small dining table and two chairs. The largest piece of furniture in the room was a six-foot bookcase lined with books ranging from Norwegian translations of American best-sellers to classics from all over the world, and of course, psychology textbooks. But her eyes widened when she saw the thin red binding of a familiar book, one she knew only too well.

"Erik! When did you get this book?" Her voice sounded unnaturally loud in the small room.

He looked up from stoking the fire, grinning. "I received it only a few weeks ago. I had a friend at G.M.U. get it for me. Believe me, it wasn't easy trying to explain why I wanted a teenage romance sent to me."

Leigh looked down at the illustration on the cover of the Deanna Harper novel. She'd still been enmeshed in the first magic of their love affair when she'd sketched the cover design. Unbelievable that Erik had gone to the trouble of getting a copy! Smiling, she gazed at the young couple on the cover. She hadn't realized before how much the football player resembled Erik. Had he noticed?

He stood up and wiped his hands down the front of his jeans. "I haven't read it," he said as he moved toward her. "But looking at the cover brought you closer to me."

A vague nervousness swept over Leigh. She turned away to gaze out the window again, feeling his approach. Suddenly she found it difficult to breathe. His firm hands clamped down on her shoulders; she could feel his chest rising and falling against her back. How she wished she could relax and lean against him, giving herself up to him, but the strange tension that gripped her body wouldn't let go.

"Doesn't it seem appropriate that it's snowing?" Erik said softly, dropping his head so his lips could just brush the tender spot below her earlobe.

Leigh shivered, not sure if it was from desire or fear.

"*Englebarn* . . . what is it?" he asked.

"I don't know," Leigh whispered. "I think I'm scared."

"Of me?" His voice was amused.

Leigh watched the falling snow, mesmerized by its beauty. "Of us. Of the situation."

Gently, Erik turned her to face him. The look in his blue eyes was so endearingly familiar that Leigh felt her anxiety melt away. "You're wondering if you made the right decision in coming here? I can't tell you if you did or not. All I know is I am very, very glad you came." His sensitive fingers traced the V-neckline of her pink lamb's-wool sweater, his eyes devouring her.

"My sexy Kayleigh," he said huskily. "It's been so long. Do you feel how much I want you?"

She smiled up at him, touching his lips lightly with her fingertips. "Convince me."

The tram hissed to a stop, and Erik stood up, pulling Leigh with him. "Here we are. Kirkeveien. There's the entrance to *Frognerparken* over there."

They stepped down from the tram, and Leigh tugged at the collar of her dark gray wool coat, futilely trying to find protection from the knifing wind. Erik turned to her and pulled the heavy collar closer around her neck and then, as an added measure, drew her wool cap down another inch over her ears.

He shook his head. "You're dressed for the American winter, not ours. We'll have to do something about that." Quickly, he unwound a scarlet woolen scarf from his neck and wrapped it around hers. "That will have to do for now."

"But Erik!" Leigh protested. "I don't want *you* to freeze."

"Freeze?" Erik laughed. "*Kjareste*, this is what we Norwegians call a mild December." He pulled up the fur-lined hood of his flight jacket. "Come. Let's go see Vigeland's sculptures."

The gates of Frogner Park loomed before them, a formidable structure made from wrought iron and twisted into strange geometric shapes. An ugly reptilian figure glared down from the center of the entrance as if holding a ferocious guard over the treasured works of art by Gustav Vigeland.

Doubtfully, Leigh eyed the strange creation of the famous Norwegian sculptor, hoping the entire park wouldn't be devoted to such monstrosities. But her mind was immediately put to rest as they approached a three-hundred-foot bridge peopled by groups of bronze figures involved in everyday activities. Running, jumping, laughing—the lifelike statues appeared to be squeezing every precious drop out of life. Leigh was astounded by the realistic expressions. It was almost as if they'd been frozen in time, as if a sorcerer had waved his magic wand and real live people had suddenly turned to bronze. Amazed, she walked from one figure to another, delighting in every new and immediately recognizable expression of human emotion. Erik followed behind her, watching her face and sensing her profound awe.

"Life from the cradle to the grave . . . ," Erik said. "Vigeland was obsessed with that theme."

"Oh, Erik, look at this. . . ."

She'd stopped before an exquisite statue of a little boy

stomping his foot, obviously in the middle of a violent temper tantrum. "He looks just like Aaron. . . ."

"*Sinnataggen.* It means 'hothead' in English. This is one of Vigeland's most popular sculptures. Most everyone sees a little boy they know in him. *Mor* has always said it's the image of Mags. But I think when you meet him tonight, you'll see he's grown up quite a bit."

Leigh felt a ripple of apprehension run through her at the thought of meeting Erik's family. Of course, the Haukelands had no idea of their true relationship. They only knew her as the American woman who'd hosted their son during his year in the States.

"Do you think Mel told Mags about us?" she'd asked. Mel had been writing to Erik's brother for over a year.

"No." Erik shook his head. "Believe me, if Mags suspected anything, he'd never let me hear the end of it. Come on." He took her hand, and they left the bridge. "In the summer, this is a beautiful rose garden. I'll bring you back here when it is blooming. But then we won't have the park to ourselves. Come! Let me take you to the Labyrinth and the Fountain of Life."

In the gray morning light, Leigh saw a mosaic of black-and-white granite slabs looming ahead. She wondered if Erik actually intended to take her through the maze. Although she was enjoying the sights of Vigeland Sculpture Park, her nose and lips were numbed by the relentless wind, and her feet felt like blocks of ice, even encased in fur-lined leather boots.

"We'll have to go through the Labyrinth another day," Erik said. "Just hold my hand, and I'll take you to the center to see the fountain."

Carefully, they made their way across the huge slabs. "This labyrinth is Vigeland's rather ironic view of the course of life," Erik said. "Curves, corners, dead ends. I believe he is saying that life is nothing but a puzzle."

They reached the center of the Labyrinth. Erik placed his hands on Leigh's shoulders and turned her to face him. "It is, you know." His blue eyes were serious. "Life is but a puzzle."

He stared down at her a moment longer and then bent his head to kiss her.

His mouth was warm and wonderfully intoxicating as the icy wind whipped around them and stray snowflakes whispered down from the slate sky. Erik drew away and once again adjusted the wool cap around her ears. "I love you," he said. Then abruptly, "Well, there's the Fountain of Life. Of course, it's more magnificent when it's working."

It was beautiful even without the water. Fascinated, Leigh gazed at the six bronze males bearing a huge bowl on their shoulders, from which cascades of water would flow when the fountain was working.

"Look at their faces, Erik." Leigh moved closer. "Look at this poor old man, the pain in his eyes."

He grabbed her hand as if anxious to move on. "Come, let's start over in the northeast corner and follow the cycle of life. I believe there's sixty bronze reliefs in all."

Because of the enervating cold, Leigh and Erik strolled quickly, barely giving more than cursory glances to the beauty of Vigeland's work.

"Frogner Park is a very philosophical place, isn't it?" Leigh said when they reached the spot where they'd begun.

"I guess that is one reason I wanted to bring you here. Being an artist yourself, I knew you would appreciate it." Erik placed his arm around her and drew her close. "Let's go. I shouldn't think we'll have to wait long for the Holmenkollen tram. Are you hungry?"

"You know me. I'm always hungry."

"Good. I'll treat you to a genuine *Norsk lunsj*."

Leigh wished the weather had permitted a more leisurely tour through the sculpture park. She wanted to give Vigeland's work the rapt attention it deserved. Well, as Erik had said, maybe next summer. Startled at her unbidden thought, Leigh felt a cold lurch of fear inside her heart. Was she about to make the decision to stay?

It was dark and cold in Erik's flat when Leigh awoke in the late afternoon. Their day of touring Oslo had ended abruptly after lunch when they'd exchanged a smoldering glance and decided love was more important than reconstructed Viking ships.

Leigh reached for him, but his side of the bed was empty. She sat up and pulled the luxurious down comforter closer around her. The fire had died to faintly glowing embers. Wrapping the comforter around her naked body, she stepped onto the hardwood floor and shivered at the icy contact. She found the poker near the hearth and prodded the embers, sending tiny orange sparks flying up toward the chimney. Carefully, she nudged another log onto the grate and poked at it until it began to burn.

Satisfied that the fire was beginning to burn steadily, she wandered over to the window to gaze out onto the quiet street. The snow had stopped sometime while they'd been in bed and now the sidewalks and streets glittered in the lamplight as if they had been sprinkled with star-dust by thousands of magical fairies. But it looked bitterly cold. Leigh shivered and moved back to the fireplace. A key rattled in the lock, and Erik came in, his cheeks and nose red and his blond hair windblown. He wore a huge grin and carried an even larger box.

"*God aften*, Kayleigh, my love. What are you doing standing there in that eiderdown?"

"You mean besides freezing my buns off?" Leigh edged nearer to the fire.

He placed the box on the dining table. "Did you think of turning the thermostat up?"

Leigh gave a short laugh and shook her head. "I didn't even think to *look* for a thermostat. I thought the fireplace was the only source of heat."

Erik grinned. "*Kjaereste*, this is the city! Of course we have central heating. But no matter. I have something for you. And I promise, you will never be cold again. Here. Open this."

With unconcealed curiosity, Leigh approached the box. "What have you gone and done now?"

"Just open it."

She did and gasped. "Oh God! Erik!"

"It's blue fox." His eyes twinkled. "Imitation, of course. My conscience would not allow me to buy a real fur . . . nor would my wallet. Do you like it? Drop the eiderdown and try it on."

As if in a trance, Leigh let the comforter drop around her as she drew the soft fur jacket from its tissue-lined box. It was gorgeous! She'd never have guessed it wasn't real, either. She slid her bare arms into the sleeves and trembled slightly at the sensation of the cool satin lining against her body. "Mirror! Where's a mirror?"

"Here, behind the *toalett* door." He followed her into the bathroom. "You look so sexy with your bare legs showing beneath the coat. It makes me want to make love to you until it kills both of us."

"*That* will never kill us," Leigh said, eyeing herself in the full-length mirror and coquettishly pulling the shawl-like collar up around her neck. She turned quickly and threw her arms around him. "Oh, Erik, I love it . . . and I love you." She pulled his head down to hers. Their lips clung for a long moment.

Slowly, she drew away, smiling mischievously. "When did you say we have to leave for your parents?"

A fire leapt in his eyes. He shrugged. "We aren't expected until eight."

15

On the drive to the Haukeland's home, Erik went over some last-minute lessons on Norwegian customs. He drove slowly because the streets were icy from the afternoon's snowfall.

"Now, we've got the flowers to give *Mor*. What else? Oh, there's *Skal. Fordamme!* I should have had you try aquavit last night. I didn't think of it because I only drink it when I visit home. Hate the poisonous stuff! You see, one of the best ways to impress a Norwegian is to drain your aquavit in one gulp. But I wouldn't recommend trying it without practice."

"So, what do I do?" Leigh asked, brows knitted.

"Just swallow as much as you can and don't worry about what's left in the glass. Whatever you do, don't try to sip it."

"Anything else I should know?" She felt as if she were on her way to a guillotine . . . or worse, a dental appointment.

Erik pumped the brakes and brought the Volkswagen to a gentle stop at a traffic signal. He reached over and covered her gloved hand with his own. "You'll do fine," he said with a smile. "They'll love you . . . even if you *are* an American."

Alarmed, her eyes flew to his. He laughed. "Just kidding, *kjareste*. Come on, loosen up. It won't be so bad."

Leigh tried to believe him, yet her stomach fluttered with butterflies. Why, suddenly, was it so important for Erik's family to approve of her? Did it really matter? If they ever found out about their true relationship, the point would be moot.

They'd been driving for twenty minutes and were now in the countryside surrounding Oslo. As they climbed into the hills, the condition of the roads worsened. Rounding a sharp curve, Leigh felt the back wheels of the Volkswagen slide on the ice, and she stifled a gasp. Erik handled the skid with ease and glanced over at her, smiling. "Don't worry. Almost there."

He turned into the driveway of a wood beige house and parked next to a red Saab. As he switched off the ignition, he looked at the car and said clearly, "Shit."

"What is it?" Leigh asked.

Erik shook his head, a distracted expression on his face. "It looks like everyone else is here already. I just hope we aren't late. *Mor* is adamant about being on time."

Mor *sounds like a tyrant,* Leigh thought. She drew back the sleeve of her fur to check her wristwatch. "It's five till eight. Five minutes early."

Her heart thudded as they made their way up the slippery walk. Erik squeezed her arm reassuringly while they waited at the door. A huge gray-haired man opened the door and beamed at them. "Erik! *God kveld. Velkommen! Det gleder meg a treffe Dem, Fru* Fallon."

Leigh smiled blankly as Erik hugged his father. "Kayleigh doesn't speak Norwegian, *Far*, as you well know." He grinned at Leigh. "My father can speak perfect English when he's in the mood."

From another room, Leigh heard a feminine voice speaking

in Norwegian. A lovely white-haired woman came into view, wearing a red blouse and a long red and black hostess skirt.

"Erik?"

Erik bent down to receive his mother's light kiss. "*Mor*, this is Kayleigh."

Immediately, the woman turned to Leigh and smiled regally, holding out her hand. "Good evening, Mrs. Fallon. I'm Grethe."

"*God kveld,*" Leigh said, hoping her pronunciation wasn't too far off. Erik had spent twenty minutes coaching her on it.

"Ah, so you speak a little *Norsk*?" Grethe Haukeland smiled, yet Leigh imagined a coolness in her eyes. It was almost as if she'd been assessed by Grethe and was found wanting. Was it possible his mother suspected their relationship wasn't what it should be?

"*Litte grann Norsk,*" Leigh said. A little Norwegian. "In fact, that's about it. Oh, these are for you." She gave Erik's mother the bouquet of fresh flowers they'd bought at the florist that afternoon.

"*Tusen takk*. Please, come into the family room and meet everyone."

The Haukeland's home was comfortably furnished in the sleek, no-frills style common to Scandinavia, and complemented with a variety of large leafy plants growing in every available spot. As they followed Grethe down a short hallway, a delicious aroma wafted from the kitchen, making Leigh's stomach growl in anticipation. They entered a large room, and her eye was immediately drawn to the tall blue spruce Christmas tree in the corner, alight with what appeared to be antique ornaments of glass and wood and tiny Norwegian flags. Adjacent to the tree, a hearty fire crackled in a stone fireplace. Her attention turned to Erik's relatives, and she was struck by how much the scene resembled a family Christmas card. Conversation halted, and blue eyes and blond heads turned in unison to inspect the newcomer. Leigh suddenly felt as if she were on display.

Erik came to the rescue. "Everyone, this is Kayleigh Fallon," he said in English. "Kayleigh, this is my brother, Bjørn, and his wife, Anne-Lise, their daughters, Marit and Inger-Lise. My sister, Dordei, and her husband, Hakon. And my brother, Mags."

Erik's older brother, Bjørn, stood up and extended a hand to Leigh. This seemed to be the signal for everyone else to move. They gathered around her, all of them smiling and talking at once. A feeling of relief settled over her. It was going to be okay. She liked them, and she was sure they felt the same way. Bjørn, who was tall and balding, had a smile that was uncannily like Erik's. His wife, Anne-Lise, an elegant bespectacled blonde, greeted Leigh warmly, saying she hoped to visit the United States someday. Erik's sister, Dordei, was a somewhat washed-out version of her mother. She stood quietly nearby, eyeing Leigh curiously, but speaking very little. Leigh smiled politely, her mind awhirl with everyone talking to her at once. She was sure she would never be able to put names to faces.

"Erik?" Grethe spoke to her son in a voice that instantly put a stop to all the conversation around them. "Aren't you going to introduce Margit to Mrs. Fallon?"

For a second, Leigh saw a strained expression on Erik's face, but it was gone so quickly she thought she must have imagined it. "Of course, *Mor*," he said smoothly, drawing a young red-headed woman to Leigh's side. "Kayleigh, meet Margit Lovvig, an old friend of the family. And that adorable little boy with her is her son, Gunvor."

Margit stretched out her hand as Erik moved away to the other side of the room. "I'm happy to meet you, Kayleigh." She smiled warmly. "Erik has told me so much about you and your family since he returned home."

Just as Leigh opened her mouth to respond, a loud clinking sound came from behind her. Erik's father grinned, tapping a spoon against a large brandy snifter to draw everyone's attention. Erik appeared at Leigh's side, handing her a snifter of her own. Arne lifted his glass and solemnly gazed around the room. An expectant silence had fallen.

"*Skal,*" he said softly.

Immediately, everyone else repeated the same word and

drank the contents of their snifters. The smooth brandy slid
down Leigh's throat. She wondered how she was ever going
to make it through the evening without getting dogfaced
drunk. Boy, would that make an impression on Mother Haukeland!

After they'd finished their brandy, the party moved into the
dining room, and Leigh found herself seated between Mags
and Dordei's husband, Hakon. On the other side of Hakon sat
Anne-Lise, looking stunning in a red velvet jumpsuit with
rhinestone buttons. Leigh felt almost dowdy in comparison,
even though she wore a new emerald silk dress she'd bought
at Bloomingdale's before leaving New York. As if reading her
insecure thoughts, Erik's eyes met hers across the table where
he sat opposite Anne-Lise. At his reassuring smile, she felt a
bit calmer.

Bjørn was seated opposite Leigh between Margit Lovvig
and Dordei. Arne and Grethe rounded out the long table at
each end. The children had been relegated to the kitchen,
where their voices rang out occasionally in outbursts of excited
Norwegian.

Leigh gazed at the array of food on the table. Most of it
was unfamiliar, but she did recognize various cheeses on the
relish tray. The aroma of the unusual Norwegian dishes tan-
talized her senses. She couldn't wait to try them. If only she
weren't so nervous about *skal*. She knew it would be coming
up any time now.

Almost immediately, the dreaded moment arrived. Arne
lifted his tiny glass of aquavit and looked directly at her.
"Skal," he said, his eyes firmly fixed upon hers.

With trembling fingers, Leigh picked up the shot glass near
her beer chaser and glanced at Erik. He gave her an encouraging nod. God, what if she screwed up? Everyone in the room
watched. Leigh raised the glass and looked squarely into
Arne's friendly blue eyes.

"Skal," she said in a near-whisper. In a synchronized movement with Arne, she threw back her head and downed the
contents of the shot glass.

Liquid fire burned down her throat and into her lungs, finally hitting her stomach with a smoldering explosion. Gasping, she grabbed the beer and gulped it down, praying she wasn't going to embarrass herself any further. Through the roaring in her ears, Leigh heard a warm applause from around the table.

"Very good, Kayleigh," Bjørn said approvingly. "There are not many Americans who could do that like you just did. You must have some Viking blood."

Through blurred eyes, Leigh looked at Erik and saw him grinning at her proudly. Everyone at the table smiled their approval at her, but Leigh didn't miss Grethe's expression of remote skepticism. Dimly, she wondered why Erik's mother seemed so cool toward her, but then she forgot about her as the warm glow of the aquavit spread through her body. Everyone began helping themselves to the food.

By the time dinner was finished, and several more *skals* had become history, Leigh's head buzzed with all the liquor she'd consumed. As she stood to help Grethe and Anne-Lise clear the table, a wave of dizziness engulfed her. She sat down again abruptly. Anne-Lise smiled and placed a light hand on her shoulder.

"Sit, Kayleigh. Dordei and I will take care of the table. You aren't used to the aquavit. Margit, why don't you take her into the library for a few quiet moments before we join the men for coffee."

"Of course." Margit smiled and stood up. "Kayleigh, I hear you're an artist. You must see Dordei's charcoals. She was very dedicated to her art before she married Hakon."

Feeling disoriented, Leigh followed Margit into the library, a beautiful room with a soft mauve sofa and several dove-gray chairs. Except for one corner where Dordei's charcoals hung, the walls were lined with books on all sides. Like Erik, the other Haukelands were voracious readers, judging by the amount and variety of the books. Leigh politely admired Dordei's charcoals, wishing she could fall onto the inviting sofa and give herself up to sleep. Jet lag had caught up with her.

"You'd better sit down," Margit said. "That aquavit is quite potent. Especially if you're unused to it."

Gratefully, Leigh sank onto the sofa. Margit snuggled into a chair and kicked off her shoes with a sigh. "I'm very tired myself. I work at a child care center. The children wore me out today."

"You must really enjoy children if you can spend all day with them," Leigh said. "How old is your son?"

"He'll be three in March." Margit ran a slender hand through her long reddish-blond hair. She had an open, friendly face dusted with freckles and a warm smile. A straight-haired girl-next-door version of Nicole Kidman. "My husband, Gunvor, was killed in a helicopter crash in the North Sea before he was born. He worked at an offshore oil platform for Phillips Petroleum."

"How terrible for you!" Leigh said, shocked. Margit was so young to be a widow.

"*Ja*. It was an awful blow. But Gunny and I are starting to get our life back together. If it weren't for the Haukelands, I don't know how I would have made it. They've been so good to us. I've known them since I was a child. And recently, when Gunny was ill, Grethe and Arne were so supportive."

"What was wrong with Gunny?" Leigh asked.

"He had hepatitis, and was extremely ill for a while, but Bjørn brought him through it. He's a wonderful doctor." Margit's freckled face glowed.

"I'm sure he is. He seems great with his daughters."

"And you, you must miss your children, being so far away from them at this festive time of the year." Curiosity glimmered in her green eyes.

Uneasy, Leigh looked away from her. "Yes, I do miss them."

"Mummy!" Gunny ran into the room, his chubby arms outstretched toward his mother.

Margit smiled and spoke to him in Norwegian. He crawled onto her lap, cuddling against her breasts. Leigh smiled at him. He gazed back at her with huge blue eyes, his thumb firmly inserted in his mouth. How adorable he was! With those reddish-gold curls and chubby cheeks. As she watched mother and son together, Leigh thought of the tender moments she'd shared with Aaron. But he didn't need her anymore. None of her children did.

Margit gazed at her over Gunny's silky head. "Gunny wants me to take him to see the *jul* tree. Would you like to join us? I'm sure coffee will soon be ready."

Coffee sounded like a godsend. When she stood up, Leigh found her vision wasn't quite as blurred as it had been. The short rest had helped. A few minutes after they arrived in the family room, Grethe, Anne-Lise, and Dordei entered, carrying luscious desserts and coffee.

Although Leigh had thought she was too stuffed to eat another bite, the desserts looked so tempting she immediately relented. Anne-Lise pointed out each confection—a ring-shaped cake made from crushed almonds and egg whites called *kransekake*, and two different kinds of cookies. For the guests who still hadn't had enough holiday spirits, Eggnog Viking was served, heavily laced with brandy. Leigh wisely decided to bypass it, but helped herself to a small portion of each dessert and a cup of strong black coffee.

The children had rejoined the adults in the family room and had filled their plates with sweets. Leigh watched as little Gunny grabbed a cookie from a plate, took one bite of it and handed it to his mother. Immediately he returned to the buffet table and reached for a different kind.

"*Nei*, Gunvor," Margit said sternly.

The little boy scampered away, his eye having been caught by a pull-toy that two-year-old Inger-Lise dragged behind her. Across the room, Erik's eyes met hers and he smiled, lifting his eggnog glass and silently mouthing, "*Skal.*"

Leigh grimaced and lifted her coffee cup in an ironic toast. Just then, Bjørn drifted over to Erik's side to begin an animated conversation. Smiling, Leigh turned away and glanced about the room at Erik's family. They were almost exactly as he'd described them, except he hadn't prepared her for his mother's frostiness. But the visit would soon be over, and she'd have Erik to herself again. That was all she wanted. Just Erik . . . and if possible, her kids.

"*Gunvor, stoppe! Nei!*"

Leigh looked up to see what had prompted Margit's harsh command. Gunny stood on his tiptoes, reaching up with stubby fingers toward a fragile glass dove hanging from a branch of the Christmas tree. With a look of mischievous guilt, he pulled his hand away from the ornament and smiled up at his mother.

"Krumkake!" he said clearly, lifting his cookie toward her, as if it were a peace offering.

Laughing, Margit gathered the little boy into her arms. He allowed her embrace for a brief moment, then struggled out of her arms and trotted away.

Anne-Lise appeared at Leigh's side. "Kayleigh, are you feeling okay? You look a bit pale. Would you like some water?"

"Yes, thank you," Leigh said hoarsely, unable to look away from Gunny and his mother. A trembling had begun in her limbs as she'd watched the scene at the Christmas tree. She could still see the expression on the little boy's face as he'd been reprimanded.

He'd looked exactly like Erik.

16

Leigh wasn't sure how she'd managed to get through the rest of the evening after coming to her startling conclusion. Somehow, she'd been able to carry out her social obligations, but her mind had been in a trancelike fog. She couldn't keep her eyes off the little boy.

Erik's son. It didn't make sense. Of course it didn't. But deep in her heart, she knew it was true. The phone call in October. The one where she listened to Erik's voice on the answering machine. "Something has happened here . . . it's imperative I talk to Kayleigh." Had that been what he was calling about? But no, that didn't make sense either. The boy was three years old. If it was true that Erik was his father, surely he would've known about it all along, right? Which meant . . . all this last year . . . every time he slept with her . . . Oh, dear God. She felt nauseated.

Naturally, Erik realized something was wrong during the cautious drive back to his apartment. Several times, he asked her why she was so quiet. Too much liquor, she told him, aware that her voice carried a revealing edge. But she wouldn't say more. There was no point in getting into it while they were driving on icy streets.

Erik refused to drop it. "It's more than the aquavit, isn't it? What is wrong?"

Her control broke. "Nothing! Just leave me alone!"

His hands tightened on the steering wheel, but he didn't speak again during the drive. Inside his apartment, he went straight to the fireplace as Leigh stood at the window, shivering in the fur coat he'd bought her.

After building a fire, he stood up and turned. Leigh was still at the window, staring out at the snow that had started to fall again. He moved toward her. "Kayleigh, is it *Mor*? Is it because she was so aloof? It takes her a while to get to know someone. You should not take it personally."

Leigh whirled on him. "It's not your mother, Erik! It's Margit!"

If she had not been watching his face so closely, she might have missed the sudden wariness in his eyes, the faint flush that appeared on his cheeks. She felt her heart sink. Here was the final proof. But would he lie to her . . . or admit the truth? She took a deep breath and asked the question. "Gunny is your son, isn't he?"

He didn't answer. Leigh waited, knowing his silence was answer enough.

Finally, he spoke. "Yes."

The word hung in the air, echoing inside her brain, traveling down through her consciousness and finally stabbing deep into her heart like a razor-edged poison dart. How could one little word hurt so much?

Erik moved closer, but made no attempt to touch her. "Kayleigh, will you let me explain?"

Leigh turned away. What possible difference could an explanation make? "Just tell me one thing," she said. "Are you in love with her?"

"No." His answer was swift and firm. "But you must let me tell you what happened. I didn't know myself I was the father until I got back from the States."

She stared at him. "How is that possible? The kid is three years old."

"I will tell you. But first, I'm making you some tea. You're still shivering. Sit down, *kjareste*. It will only take a moment."

Wrong, Erik. Tea is not going to fix this. Was it to always be her fate to be betrayed by the man she loved? But overcome by a sudden lethargy, she allowed Erik to lead her to the bed where he tucked her into the rumpled covers. Without speaking again, he walked into the kitchenette and placed the kettle on the stove. She leaned back against the wall, hugging the fur coat to her. God, she was so cold. Was it only this afternoon she and Erik had made love in this very bed? How different it all seemed now.

As if from a great distance, she heard him clanging away in the kitchen and wearily, she realized the tea was just an excuse. He was in there thinking up a reasonable story to get himself off the hook. And she shouldn't let him get away with it. If she had any brains, she would get out of bed, pack her clothes, and take the first plane home to the States. But she knew she wouldn't do it. She had to listen to what he had to say; even now, he still had a mysterious power over her and she couldn't fight it.

Erik returned to the bed, carrying a tray with two mugs of steaming tea. He placed it on the nearby table, gingerly sat down on the edge of the bed, and handed a mug to her. Silently, she took it, refusing to make it easy for him.

Leaving his tea untouched, he spoke in a low voice, "Margit was married to my best friend, Gunvor. The three of us practically grew up together. I loved her like a sister . . . loved them both. I'll never forget the day I found out about the helicopter crash. It was the seventeenth of May, Constitution Day. I was at university, celebrating with all the other students. Bjørn found me there, told me what had happened to Gunvor.

I was devastated. We'd been best friends for years, going through elementary school and the *gymnas* together. I couldn't believe he was dead." Erik paused, his voice husky. "I didn't know what to do . . . except get sloshed. And that, I did. Then I got it into my head that I had to see Margit. She was the only one who loved him as much as I did . . . who could understand my pain. My roommate tried to discourage me from driving, but he couldn't stop me. I was determined to see her."

He paused again and took a sip of his cooling tea. His eyes wore a haunted expression. Leigh sat motionless, trying to hold onto her anger, yet she felt her heart softening against his naked vulnerability. *No!* She couldn't let him get away with this; she was hurt, too.

He continued, "Margit looked frightful when she answered the door. Her hair was tangled, her eyes red and swollen from crying. But even in her grief, she saw how bad off I was and took me into her flat. She made coffee and we cried in each other's arms. We were both lost without Gunvor." He looked straight into her eyes. "What happened between us that night was a result of our grief. We were reaching out for comfort, but it was an empty gesture. We both realized it was a mistake as soon as it happened. And we agreed to forget about it, to pretend it *didn't* happen."

"But nine months later, there came a little reminder, right?" Leigh couldn't hide the bitterness in her voice.

"No, that's not right," Erik said. "*Ja*, she found she was pregnant, but Gunvor had been home the weekend before he died, and she refused to believe the child wasn't his. She found out the truth while I was in Virginia."

"And how did she do that?"

"Gunny became ill with hepatitis and needed a blood transfusion. Bjørn discovered his blood type was incompatible with Gunvor's, making it impossible for him to be the father. Somehow, Bjørn had found out I'd been over there that night, and he made an educated guess about what had happened. After he confronted Margit with the blood test results, she admitted that I . . . that we had . . . intercourse that night. She begged him not to tell me, but he couldn't make that promise to her.

He believed I had the right to know Gunny was my son."

"And does everyone . . . all your family know about it?" Leigh asked.

"Only my parents and Bjørn."

Leigh drew her hands through her rumpled hair. "God! I feel like such a goddamn fool!" A riptide of fury washed over her. "*Damn* you, Erik! Why didn't you tell me?"

"I didn't know Margit was going to be there tonight. That was my mother. She has been trying to play matchmaker. Kayleigh, you have to believe I didn't want you hurt. I thought we could be together, and you would never have to know about Margit and Gunny."

"And if I decided to stay here? To be with you? Then what? Were you going to hide them from me forever, Erik? How were you going to manage that?"

"I hadn't thought it out. *Kristus,* Kayleigh! Can't you see what you've done to me? I love you so much I'll do anything to keep you." His face was anguished. "I was so afraid of losing you. That's why I couldn't tell you."

"I don't want to hear it!" Leigh shouted. "You're a selfish jerk, Erik, and I hate you!" A strangled sob caught in her throat, and quickly, she scrambled up from the bed.

"Kayleigh, how can you blame me for something that happened years ago, before I even met you?"

She whirled around. "I don't give a *shit* about what you did years ago! It's *now* that concerns me. And you lied to me! Yes, by omission, true, but it's still a lie! You should have told me about Margit and Gunny."

"How?" Erik fired back. "You wouldn't even answer my letters! The first thing I heard from you was that telegram saying you were arriving. What did you expect me to do? Wire back . . . 'Kayleigh, so glad you'll be here . . . guess what . . . I'm a father?' Don't be stupid!"

"But you could have told me after I arrived . . . at least before you took me to your family's home."

"*Ja*, I admit I made a mistake. I can only plead that I wanted to have more time with you before we had to face it." Erik moved off the bed and approached her. "Kayleigh, there's more . . . I want to be straight with you this time. But first, you must believe that I love you." He stopped inches away from her, his blue eyes solemn, his arms at his side, making no attempt to touch her. "I have to marry Margit."

She felt as if he'd plowed his fist through her stomach. Turning away from him, she sat down at the small dining table. "I see." Her voice was oddly unemotional.

"Do you?" Erik whispered, joining her at the table. "Kayleigh, will you at least look at me?"

She lifted her chin and forced herself to meet his eyes.

"To be blunt, I am honor-bound to marry her. I know that must sound old-fashioned to an American, but it's the way I feel. Gunny is my son, and it is my responsibility to give him and his mother a good home. I can do nothing else now that I know the truth."

There was a long silence. Leigh could only stare at him, speechless. A pulse throbbed heavily in her temple, foretelling the onslaught of a migraine. Erik's eyes dropped to the table as his fingers stroked the varnished grain of the wood.

"So far, Margit is refusing to marry me. She thinks of me as a brother."

Leigh's harsh laugh broke the stillness in the room. "Yes, it was real brotherly of you to screw your best friend's widow on the night he died." The barb struck home. She cringed inside at the wounded look in his eyes.

He stood up. "I was a fool to think you'd understand." He strode into the kitchenette and opened a cabinet, from which he pulled out a bottle of wine. "Why don't you get some sleep?" he said over his shoulder. "We have an early start tomorrow."

Leigh stared at his broad back in amazement. "An early start?" she echoed. Realization set in. "Do you actually expect me to travel through Norway with you after tonight?"

Erik had arranged for them to spend Christmas in his family's cabin in southern Norway's Setesdal Valley.

He turned around, a surprised look on his face. "What else are you going to do?"

"I can get a flight home tomorrow."

Erik shrugged. "If that is what you want . . ."

Bitter tears sprang to her eyes. That wasn't what she wanted. She wanted for it to be like it was before . . . just her and Erik, with no Margit and no little blue-eyed boy with bright red-gold curls standing between them. But she wasn't going to tell him that. Why should she let him see how much she was hurting? She looked away from him so he wouldn't see her tears.

"And I really think I should leave here now. Get a hotel room."

Erik shook his head. "It's after one o'clock. You would never be able to find a room. And Kayleigh, I think you'd better forget about a flight home tomorrow. Christmas is only a few days away, and I'm positive they are fully booked."

She knew he was right. So then, what could she do? She felt him approaching and stood up to move away. But she couldn't evade him. His gentle hands dropped onto her shoulders, and he turned her around to face him. His thumbs brushed away the tears sliding down her face. "My Kayleigh," he said. "We'll work this out. Find a way to be together."

Silently, Leigh shook her head. Still, his touch had broken through the rigid wall she'd erected between them. She allowed him to hold her closer until finally, her face rested against his comforting chest. It was simply impossible for her to remain angry with him, especially since she could see how miserable he was, too. But nothing was resolved. A decision had to be made, and she knew there was only one choice.

"Let me make love to you," Erik said, and drew her mouth up to meet his. His kiss was achingly sweet, and once again, Leigh gave herself up to it. She couldn't resist him; she was drawn to him as if he were a magnet and she was just one of a clump of pins that clung tenaciously to it.

One choice. For the sake of her sanity, she had to find the strength to draw away from this powerful magnet.

"Kayleigh, have you ever heard the story, 'East of the Sun, West of the Moon'? It's an old Norse legend."

"No."

Beneath her left ear, she could hear Erik's heart beating, deep and steady now that the lovemaking was over. He held her tightly, one hand stroking her back, almost as if he was afraid to release her.

His room was dark except for the flicker of the fire burning low in the grate. Outside, icy particles of snow chattered against the window. Erik's body was warm wedged against hers, yet she still felt cold. It was a cold that emanated from the inside out. And no amount of sweet lovemaking was going to warm her up.

"I will tell you this legend."

"Erik, I think the time for fairy tales is over."

His arms tightened around her. "I will tell you this legend, Kayleigh. Please."

She released a sigh. "Okay."

"A poor man sold his youngest daughter to a white bear so that he could feed his family. The daughter went to live with the bear in his castle inside of a mountain. On her first night there, after she went to bed, a man came into her dark chamber and slipped into her bed. The young woman never saw his face, but she grew to love him when night after night, he came to her bed and made love to her. After several months, the bear gave her permission to go home to visit her family, but he warned her not to tell her mother about the man who visited her chamber every night. Of course, the girl did just the opposite. She told her mother about the nightly visits, and how she had fallen in love with the man whose face she'd never seen. She wished desperately to see what he looked like, so her mother gave her a piece of tallow and told her to light it after the man had fallen asleep, but to be careful not to drop any on him. So, this is what the girl did. When the man came to her bed the next time, she waited until he fell asleep, and then lit the tallow." He paused.

Despite herself, Leigh was intrigued. "So, what did she see?"

There was a smile in Erik's voice. "A handsome prince. The girl was overjoyed and even more in love than she was before. But then, something terrible happened. A drop of tallow fell upon his nightshirt, and in the blink of an eye, the prince disappeared, and in her bed was the white bear. In a sad voice, the bear told her that he'd been bewitched by his wicked stepmother; by day, he was a bear and by night, a prince. And if only the girl had held out for a year without discovering his secret, he would've been free. Now, he had to return to a place east of the sun and west of the moon to marry an ugly princess chosen by his stepmother."

Leigh frowned. "God, I'm beginning to hate your tragic Norse legends. But I'll bite. What happened?"

"Well, it is a long story, but I will make it short. The girl loved her prince so much that she found her way east of the sun and west of the moon, reaching there on the eve of his wedding. He was overjoyed to see her, telling her that she was the only woman in the world who could set him free. On the morning of his wedding, he told his stepmother that before he wedded the ugly princess, he had to know what she was good for. He brought out his nightshirt with the drop of tallow on it. 'I will take only the woman to wed who can remove this tallow.' Well, the ugly princess scrubbed and scrubbed, but the tallow remained. The prince then called in a beggar lass from outside, who of course, was our heroine. And as soon as she began to wash the shirt, the tallow stain disappeared. So, the prince married the woman he loved and they lived happily ever after."

"Ah, a happy ending," Leigh said after a moment of silence. "Unusual for a Norse legend, wouldn't you say?"

Erik's hand fastened on her chin, and he turned her toward him. She saw his face, solemn, in the muted glow of the fire. "Kayleigh, you are the only woman who can remove the tallow from my shirt."

Her eyes welled with tears, and her voice was tremulous when she spoke, "Even if that *is* true, Erik . . . you're *still* going to marry the ugly princess, aren't you?"

He gazed at her but didn't answer. She pulled away from him and rolled onto her side, staring into the darkness and blinking back tears until sleep finally claimed her.

*   *   *

"I don't understand how you can make love to me like you did last night . . . and still go back to America."

Leigh turned away from the snowpacked beauty of the Aust-Agder countryside and glanced at Erik's grim profile. His hands were clenched tightly on the steering wheel of the Saab they'd rented in Kristiansand that morning.

"Erik, we went through this last night," she said. "Do we really have to keep discussing it?"

"We still have six days before we go back to Oslo," he said softly. "And I am going to do everything I can to make you change your mind."

Leigh sighed and gazed out the window again. Early that morning, they'd left Kristiansand and traveled north into the Setesdal Valley. Their final destination was the tiny hamlet of Ose where the Haukeland family owned a cottage on the By-glandsfjord. If circumstances were different, Leigh would've been filled with anticipation at the thought of several days alone with Erik in an isolated cabin. But she felt only pain. Last night, he'd again tried to convince her to stay. She could still hear the anguish in his voice as he pleaded with her.

"Margit and Gunny are *my* problem." His turbulent blue eyes gazed imploringly into hers. "You won't ever have to see them. They will be one part of my life and you will be the other . . . the good part. *Kjareste*, we can make this work. There is no reason why we should have to give each other up."

Leigh's mouth dropped open. "Oh, my God. I don't believe I'm hearing this. You're saying you're going to marry Margit, yet, you want me to stay here in Norway and be your kept woman. Your mistress. Have I got that right?"

Erik stared at her, amazed. "You are the woman I love! If anything, Margit would be the kept woman, not you."

"Are you *insane*?" Enraged, Leigh shoved him in the chest as he tried to touch her. "Do you realize what I've given up for you? I walked away from my marriage. I left my *kids* behind for you! My whole life has been turned upside down because I fell in love with you. And all you're offering me is the chance to stay here and be your mistress? You need your head examined, Mr. Psychologist!" She whirled away from him, heart thudding with anger.

He crossed the room to her, stopping just inches away. His voice lowered insistently. "Can't you see, Kayleigh? I'm clutching at straws here, trying to find an answer for us. An answer for all of us. Please, I'm just asking you to think about it. You said you wouldn't come to Norway, yet here you are. Once you go home, you won't be able to get me out of your mind, and soon, you'll realize you have to come back."

"It's not going to happen." Leigh shook her head, standing rigid. She wouldn't turn and look at him. "I know you don't believe it, but I'm stronger than that, Erik. I won't share you with another woman. I can't."

"I'll change your mind." He reached out and touched her hair.

She tensed, as always, feeling her limbs melt at his touch. She willed herself to move away from him, fought to hold on to her anger.

His voice lowered, "Please, Kayleigh. Let me hold you. Just for a little while."

She felt herself weakening, and hated herself for it. *Just a few more days,* she told herself. He was her drug. She knew that. But soon enough, she'd have to wean herself from him. But not tonight.

He turned her around, aligning her body against his. "How can you live without this?" he whispered, entwining his hand in her hair, drawing her head backwards so his mouth could sear a possessive brand into the tender slope of her neck, making her ache with the ever-present desire he awakened in her. "And *this?*" His fingers impatiently brushed away the thin satin strap of her camisole as his lips trailed down her neck and onto her shoulder. "Can another man ever make you feel like I do?" he whispered, just before his mouth captured hers in a silken kiss.

Wearily, Leigh dragged her mind back to the present. Their arguments always ended the same way. She, in his arms, thrilling to his touch, with nothing really resolved.

The landscape had changed dramatically from the rolling

hills and valleys of Sørlandet to a rugged snow-covered terrain. Gradually, the valley had narrowed, and now the highway was hemmed in by dark gray cliffs that loomed over them in a menacing beauty. On their left, the Byglandsfjord glimmered in the midday light; it looked deep and icy. Leigh shivered, suddenly uneasy for no apparent reason. Perhaps it was because of the ominous black clouds marching in from the west over the crests of the mountains. Bad weather ahead. She opened her mouth to mention it to Erik when he spoke.

"In the summer, you can catch dwarf salmon in Byglandsfjord. In fact, this area is the only place they can be found. Have you ever fished, Kayleigh?" When she shook her head, he grinned. "I'll teach you next summer."

He glanced at the leather-banded watch on his wrist. "We're making good time. The shops will still be open in Ose."

In the little village near the fjord, they stopped to buy food and supplies for a couple of days.

"We live quite rustically at the cabin," Erik said as he paid for the groceries at the small family-owned store. "There's a small icebox. No electricity. We'll have to come back to Ose for more food in a few days."

Leigh stared at him. "You didn't tell me there was no electricity."

Erik grinned. "You'll love it. The kerosene lamps are very romantic."

"I suppose you also think outhouses are romantic." She tried to summon a spark of gaiety into her voice.

Erik gave a lascivious chuckle. "Why not? An outhouse can offer all kinds of interesting possibilities. After all, look what happened in your outdoor shower!"

"Erik, you're gross! Seriously, is there an outhouse?"

"Seriously, there is." They returned to the car. "But not to worry. We don't use it anymore. The first time *Far* brought my mother here, she was horrified. She refused to come again until he had a well dug and plumbing installed."

"So, why not electricity and a refrigerator?"

"*Far* drew the line at that. He told her if she wanted electricity, she could spend her holidays at the Grand Hotel in

Oslo, but he intended to get back to nature. And that meant no electricity. I must say, I fully agree with him. It wouldn't be nearly so charming if it were all lit up with electric lights. You'll see."

For the last five minutes, the Saab had been climbing a winding, snowpacked road. Huge spruce trees towered over them, blotting out the feeble afternoon light to an almost early evening twilight. They rounded another curve, and there, tucked into a small clearing, was the tiny stone cabin. From the outside, it presented a quaint picture with its brown wood trim and thatched roof, but Leigh had her doubts about the interior. She'd never spent any time in a place without modern conveniences. Yet, she felt oddly excited, as if she were on a new adventure. A year ago, she'd been fantasizing about being with Erik in a remote place such as this. Now, the fantasy had become reality.

Erik parked the Saab around the back of the cabin, where the clearing ended in a steep ravine. Leigh gasped at the sheer beauty of the mountainside. The bluish-green spruce trees, laced with a powdery dusting of snow, carpeted the slope. Nearby, a crystal rush of water tumbled down through the dense underbrush, cutting its way toward the deep pewter of the fjord below. Except for the musical surge of the brook and the lowing wind in the trees, a majestic silence surrounded them.

Leigh gazed around in awe. "What a view!"

"Believe it or not, it's even lovelier in the summer when everything is green and the flowers are blooming. The fjord is deep blue . . . you can't believe how blue. I can't wait to bring you here then . . ." He stopped, an almost unbearable look of pain on his face.

Leigh swallowed hard, trying to dislodge the sudden lump in her throat. So, he really wasn't as confident as he'd pretended. He was beginning to believe she really wasn't going to stay. *But God, the look on his face!* It broke her heart. She turned away. "Shouldn't we get this car unloaded before it gets completely dark?"

It didn't take long before they had everything in the cabin.

Erik went out for one last trip to unstrap the cross-country skis from the top of the car.

"Tomorrow we'll ski over to Reiardsfossen. I've been wanting to show it to you since I told you about the legend last Christmas. Do you remember?" Erik asked, placing the skis in the corner of the room.

"Of course! The one about Ann and Reiard and the ravine." For the first time, Leigh took a good look around the tiny three-room cabin. "Erik, this is really very nice!"

Despite the simplicity, the living room was cozily arranged with sturdy wood furniture, homespun rugs, and a large sofa bed placed in front of the stone fireplace. The other half of the room was devoted to food preparation with an old-fashioned woodstove, a water pump, and a sink. In the tiny bedroom, there was only room for a full-size bed covered with a down comforter and a small wardrobe. The bathroom consisted of a toilet, sink, and a deep claw-footed tub.

"We'll have to heat the water on the stove for bathing," Erik said, following her into the bathroom. "Of course, when we stayed here in the summer, we boys took our baths in the fjord."

"Well, I bet you won't be taking any baths in it in this weather. Listen to that wind blow. It's really picking up." Shivering, Leigh moved back into the living room. "Maybe I should see about fixing some dinner while you get the fire going."

"I'll get the fire started later," Erik said. "First, I'm taking you out to dinner."

"Erik, we're in the middle of nowhere! How can you take me out to dinner?"

"Ose is only a few miles away, and we have a car. I have something special planned for you tonight."

Erik instructed her not to dress up because the inn was a tiny family-owned place, usually frequented by local Norwegians who stopped in for aquavit, good food, and traditional music. With that in mind, Leigh dressed for warmth instead of style, pulling on her new Norwegian sweater and navy wool slacks over thermal underwear. Erik was similarly attired in sturdy warm clothing. He nodded approvingly when he saw her.

"You're learning to dress for the Norwegian winter."

The tiny inn was tucked into a side street of the village where a typical tourist would have easily passed it by, not realizing it served the best Norwegian food in the area. The decor was practically nonexistent, just a few tables scattered throughout the small room with a space cleared at one end for entertainment.

The proprietor led them to a table near the inevitable blazing fireplace. Leigh settled back in her chair to enjoy the warmth while Erik rattled off a stream of Norwegian to the waiter. She noticed that all the other tables were filled with cheerful customers, some of them in traditional Norwegian costumes.

"I ordered *kjottkaker* and *kulruletter-fylt blomkol*, meatballs and stuffed cauliflower," Erik told her. "And for an appetizer, various cheeses and fish balls."

"Not *gammelost*, I hope?" Leigh couldn't understand how anyone could eat the foul-smelling cheese from the West Country, but Erik loved it.

He smiled. "We'll see."

They sat in companionable silence for a few moments, listening to the lively music of Norwegian folk dances playing in the background. Suddenly Erik excused himself and disappeared into the foyer of the inn. He was gone for only a moment.

"A surprise," he said when he returned.

The food arrived, and as Erik had predicted, it was wonderful . . . except for the *gammelost*, which Leigh declined. As they were finishing, a blond man in traditional dress stepped into the room, carrying a strange-looking instrument that resembled an ornate violin with four extra strings.

"That's a Hardanger fiddle," Erik said. "I guess you could call it the Norwegian national instrument."

The tune was a lively one, and the blond man sang along to the accompaniment of clapping hands from the guests. The music of the Hardanger was unlike anything Leigh had ever heard before, similar to bagpipes, yet unmistakably different.

At first, it was rather grating on the ears, but soon Leigh found herself enjoying it, and when the fiddle player finished, the customers applauded loudly and called for more. He launched into another song, this time a plaintive ballad. After the waiter swept away the remains of their meal, Leigh and Erik settled back to enjoy the music. Erik reached for her hand and smiled at her warmly, then looked back at the singer. After another ten minutes, the entertainer took a bow and disappeared as quietly as he'd arrived.

"That was Hans Wenche, the son of the innkeeper. We were lucky to see him tonight. He only performs when he is in the mood." There was a sparkle in Erik's eyes as he looked across the table at her. "I have something for you." He drew out a small white box and placed it in front of her.

Leigh lifted the lid and gazed down at a slender silver ring delicately shaped into the entwined initials of *E* and *K*.

"We're in the land of the silversmiths," Erik said. "I called Herr Wenche when I first got home and described what I wanted. I thought I would have to post it to you. I'm glad I didn't have to. Do you like it?"

Leigh studied the beautiful ring, an invading sense of despair sweeping through her. She sighed. "It's lovely, Erik, but I don't know how I can accept it now."

His eyes darkened. "What do you mean, *now*? You said your feelings for me haven't changed."

"They haven't. But don't you see we're just prolonging the pain?"

A closed expression settled on his face. He reached out to take the box. "I'll return it."

"Erik, no." Leigh's hand covered his. "I'm sorry. I was thinking of myself, how hard it would be to wear it and think of you so far away."

Erik's face softened. "It doesn't have to be like that."

It was Leigh's turn to withdraw. "Yes, it does."

He stared at her a moment longer and then slowly sat back in his chair. Nothing was right after that. The charm had gone out of the evening. It wasn't long before Erik suggested they leave.

An icy wind howled around them as they left the inn, and tiny flakes of snow swirled haphazardly to the ground. Leigh saw a flicker of greenish-orange light in the dark sky. "That's strange! Lightning while it's snowing."

"It's not lightning," Erik said. "That's the aurora borealis—the northern lights. Make a wish. Legend has it that if you wish upon your first sight of the northern lights, it will come true before the year is out."

"Okay. I wish I could be warm again."

They got into the car. Erik sat still for a moment before starting the engine. "Too bad I cannot have your wish. I think you know what I would wish for." He turned on the ignition, and cold air blew out of the vents.

Leigh shivered uncontrollably and thought longingly of the cozy inn they'd just left. "I don't think I'll ever be warm again," she mumbled, her teeth chattering.

He didn't comment, but just turned off the flow of air and put the gearshift in reverse. Leigh felt a tickle rising in her throat and tried to suppress it, but it was no use. The nagging cough she'd been battling for the last two days had returned with a relentless fury and the cold seemed to intensify it. Erik glanced over at her.

"I think I have something for that cough back at the cabin. And I'll heat up some water for a bath just as soon as I get the fire going."

Out of the corner of her eye, she gazed at him. Was he making an attempt to shrug off his moodiness? But he didn't speak again on the short drive back to the cabin. As soon as they arrived, Erik started a fire in the grate and placed a huge pot of water on the woodstove to boil. Leigh huddled near the fireplace, trying to get warm while he prepared a concoction for her cough. Outside the stone walls of the cabin, the wind howled as a mixture of sleet and snow beat against the windows.

"Here, try this." Erik handed her a mug of hot liquid. "It's lemon tea with honey and a dash of aquavit."

She thanked him and tasted the tea. It wasn't bad, in spite of the heavy dose of aquavit. It pleasantly tingled her insides as it went down. By the time she finished it, the water was hot for her bath.

"Won't you join me?" Leigh asked as she headed toward the bathroom.

He looked at her, an implacable expression on his carved Nordic face. "I have to go out and bring in more wood for the fire tonight."

Leigh shrugged and stepped into the bathroom, irritated by his coolness.

In the tub, the caressing warmth of the hot water seeped into her chilled bones; she stretched out and closed her eyes, allowing all conscious thought to flow from her mind. The sound of the wind was muffled inside the tiny bathroom, lending a womblike tranquillity to the atmosphere. But as the water cooled, reality returned, and Leigh sat up to soap her body. As her hand moved over her nipple, she experienced a rush of heat between her thighs. An overwhelming longing for Erik swept through her.

It was almost as if he read her thoughts. Only a few seconds later, he stood at the door of the bathroom, holding another kettle of hot water. His smoldering eyes roved hungrily over her.

"I thought you might be ready for more hot water."

"Yes. It's starting to cool off." Her eyes issued an invitation to him, but he chose to ignore it. She moved toward the head of the tub to allow him to pour in the water. He turned to go.

"Erik?" Her heart pounded, her breathing shallow.

He stopped. *"Ja?"*

"Don't go."

He turned back to face her. She could see him wrestling with his emotions. It was obvious he wanted to stay, but for some reason, he was fighting it. She held out a supplicating arm, whispering, "Please, Erik . . ."

Slowly, he moved toward her, his hand reaching down to curl into the soft tendrils of her damp hair. "I've got to learn to resist you," he said almost angrily, a fire in his eyes.

Leigh smiled with satisfaction and trailed her wet hand up the front of his crotch, lightly caressing the rock-hard bulge evident under the thick denim. She got to her knees in the bathwater and brought her other hand up to unzip his jeans. Abruptly, he pulled away from her, his face stony.

"I must go see about the fire." Before she could speak, he was gone.

Leigh sank back into the water, baffled. Was this a new game of his? Did he think if he withheld sex, she would change her mind and stay with him? Surely he wasn't that immature! With a grunt of exasperation, she pulled the plug from the drain and stood up, reaching out for the towel that hung on a rack nearby. It was time to have it out with him.

The fire glowed brightly in the small living room. She found Erik busily making up the sofa bed.

"Oh, good. We're going to sleep in here near the fire."

He straightened up. "You'll be sleeping in here where it's warmer. I'm taking the bedroom."

Leigh stared at him in amazement. "Are you serious?"

His eyes flicked to her for a second and then back to the comforter he was smoothing. "Quite serious."

That did it. The fragile control on her anger broke. "Well, *shit*, Erik! What is wrong with you all of a sudden?"

Icily, he stared back at her. "Nothing, that I'm aware of. You are the one that seems to have a problem. You've decided you want nothing more to do with me. You're going back to the States in a few days, and we'll never see each other again. So, why should you want to sleep with me?"

"Because I love you. And I want you. Besides, you've known about my decision for the last few days, and that hasn't stopped you from making love to me. Why now?"

He shrugged. "Perhaps I've finally realized you *don't* love me. I don't think you ever did. Maybe I was just a convenient excuse for you to leave your husband."

Leigh stared at him a long moment, not quite believing she'd heard him correctly. He gazed back, a challenging light in his eyes. Her breath exploded from her in an exasperated sigh. "You know something, Erik? You really act your age sometimes."

His face paled, but he didn't speak.

"And how dare you try and turn this around on me?" She bristled anew. "You're the one who is in the wrong here, and you know it. I came here because I love you, and because I thought you loved me. Well, maybe you do, but it's not enough, Erik. Not if you're going to marry Margit. There's no place for me here. By this time next week, I'll be out of your life." She took a deep shuddering breath, trying to calm herself. "We only have a few days left together. It's up to you. Do you want to spend them going around in circles like this? I'm not going to change my mind. So, wouldn't it be better if we just enjoy what little time we have left together?"

He eyed her somberly, his jaw tight. "Don't you see, Kayleigh, every time I make love to you, it breaks my heart. I cannot do it."

He walked out of the room, closing the door firmly between them.

17

The firelight cast an eerie glow on the wood paneled walls of the cabin. In the corner of the room, a grandfather clock ticked monotonously. Leigh lay stiffly in the warm bed and stared up at the ceiling. *Useless to try to sleep*, she thought. It wasn't just the horrendous sound of the wind or even the occasional mournful howl of a faraway wolf that was keeping her awake. In her mind, she kept hearing the tone of Erik's voice. Scathing, bitter. She simply couldn't believe he'd chosen to stay in that cold bedroom, when she was right here, alive and warm and wanting him so much. Didn't he realize they only had a few more nights together? Abruptly, she turned on her side and drew her knees up toward her chest. She had to try to get some sleep. They planned to leave early for the trek to Reiardsfossen.

Outside, there was a sudden hush as the wind took a momentary respite. Suddenly, the quiet was broken by an eerie howl from just outside the cabin. Leigh's heart paused in mid-

beat and then galloped. When her momentary paralysis subsided, she sat up, trembling, and threw off the covers.

"That does it," she muttered. "I'll be damned if I'm going
to sleep alone when there's a hungry wolf on the doorstep."

Her feet whispered across the icy wooden floor. A few seconds later, she stood at the door of Erik's room, experiencing
an odd sense of déjà vu as she remembered that snowy January
morning when she'd also hesitated outside his door. Hard to
believe almost a year had passed since that day. But this time,
she was no married housewife, wrestling with her conscience
and berating herself for lusting after a younger man. This time,
she was downright horny and more than a little resentful of
his sudden attack of conscience. Where was his conscience
when he slept with Margit? How *dare* he refuse to sleep with
her—the woman he professed to love? What kind of affair
was this anyway?

"Damn it, Erik!" She waited until her eyes adjusted to the
total darkness in the room and then moved toward the bed.
"Erik?"

She couldn't believe it. He was actually asleep! *He* obviously wasn't having any trouble with his hormones tonight.
Shivering in her sheer nightgown, Leigh stared at him as he
lay flat on his back, a contented expression on his face.

"You shit," she whispered, then quickly slipped under the
down comforter and snuggled up to his warm body. "Stubborn
Viking . . . you can't ignore me like this."

Her fingers slid through the bristling hairs on his chest and
down his flat stomach to his navel, while her lips nibbled at
the sinewy cords of his throat. He made no response, but when
her roaming hand reached the band of his briefs, she imagined
she heard a slight intake of breath. She lay still against him
and continued her exploration of his body, skipping over his
groin to run her hand lightly over his powerful thigh muscles,
conditioned by years of cross-country skiing. Slowly, almost
imperceptibly, she moved her hand back up until once again,
it was at the band of his underwear. This time, she didn't
hesitate, but slid her hand under it and found, as she'd expected, a healthy erection.

"It isn't polite to call someone a shit," Erik said. In a lightning movement, he turned over, pinning her flat to the bed. "You don't take no for an answer, do you?"

Leigh smiled up at him, just happy to be in his arms again. "You really didn't want me to, did you?"

He pulled away slightly. "Let's get that damn thing off you." He yanked at the nightgown and Leigh heard it rip.

"Erik! I just bought that at Saks!"

"I'll buy you another. *Fordamme!* I love your breasts." His mouth devoured her hardened nipples, even biting one until she yelped.

"Babe, you're hurting me!"

"You make me want to hurt you," he mumbled, but he became gentler, his tongue trailing down her firm torso to her belly. The fires inside her erupted into sweet spasms of pleasure as his expert tongue brought her to a quick climax. As she struggled to bring her erratic breathing under control, Erik slipped out of his briefs.

"I want to be inside you," he said hoarsely.

"No. Not yet." Slowly, Leigh slid down his hard body and cupping him in one hand, she stroked him with the other and took him into her mouth. He groaned, arching his body as her tongue worked magic on him. It didn't take him long to reach the peak. After his shuddering had stopped, he pulled her up to him, entwining his legs around hers, his semihard penis wet against her bare stomach. She snuggled against him, suddenly feeling more fulfilled than she'd ever been in her life. Even the black thought of her departure didn't diminish the glow of the moment. As their heartbeats settled to a normal rate, the frosty temperature of the room chilled their sweat-soaked bodies. Erik pulled the comforter up around them.

"Don't you dare fall asleep now," he said, as Leigh felt her eyelids grow heavy. His hand moved caressingly to her breast. "I'm not done with you yet."

And he wasn't. This time, their lovemaking was slow, poignant, bittersweet. In a way, it reminded Leigh of that night in New York when he'd loved her so desperately, as if he were a doomed soldier leaving for battle the next day. When finally they lay spent in each other's arms, she felt a teardrop roll down her face, yet she couldn't bring herself to speak, to share her pain with him.

It was as she was falling asleep that she heard his voice. But perhaps she was already dreaming because his words didn't make sense.

"Damn you, Kayleigh. You're poisoning me."

A violent coughing spell woke Leigh the next morning. Even through the thickness of the down comforter, she felt the penetrating chill of the room. She burrowed down in the bed, dreading the thought of throwing the comforter off and getting up. But finally, the coughing forced her to sit up and put her feet on the icy floor. Erik appeared in the open doorway, dressed in jeans and a thick turtleneck sweater. He held out her heavy fleece robe and slippers.

"Better get in by the fire. I've prepared some more cough remedy for you."

Growing warm now that she was beside the fireplace, she sipped the hot doctored tea while Erik arranged a platter of sliced meat and cheese for breakfast. Her eyes roved to the beautifully polished rifle hanging above the mantel. "What do you use that for?"

He glanced up from slicing a loaf of dark bread. "The rifle? I don't use it at all. It's *Far's*. Occasionally, we have a problem with fox raiding our garbage." He brought the platter over and placed it on the table.

"Oh, no! He doesn't shoot them?" She reached for a slice of *mykost*, the creamy brown goat's-milk cheese she'd tried with some trepidation at his parent's house. Surprisingly, she'd found it sweet and delicious.

Erik shook his head, biting into a bit of the inevitable *gammelost*. "Fires over their heads to scare them off. There are no hunters in my family."

The scent of Erik's pungent cheese wafted over her, and Leigh clutched her stomach, suddenly nauseated. She stood and hurried to the bathroom. The cold of the room helped to settle her stomach, and after a moment, she felt almost normal except for the warning twinges that signaled the onset of a headache. She swallowed two Tylenol tablets and returned to the living room. Erik watched her as she dropped the pain reliever bottle into the side pocket of her purse.

"Headache?"

"Just beginning. But I think I caught it in time." A paroxysm of coughing shook her.

A worried frown creased Erik's brow. "Maybe we shouldn't try to go to Reiardsfossen today. Your cough is worse."

"I'll be okay. I haven't finished the tea yet." Leigh sat down near the fireplace and picked up her cup. "Besides, you know how much I want to see the waterfall."

"I know. But it's very cold outside. It won't be good for you to be out in it."

Leigh glanced out the window. "It's almost stopped snowing. Come on, Erik, you said it isn't far. We won't have to be outside too long."

Erik shrugged. "Okay. If you are sure . . ."

Leigh realized he hadn't smiled once this morning. It looked like he was in another of his moody spells. What was with him? Did he think he was the only one who was hurting?

It had been a mistake to come to Norway. Yes, it was wonderful to be in his arms again, but was it worth it? The pain of their first separation would be magnified many times over when the final break came, only a few days away. Tomorrow was Christmas Eve. They were leaving for Oslo on the twenty-sixth. She hoped it wouldn't be too difficult to get an earlier flight back to the States. Staying with Erik in Oslo would only prolong the agony.

After helping him clear away the remains of breakfast, she pulled on her clothes before the fire. Stepping outside with Erik, she glanced up at the dark gray sky. Stray snowflakes floated down halfheartedly, but the wind had eased. It didn't feel quite as cold as yesterday, Leigh thought.

Before stepping into his skis, Erik attached a bright red cord around Leigh's waist and another around his own. "In case of avalanche," he explained. "It trails along behind you. Should you get buried, the end of it will probably be above the snow. That way, the rescuers know where to dig."

Leigh stared at him. "Are you serious?"

"Quite." Erik said grimly, clamping the toe of his ski boots into his skis. "Ready?"

She nodded, her mind still on the threat of avalanche. Surely, he wouldn't take her out if there were any real danger. He was just being cautious. Feeling somewhat awkward on her cross-country skis, Leigh followed Erik as he skied through the giant pine and spruce trees in a southeasterly direction. She tugged the wool cap down over her ears and gamely tried to forget about the throbbing of her head. It was only the third time she'd been on cross-country skis, and it took all of her concentration to follow Erik's lead. Just as she thought they'd never find their way out of the silent forest, Erik slid to a stop in front of her.

He turned with a smile and said, "Listen . . ."

Then she heard it, too. The deep roar of water cascading down a rocky gorge.

"It's not far now. Come on."

Five minutes later, as the music of Reiardsfossen grew deafening, they broke out of the forest into a clearing, and there in front of them, Reiardsfossen fell straight down in an icy plunge from the top of the mountain to the river below. On the other side of the waterfall and directly below, nestled the village of Ose. It looked very close, but Erik told her it was still several miles away by skis.

"My brothers and I like to ski down to the village for sport on winter vacations."

"Why don't you go by the road past the cabin?" asked Leigh.

"The grade is too steep. This is the only way down to Ose by cross-country skis."

"But how did you cross the river?"

"That's part of the adventure. About a mile from the village, there's a narrow ford. It's not too dangerous, except in spring, of course."

A sudden rustling came from the woods behind them.

"Kayleigh," Erik whispered. "Quietly . . . look behind you."

Leigh turned and gasped. A beautiful red fox stood frozen in startled caution, eyeing them from the thickness of the trees. Involuntarily, she took a step closer to Erik. At her movement, the fox bounded off into the forest. Erik laughed and reached for her hand.

"Well, what do you think of Reiardsfossen?"

Leigh's eyes returned to the thrilling waterfall. "So, this is where old Reiard fell to his death," she joked.

"And where Ann followed him to hers." A shadow passed over his face. He dropped her hand. "Perhaps she had the right idea."

"To kill herself?" Leigh said. "It's romantic, but stupid."

"Maybe so. But if you don't have anything to live for, why not? When she saw Reiard die, she knew she couldn't go on."

Leigh flashed a quick look at him. He sounded so grim. "Erik, you're just being melodramatic, aren't you? You're not . . . I mean, you wouldn't . . ."

"Kill myself?" Erik permitted himself a cynical grin. "No, I wouldn't kill myself. Actually, I was thinking about pushing *you* off. It might be easier to think of you dead rather than living in America with some other man."

"That's not funny." Leigh glared at him. "You really have a sick sense of humor sometimes." She would've gone on, but a fit of coughing interrupted her admonishment. When it passed, it left her head feeling as if it were being pierced by nine-inch nails.

"Come on, let's go back." Erik pushed off on his skis.

"Are you sure you know the way back?" Leigh called, following him. Snow fell from the sky, more steadily now, and the visibility was diminishing. "It's so confusing."

"It would be easy for a stranger to get lost in this area," Erik called back to her. "But I've been coming here for years. I'll get us back to the cabin."

The snow blew directly in their faces, making it almost impossible to see. Even so, Leigh had complete trust in Erik's ability to guide them back to the cabin. He was a seasoned outdoorsman, accustomed to hiking and camping. She just wished they'd get there soon. Her head throbbed. Again, a wave of nausea assaulted her. She coughed, and for a moment, her lungs felt like they were on fire. A vision of the warm bed near the fireplace played in her mind, and for once, it wasn't because Erik would be in it with her. She just wanted to sleep, to rest.

The icy wind whipped up again, hurling snowflakes into her eyes, stinging her exposed cheeks and chin. Would they never get back? She lowered her head against the onslaught of snow and watched her skis as they slid forward, one after the other, on and on, monotonously. Why did she seem to be moving at such a ridiculously slow speed? She glanced up to see Erik far ahead of her, and strived to find her voice to call him to wait up. But she couldn't summon the strength to make a sound. When she looked back down at the ground, she was amazed to find her skis had stopped moving. Try as she might, she couldn't slide forward another inch. Another deep cough rumbled from her sore chest, and her body shuddered. Swirls of gray mist formed in front of her weary eyes, shutting out the reality of the stinging snow.

"Erik . . . ," she whispered, and crumbled to the white carpeted ground.

An enveloping warmth encircled her body. She stretched out her legs and wiggled her toes. Her mouth parted in a soft moan. She sensed movement at her side.

"Kayleigh?" Erik gazed at her, his eyes worried. "How do you feel, *kjareste*?"

Bewildered, she focused upon him. "I thought you left me in the woods," she whispered. Her throat was so dry. "Where are we?"

"In the cabin," he replied, clutching her hand. "I thought you were right behind me. When I called to you and there was no answer, I went back and found you passed out in the snow. What happened?"

Leigh shook her head. "I don't know. I was so tired . . . couldn't go on. I'm thirsty. Can you get me some water?"

Gingerly, she sat up. A pulsating pain stabbed through her head. "Oh, shit!"

Erik returned with the water. "Your head?"

"It hurts like hell," she said after greedily swallowing the water. "And I think my throat is getting sore, too."

"It's a good thing we got back when we did," Erik said. "Take a look outside."

"Oh, my God!" Her eyes widened at the sight of the window nearly obscured by thick wet snow. The small cabin was trembling from the force of the wind.

"I'm going to have to get down to the village sometime this afternoon," Erik said. "We'll need more food, just in case the storm keeps us holed up here for a while."

"In this weather?" Leigh exclaimed. "Erik, that's crazy!"

He shrugged. "Perhaps it will let up soon. Where's your Tylenol?"

"I think I put it in the side pocket of my purse this morning. Just how serious is the food situation?"

"Not bad yet. But we only bought enough to get us through today." He rummaged in her purse for the pain reliever. "We have a few cans of soup left and a little cheese. The bread is gone, but I think *Mor* has some basic staples in the cupboard. I remember seeing a tin of popcorn and plenty of coffee and tea. What's this?" He held out a small white card. "Who is Knut Aabel?"

"Oh! Just this man I met on the flight in. He was going home to Tromsø to spend Christmas with his daughter."

"I see." Erik's face was inscrutable. "And he works for the Norwegian Embassy in Washington?"

"Yeah."

"And why did he give you his card?"

"Well, I don't know. We got to talking, and he said maybe we could get together if I ever went back down to Washington." Although his face was expressionless, Leigh sensed he was livid. "Please, Erik, the Tylenol." With her fingertips, she massaged her aching temples.

Silently, he flicked two of the pills onto his palm and

dropped them into her hand. She swallowed them with the rest of the water.

"Why did you take his card? At the time, you didn't know if you *would* be returning to the States. Or perhaps you never planned to stay here with me. . . ."

"Get real, Erik!" Leigh cried out. "I bought a round-trip ticket. Even if I *had* decided to stay here with you, I would've had to go back to tie up the loose ends back home. I never once led you to believe this was a done deal. So *what* if I took this man's card? I did it to be polite. Get *over* it! It's history!"

Erik stared at her broodingly. Suddenly he tore the card into tiny pieces and dropped the fragments to the floor. "*Ja*. It is history."

"Why did you do that?" Leigh asked quietly.

"You won't be needing it, will you? After all, it would be really stupid for you to see another Norwegian. He will only remind you of me."

"Oh, don't be so conceited! It's not up to you to decide who I'll see. You had no right to tear that card up."

"But it's done," he said matter-of-factly. "I can't bear the thought of you with someone else, *especially* a fellow countryman."

"Tearing up a card isn't going to stop me from dating other men, Erik. I'm sure it would be easy enough to look him up through the Norwegian Embassy. And I just might do that. Once I leave here, I'll be starting a new life." She closed her eyes, rubbing her forehead with her fingertips. "You surely don't expect me to sit around in a lonely apartment and pine over you for the rest of my life. I'm hurting as badly as you are, but there's a difference between us. I'm facing reality, and you're not." She opened her eyes and gazed at him. Her vision was blurred from the pain. "Erik, don't you realize, we never had a chance for a life together. I always knew that, but I listened to my heart instead of my head."

"You listened to your heart?" Erik said. "Or was it your pussy that was talking to you?"

Leigh slid down into the bed and rolled away from him. "Go to hell," she said wearily, closing her eyes.

A few minutes later, the door slammed, and she knew she was alone in the cabin. She must have slept a long time, for when she awakened, it had grown dark. Although she saw that the fire burned briskly in the grate, her teeth chattered, and her entire body trembled with cold. Stark terror washed over her. Had Erik left her here alone? It was too quiet; only the sound of the moaning wind broke the stillness.

"Erik?" she called out. But the wind was the only answer, howling mournfully through the firs. She sat up, her eyes searching the room for his familiar presence. Another cough rumbled up from her lungs, sending knifelike stabs of pain through her chest wall.

The front door opened, and an icy draft of wind and snow blew into the room as Erik entered, carrying an armful of wood. His down parka and bright red plaid hat were caked with snow.

Tears of relief sprang to her eyes at the sight of him. "Oh, Erik, I thought you left me."

He stomped the snow from his boots and took off his coat. "I tried to take the car down to the village, but it won't start. Too cold, I guess." He flung his hat onto the table and ran his fingers through his tousled hair. "Tomorrow, I'll try to ski down." He approached the bed, his eyes solemn. "*Kjareste*, I'm sorry about what I said earlier. It was unbelievably crude." He sat down on the edge of the bed. "I've been thinking about what you said. And you're right, of course. I haven't been taking this whole thing very well. I'm not used to losing, and I haven't been a good sport about it."

A tear rolled down Leigh's face. "It hurts me, too. I don't want to leave you, Erik. But I don't have any choice. Can't you understand that?"

"I'm trying . . ." His hand reached out to brush away her tears. "*Fordamme!* You're on fire!" He felt her forehead. "I had no idea you were so ill. I'll get you some water."

"No, Erik. Don't leave. I'm so cold." She reached out to him. "Just hold me."

Quickly, he slipped out of his clothes and crawled into bed.

With a soft shuddering sigh, Leigh nestled against him, drawing the heat from his skin like a thirsty animal lapping fresh spring water. Moments later, safe in his loving arms, she sank into a deep dreamless sleep.

18

Through a layer of white cottony fog, Leigh heard Erik's voice. She struggled to open her eyes and focus on him. Gradually, the mist cleared, and she saw him staring down at her, his blue eyes concerned and his hands clutching hers tightly. She wanted to reassure him that she was okay, but couldn't summon the energy to speak.

"I'm leaving for the village now, Kayleigh. Do you understand?"

His voice came through clearly. She felt a sudden panic, but still couldn't find her voice to beg him to stay. His hand tightened upon hers for a moment, and his face drew away. A moment later, the fog closed around her again, drawing her back into the mists of unconsciousness.

They were out in the woods. Leigh wore only her light satin nightgown from Saks. She shivered in the frigid air. The icy wind whipped around them as the snow fell in flakes the size of quarters, landing with noisy, wet plops on the covered ground.

"Erik, I'm so cold!" Leigh reached out to him. "Please, can't you give me something to wear?"

He stood before her, dressed in bulky ski wear, mirrored goggles covering his eyes. He smiled, his teeth white and straight against the golden tan of his face.

"Of course." He tossed her the blue fox jacket he'd bought in Oslo.

She slipped into it, but it did nothing to protect her from the cold.

"Now, I must go." Erik turned on his skis and moved away.

"There's no use in trying to follow me. You could never keep up without skis. And if you don't know this forest, you could walk in circles for months before finding your way out." Then he laughed. "But no need to worry. The wolves will find you long before that."

"Erik!" she screamed at his retreating back. *"Don't leave me here!"*

But he kept going. Leigh sank to the snow-covered ground in tears. Just when she'd given up hope, Erik turned and skied back to her. He pulled her to her feet, his face expressionless.

"I knew you couldn't leave me here," she sobbed.

"You were right," he said quietly. "I couldn't do that to you. Come."

"Are we going back to the cabin?"

"Not yet." He smiled. "I want you to see something very beautiful."

They stood on the cliff overlooking Reiardsfossen. The view was as magnificent as before, but Leigh didn't want to be there. She was cold. She wanted to return to the cabin.

"Let's go back, Erik," she pleaded. "I'm freezing."

"Give me your ring." He held out his hand as he gazed out over the waterfall. "The one I gave you in Ose the other night."

She twisted it off and dropped it into his outstretched palm.

"You see, the other way was too slow." He hurled the ring into the abyss. "Please try to understand—I can't let you go." He grabbed her shoulders and his mouth clamped down on hers, his tongue searching.

As always, she responded to his electric kiss, her mouth becoming soft and pliant under his. But then, she realized something was wrong. The pressure of his body was forcing her backward. Her footing became unstable. Erik ripped himself away from her and pushed her hard.

The blood drained from her face as she felt the ground crumble beneath her feet. Desperately, she lunged at him, but it was too late. Her clawing hands grasped at the brittle rock at the cliff edge, and for a moment, she hung there suspended in a void between life and death, her frantic eyes staring in shock at Erik's impassive face. Suddenly the rock gave way beneath her desperate fingers.

"Ehhrrriiikkk!" she screamed, hurtling toward the violent cauldron of water below.

"Erik!" Leigh bolted up and found herself in the sofa bed at the cottage.

Tears streamed down her flushed face as her eyes darted wildly around the empty room. She couldn't stop shivering. When she saw the dark fireplace, she realized why. Where was Erik? Then she remembered the nightmare. It had been so real, so frightening. Where had he gone, and why was the fire out?

Her arm felt as if it were weighted with iron bracelets as she threw back the covers. She managed to drag herself up, and for a moment, she sat on the edge of the bed, summoning the strength to stand. There was something different in the room. Her eyes fastened on the snow-caked window, where a feeble sun cast a soft glow through the gloom. The blizzard had finally blown itself out. Her brow furrowed as she tried to remember what Erik had said before he'd left. It was so vague in her mind. Something about going for help?

Trembling, she stood and moved like an old woman toward the fireplace. She breathed a sigh of relief when she saw a few burning embers in the bottom of the grate. After she prodded the fire back to life and added more wood, it began to burn brightly. As she turned to go back to bed, a wave of dizziness washed over her. She stood still for a moment to let it pass. When her vision cleared, she saw the white scraps of paper on the floor.

Knut Aabel's business card. The one Erik had ripped in a fit of anger. Leigh climbed into bed, still shivering. She remembered the ruthless expression on his face as he'd destroyed the card. Rarely had she seen that side of him . . . except lately in the ominous nightmares she'd been having. The one at Reiardsfossen had been especially vivid.

How long had he been gone? She was sure he'd gone to Ose for help. When had he told her that? Hours ago, it seemed.

Or had that been a dream? She was so confused. The coughing began again. With every heave of her diaphragm, the pain in her chest worsened, stabbing through her lungs and bringing tears to her eyes.

Oh, Erik, where are you?

On the table nearby, she saw the half-empty cup of doctored tea she'd been drinking earlier. Between racking coughs, she gulped it down, hoping it would work fast. The pain was becoming unbearable.

Twenty minutes later, the cough still hadn't eased. In a near panic, she sat up, wondering what she could do. If she could make it to the kitchen nook, she could drink some water; maybe it would ease the burning sensation in her throat and lungs. Again, she managed to get out of bed. Moving as if walking in thigh-deep water, Leigh finally reached the kitchen area and threw her weight against the counter near the stove. A loud crash jerked her to awareness. She'd knocked over a bottle of aquavit.

Aquavit. She stared at the bottle. The booze would probably work better than water. After all, Erik had admitted his mother's medicinal tea was half-aquavit. Without hesitation, she unscrewed the cap and brought the bottle to her lips. The liquid fire burned down her scratchy throat and hit her empty stomach like an explosion. She gasped, struggling to catch her breath and then leaned weakly against the counter. She'd forgotten what a kick the Norwegian liquor had. But already, she felt a calmness stealing into her chest, suppressing the vicious cough. With the aquavit bottle in hand, she stumbled back to the bed and fell into it gratefully.

Maybe if she could fall asleep again, Erik would be here when she woke up. And hopefully, he'd have a doctor with him. She took another swig of aquavit. It went down easier than before. Leigh collapsed flat onto the bed, staring up at the ceiling. It was unnervingly quiet. No wind, no noise anywhere. Only the monotonous ticking of the grandfather clock in the corner. How much time had passed since Erik left her?

Apprehension swept over her as she realized just how alone she was. What if something had happened to Erik as he made his way down the mountain? Suppose he'd had a skiing accident? Did anyone know she was here alone in the cabin? Would the innkeeper remember she'd been with Erik that night in Ose? Had he even noticed her? But deep inside, Leigh knew the truth.

Only Erik knew she was here.

It was an exhausting effort just to get dressed, but finally she tugged on her boots and stood shakily. Shivering in spite of the thermal underwear, a bulky sweater, and her parka, she glanced around the room, wondering if she should take anything, but her mind refused to cooperate. All she could think about was getting out of this isolated cabin . . . finding Erik, or someone.

Pausing at the door of the cabin, she took a long tremulous breath before struggling to get the heavy skis through the doorway. Just as she was about to close the door behind her, a mournful howl echoed from the forest. Leigh froze. She'd forgotten about the wolves. Indecision plagued her. Would it be safer to go or stay? Then she remembered the rifle hanging on the wall in the cabin. A vague memory of her father teaching her to shoot fluttered through her mind. Could she do it now if she had to?

The rifle was already loaded, and although it was a heavy burden, Leigh decided to take it. The thought of those slinking carnivores filled her with terror. At least with the rifle, she felt somewhat protected.

Outside, the cold air wrapped around her body like an icy glove as she stepped into the skis. A phlegmy cough rumbled up from her chest, and she spat a glob of yellowish-green sputum into the snow. Her head still throbbed, but fortunately, it didn't seem as intense as before.

"I just might make it," Leigh muttered as she turned in the direction Erik had taken two days before. If she could get to Reiardsfossen, she was sure she could find her way into the valley below. She worried about crossing the river, but she'd deal with that when she got to it. Maybe she'd be lucky, and it would be frozen. Right now, her biggest concern would be finding her way to Reiardsfossen. In the deep forest, it would be easy to become confused and lose all sense of direction. Hadn't Erik said the other day that even experts get lost sometimes in Norway's great forests?

Damn Erik, anyway! He was probably relaxing in front of a fire right now, sipping a cup of hot coffee. Or maybe he was on a rail express speeding back to Oslo to be with Gunny and Margit.

Only a few minutes had passed, and already, she could feel her strength ebbing. Pausing, she leaned on her ski poles, trying to calm her racing heart. The trees appeared thicker than she remembered, thrusting their great trunks up toward the afternoon sky, their branches laden with meringued dollops of snow. It was strangely silent now that the wind had died. With the back of her gloved hand, Leigh wiped the beaded drops of perspiration from her brow and looked up at the path in front of her. Her torturous gulps for air were magnified in the stillness. She wasn't sure she'd be able to go on. But what choice did she have? If she stayed, she'd freeze to death.

Far away, a wolf howled in the stillness. Another incentive to keep going. She summoned the strength to move her legs and once again, she was sliding down the path that, she hoped, led to Reiardsfossen.

The only sound she could hear was the whistling of her lungs as she gasped painfully for air. Eyes fastened upon the tips of her skis, she slid along the trail. Somehow, her feet were moving—one ski before the other in never-ending repetition. Faintness swept over her, and she squeezed her eyes shut, gritting her teeth to force herself not to give into it. *I have to keep going. If I stop now, I'll die.* She tried using psychology, imagining she was a long-distance cross-country skier vying for the gold medal in the Winter Olympics. But it didn't work. Her ears roared, and dark spots appeared before her eyes. *I'm going to pass out.* Yet, like a mindless automaton, she forced herself to keep going. The trail descended, and her speed picked up. She saw the slight bump ahead, but it was too late to do anything about it. With a thud, her right ski hit it, and she was out of control. In a blur of snow and black trees, she rolled across the snow-covered ground and came to a stop facedown. She lay still, pressing her face against the snow. It felt so cool against her flushed skin. A comforting pillow of softness. Why was she in such a hurry anyway? She was too tired to be skiing. A little rest. That's what she needed. Just a few moments to sleep . . .

Her eyes closed. The roar in her ears had diminished to a peaceful murmur. It was a lovely sound. Reminded her of something . . . a place of sanctuary . . . but what? . . . where? . . . something to do with home . . . Virginia . . . yes . . . the back-yard . . . the brook and the waterfall. Slowly, her eyes opened. The roar was louder now.

A waterfall. Of course! Reiardsfossen! If it was the water-fall, that meant the village wasn't too far away!

With all her strength, Leigh pushed against the ground and finally brought herself to a sitting position. She brushed the snow from her face and looked around for her skis. They were several feet away. It seemed to take forever to crawl toward them. Then another agonizing moment passed as she stumbled to her feet. Forcing herself to concentrate, Leigh snapped one boot into her bindings, then the other one. She pushed off. The trees thinned out, and soon, the roar of the waterfall grew deafening.

The clearing was ahead. She slid into the sunshine and blinked. The village of Ose lay below like a scene from a Christmas storybook. If it weren't for the thin streams of smoke coming from the chimneys, Leigh could almost imagine Ose was a gingerbread village dolloped with white royal frost-ing, just like the ones she'd often prepared for the holidays. Surrounding her, the mountains rose majestically, blanketed with the heavy snowfall of the last two days. To the east, a wide snowfield sloped gently down toward the village. It didn't look too difficult, especially if she took it slowly. She took a deep breath and eased her way across the snowfield. The weight of the rifle bit into her shoulder, and she thought briefly of leaving it. But then she remembered the howl of the wolf.

Her mind was still on the wolves when she saw a movement out of the corner of her eye. Her heart lurched. A few feet away stood a man dressed in a bright colorful costume. It was the man from Ose who played the Hardanger fiddle. He smiled and waved.

"Oh, thank God!" Leigh moved toward him. "Please, you have to help me!"

He nodded, pulled his fiddle from his coat and began to play. Confused, Leigh stopped. What was wrong with him? She needed help and he was playing his damn fiddle!

"Do you speak English?" she shouted.

His head bobbed as he played a lively tune on the Hardanger. He smiled at her. Then he turned to go.

"Hey!" Leigh cried out. "Don't go!" He disappeared. Right in front of her. He simply wasn't there. She rubbed her gloved hand across her eyes. He was gone—or had never been there at all. A sob escaped her throat. Maybe none of this was real. Maybe she was still back at the cabin, dreaming. Waiting to die.

She turned back toward the village. It was still there, bright and sparkling in the afternoon sun. She knew she had to keep going. Dream or no dream, there was nothing else to do. Her chest burned with the effort of skiing through the heavy snow. Suddenly she remembered Erik saying that the village looked much closer than it actually was. But he was wrong! Had to be. It couldn't be that far. The onset of another coughing attack forced her to stop again. It quieted after a few moments, but it had exhausted her so much she almost gave in to the irresistible urge to drop to the snow-covered ground and close her eyes for a few minutes. Somewhere in the back of her fever-fogged brain, she realized the danger in that compulsion. She'd almost given in to it once before. This time, she wouldn't. She fixed her eyes ahead to the open snowfield.

That was when she saw it. Something dark sticking up out of the snow in the middle of a patch of white. She blinked groggily, thinking it was another hallucination like the Hardanger man. But something inside her, some sixth sense, told her this was real, and whatever it was signaled urgency.

Like a parting curtain of fog, her mind became clear and lucid. It spurred her forward. Long before she was close, she'd registered the object as a ski, and as she drew nearer, she knew in her heart it belonged to Erik. Another fact was clear. The snow was different—no longer a smooth landscape of unmarked nature, but showing signs of recent turmoil, as if a celestial truck had dumped several tons of hard-packed snow in the spot. Leigh stared around her, a tight knot of fear in the pit of her stomach. Her eyes fastened on the odd appearance of the slope to the north. It was as if a huge gash had been cut into it, leaving a cracked wall of snow hanging perilously to the mountainside.

Avalanche. The thought sent terror shooting through her heart. Her frantic eyes returned to the ski lying half-exposed above the snow. Erik's? Stifling a sob, Leigh dropped the rifle and hit the release of her binding. Stepping out of her skis, her feet sank into the deep snow. She dropped to her knees near the half-buried ski and began digging. It surfaced easily, but there was nothing more.

"Oh, God." Leigh sank back on her heels, tears streaming down her face. Then she saw a few inches of a bright red cord. She remembered the avalanche cord Erik had attached to her when they'd skied to Reiardsfossen. With a grateful sob, she stumbled over to where part of it was exposed and frantically, wildly, began to dig. Her breath steamed out in frosty clouds as she clawed at the snow, panic urging her on. From somewhere, the strength of determination flowed through her, and she knew she would never give up. Not until she found him. There was no doubt in her mind it was Erik. She refused to entertain the possibility that he might be dead.

Even with her thick gloves, her hands were numb when she finally reached his body. With all her remaining strength, she dug away the snow above his waistline. Gasping with exertion and fear, she could only cry out his name as she brushed away the last of the snow from his waxy, bloodless face. She fumbled to feel for a pulse at his throat. It was faint, but his heart was beating. Quickly, she adjusted his head, pinched his nose and began to give him mouth-to-mouth resuscitation.

For an eternity, there was no response. Nothing. But she refused to give up. And while she paused to grab another breath, she felt him move. Then he coughed. Leigh clutched at him. "Erik. Oh, thank God."

His eyes fluttered. He stared at her, dazed. "Kayleigh," he murmured. "I've brought the doctor."

"You were caught by an avalanche. I saw your ski."

Slowly, comprehension dawned in his eyes. He tried to move. "Where's the doctor?"

"Was he with you?"

Erik nodded, grimacing. "We were on our way back to the cabin when . . ." He groaned softly and his face twisted in pain.

"Where do you hurt?"

"My leg . . . I think it's broken."

"You're still half-buried. . . ." She began to scoop the snow away from the lower half of his body.

Erik shook his head weakly. "Not now. Find the doctor . . . he's somewhere near."

"Was he wearing an avalanche cord?"

"*Ja*. On the way down, I saw . . . that the conditions were very bad."

"Yet, you went for help anyway," Leigh said, overcome with shame. How could she have believed he'd deserted her? She moved away from him and started to get to her feet, but froze when she heard a growl behind her. Her heart jumped into her throat as she turned and stared into the great yellow eyes of a large gray wolf twenty yards away. The animal stared at her warily, his mouth opened in a menacing grin.

"What is it?" Erik asked.

"A wolf," she said softly. *Where had she dropped the rifle?* Frantically, she looked around and saw it only a few feet away.

"Don't make any sudden moves," Erik warned. "He's just curious."

She edged closer to the rifle. Curious or not, she would feel better with that gun in hand. The wolf didn't move, but continued to watch her. Her hand closed on the rifle butt. She dragged it to her and hoisted it into firing position, planning to fire above his head to scare him off. A sudden movement from Erik arrested her.

"No!" With superhuman effort, he wrenched his upper torso toward her and with one large hand, knocked her to the ground. He fell back, writhing in agony.

The rifle dropped out of her hands and skidded over the snow as she fell sideways onto an elbow. As she lay there gasping for breath and wondering why Erik had knocked her down, she became aware of the growl of a snowmobile growing closer from the direction of the valley.

The crushing pain in her chest intensified. She closed her eyes in agony. *Please God, I don't mind dying—just make the pain go away.* As if from a great distance, she heard voices speaking in Norwegian. She struggled to open her eyes, and in the disappearing afternoon light, she saw shadowy forms surrounding them. Good. Help was here, and now she could just relax . . . and sleep. Funny, she no longer felt the cold.

19

Vivid scenes played behind Leigh's closed eyelids, scenes of blinding white snow, swirling avalanches, and hungry wolves. Erik, his face ravaged by pain, called out in a panicked voice. Suddenly she found herself rolling in the wet snow, tumbling haphazardly down the mountainside, clutching futilely at sparse bushes that evaporated on contact.

Her eyes flashed open. She found herself staring at an anonymous white ceiling. A peaceful silence filled the room. She was safe and, most important of all, warm again. Her eyes moved upward to a plastic bag hanging on an IV pole, following the clear tubing down to where it was attached to a heavily taped needle inserted into the back of her left hand.

Was she still in Ose? And where was Erik? She didn't remember anything after the rescuers had arrived. Erik had just knocked her to the ground to stop her from shooting at the wolf. At the time, she'd been shocked. Only now did she understand why he'd done it. A shot from the rifle would have brought another avalanche hurtling down. How stupid of her not to have realized that. Yet, she'd been panicked and fever-ish. Thank God Erik had stopped her, or they might both be dead.

It was incredible enough that he'd survived the avalanche. She'd read somewhere that if an avalanche victim was knocked unconscious and buried, the odds for survival were increased because less oxygen was used up. That must have been what happened in Erik's case.

"Oh, God, thank you for letting me find that ski," she whis-pered. Where was he? She needed to see him, to assure herself that he was, indeed, alive. She felt a call button at her side and pressed it.

After an anxious moment had passed, a uniformed nurse appeared at the door. *"Ja?"*

Oh, Jesus, please let her speak English. "The man that was brought in with me? Erik Haukeland. I must see him. Please, is he all right?"

The woman stared at her impassively. "Very soon," she said firmly. "The doctor will see you very soon."

"No, I don't care about a doctor. I want to see Erik Hau-keland."

Her expression remained unchanged. *"Ja.* Soon," she re-peated. The nurse turned and left the room, leaving Leigh beat-ing her fists against the bed in frustration.

"Mrs. Fallon? I'm Dr. Svendsgaard. You're here at the com-munity hospital in Byglandsfjord."

He was a middle-aged man with slightly graying hair, a neatly trimmed goatee, and twinkling blue eyes. "You've had quite a rough time of it in the last few days, haven't you?"

"Not exactly jolly," Leigh agreed.

"You've probably guessed you're suffering from a mild case of pneumonia."

"Mild? I'd sure hate to know what a severe case would feel like."

Dr. Svendsgaard smiled. "My dear woman, you would

never have made it down that mountain if it had been worse than mild. We've started you on antibiotics, and I can guarantee you'll be feeling fine in a week or so. That is, if you will agree to no more cross-country skiing through avalanche country. What on earth were you doing out on the mountainside when you were so ill?"

"I'm not sure myself," Leigh said. "I guess I was delirious from the fever. Doctor, when can I see Erik Haukeland?"

"Soon, my dear. Young Haukeland is a very lucky man. Just a concussion and a fractured tibia. Indeed, he will be fine in a few months. Thanks to you, I might add. You saved his life. He wouldn't have lasted much longer without air." He shook his head. "These tourists. They do not know what they're doing. An inexperienced hunter from London fired a shot, which set off the avalanche. Can you imagine the stupidity of such a person?"

Leigh felt her face grow hot. She'd come close to doing the same thing.

"Oh, but listen to me going on! You want to see your young man." Dr. Svendsgaard beamed. "Just let me find a nurse who can wheel you down to his room. You're still too weak to be walking around. You were very badly dehydrated when you were brought in, you know. Pneumonia's high fever will do that to you." He turned to go. "I'll send a nurse or an orderly down right away."

Twenty minutes passed before a student nurse appeared in the doorway. She smiled brightly and spoke in perfect English. "Mrs. Fallon? Dr. Svendsgaard said you wish to visit Mr. Haukeland? He has a visitor right now, but as soon as she leaves, I'll take you down to see him."

"She?" Leigh asked, startled. *Who is it? Margit? His mother?* But how could she find out without appearing nosy? "Oh, it must be his mother."

The girl shook her head, smiling. "Oh, no! Not unless she's a twenty-year-old redhead!"

So, it *was* Margit.

"I'll come down for you as soon as she leaves."

"Never mind," Leigh said slowly. "I'm beginning to feel tired. I think I'll sleep for a while."

After the nurse left the room, Leigh stared at the drip of the IV bottle, imagining Erik and Margit together, planning their future. It was better to leave things as they were. If he wanted to see her again, he'd come to her.

"Yes, Mrs. Fallon? Is there something I can do for you?" It was the perky student nurse who answered her call.

"I was just wondering . . . has Mr. Haukeland's visitor left yet?" It had been several hours since Leigh had first heard Margit was visiting Erik. Finally, she decided she couldn't wait any longer for him to come to her. She had to see him. Somehow, she had to touch him once more, assure him of her love, and say good-bye. There was so much guilt in her for thinking he'd deserted her—left her in the cabin to die. Of course, she'd been half out of her mind with fever, but still, she couldn't help feeling the twinge of conscience when she thought of Erik struggling up that slope with the doctor. He'd risked his life for her. She just wanted to see him one last time before she left for home.

"Oh, yes. They left about thirty minutes ago," the nurse said. "Mr. Haukeland is being transferred to a hospital in Oslo."

"He's gone?" Leigh asked, stunned. *Without saying good-bye? No! It isn't possible! Erik would never do that.* A message. He must have left a note for her. "Did he leave a message for me?"

She looked blank. "Why, no. Not with me. But I'll go check at the front desk."

"I'm sure he left some kind of message for me," Leigh said, her stomach churning. "Please ask everyone."

Her mind whirled as she waited. She couldn't believe he'd left without seeing her. It was so unlike Erik! Could it have been Margit's doing? But how could she possibly have that much power over him?

The nurse returned, and by her face, Leigh knew at once

the news wasn't good. "No message," she said. "I'm sorry. I asked everyone on duty."

Leigh blinked back tears. "Thank you," she said softly. With a sympathetic smile, the nurse left the room. Leigh's eyes blurred as she stared down at the delicate silver ring on her finger with the entwined initials *E* and *K*.

"Oh, Erik . . . how could you?" she whispered.

She'd been trying to prepare herself mentally for the moment they'd say good-bye. And now, it was all over. No good-byes were to be said. "I needed to say good-bye to you, Erik. Didn't you realize that?"

She didn't know how long she sat in that hospital bed, staring at nothing. The shadows lengthened in the room as the feeble sun slipped behind the mountains. Still, Leigh couldn't summon the will to move. What was there to do anyway? Erik was with Margit, flying home to Oslo. Slowly, her eyes moved to the telephone on the bedside table. With a trembling hand, she reached for it, and quickly, before she could lose her nerve, she dialed the operator.

"Yes. Do you speak English? Thank you. I'd like to make a call to the United States. The number is 703-759-6384."

A few minutes later, she heard the ring of the phone in a house an ocean away and could imagine the ultramodern kitchen where just a year ago, she'd been preparing a family meal. It seemed like a *thousand* years ago. The phone was picked up in midring. Leigh's heart leapt when she heard Melissa's familiar soprano.

"Mel, this is your mother," she spoke with a tone of quiet determination. "Don't hang up. I'm calling from Norway. No . . ." She paused. "He isn't here with me. I won't be seeing him again." A sob caught in her throat, but she went on, "Melissa, I'm going to fly back home next week. No, not Virginia. I'm living in New York, remember?" She felt a spark of hope in her heart. "Mel, is it my imagination, or do you sound disappointed? . . . Oh, then I guess it *was* my imagination. Anyway, I'll be coming down to visit as soon as I get in. . . . Yes, I'm aware you don't want to see me, but that's too bad. It's time you and the boys sit down with me and get this thing straightened out. We're going to get our relationship back on track, even if it kills all of us. . . . *Why* should we?" Leigh was silent for a moment, flabbergasted at her daughter's insolence, yet she was almost sure she sensed a vulnerability beneath Melissa's caustic words. "Because—damn it—I'm your mother, and I love you." She waited but there was no response on the other end of the line. "I'll take a taxi from the airport. Tell Mark and Aaron I'm coming. Bye, Mel."

A slow tear slipped down her face as she gently replaced the receiver in its cradle.

Part Two

West of the Moon

20

January 1991

The Mediterranean sun baked down from an azure sky, glimmering like diamonds onto the pure turquoise of the sea. Erik, wearing a cast on his right leg, stared broodingly out at the horizon where the two shades of blue merged into one. Somewhere out there was Turkey.

Escape crossed his mind. It was a totally whimsical thought. Of course, there was no escape. He'd known that from the beginning. Or at least from the moment Margit had entered his hospital room to tell him she would marry him. Right now, she was asleep in a whitewashed stone cottage in the Greek village below. It was early, only seven o'clock, and last night had been the first one they'd spent as man and wife.

If only she hadn't walked into his hospital room that day, he'd be a free man right now. How ironic that just as he'd decided to go to Kayleigh, tell her he loved her enough to give up all claims to Gunny and return to the United States with her, Margit had turned up. But *was* it coincidence? Had she suspected his relationship with Leigh, and had that been the deciding factor in changing her mind about marriage? Whatever, Erik knew he had to be up front with her. He'd told her everything, even admitted that he loved Kayleigh, hoping Margit would let him go. But incredibly, it hadn't changed her mind. She'd insisted their marriage would be the best thing for everyone. What could he do but agree? Now, too late, he knew that of all the mistakes he'd made, marrying Margit had been the worst.

Erik turned from his contemplation of the sea and limped over to the six-columned ruin that had stood guard over the Rhodean village of Lindos for centuries. The Sanctuary of Athena, Greek goddess of war. His hand caressed the sun-kissed smoothness of a column as he gazed around him, wondering why he couldn't shake off his moodiness and just enjoy this holiday in Rhodes. It wasn't every day a man was able to honeymoon on a Greek island. Yet, Erik knew he had a right to feel the way he did. He was on a honeymoon, but he wasn't in love with his wife.

Last night, when he'd made love to Margit, the only way he'd been able to attain an erection was to think of Kayleigh. Halfway through, when Margit had murmured an endearment in Norwegian, he'd immediately gone limp. Reality had returned. Margit had been understanding, of course, attributing it to fatigue and jet lag. But how much longer could he keep up the pretense? How would he ever be able to think of her as a lover instead of a sister? In two weeks, they would return to Oslo and start their married life together. Gunny would be there, thank God. Perhaps that would help bring some normality to their lives.

A breeze quickened off the Aegean Sea and rippled through his hair. He should go back. Margit would probably be up by now. But still, he lingered, basking in the warmth of the morning sun. He wondered what she'd want to do today. Swim in the bay, perhaps. It would feel wonderfully warm to her Scandinavian-bred body, even in January. Perhaps she'd want to take a paddleboat out onto the glasslike sea. He was sure she wouldn't want to do what he preferred . . . sit in a beachside taverna, sip retsina, and get comatose-drunk.

Erik made his way down from the acropolis toward the tiny white village nestled below. It had been an effort to climb up here with crutches, but he'd felt such a need to get away. To find space. But it hadn't worked. Even at the top of the Lindos acropolis, the ghosts hadn't stopped haunting him.

*   *   *

Leigh stood in the airport ladies' room and retouched her lipstick. Unfortunately, the warm russet color did nothing to relieve the pallor of her skin. The bout with pneumonia had taken its toll, revealing itself in the gaunt lines on her face and the smudged circles ringing her eyes. She'd lost over ten pounds, and even now, after two weeks spent in the Norwegian hospital, her appetite hadn't really returned. The kids probably wouldn't recognize her.

She ran a comb through her rumpled hair and sighed. It was the best she could do.

Outside, in the cold January afternoon, she hailed a taxi and gave the driver the familiar address.

The place where home used to be.

The taxi pulled up to the house. Leigh stepped out and waited while the driver took her suitcase from the trunk. "Just put it there on the driveway, please." She paid him and waited until he drove off before turning around to look at the house. Ruefully, she glanced down at the suitcase. A mistake. She should've found a hotel room before coming here. The kids would think she was back to stay. She glanced at her watch. They'd been home from school for an hour. Leaving her suitcase behind, Leigh walked up the familiar driveway.

Halfway there, the front door opened. Leigh saw a small figure with blond hair. Her heart skipped a beat, and she stopped, staring. "Aaron," she whispered, unable to move. Almost as motionless, Aaron stared at his mother for a moment. A movement beside him caught Leigh's eyes. Ivan, their golden retriever. The dog slipped past Aaron and gave one sharp bark. Then he was running toward Leigh, his tongue lolling in a friendly grin.

Leigh extended a hand toward him. "Hello, Ivan." The dog licked her palm in welcome and tried to jump on her. "No. Don't jump. But it's good to see you, too."

"*Mom!*" Aaron shouted. His paralysis left him, and he began to run toward her.

It was all Leigh needed. With Ivan at her heels, she ran to

meet him, tears of joy streaming down her face. Aaron threw himself into her arms. She clutched his wiry body tightly and smiled into his golden hair. "Oh, Aaron, baby, I've missed you so much."

The eleven-year-old boy held on to his mother as if he were afraid she would disappear . . . again. "I *knew* you'd come back," he said. "Mel said you never would. That you didn't love us anymore. I called her a lying sack of dogshit and she hit me. Dad grounded both of us."

With difficulty, Leigh pulled away and gazed into his blue eyes. "I *never* stopped loving you. And it was wrong for Melissa to tell you that. But when people are angry and bitter, sometimes they say things they don't mean."

Aaron clutched her hand and pulled her toward the house. "Mark isn't home, but Mel is in the kitchen."

Leigh marveled at how much Aaron had grown since she'd last seen him. He was at least two inches taller. Her throat tightened. He was no longer her baby.

As they went in through the front door, Leigh inhaled the familiar scent of lemon oil furniture polish. She looked around and was amazed to see the cherry wood furniture freshly polished, including Grandmother Kayleigh's grandfather clock. The sea-green cushions on the floral sofa looked as if they'd been recently plumped, and the delicate mauve and sea green Oriental rug had definitely seen a vacuum cleaner recently. Had Bob—?

As if in answer to her unspoken question, Aaron spoke. "You should see Mel. She comes in here every day after school and dusts and vacuums. And Dad doesn't even *tell* her to do it. She gets weirder every day."

"Maybe you should tell her I'm here."

Aaron pulled on her hand. "No, let's surprise her."

Leigh allowed herself to be pulled along, thinking maybe he had the right idea. If Melissa were warned, it would be just like her to barricade herself in her room. From the hallway leading into the kitchen, Leigh heard a television blaring. They walked through the doorway, and she saw Melissa sitting on a countertop, munching a sandwich, her eyes glued to a soap opera on the small color TV on the opposite counter. A new addition to the kitchen, Leigh realized, and it immediately aroused the cynic in her. Bob, up to his old games, substituting material goods for attention.

"Mel . . . ," Aaron began.

"Quiet, bozo-breath. Dominic is about to rescue Alexandra from Zebulon."

"Mom's here."

At first, Leigh thought Melissa hadn't heard Aaron's announcement, because her eyes remained fixed upon the television screen. But then, slowly she turned her head, a curtain of long blond hair falling gracefully over one curved cheekbone. Leigh drew in a sharp breath. How beautiful her daughter had become. Her face was clear of blemishes, and her girlish body had ripened into womanly curves. Had her breasts thrust out so pertly six months ago? Likely, they had, but in those final passionate days with Erik, Leigh had probably been too preoccupied to notice.

Leigh saw Melissa try to keep her face impassive, but there was an unmistakable light in her eyes as she looked at her mother. What did it mean? She swallowed the bite of sandwich she'd just taken and said, "Oh, hi. Want a Coke?"

Leigh was speechless. It was as if she'd just come in from a PTA meeting. Finally, she found her voice. "Yeah, thanks."

Melissa's eyes slid back to the TV. "Aaron, get her a soda."

Leigh didn't miss the *her*. It was as if she couldn't bring herself to say *Mom*.

"Sit down," Melissa said. "This is almost over. See, Zebulon—he's the bad guy—has the house rigged with a bomb, and Dominic and Alexandra are inside."

Leigh glanced over at the TV, feeling like she'd just stepped into the twilight zone. With the exception of the phone call from Norway, the last time her daughter had spoken to her had been when she'd screamed invectives across the kitchen at the beach house. Words like: *old woman, slut, whore*. Or had that last one been Bob's word?

On the screen, a house blew up, and Mel jumped down from the countertop. "That's it. They always leave you hanging on

Friday." She switched off the television and turned back to Leigh. "So, how was Norway?"

Uneasily, Leigh glanced over at Aaron, who'd sat down at the table beside her, nibbling an apple. "It . . . wasn't exactly what'd I'd expected."

"Oh, really?" She flipped a long strand of hair around in front of her and examined the ends. Then, softly, she said, "And Erik? How is he?"

Leigh felt the color rise on her face. "He's getting married."

For the first time, Mel's eyes met hers. "Who to?"

"An old girlfriend in Oslo. I met her. She's very nice."

"So . . ." Melissa stretched out her legs under the table and studied her lavender fingernails. "You won't be seeing him again?"

Quietly, she said, "*No.*"

"Is there a chance you and Dad—?"

"*No,*" emphatically this time.

"Well." Melissa stood up. "You *will* stay for dinner, won't you? Dad won't be home. It'll be just the three of us."

Before Leigh could answer, she heard the back door open. "Hey, Mel, what's cooking? I'm starved."

Leigh's mouth went dry at the sound of Mark's voice. Without being able to see him through the walls of the utility room, she could only imagine what he looked like, shrugging out of his coat and talking to Melissa over his shoulder. "Vicki sent me home because she wasn't feeling well. I think she's coming down with the flu." He walked into the room and stopped dead upon seeing Leigh.

Gravely, Melissa eyed him. "We have a visitor."

"She's not a visitor," Aaron said, glaring at Melissa. "She's our mom."

A cold look settled on Mark's handsome face. "What brings *you* here?"

"I wanted to see all of you. We can't go on the way it has been."

"Why not? We're doing okay without you."

"Well, I'm not doing okay without you."

Mark's sneer reminded her of Bob. "What's the matter? The Norwegian stud wasn't enough for you?"

Even Mel looked shocked, but Leigh sat stoically, not giving him the satisfaction of showing how much the barb had hurt her. "I want us to try to get our relationship back on track. I know it won't be easy. But don't you see, this bitterness has to stop."

An uneasy silence fell in the room. Aaron gazed at her with a look of adoration, and Mel scrutinized her shoelace. Mark stared mutinously.

"Look," Leigh went on. "Why don't we call out for pizza? I'll treat."

Melissa's foot dropped to the floor. She stood abruptly. "Great idea." Aaron slipped out of his chair and draped his arms around Leigh's neck. Mark's expression didn't change.

"Count me out," he said. "I'm going over to the university."

"But you said you were starved," Melissa protested.

"I just lost my appetite." He turned and walked out to the utility room. A second later, the slam of the back door reverberated through the room.

"Erik, you should've listened to me when I suggested we postpone our honeymoon until summer." Margit waved away a second cup of thick, sweet Greek coffee and watched morosely as the waiter filled Erik's empty cup.

"Oh, and can you bring me a bottle of retsina, please?" Erik asked as he buttered a breakfast roll.

Margit's green eyes widened. "Wine at breakfast?"

A cynical smile came to Erik's lips. "It's after eleven. And I don't believe we've been married long enough to give you the liberty to start nagging."

"Nagging?" Margit pretended to be shocked. "I'm hurt you would think such a thing!" A breeze from the sea rippled through her straight reddish-blond hair. She gazed out at the turquoise bay. "Oh, Erik, isn't this wonderful? I could stay here forever. Having breakfast in an open-air café, lazing in the sun all day. Why do people live anywhere else?"

"Because they were born somewhere else." His eyes fastened on his newspaper—the only English-language one he could find. "Oh, the krone has dropped again. If we keep spending money here in Greece, we may be penniless when we get home."

"Did you hear what I said? We should've waited."

"Why?"

"Your cast, of course. Look at you. You can't go into the water with me. You can't even get a tan, or you'll be two-toned when the cast comes off."

"Don't worry about me," Erik said, flipping to the sports page. "I'm enjoying myself."

"But *I'm* not! I mean, I want to do things together. Here I am going to the beach, and you'll be hanging around this café getting drunk on Greek wine."

Erik dropped the newspaper and looked at his wife. "Do you want me to come down to the beach with you?"

A chastened expression crossed her freckled face. "No, of course not. You'd be miserable. Look, I'll just go out for an hour or so. Just enough to get a little color. Then we'll meet for lunch." She stood up and bent toward him for a kiss. "I'm going to change into my swimsuit. You sure you won't be bored?"

"Not at all," Erik said. "I'm going to write some postcards. I'm sure everyone back home wants to know how we're doing."

"Okay." She smiled. "Try not to miss me too much."

Erik's eyes followed her trim figure as she headed back to their cottage, her long reddish-blond hair swinging past her shoulders. She was an adorable girl, really. There would be many interested male eyes upon her down at the beach, and he knew he should feel jealous. But that emotion just wasn't there.

He glanced down at the pile of postcards on the table. Usually, he loved writing notes and letters to his friends and family, but today, he just wasn't in the mood. There was only one person he wanted to write to. Quickly, he took out the ink pen from his shirt and in sweeping letters, wrote, *Dear Kayleigh,* onto the back of a postcard. He stared down at it, feeling a wash of emotion spread through him. God, it hurt so much just to see her name. And what could he write to her? "I hate my life, I don't love Margit, and the only thing I want is you." No. It would only make her feel as horrible as he did. Besides, there was nothing he could say now that he hadn't already said in that final letter he'd written in the hospital.

Another mistake. His life had been full of them lately. He shouldn't have listened to Margit. Instead of writing the good-bye letter and giving it to Margit to leave at the nurse's desk, he should've followed his instincts and said good-bye in person. Kayleigh had saved his life on that mountain above Ose. His last sight of her had been as she'd collapsed onto the snow after he'd stopped her from firing the rifle.

Abruptly, he slashed through her name and then tore the card in half. It was time to face the fact that Kayleigh was gone forever.

He glanced up to see a woman walk by on the sidewalk in front of the café. He saw her only from the back, but her ash-blond hair was styled exactly like Kayleigh's. His heart raced. He moved up from his chair so quickly that one of his crutches fell to the floor with a crash.

"Kayleigh!"

The woman stopped and turned to look at him, a question in her eyes. He stood still, one hand grasping the back of the chair as he struggled to retain his balance. His heart pounded like a kettledrum. "Sorry," he mumbled. "I mistook you for someone else."

Erik settled back into his seat. With a trembling hand, he poured himself a glass of retsina and gulped it down. He stared down at the postcards, blinking quickly to restore his suddenly blurred vision.

Margit settled herself onto a beach towel and tugged her sun hat down to protect her face. With her pale complexion, she'd have to be very careful out here on her first day in the sun. She wished Erik could have joined her. Some honeymoon! Last night, something had gone wrong with their lovemaking. It had been the first time since the night they'd learned Gunvor was dead. Thinking about it, she blushed. It had been so awkward. And then, Erik had—well—lost it. She'd tried to reassure him it was jet lag, but she wasn't sure it was.

Was it Kayleigh? How she wished she'd never heard of that woman! She knew Erik had loved her. He'd admitted it. But did he still? She was so sure it had just been sexual attraction. What else could it be? The woman was at least a decade older than he! Good-looking, yes. She could understand why she'd be attractive to Erik. But love? Impossible! They had nothing in common.

It was a good thing she'd torn up that letter he'd written to her. No loose ends.

The break had been sudden—and permanent.

21

Half-drunk from the retsina, Erik lurched back to the cottage, wanting only to fall into bed and sleep. He was relieved to see Margit hadn't returned from the beach. With any luck, she'd stay there for a while, at least long enough for him to take a nap. Inside, the room was a peaceful haven. Erik sank down onto the cool white sheets with a sigh of relief and stared up at the paddles of the electric fan spinning lazily on the ceiling. Wooden slats at the window protected the room from the sun yet allowed in a fresh sea breeze. Erik closed his eyes, enjoying the blissful quiet. The only sounds were the whisper of the fan and, in the distance, the crashing surf.

A little bit of heaven, he thought, as he sank into sleep and immediately began to dream. He was back at the beach house in Rehoboth. There, in front of him, stood the outdoor shower, and beneath the door, he could see a pair of trim feet. Slowly, he moved toward it and pushed the door open. Inside, he faced a wet, naked Kayleigh. Her hair was white with the lather of shampoo, and some of the rich suds had slid down her neck and onto the swell of her breast. When she saw him, her eyes grew wide. He reached out for her, and she melted toward him, feeling very warm, very real. They kissed deeply, his tongue probing the tenderness of her mouth. He felt himself grow hard, and he knew he couldn't wait much longer to have her. He moaned as her warm silky hands closed upon his erection. Then he plunged into her, and out of control, came to a quick climax.

"I'm sorry," he murmured. "I couldn't wait."

"Don't be sorry, *kjareste*. It was good for me. Not at all like last night."

Erik's eyes flashed open. He found himself staring down into Margit's heated face. *Kristus!* He'd thought he was dreaming. But obviously, it had been real enough for her. He withdrew from her and rolled over onto his side, his face flushed with embarrassment. He'd been dreaming about Kayleigh, and somehow, during it, Margit had come in and slipped into bed with him. Had he called out Kayleigh's name? No—if he had, Margit would surely not be wearing that pleased expression on her face.

She giggled and ran a finger up the mat of blond hair carpeting his chest. "When I got into bed, you were hard as a rock. Having erotic dreams, were you? About me, I hope."

"Of course," Erik said lightly, and turned over on his back to escape her cloying hands.

"Tell me about it, Eriksen. Perhaps we could reenact it."

"Sorry. It's already slipped away."

He stared up at the ceiling, his jaw tight.

You may own me, Margit Lovvig, but you don't own my thoughts and dreams.

As Leigh and Melissa cleaned up the remains of their pizza, they heard Bob's Mercedes pull into the driveway. Leigh felt her stomach take a sickening plunge. She'd hoped she'd be able to get away before he came home.

Melissa stared at her warily. "Maybe you'd better go. Dad hasn't adjusted well to . . . this whole thing."

But Leigh knew it was too late. He came in through the back door. Immediately, they heard the thud of his briefcase hitting the floor of the utility room. It was followed by an exasperated growl.

"Who left a goddamn suitcase on the driveway? I almost ran over it!"

He strode into the kitchen and stopped short when he saw Leigh. "What the fuck are you doing here?"

She stared into his glowering face and then said something that surprised even herself. "You might as well get used to it, Bob. I'm back to stay."

Bob's lips twisted in a sneer. "What do you mean, you're back to stay?"

Melissa and Aaron stared at Leigh, waiting for an answer. She saw the hope in Aaron's eyes and immediately felt guilty.

"I didn't mean it the way it came out," she explained, her eyes upon Aaron. She turned back to Bob. "I've decided I'm moving back here to Washington. Seeing the kids again has made me realize there's no hope for us if I stay in New York. And they are more important to me than my career."

Bob laughed. "How touching! You're really something, you know that? Do you think they're so naive they're going to believe that? Where was your concern for the kids when you were screwing that Norwegian commie?"

Something snapped inside her. "Don't talk like that in front of them!"

"Hey, lady. This is my house, or have you forgotten? I'll say whatever the fuck I want to in it. And who the hell are you to come off with that holier-than-thou attitude? The kids know what you are! They know *I* wasn't the one who was sleeping around."

Her mouth opened to put an end to that fantasy once and for all, but then she remembered the kids. They had to live with him for now. Why give them more pain? Her face set, she turned away and went to the phone.

"I'll be out of your way as soon as I can get a taxi." She called information, and a moment later, gave the address to the dispatcher. When she hung up, she saw Bob had taken off his coat and sat down at the kitchen table, still staring moodily at her. "I just wish you and I could be civilized," she said. "You know, it *can* be done."

"Oh, yeah? Well, if you think we're going to get all cozy like they do on the soap operas, forget it. It's not that easy for me to forget what you did."

"I'm not asking you to forget. I just think we should be able to talk without throwing insults at each other."

Bob was silent. Aaron moved over to his mother and took her hand. His eyes were sad. "Do you really have to go, Mom?"

"Yes. For now." Leigh touched his cheek. "But I meant it when I said I'm going to move back here. First, I have to go back to New York and move out of Deanna's apartment. But I'll be back in a couple of weeks to look for a place to live."

An abrupt laugh escaped Bob's throat. "That should be cute. You'll have to live on your own without that novelist to support you."

Leigh bristled. "I paid my way while I lived at Deanna's."

"Really? Don't tell me she was charging you rent for that Central Park penthouse? Oh! I forgot. She's a Jew, so she probably was. So, how did you afford it? Maybe Erik Haukeland was helping you out?"

Leigh couldn't hide her disgust. "God, you're such a bigot. Too bad your constituents don't know the *real* Bobby Fallon."

Bob ignored her gibe. "So, how do you plan to support yourself here in Washington? Besides freelancing your kiddie pictures?"

"I'll manage," Leigh said stiffly. "Not that it's any of your business."

Bob grinned viciously. "Hell! If I know you, you won't be able to make it without a man for long. We'll probably all be hearing wedding bells in the not-too-distant future."

"Don't count on it," Leigh said between clenched teeth.

"Well, I can't say I'm surprised you didn't stay in Norway. What happened? Once your lover compared you with all his hot Norwegian bimbos, did he lose interest?"

Leigh's stomach churned, but she held back a retort. Sparring with Bob would be a losing battle.

An uneasy silence fell, and was finally broken by the sound of a car pulling into the driveway. Bob stood. "Your ride is here."

Leigh pulled on her coat, kissed Aaron, and said good-bye to Mel. She'd just reached the door when Bob spoke again. "Oh, by the way, Leigh . . . what did that Norwegian do to you anyway? You look like hell."

The wrought-iron latticed elevator rose smoothly to the top of the luxurious apartment building and stopped at Deanna's penthouse. Leigh pushed the alabaster doorbell button and waited.

The door opened. A uniformed butler met her in the foyer. "Ah, Ms. Fallon. It's so good to see you again. Miss Harper is waiting for you."

"Leigh?" Deanna's strident Brooklyn voice called from the living room. "Get your skinny ass in here!"

Leigh stepped into the living room to see a bald Deanna, dressed in gray sweats, her face a mask of green slime and riding a stationary bicycle like a possessed demon. She stopped when she saw Leigh staring at her.

"Okay, damn it, *look*!" Deanna sat up straight and thrust out her chest. But there was nothing there to thrust out. "The new Deanna Harper! I can give Twiggy a run for her money. And what do you think of my hairstyle? I figure if Sinead O'Connor can get away with it, I can, too. Lost every damn bit of my hair after the first radiation treatment, but the doc says it'll grow back."

Leigh grinned. "What happened to the Dolly Parton wig?"

Deanna shrugged. "Tried the friggin' thing, but it made me feel like a cast member in *Clan of the Cave Bear*." She jumped off the bicycle. "Jesus Christ, Leigh! What happened to you? You look like—"

"Hell?" Leigh said dryly. "Yes, so I've been told. If you have a few years, I'll tell you all about it."

"Okay. Just let me get this shit off my face. Have Jackson bring us some coffee."

A few minutes later, Deanna returned to the room, her face

freshly scrubbed. She dropped into a mauve easy chair and stared at Leigh through teal-shaded glasses. "I almost died when you called from Washington. I thought you were still in Norway. Here I am talking to you and I'm thinking, 'Jesus, this overseas line is good.' Then you said you were in Washington! What the hell happened?"

"Well, you know that blizzard shut down JFK just as my flight was heading in, so they diverted us to Dulles. I look at it as fate. It didn't give me a lot of time to get nervous about seeing the kids again."

Jackson arrived with the coffee. Deanna sat up straight to take a steaming mug. "Jackson, you're a sweetheart." She waited until he left the room before speaking again. "I'm not talking about your airline problems, you numskull! What happened with Erik?"

Leigh took a sip of coffee. "I'll get to that. But what about you? You seem to have recovered from your surgery pretty well. Should you be exercising like that, though?"

Deanna shrugged. "Probably not. But I'll be damned if I'm going to get fat just because I don't have any boobs. I'm doing okay. There were some moments I was depressed as hell, but Carrie was here and helped me through it. It really wasn't as bad as I'd expected. Even the radiation treatments. No nausea or anything—and here, I was expecting to be sicker than a drunken sailor. But my worst problem is just this enormous fatigue after the treatments. I'm so weak I can barely pull down my panties to go to the bathroom. But I feel better after a few days."

"I should've been here," Leigh said glumly. "Then you would've had me *and* your daughter."

"Ah, cut the crap! You wouldn't have done me any good in the condition you were in. Shit! You *had* to go to Norway, Leigh. And no matter what happened there, aren't you glad you did?"

"Oh, yeah. It certainly woke me up to a few facts." Leigh stood up and walked over to the full-length windows overlooking Central Park. A wave of anguish passed through her, remembering the wonderful moments with Erik in that park.

In this apartment, too. She thought of the water bed in Deanna's room and winced.

"Surely Erik hadn't changed that much in six months," Deanna said.

Leigh turned around. "Oh, no. He hadn't changed at all. He was loving and attentive. Boy, was he attentive!" Leigh's cheeks grew warm at Deanna's bawdy laugh. "But one night at his family's house, he introduced me to a woman named Margit Lovvig. She had a little boy about three who, would you believe it, looked exactly like Erik." Leigh told her the whole sorry story, ending with Erik's abrupt departure with Margit.

"Damn him!" Deanna's brown eyes blazed. "How could he just leave without seeing you again? Not even a note, or anything?"

"Nothing." Leigh blinked quickly, feeling very close to tears. "So, that's what I got out of my trip to Norway. Just my heart stomped on." She shook her head and muttered, "I was so stupid. Thinking I could make a life with a man so much younger than me."

"It wasn't your age that was the problem," Deanna said. "It was just circumstances. And Erik's reckless libido. If it weren't for that night with—what was her name? Margaret?"

"Margit. Oh, Dee, you should see her. Long reddish-blond hair. Petite. Looks like Nicole Kidman playing the girl next door. How could I compete with that?"

"Did Erik say he's in love with her?"

"No. Just the opposite. He says he thinks of her as a sister. That's a laugh, isn't it? He swore he still loved me. I guess I believe that. Well, I *did* until he left without seeing me. Now, I don't know what to think. Damn!" Leigh plopped down into a chair. "It doesn't matter now anyway, does it? I have to get on with my life."

Deanna looked at her closely. "So, have you decided what you're going to do?"

Here it was. The moment to tell her she planned to move back to Washington. Yet, Leigh didn't speak. The sight of Deanna in that gray sweatshirt, the now boyish chest flat against the soft fabric, sent a sharp pain through her heart. It wasn't fair! She never expected to see Deanna Harper look so vulnerable.

"Leigh, don't take this wrong, okay? But I think you'll be happier back in Washington."

Leigh's mouth dropped open. Deanna *wanted* her to move out!

"You're taking it wrong. I can see it on your face," Deanna said. "Look, darling, I know you're miserable here. And I don't think it was just because Erik wasn't around. You hate living in New York, don't you? Come on, admit it. Remember Christmas? Remember how you couldn't stop talking about your old-fashioned Virginia Christmases?"

"I guess I was a real pain in the ass, wasn't I?"

"Damn it, you're one thickheaded broad! Just tell me the goddamn truth. Do you like living here in New York with me?"

Leigh stared at her; then finally, her eyes dropped. "You're right. I hate New York. Living here, I mean. But Dee, you're my best friend, and I don't know what I would've done without your support these last months. And I don't want you to feel like I'm running out on you—especially now while you're going through the treatments."

"Chicken-feathers!—as my grandmother would've said. Sweetie, you're not running out on me. If anything, I'm kicking you out. For your own good. I want you to be happy. And I don't think you will be unless you're close to your kids. How did it go with them, by the way?"

"Not bad with Melissa and Aaron, but I'm afraid Mark is another story. He took one look at me and walked out. But I think you might be right. If I'm living there close, maybe it'll just be a matter of time before he comes around."

"You see. You know I'm right. Now, it's time for me to go into my noble act because I'm sacrificing myself so you can go live near your kids."

"But Dee, we'll still see each other, won't we?"

"Of course. I'll be staying with you when I come to Washington. You don't think I'd go to one of those stuffy hotels when I can stay with you in Georgetown, do you?"

"Boy, are you dreaming! How do you expect me to live in Georgetown? I don't even have a job."

"You will," Deanna said. "In fact, I have the perfect one for you. Did I ever tell you about my friend, Ward Radcliffe? He owns an art gallery in Georgetown, and it just so happens he's looking for someone to manage it. I'll give him a call tonight if you're interested. What do you think?"

"I think you're the best friend anyone could hope for," Leigh said, blinking away grateful tears. "Why are you so good to me?"

"Hey, I take care of my friends." Deanna smiled. "You're like a sister to me, Leigh. You know that. I'll get Ward's card for you. I'm sure he'll expect you to drop by as soon as you get back." Deanna stood and moved toward the door leading to her office. At the threshold, she paused. "Oh, by the way, Ward is gay. That doesn't bother you, does it?" Without waiting for an answer, she disappeared into her office. In a few seconds she was back, and still talking. ". . . and he mentioned that there's a vacant apartment in his building. A brownstone."

"But I can't afford to live in Georgetown!" Leigh protested.

A thin penciled eyebrow rose. "Really? Well, maybe you'll change your mind when you see the salary Ward is offering. My dear . . ." She faked a horrible British-gentry accent. "Ward Radcliffe just happens to be from a titled English family. He claims he's linked by blood to the Queen Mother." She resumed her normal Brooklynese. "In other words, he's loaded. You're going to love the man, Leigh. Everyone does. I swear, if you cut him with a knife, he'd *bleed* charisma. Now, how about if we get Jackson to serve us some lunch, and then I'll let you critique the first three chapters of my new novel." A mischievous grin lit up her face as she added, "But only if you promise to like it."

22

The yellow Volkswagen Rabbit slowly nosed its way up the winding snowpacked road leading to the Haukeland family home. Margit peered anxiously out the passenger window; she could barely wait for her first glimpse of Gunny.

Erik glanced over and grinned. "Settle down. It hasn't been *that* long."

"Two weeks! Remember, darling, I haven't been separated from my baby before. I just hope he wasn't a terror for your mother."

"I don't think you need to worry about Mother. She raised four of us, you know."

"That's true. But sometimes I believe Gunny can be equivalent to six boys his age."

Erik turned into the driveway of his parents' house. "You worry too much, Margit. I'm sure he's been an angel."

As they were getting out of the car, the front door opened, and Gunny stepped out onto the porch. When he recognized his mother, he cried out in excitement and ran toward her. Grethe Haukeland followed behind, smiling. "Well, look at the two of you. Such lovely tans! Come on in now, and I'll warm you up with some good black coffee."

Margit had already run over and scooped Gunny into her arms. He buried his head into the fur of her collar, clinging to her tightly. "How was he?" she asked Grethe over his silky golden-red hair.

"Oh, we had lots of fun! Of course, he asked, 'Where's Mama?' every day, but when I told him you were on holiday with his new daddy, he went right back to playing."

Inside the house, Grethe took their coats as Gunny kept up a running stream of chatter about everything he'd done while she was away. Finally, the toddler turned to Erik and said, "Hi, Uncle Erik. Did you bring me something?"

Margit gave him a stern look. "Gunvor, that is a very rude

question. And didn't I tell you that Erik is your father now? You must call him Father."

Gunny thrust out his bottom lip. "I don't want a father. Just want you." He reached his arms up to her.

She bent over and picked him up, casting an apologetic glance at Erik.

"Don't worry, you two," Grethe said. "It will take him a little while to adjust. He's never had to share his mother before."

"Well, we'll have to do something about that, won't we, Erik?" Margit smiled up at her husband.

Erik looked at her blankly. "Did I miss something?"

Grethe gave him a wry smile. "I think she's talking about a baby brother or sister, Erik."

Erik hadn't thought of more children. Curiously, the idea appealed to him, despite his platonic feelings for Margit. He'd always loved being a part of a large family; he especially enjoyed children. Perhaps having another child would put a spark into his life. God knew he needed one.

"Come on," Grethe said. "Dordei and Hakon are in the family room, and Bjørn and his family should be arriving soon. They all knew you were coming home tonight."

As they walked into the family room, Hakon raised his glass of aquavit and called out in an overly jovial voice, "Ah, the newly wedded couple are here!" He gave Erik a hard slap on the back.

Erik grimaced. One of these days, he was going to lose his patience and haul off and slug his insufferable brother-in-law. How Dordei could stomach him, he'd never understand. But women loved that classic male-model look, and that was about the only thing Hakon had going for him. Erik thought he was a pompous know-it-all. After exchanging a word of greeting with him, he moved on to his sister and gave her a hug. She held him tightly for a moment, then pulled away and gazed up at him, her blue eyes serious.

"Is everything okay, Erik?"

"Yes. Just fine." He could tell she didn't believe him. But then, why would she? Erik and Dordei had always been especially close. He was the one she'd always turned to when she had a problem. And in the last few years, he'd been turning to her more and more. She'd grown to know him almost better than he knew himself. Only a few days before the wedding, she'd cornered him and demanded to know why he was marrying Margit.

"It's not because you love her. Not in the way a man is supposed to love his wife."

There was no way he could pretend with her. "Dordei, I know it must look odd to you, but I have a good reason for marrying her. You see, Gunny is my son."

Dordei didn't raise an eyebrow. "I know that. Bjørn told me. But Erik, we're talking about your life here. Is this what you really want?"

Erik's lips tightened. "It doesn't matter what I want at this point. What I wanted wasn't possible."

"Kayleigh?"

"How did you know?" Erik asked.

"I remembered our discussion about a woman you'd fallen for when you came home for Christmas last year." Dordei shook her head. "I knew it was Kayleigh the moment you two walked into the room. Anyone with half a brain could've seen it in the way you looked at her that night. And I got the feeling she was pretty taken with you, too."

"She was."

"You're still in love with her, Erik. How can you marry Margit?"

In frustration, he spoke harshly to his sister. "What do you suggest I do? I have a responsibility toward Margit."

Dordei's eyes hardened. "And what about the responsibility to yourself? To Kayleigh? There is only one thing I know, Erik. A bad marriage is a living hell. I'd hate to see it happen to you."

Now, as Erik looked down at his sister, he could see the doubt in her eyes at his curt answer. A silent message passed between them as she squeezed his hands tightly before letting go. He wanted to ask her about Hakon and their relationship. She'd never discussed it with him, but he was sure she was desperately unhappy in her marriage. Of course, he had no proof, but he had the distinct feeling the man was a blatant philanderer. He'd even flirted outrageously with Kayleigh that night right in front of Dordei. God help him, if Erik ever found out for sure he was playing around.

"Son, you're home!"

Arne had arrived home from work at the shipyards. Everyone took seats and immediately began bombarding Erik and Margit with questions about Greece. Grethe entered the room with hot coffee and *goro*, cardamon-flavored cookies with a hint of cognac.

"Where's Mags?" Erik asked during a pause in the conversation. It was unusual for his younger brother not to be around during a family gathering.

"Oh, he went to Holmenkollen for ski-jumping," Grethe said. "He is very serious about making the Olympic team this time."

The doorbell rang, and Arne went to answer it. Margit moved to the sofa to sit down next to Erik. She smiled at him warmly and took his hand. There was a great commotion at the front door and a few seconds later, two little blond girls rushed in and flung themselves onto Erik's lap.

"Oh, what have we here?" He laughed, hugging them. "My two little princesses."

Five-year-old Marit and three-year-old Inger-Lise were crazy about their uncle Erik. In their young eyes, there was no one in the world like him. Bjørn and Anne-Lise entered the room, followed shortly by Mags. The family exchanged boisterous greetings and kisses.

Erik felt his heart lifting. Home. It felt good. But later that evening, as he saw Bjørn and Anne-Lise exchange a tender glance, he felt a pang in his heart as his thoughts returned to Kayleigh.

It should be *her* on the sofa next to him, not Margit. This was all wrong, but there wasn't a goddamn thing he could do about it.

*   *   *

Margit drew a comb through her hair and stared at her reflection in the bathroom mirror. The Mediterranean sun had done wonders for her skin, giving it a subtle golden glow. She didn't care what those stupid medical people said. In her opinion, having a good suntan was the epitome of health. She opened the bathroom door and stepped out into the hall.

Bjørn was leaning against the wall.

Her eyes connected with his. "Oh, were you waiting for the lavatory?"

He smiled. "Don't be cute. How was the honeymoon?"

"Okay."

His gaze moved lazily over her. "Was Erik the great stud he thinks he is?"

Her lips lifted in amusement. "That's a rather rude question, Bjørn."

"Is it?" He moved over to her and pushed her back inside the bathroom. Smiling, he stepped in after her, closed the door and locked it, then turned to face her. Her heart raced as she stared into his intent blue eyes. He grabbed her shoulders, and his mouth came down hard on hers, his tongue thrusting. Her hands locked on to the back of his neck as she returned his kiss urgently. Finally, she pulled away from him, nipples taut, panties moist. A cynical smile touched his lips. "You want rude, baby? You've got it!"

Breathlessly, she spoke, "Bjørn, you must be mad! Anyone could be waiting out there for the lavatory."

He chuckled softly. "I'm mad for *you*. When can we meet?"

"I don't know. I'll have to call you."

"Make it soon." One large hand reached under her hair to the back of her neck and then slid slowly down her shoulder and onto the swell of her left breast. A shudder ran through her. "I can't wait to hear all about your honeymoon." Then, as quickly as he'd entered the bathroom, he slipped out and was gone.

Trembling, Margit flushed the toilet and washed her hands again, gazing at herself in the mirror. Her face glowed from the encounter; her green eyes held a spark of excitement. She hoped no one would notice.

*   *   *

Leigh opened the door of the Georgetown art gallery and walked in. It was quiet inside. Only one other person stood in the elegant room—a rather dumpy-looking middle-aged man studying a painting of a little girl dressed in white. She looked around but didn't see anyone who might resemble the owner, Ward Radcliffe. Her attention moved to the paintings on the wall. Although she'd worked only as a freelance illustrator for years, she'd never lost her love for watercolors and charcoals. She'd always intended to concentrate on those media someday, but time had slipped away, and she'd never done it. Perhaps now was the time. If she made a decent salary working in the gallery, she might get the chance to branch out with her art. Assuming she got the job, of course.

"It's not *that* good, is it?" The voice behind her had a slight British accent.

Startled, Leigh turned to meet a pair of friendly brown eyes and an amused smile. It was the man who'd been eyeing the painting when she walked in. His salt-and-pepper hair suggested he was in his early fifties and a slight paunch under a burnt-orange sweater told her that here was a man who enjoyed his meals. But the most extraordinary thing about him was the warmth of his smile. It reached out and cloaked her in a blanket of goodwill. And she knew immediately who he was.

"The painting." He gestured toward a charcoal of a nude man holding a huge pumpkin in front of his crotch. "Personally, I hate that one, but the artist is a friend. And if you don't have friends, what's the use in living?"

Leigh smiled. "You're Ward Radcliffe, aren't you?"

His smile grew wider. "And you must be Leigh Fallon. Deanna told me you were drop-dead gorgeous, but I thought she was exaggerating. So, are you ready to start working for me?"

"Without an interview?"

Ward shrugged. "Deanna recommended you. That's enough for me. Can you start next week?"

Leigh felt like a character in one of Deanna's books. It

wasn't supposed to be this easy. She extended a hand to Ward. "I sure can. That gives me a chance to start looking for an apartment."

"No need." Ward enclosed her hand in his in a warm clasp. "Shall we say an apartment comes with the job? I have to charge a minimum rent, of course. Just to keep it legal. I own a brownstone a few blocks away, and one of my tenants just moved out. The question is . . . can you stomach me as your boss *and* your landlord?"

Leigh laughed. "Oh, I think I can." Unbelievable. She'd been talking to the man for only a moment, yet she felt as if she'd known him for years. Just like it had been when she'd first met Deanna. Instant friendship.

"Great. We close shortly, so if you'd like, we can walk over and take a look at the apartment." A thought seemed to occur to him. "Oh. Did Deanna mention I have a friend who lives with me? A male friend?"

Leigh couldn't control a blush. She'd completely forgotten Deanna had warned her Ward was gay. "Uh . . . well, yeah, she did say something . . . like that."

"I find it best to be up front about it. To use a well-worn cliche, Honesty is the best policy, I think." Ward peered at her, a speculative light in his brown eyes. "Egan and I have been together for years. No problem with that?"

"Of course not." Leigh said, shocked. "Mr. Radcliffe, your personal life is none of my business."

Ward smiled. "You'd be surprised how many people don't go along with your philosophy. And by the way, it's Ward, not Mr. Radcliffe." He smacked his palms together. "Okay. Shall we go take a look at your new apartment?"

Leigh turned around in the empty living room and tried to suppress a shout of pure delight. It was a dream apartment. Freshly buffed parquet floors sparkled beneath her feet. On the ceiling, heavy wooden beams lent a rustic flavor to the room and complemented a large stone fireplace that took up most of one wall. To the right of the fireplace, a window seat added to the charm, looking out onto a small rock garden. Across the room, varnished French doors opened onto a flagstone patio, and opposite them, burnished wooden stairs led to a bedroom loft overlooking the living room.

Off the hallway, a powder room done in blue ceramic tiles and pine was tucked into the nook under the stairs. As if that and the modern kitchen with oak cabinets and cinnamon-colored Mexican tile weren't enough, the apartment boasted a small "maid's room" in the back—perfect for the kids if they wanted to spend the night.

Leigh knew right away she had to have it; she couldn't believe how lucky she was to get it at such a ridiculously low rent. Once again, she had Deanna Harper to thank. Grandmother Kayleigh's grandfather clock would look perfect in that corner there. This weekend, she'd hire a rental truck and pick it up. She'd have to start shopping for furniture. She'd have to charge it, of course, and pay it off as the paychecks arrived.

"So, this will do?" Ward asked at her side.

Leigh felt like hugging him. But she didn't. Her smile said it all. "I think I can live with it."

Ward reached out and squeezed her hand. "Wonderful. Come on. Let's go upstairs. I want you to meet Egan. Now that we're neighbors, you have to come up for dinner."

"Tonight?" Leigh asked.

"Unless you have plans."

"Well, no, I don't, but Egan might not . . ."

"Oh, he loves guests. He likes to show off his cooking. He's a chef at Quillen Fein's Irish Pub. Luckily, it's his night off." As he spoke, he locked the door to the apartment and handed her the key. "It's all yours." He led the way up a flight of stairs. "We're just above you, so if you ever need anything, just bang on the ceiling."

A flutter of nervousness swept through Leigh as Ward unlocked the door to his apartment. She didn't quite know what to expect. How did male lovers act in front of company? They walked into a tastefully decorated apartment that had the same floor plan as hers. But instead of a patio, a balcony overlooked the tiny yard below. Ward grinned as he saw her glance out the French doors. "No nude sunbathing out in your backyard," he said. "Egan, we have company."

A slight, red-haired man in his mid-thirties stepped out of the kitchen. He wasn't anything like Leigh expected. Somehow, she'd imagined an effeminate man with a handlebar mustache wearing an apron and a chef's hat. Egan Allister looked like an ordinary young man; the only thing exceptional about him was his smile. It was so sweet that Leigh was immediately under his spell. And when he spoke, she was surprised by his thick Irish brogue.

"Ah, Durward. You've brought home another stray cat, have you, now?"

Durward? Leigh looked at Ward curiously.

He sighed. "For God's sake. He says that to annoy me. Yes, it's my true name, and he won't let me forget it."

"Ah, but you're a lovely colleen." Egan grinned at her. "What's your name, child?"

Leigh laughed. The man was younger by at least five years, yet, he called her child.

"This is Leigh Fallon, our new neighbor," Ward said. "And my new employee at the gallery."

"Fallon, is it? A good Irish name. Does me heart good."

Leigh smiled. "Well, I can't take credit for it, since it's my married name. But my maiden name *is* Connelly."

"Ah, even better! Some of me best friends are Connellys. Sit down, darlin'. Do you like Irish stew? It's a cold night out, and it'll warm up yer insides."

"Sounds wonderful," Leigh said. But she didn't think she needed any stew to warm her up. Egan and Ward had already done it. For the first time since she'd left Norway, she felt optimistic about the future.

After the last customer disappeared through the doorway of the gallery, Leigh glanced at her wristwatch. Thank God. It was almost closing time. She was looking forward to a long soak in the bathtub. For some reason, it had been especially busy since opening; she'd been on her feet most of the day. Had bonuses been handed out on Capitol Hill or something?

More paintings had been sold today than in her entire first week. When she'd mentioned it to Ward, he'd laughed.

"Yeah, that's how it is here. Feast or famine. It's all these Capitol Hill parties. One senator's wife sees a painting at another wife's party and decides she has to have something even better. It's all a frivolous game to them. After you've been here awhile, you'll be able to tell the difference between a pseudo and a true art lover. That's what I call the society people. *Pseudos.* God, I detest them."

Leigh smiled. Apparently, Deanna hadn't told him she'd once been a congressman's wife. That she'd experienced that kind of game-playing firsthand. Thank God, she was seeing it all from a new perspective these days. Just this morning, an elegant blonde had entered and without even glancing at Leigh, drew out her American Express Gold Card and said, "I want the most expensive painting you have. Have it sent around to my house at four o'clock." One of Ward's pseudos.

"You worked hard today," he said now. "Why don't you go ahead and take off early. I'll close up."

"That's okay," Leigh said. "I only have fifteen minutes to go."

The bell at the door tinkled, signaling a last-minute customer. Leigh resisted a sigh. She hoped this wasn't going to be one of those long drawn-out sales, or worse, a long drawn-out contemplation, and then no sale. A man of medium height with thinning brown hair walked toward her. He looked vaguely familiar, but then again, his face was rather ordinary. His blue eyes stared at her intently, and then he smiled. Leigh's eyes widened in recognition.

"Hello, Leigh Fallon," he said. "Remember me?"

Her heart thudded at his familiar Norwegian accent. "Yes. Your first name is Knut, but I can't quite remember the last name."

"Aabel. I'm pleased you remember me at all." He placed his hands in the pockets of his woolen overcoat and rocked back on his heels.

Leigh smiled, startled at how pleased she was to see him. "Well, we talked for an hour on the flight to Oslo."

"*Ja.* And I really enjoyed our conversation. When I returned to Washington, I'd rather hoped you'd call. I *did* give you my business card, didn't I?"

"Yes, you did but . . . it somehow got misplaced." Her eyes lowered. *Yeah, it had been misplaced, all right.* "I was disappointed because I really had planned to call."

Knut smiled wryly. "Well, you certainly are a hard woman to find. I had to employ a bit of detective work. First, I called that art gallery in SoHo where you told me you worked. They gave me a Deanna Harper's number, and she told me you'd moved back to Washington. At first, she was reluctant to tell me where I could find you, but then she suddenly changed her mind and gave me the address of this gallery."

It was the Norwegian accent, thought Leigh. She probably thought he was a friend of Erik's with a message. She became aware of Ward's eyes upon her and, remembering her manners, introduced the two men.

After they shook hands, Ward turned to her. "Go, Leigh. Take your friend out, and get him some dinner. I'll close up."

This time, Leigh didn't argue with him. She pulled on the blue fox jacket Erik had bought her in Norway, and together she and Knut stepped out into the frigid February evening.

23

It seemed only natural to invite Knut into her apartment. He took one look at the cold stone fireplace and asked if he could build a fire. Leigh smiled, ignoring the pang in her heart. Typical Norseman. Erik had always headed straight to the fireplace, too.

"How did you ever find such a great apartment?" Knut asked as he lit the match.

"Connections," Leigh said. "Ward owns the place. Are you hungry? I can heat up some leftover chili." She was rather embarrassed there weren't more choices to offer him. Her eating and cooking habits had changed drastically now that she lived on her own.

"I'd love some," Knut said.

In the small kitchen, Leigh put the chili in the microwave and reached up into the cabinet for soup bowls. All at once, she wasn't sure that seeing Knut was such a great idea. It was difficult enough to keep Erik out of her thoughts; with another Norwegian around to remind her of him, it would be impossible. Yet, she really liked him. On the flight to Oslo, he'd worked wonders in calming her down for the meeting with Erik. She opened the door of the microwave to give the chili a stir.

From their discussion on the plane, she knew they had a lot in common—love of the symphony, art galleries, and literature. Why not cultivate a friendship with him? It didn't have to be more. Lately, she'd found herself missing male companionship. And it wasn't just the sex. Somehow, she knew she'd never again have a sexual relationship like she'd shared with Erik. But there was a need in her just to have a male voice around . . . a warm smile and an affectionate touch. Someone to talk to, relax with. Of course, she had that to some extent with Ward and Egan. They had been wonderful . . . inviting her up to eat with them and sometimes to play trivia games— which she always lost because they were so damn intellectual. But Ward and Egan's company didn't quite fill the void.

All in all, she was glad Knut had shown up tonight. She guessed his age to be around the mid-forties. His blue eyes were covered by tortoiseshell glasses that gave him a distinguished professorial look, but it was his smile that really took away his mediocrity. His teeth were white and straight, attractive enough for a toothpaste commercial.

Leigh placed the steaming bowls of chili onto a tray and carried it into the living room; it would be more informal to eat in front of the fire. Knut was on the floor, perusing her compact-disc collection.

He looked up and grinned. "I see you're a well-rounded woman. Classical, country, jazz, rhythm and blues. Even some rock. Where's the hip-hop and heavy-metal?"

Leigh set the tray on the coffee table and shrugged. "I guess I'm not *that* well-rounded. What would you like to drink? Beer, wine, or a soft drink?"

"I suppose it would be rude of me to ask if you brought any aquavit back from Norway?"

Leigh shook her head. "Not rude, at all. But sorry to disappoint you. I don't have any. To be honest, I wasn't real taken with the stuff. But it did do wonders in taking away a cough."

Knut grinned. "If you drink enough of it, it'll pretty much cure anything. Or at the very least, make you forget you've got something that needs curing. But since you don't have any, I'll have a beer."

Leigh turned back to the kitchen. "Why don't you go ahead and pick out some music. I'll be right back."

When she returned to the living room with two Killians, Handel's *Water Music* was playing. Knut ate heartily, praising her chili as if he hadn't had anything so good in years. Leigh knew better, but thanked him anyway. Afterwards, he leaned back against the sofa and sighed contentedly.

"Nothing like a hot dinner on a cold night," he said. "I'm afraid I'm rather inept at cooking. I eat most of my meals out at this little café near my flat. It's not great, but it's better than sandwiches."

"I'll have you over for a real dinner sometime," said Leigh, surprising herself. "That is, if I can remember how to cook one. It's been a long time since I had someone to cook for."

"How long have you been divorced?" He rummaged in the pocket of his jacket and pulled out a pipe. "Do you mind if I smoke?"

"Go ahead. It's been six months, but it seems longer."

"And you told me you have children, *ja*?"

"Three. Mark, Melissa, and Aaron. They live with their father."

He raised an eyebrow at that, but made no comment.

"I moved back here to try to patch things up with them. It was pretty bitter for a while." No need to get into the reason why. "They're having a hard time adjusting to the divorce."

"*Ja.* It's tough. My Kristin would barely speak to me the first time I returned to Tromsø after the divorce. You know, no matter how fair the parent with custody tries to be, the child always seems to be bitter toward the other one. But it passes with time." His eyes were warm with understanding.

"I hope you're right."

A brief silence fell. The sweet cherry smoke from Knut's pipe mingled with the scent of the wood-burning fireplace. Leigh found that she liked the smell. It felt homey. Outside, through the French windows, hidden floodlights illuminated a light snow that had begun to fall.

Snow. She should hate it . . . with all the memories of Erik it evoked. Still, it never failed to give her a cozy feeling of security. Even during the violent blizzard at the cabin, she'd felt cocooned against the reality of the outside world.

"I hope you don't have to drive far. It's starting to snow."

Knut looked at her, amused. "You're talking to someone who used to live above the arctic circle."

"Sorry. I forgot." She searched for a topic to cover her faux pas. Her eyes fastened upon his pipe. "You were sitting in nonsmoking on the flight!"

Knut ruefully glanced at his pipe. "*Ja*, I was, wasn't I? I'm afraid I started again after my visit home. I hadn't smoked for over a year. But . . ." He shrugged. "Something snapped while I was home . . ."

"I guess it's a pretty stressful situation," Leigh said. "How is it between you and your wife? Oh, I'm sorry if that's too personal."

"Not at all. As a matter of fact, Sigurd and I get along much better now than we did when we were married. Obviously, she's very happy back in her own country." He paused for a moment, seemingly lost in thought. "I suppose I was wrong in trying to make her adopt America. Just because I love it here doesn't mean it's right for everyone. I should've realized how strongly she felt about going back to Norway."

"But would you be happy if you'd gone back with her?" Leigh asked.

"I don't know. That's the trouble with life, isn't it? You

never know if you've made the right or wrong decision until it's in the past. Sometimes, even then you don't know."

"But it's not necessarily too late, is it? I mean, you could still go back to Norway. Try to make a go of it with your wife."

Knut shook his head. "Sigurd is dating someone else. A widowed farmer who lives outside the village. She seems content with him. No, it's not possible to go back."

Leigh drew her legs up under her and turned toward him. "What about you? Have you dated much since the divorce?"

He shook his head. "Actually, Leigh, I haven't dated at all. I guess I'm too particular. To be perfectly honest, until I met you on the flight to Oslo, I just wasn't interested. But I enjoyed our conversation so much, and it made me realize how much I'd missed having that kind of stimulating exchange with a woman. That's one thing Sigurd and I always shared. Of course, we rarely agreed upon anything, but that was part of the fun."

He still loves his wife, Leigh thought. Why were people so stupid, not to be able to see what stared them in the face? And she was one of them. Believing she and Erik could make a life together. It was all so clear now, how impossible that dream had been.

"So, what about you?" Knut asked. "I seem to recall you were on your way to Norway to visit a lucky man."

Leigh stiffened, and couldn't find her voice.

"Now, I'm being too personal. I'm sorry."

"No, it's okay," Leigh said. "It just didn't work out with him. And I'm still a little too close to the situation to be able to talk about it."

"I understand. So, you're not seeing anyone right now?"

Leigh shook her head. "Just you. I mean . . ." She grimaced at her bluntness. "If you want to, I'd like to see you again."

Knut flashed a delighted smile. "You don't have to ask. What about tomorrow night? Dinner here in Georgetown? You can pick the place."

"It's a deal." Leigh returned his smile. "I know a great place a couple of blocks over. We can walk."

Knut stood up. "Well, speaking of walking, I'd better get going."

At the door, he paused before going out. "You know, I was really nervous about coming into the gallery to see you. It's been a long time since I've had to . . . well, do anything of this sort. Now, after spending some time with you, I don't know why I was so nervous. You're just as easy to be with as I remembered."

"Thank you. So are you." Leigh impulsively reached out and squeezed his hand. "I'm glad you *did* stop in, Knut."

"See you tomorrow night. Is seven o'clock all right?"

She watched him as he jogged down the steps of the brownstone and disappeared into the snowy night. After closing the door, she turned and walked back into the living room. She sat down in front of the hearth and stared into the flickering fire. Another Norwegian. Was she *insane*? How was she ever going to get rid of the memory of Erik with Knut around? Then, another disquieting thought occurred to her. Was that *why* she wanted to see Knut again? Because he reminded her of Erik?

Erik pulled into the parking lot of Margit's apartment building. He sat in the Volkswagen a moment and gazed at the snowflakes falling softly on the windshield. With the engine off, the cold seeped into the car, gnawing at him. He knew he couldn't sit here much longer. He had to go in and face Margit. They hadn't been married a month yet, and already, he felt as if his life had fallen into a monotonous rut. The thought that he would face this same scenario every day for the rest of his life made him want to scream out in frustration. Dordei had been right. He'd made an awful mistake in marrying Margit. It wasn't worth it. Not even for Gunny.

The cold finally forced him to get out and trudge up the icy stairs to Margit's flat. He couldn't think of it as his. Her personality was written all over it, starting with the beige sofa topped with salmon-colored throw pillows and ending with the pale pastel watercolors on the beige walls. Immaculate. Sterile. Erik wondered how she managed to keep everything so perfect with an active child around. Even the glass-covered accent tables were unsmudged by tiny fingerprints.

When he walked in, Gunny ran toward him and wrapped his arms around Erik's legs. Chuckling, Erik swung the little boy into his arms and hugged him. As Gunny snuggled against him Erik smiled. Thank God for him—the only good thing in his life right now. In the few weeks since he'd moved in, the little boy had grown very close to him. Yet, he still refused to call him father. Insignificant, perhaps, but it bothered Erik.

"Where's your mom?" he asked, ruffling Gunny's reddish-blond curls.

"The kitchen!"

With its cabinets of pine and gleaming copper pots and woven baskets hanging from the wood beams on the ceiling, the kitchen was the only room in the entire apartment Erik truly liked. Margit stood at the vintage-style stove frying *lefse*, the Norwegian version of potato pancakes. At their enticing scent, Erik's stomach growled in anticipation. Another good thing— Margit was a great cook. She heard him and turned, a smile on her lightly freckled face. "Hello, darling. Did you get everything straightened out at the university?"

"Yeah." Erik dropped his portfolio on the kitchen table and went to the counter to pour himself a cup of coffee. He glanced back at her. "Oh, I dropped in at the center to take you out to lunch, but you were already gone."

An odd look flickered in her eyes. She turned back to the *lefse* and deftly flipped one over. "You did? No one mentioned it to me."

"Well, I had a couple of hours to kill before my appointment with Dr. Stalsett. Where did you go for lunch? I walked over to those fast-food places close to the center. Thought you might be there."

Margit studied the browning pancakes intently. "Oh, one of the other girls wanted me to try this new restaurant over on Sorkedalsveien."

"How was it?"

"Not bad. Rather expensive, actually."

"Too bad I didn't get there earlier. I could've gone with you."

Margit moved the *lefse* to a warming platter and began frying sausage. "Perhaps next time. So, did you have a good conversation with Dr. Stalsett? Did he have any suggestions about your thesis?"

"Not exactly," Erik said quietly. "I've decided to quit."

Margit turned and stared at him. "You're not serious?"

He nodded. "It's time for me to give up this idea of becoming a psychologist. I have you and Gunny to support now, and I can't do that and work on my thesis at the same time."

"Erik! I won't allow you to quit. You've put too many years into it to just give up now!"

"I've already made my decision," Erik said. "I'm going to find a job in construction. Perhaps I can get one with the shipbuilders."

Margit stared at him, eyes wide with shock. "It's winter! What do you think you'll find in construction now? Erik! We can live on my earnings until you finish."

"That could take years." Erik stood up and threw the remainder of his coffee down the drain. It suddenly tasted bitter. "And don't worry about money. I'll find something."

"Don't worry about it?" Margit's face contorted. He'd never seen her so angry. "I didn't marry a construction worker! You have a brilliant mind. You can't waste yourself in a menial job like that. I won't let you!"

Erik's lips tightened. "It's my decision, Margit. Let's just drop it."

"No, I won't! What kind of life can you give us if you're just a construction worker? As a psychologist, you would be respected, important . . . like Bjørn! How can you do this to us?"

Fury swept over him, and he didn't try to contain it. "*How can I do this to you?* What about what you've done to me, eh? Does that mean anything to you at all? Christ, it's no wonder Gunvor chose to go up to the North Sea. Perhaps *I* should try to find a job there."

Margit's face paled. When she spoke, her voice was very quiet. "What have I done to you?"

Erik stared at her silently. Gunny walked into the room, blue eyes huge. "Uncle Erik, are you angry at Mama?"

He shook his head, already ashamed of himself. Margit still hadn't regained her color. He felt like the worst kind of scoundrel. God, it wasn't her fault he wasn't happy. Slowly, he went to her and wrapped his arms around her. "I'm sorry, darling. I don't know what's wrong with me. I've been in a rotten mood all day."

She snuggled against him, trembling. After a moment, she drew away and looked up at him, eyes swimming with tears. "Oh, Erik. That's the first time you've ever called me *darling*. Could it be you're starting to fall in love with me?"

He tried, but couldn't look into her eyes. Instead, he pulled her head against his chest and caressed her reddish-gold braid. "You could be right," he lied. He wished it were true. She was so alive and warm in his arms. And it was obvious she loved him. He would simply have to try harder.

That night, Erik made love to Margit with an abandon that had been missing in the first weeks of their marriage. Once again, he'd grasped at the image of Kayleigh to shut out the reality of Margit beneath his hungry body. He'd come to the conclusion that if it worked, he'd do it. At least Margit wasn't left unsatisfied. And neither was he. It was only afterward when his senses had returned to normal that he felt the familiar letdown. Again, he vowed silently that their marriage wasn't going to work, that he had to escape this marital prison. Of course, only seconds later, he knew it was impossible. He was in this marriage for the duration, and his only choice was to try to make the best of it. If he could just forget Kayleigh, he knew he could force himself to be happy with Margit.

24

"The birthday boy is here! Do you have a big kiss for your grandmother?"

Gunny reached up to give Grethe a kiss and then scampered off to join his cousins in the living room. She shook her white head and smiled at Erik and Margit. "It's hard to believe he's three today, isn't it?"

Margit sighed. "I don't believe he's left behind the terrible twos. He's been such a handful lately. Is everyone else here?"

"Everyone except Bjørn. He was called out on an emergency at the hospital."

Erik leaned down to kiss his mother's cheek. "Hello, Mother. I hear you have a bad cold."

"It's nothing!" She sniffed and stared at him disapprovingly. "Margit tells me you've quit working on your thesis and you're looking for a construction job."

Erik held in a sigh. "Yes, but I don't really wish to discuss it."

Margit and Grethe seemed to exchange a silent message, and then Grethe said briskly, "Well, go on in the family room and I'll bring in Gunny's cake."

Later, as the family sat chatting in front of the fireplace, Mags brought Erik a glass of aquavit and sat down next to him. *"Skal,"* his younger brother said, and raised his glass.

Erik joined him, and both of them swallowed the burning liquor. Grimacing, Erik shook his head and then grinned. "You should go easy on the aquavit, Mags. I don't think your coach would approve."

Mags laughed. "I *know* he wouldn't. But it's Gunny's birthday."

Erik looked at him closely. "You're awfully pleased with yourself about something. What is it?"

"I talked to the coach this morning. He thinks I'm his best prospect to make the Olympic team."

"All right!" Erik threw his arm around his brother, giving his shoulder a good squeeze. "Just think, this time next year, we may all be in Albertville rooting you on."

"Do you think the entire family will come to watch me?" Mags asked.

"You can count on it, Magpie." Unconsciously, he'd slipped back to Mag's childhood nickname. "We'll be the proudest family in Norway!"

"Even if I don't bring home a medal?"

"Just participating in the Olympics will be enough." Across the room, he saw Margit sit down next to Hakon and begin a conversation. "I'll let you in on a secret. I always dreamed of competing in the cross-country races, but of course, that's all it was. A dream. But you are going for yours. I admire that. It takes a lot of guts."

"And stamina," Mags grinned. "And training. And giving up sex. That's the toughest part."

Playfully, Erik punched his rock-hard shoulder. "You shouldn't even be *thinking* about sex."

"You're a good one to talk. After what I've heard about you."

Erik laughed. "What have you heard?"

"Only that you had something pretty hot going with that American woman—Kayleigh—was that her name?"

Erik's smile froze. "Where did you hear that?"

Mags looked at him closely. "Hey, Erik . . . calm down. Bjørn mentioned it one night when he had a little too much to drink. It was just between the two of us."

How did Bjørn know about Kayleigh?

Erik swallowed his shock and said, "Well, Bjørn had it wrong. At least, his idea of it was wrong. I was in love with Kayleigh, Mags. There's a big difference there. I wanted to marry her."

Mags's blue eyes widened. "Christ, Erik, I'm sorry." He glanced over at Margit. "Then, why—"

Erik shook his head. "It's too complicated, Magpie. Just too fucking complicated."

Hakon's laugh rang out in the room and Erik glanced over.

Apparently, Mags wasn't the only one whose mind was on sex. Hakon was leering into Margit's face, and one of his hands rested lightly on her knee. Erik was stunned to feel an emotion very similar to jealousy wash over him. Why? He didn't love Margit. Yet, she was still his wife.

Margit laughed, pretending to be affronted by Hakon's actions. Deliberately, she removed his hand from her knee, saying, "Hakon Fenstad, you are an incurable flirt!"

Flirting? Erik thought it wasn't quite that innocent. He recognized the look of lust on his brother-in-law's face. And he didn't like it one bit. It had only been two months ago that Erik had felt indifference at the thought of strangers approaching Margit on the Greek island. What had changed?

Dordei moved over to him. "Would you like some cake, Erik?"

His eyes remained fastened on Margit and Hakon. "Can't you do something about him, Dordei?"

She followed his gaze. "What do you suggest?"

"I suppose castration would be a bit much." It was meant to be a joke, but his voice came out humorless.

"You don't need to worry about Margit. She's totally captivated by you."

"Is that so? Look at her!"

Margit was laughing and wiping a cake crumb from the corner of Hakon's mouth.

"And what *is* it with him?" Erik went on. "The way he's dressed! Doesn't he make enough money at that travel agency to afford a decent pair of jeans?"

Dordei gave a wry laugh. "He purposely ripped the knees of his jeans so he could imitate the rock stars. I told him it was absurd, but of course, he never listens to me."

Another peal of laughter rang out from Margit. Erik decided he'd had enough. "Excuse me, Dordei." He got up and strode over to his wife and brother-in-law. "What the hell happened to you, Hakon? Did you take a fall on the ice?" He squeezed onto the sofa next to his wife and placed his arm around her.

"What are you talking about?" Hakon asked, blue eyes puzzled as he grudgingly moved over to the end of the sofa.

"Your jeans. That must've been one hell of a fall."

Hakon's face turned beet red. "I didn't fall, Erik. Apparently, you don't know this happens to be the latest look. Ragtag is in."

Erik chuckled and caressed Margit's arm. "Christ! I feel hopelessly out of fashion, don't you, Margit? And sitting next to such a trendsetter."

She giggled and hit his thigh. "Erik! Don't be rude!"

But his gibe had hit the mark. Hakon stiffly excused himself and moved over to the bar to join his father-in-law in another glass of aquavit.

"Now," Erik said firmly. "Tell me what Hakon was saying that you found so amusing."

Margit looked at him, blue eyes wide and innocent. "Why, Erik! Are you jealous of Hakon?"

"Of course not. I'm just wondering what was so funny."

But he spoke quickly and didn't meet her eyes.

Leigh unlocked the door to her apartment and Knut followed her in, carrying a large pizza box. "Here. I'll take the pizza, and you can start a fire," she said, tossing her purse onto the sofa. "Damn! I missed." The purse fell onto the floor, spilling its contents over the blue and beige Oriental rug.

Knut bent down to help. "See what you get when you starve yourself all day? You lose brain cells and it makes you uncoordinated."

Leigh laughed. Knut had been teasing her all evening about not being able to get away from the gallery for lunch. "I'll take care of that mess later. Right now, I'll get some drinks so we can eat."

Knut was already putting everything back in her bag. "I've got it. Say, what's this? You never told me that Leigh is a nickname."

He was staring down at her checkbook.

"Kayleigh. What a lovely name."

The skin on her face tightened as if it were wet leather that had been left out in the Arizona sun for two days. She knew her voice was strained when she spoke. "I don't go by it. It's strictly my legal name."

"Kayleigh," he said softly, as if trying it out. "It suits you. May I—?"

"No," she said. "I prefer being called Leigh." Then, realizing how cold she sounded, she smiled. "Hey, how about that fire?"

She went into the kitchen to get the drinks, mentally kicking herself for her curtness. She hadn't meant to snap at him. It was just that she couldn't bear hearing another Norwegian voice saying her name. Or *any* voice, for that matter. No one else but her grandmother had ever called her by Kayleigh . . . until Erik. And much as she liked Knut, she didn't want him to use the name Erik had made so special.

She'd been seeing Knut for over two months. Every few days, he'd call up, and they'd go out or he'd come over. She'd been to his apartment only once; it had been rather drab and messy, a striking contrast to his neat personality. Usually, they dined at one of Georgetown's many small tucked-away restaurants, then they'd take in a movie or sometimes a play at the Arena Stage or the Wooly Mammoth. Their tastes were really quite similar; they both enjoyed romantic dramas and light comedies. Sometimes, they went to the Kennedy Center to listen to the National Symphony Orchestra, but Leigh always found it a bittersweet experience. She couldn't help but think about the one special night she'd spent there with Erik.

Despite her obsessive memories, Leigh found herself enjoying her evenings with Knut. He was so easy to talk to. Already, he knew most of her life story . . . everything except the cause of the divorce. He believed it was the result of mutual dissatisfaction and Bob's obsession with work on the Hill.

After they'd finished the pizza, Knut made himself comfortable on the sofa and lit his pipe. Leigh began to gather up the paper plates and glasses, but he patted the sofa cushion and said, "Come and relax. We can take care of that later." He placed a casual arm around her shoulders and inhaled on his pipe. "I received a letter from Kristin today."

"Oh, how is she?" Leigh asked. He was always delighted

to hear from his daughter and eager to share the news.

"She's doing okay. It seems Sigurd has taken a job at a hospital in Oslo. She's a registered nurse, you know. They'll be moving there in a couple of months. Kristin is rather sad about leaving her friends."

Leigh caught the wistful note in his voice. "Every time you mention Kristin"—*or Sigurd,* she thought wryly—"you sound a bit homesick. Do you think you'll ever go back?"

"I might. In a few years, perhaps. But right now, I have too much on my mind to think about returning to Norway." He squeezed her shoulder affectionately. "You, for instance."

"Oh, am I on your mind a lot?" Her tone was light and amused.

He gazed at her, his expression serious. "You'll never know how much." His hand tightened on her shoulder. He leaned toward her, his eyes on her mouth.

Their first kiss was warm and gentle. Although she felt no real physical stirring, Leigh enjoyed it. After a moment, she pulled away and touched his right cheekbone. "You are such a lovely man," she whispered.

A wry smile came to his lips. "I'm not sure I take that as a compliment."

"It is," she said, and then, placing her hands around his neck, she drew his head to hers for another kiss. This one, longer and more passionate. Leigh felt a flicker of desire. Knut pulled away, breathing heavily, his blue eyes stormy. Leigh smiled. She knew he wanted her. Had known it for weeks, but he'd never made a move. Now, she knew why. No doubt, it had been a long time since he'd been to bed with a woman. He was feeling shy.

Leigh's hands moved down the front of his woolen sweater, pressing against the hard muscles of his chest. She knew he kept in good shape with racquetball two or three times a week, and jogging every morning. His thighs were built up by the Norwegian answer to bicycling: cross-country skiing. Whenever he could, he went to Canaan Valley in West Virginia for the sport. All in all, Knut Aabel was quite an attractive man.

Her fingers toyed with the bottom edge of his sweater, and then she began to lift it.

"What are you doing?" he asked huskily.

"Don't you think it's too hot in here?"

"A bit." Quickly, he pulled the sweater over his head. Immediately, Leigh unbuttoned his shirt. She leaned toward him and nuzzled the hollow of his throat just above his T-shirt. "Ah . . . Leigh . . . ," he said huskily. ". . . We shouldn't be doing this . . . right now. I mean . . . I don't quite think this is the . . . right time . . ."

She pulled away and studied him. His eyes were closed, and his expression belied his words. Besides, the thick bulge in the crotch of his gabardine slacks hadn't escaped her notice. "What's wrong with now?"

He opened his eyes and slowly, his face reddened. "Why—I don't know. We really haven't . . . been seeing each other very long and . . . ah . . . well, I'm just thinking of you . . . and . . . ah . . ." His voice drained away, and he looked totally perplexed, as if he had no idea what he was saying. Leigh stared at him, baffled.

A knock came at the door. With an obvious look of relief, Knut began to button his shirt. Still puzzled, Leigh scrambled up from the sofa. Had she misunderstood him? she wondered. Maybe he didn't want more than friendship. Another horrible thought occurred to her. What if he was like Egan and Ward? Maybe friendship was all he wanted from *any* woman.

As if her thoughts had conjured him, Leigh opened the door to see Ward standing in the corridor, grinning like a fat cat who'd sneaked into the whipping cream. "Hello, Leigh! Hope I'm not interrupting anything important. We were wondering if you could do a favor for Egan?" He turned to glance over his shoulder. "Egan! Come along!"

"Sure, Ward. What does he need?"

"Just a minute, dear. He'll be right here." Another look behind him. "Egan! We're waiting!"

Leigh looked over at Knut and sighed. He grinned back at her, his eyes twinkling. From the hallway, she heard the sound of an Irish accent singing an all too familiar song. "Oh, no . . . ," she whispered.

Egan marched into the room carrying a large decorated birthday cake lit with God knew how many candles. "Happy birthday, dear Leigh. Happy birthday to you!" As the last notes of the song died away, Knut threw his arm around Leigh's shoulder and kissed her cheek as Ward applauded happily.

"Surprised, were you?" Knut whispered.

She eyed him. "So, that's why you were so—"

He laughed and looked at Ward. "It's a good thing you got here when you did. I almost had to tell her the truth. She wanted to go . . . somewhere. In fact, she was being most insistent."

Leigh nudged him sharply with her elbow and turned to the grinning Ward. "How did you know it was my birthday?"

"Silly question. All your employment papers, of course. Oh, Egan, I left the champagne out in the hall. Would you mind getting it?"

"But you didn't say a thing all day!" Leigh said.

"Well, I talked it over with Knut last week, and we decided to surprise you. Oh, here's the champagne! Nicely chilled. How about some glasses so we can toast the birthday girl?"

After they'd finished the toast, Leigh prepared to cut the cake. "Did you make this, Egan? It's too beautiful to cut."

"I surely did. With me own two hands. It's chocolate. I heard from the grapevine it was your favorite."

"Well, you heard right. God, so many candles!" She began to pull them out.

"Only twenty."

Leigh chuckled. "I *wish*." Yet, this birthday didn't seem at all traumatic like last year's. Turning forty hadn't been pleasant; it had further reminded her of the disparity in age between herself and Erik.

As they sat eating the cake, she looked around and marveled at what good people they were, and she felt grateful for their company. She hadn't heard from the kids today. Not one of them had called to wish her happy birthday. Work and Knut's presence had combined to make her forget about their insensitivity, but now she felt a little sad. She'd been so sure they were starting to get along better.

After the remains of the cake were cleared away, Egan suggested they play a game of Trivial Pursuit. "Unless, of course, you two would be wanting to be alone?"

Leigh and Knut looked at each other and burst out laughing. Ward and Egan stared as if they'd missed something. Finally, Leigh spoke, "Trivial Pursuit sounds great—even *if* you two have a monopoly on winning."

Egan stood up. "I'll go up and get the game."

But just as he reached the door, there was a knock. "Oh, wonderful! There'll be more of us to play. Oh, who might you be?"

In the living room, Leigh heard a voice that made the hair rise on her arms. "I'm Leigh's ex-husband. And who are you?" She exchanged a worried glance with Knut and stood.

Bob walked into the living room. His eyes swept casually over Ward and Knut and then around the elegant room. "Nice place," he said. "You've certainly come up in the world, Leigh. Who're your friends?"

She introduced everyone in a stiffly controlled voice. Bob made no move to shake their hands. An uncomfortable silence fell, then Egan spoke, "Ward, I'm thinking maybe we should get going. Leigh, happy birthday."

Leigh kissed Egan on the cheek. "Thanks for the cake. It was so sweet of you."

Ward stood up and hugged Leigh. "Happy birthday, darling. I'll see you at work early Monday morning."

Leigh walked them to the door and returned to the living room to find Bob and Knut eyeing each other. She wondered if they'd exchanged any conversation while she was gone.

"Leigh, I need to talk to you," Bob said. Pointedly, he glanced at Knut. "Privately."

Knut didn't move. One eyebrow rose as he looked at Leigh. "Do you want me to go, Leigh?"

An odd expression flashed across Bob's face as his eyes zeroed in on Knut. "Where are you from?"

Knut's lips quirked in an ironic smile. "I live here in Georgetown. But I'm a Norwegian citizen."

Bob glared at Leigh. "Oh, did she bring you home with her?"

With typical Nordic composure, Knut ignored the rude question. "Leigh? Shall I stay?"

"I think maybe you should go," she said. "I'll walk you to the door." Knut's presence would only exacerbate Bob's obviously foul mood.

But she could tell he was hesitant to leave. At the door, he searched her face, his eyes clearly worried. "Are you certain you'll be okay with him?"

She nodded. "Don't worry about me. I can handle Bob." She leaned against him and planted a kiss on his lips. "I'm sorry about this. I was looking forward to spending some time alone with you."

"Me, too. Oh, and Leigh? Just so you know. I wasn't at all unenthusiastic this evening—you know, before Ward came to the door. I don't want you to think I didn't want to—"

"I know." She kissed him again. "We're going hiking tomorrow, right?"

"Right. Oh, here." He pressed a small wrapped box into her hands. "I was waiting to give it to you when we were alone. You can open it later."

"I'll open it now," Leigh said. "Let him wait." She drew off the wrapping paper and opened the hinged box. "Oh, Knut!" It was a necklace she'd admired in a jewelry store window, a gold dolphin with a diamond chip eye. She gave him a radiant smile. "I love it! Will you put it on for me?"

His fingers were warm against her neck as he fastened the delicate chain. He bent down and kissed her just above where it rested against her skin. "I should go. That is, if you're sure?" His apprehensive eyes moved toward the living room.

With a gentle push, she said, "Go! I'll be fine." She touched the necklace. "And thank you, Knut." With a final kiss, he went out the door. Leigh's tender smile disappeared as she closed the door behind him.

Bob had poured himself a glass of chilled champagne and

was ensconced in an easy chair, appearing perfectly at ease. He looked up and grinned sardonically. "Well, I was beginning to think you'd left, too." He looked around at the living room. "So. You're doing pretty well. Nice place in Georgetown. Good job. Three boyfriends. Not bad at all."

"Ward and Egan are not my boyfriends. As a matter of fact, they aren't at all interested in me like that."

"Oh, but the Norwegian is, right? What *is* it with you and Norwegians? Do they hold some special power over you?" He drained his glass. "Or are they just good in bed?"

Leigh sat down on the sofa and tried to control her anger. "What is it you wanted to see me about?"

A speculative look appeared in his eyes. He got up from the chair and moved to the sofa. "It's your birthday, isn't it? I wanted to let you know I hadn't forgotten."

Leigh stiffened at his closeness. "Bob, don't play games with me."

"I'm not." He tried to look innocent, but failed. As he leaned toward her, Leigh caught a whiff of liquor, and she was sure it wasn't from the champagne he'd just consumed. Now that she looked at him closely, she saw his eyes were bleary as if he'd been drinking for hours. That was unusual; Bob had never been much of a drinker, even at parties; he was always too involved in buttering up his constituents. Leigh decided not to mention it. With any luck, he wouldn't stay long. "Actually, I wanted to talk to you about Melissa."

"What about her? I was wondering why I hadn't heard from her today. I thought she'd at least call on my birthday."

Bob shrugged. "Oh, she's probably too busy. That girl's social calendar must rival Princess Di's. She's never at home anymore. Always out with some boy. Every week, it's a new one."

"That doesn't sound good. Why so many different ones?"

"How am I supposed to know? I thought maybe you could talk to her."

Leigh sighed. "I'd love to. Only problem is . . . she's not exactly buddy-buddy with me these days. But I guess I should consider myself lucky that she talks to me at all." She regretted the words as soon as she'd uttered them. Bob would have a field day with the remark. Incredibly though, he just shrugged and drained his flute of champagne. Leigh felt her stomach tense. He was really worried about Melissa! "What, exactly, do you think is going on with her, Bob?"

His answer was abrupt. "I think she's screwing them. *All* of them."

Leigh was shocked. "No way. Melissa isn't like that."

"She's changed, Leigh. Almost overnight since she found out about you and that Norwegian."

"Oh, so now it's *my* fault our daughter is sleeping around?" Leigh stood. "First of all, I don't believe Mel is doing it. And second, why would our divorce drive her to that? Bob, I think you'd better go home and sleep it off. You're going to have one hell of a hangover tomorrow."

He stood, smiling lazily. "Well, like they say, like mother, like daughter."

Fury coursed through Leigh's veins. "I've had it up to *here* with your vulgar digs. Yes, I behaved less than honorably while we were married, only because someone came into my life who treated me like a person, not a . . . a decorative object or a live-in housekeeper. But I paid for that weakness with the loss of my kids. I'm only now beginning to win back Melissa and Aaron. Mark *still* won't have anything to do with me. And I wonder, why? Because you're constantly belittling me? You won't let him forget, will you, Bob?" She stopped and tried to regain control of her temper. When she spoke again, her voice was icy. "You should count yourself lucky I'm not so vindictive that I'd tell the kids the truth about you and your little AA."

His face whitened. "What the hell are you talking about?"

Leigh gazed at him, a smile of satisfaction on her lips. If she'd ever had doubts before, she had none now. His expression was proof enough she'd been right all along. She stood and faced him.

"I know about you and Rebecca D'Andrade. I'll bet you didn't have any trouble getting it up with *her*, did you? I don't know how long you were screwing her during our marriage, and I don't care anymore. But I'm *not* going to stand here and watch you play the innocent wronged husband another second. The curtain is down, Bob. Why don't you take your bows and get the hell out of here!"

It was amazing how fast he recovered. The color had returned to his face, along with a sardonic smile. "Not quite yet. It's over with Becky. Senator Osborne made her an offer she couldn't resist, and she moved on. And babe, I'm a lonely man." Deliberately, he moved against her. "If you give out to every Norwegian you meet, why not me? After all, it's not as if we're strangers." His hands tightened on her arms, and he wrenched her to him. Leigh twisted out of his grasp and slapped him hard.

It was the last thing she remembered. A moment later, she lay prone on the floor, a crushing pain in her jaw and exploding fireworks in front of her eyes. Then, through ringing ears, she heard his disdainful voice.

"You slut."

25

With a brisk gait, Leigh walked through the entrance of the Rayburn Building, placed her purse on the conveyer belt of the X-ray machine and passed through the metal detector. Grabbing her purse, she strode to the elevators and pushed the button. On the fourth floor, she stepped out and swept down the hallway, passing one massive wooden door after another, each emblazoned with a state seal. Indiana. Georgia. Texas. And finally, Ohio. She went in.

An attractive blond receptionist looked up and smiled. "May I help you?"

Ignoring her, Leigh headed for Bob's office.

"Wait a minute, miss. The congressman is in a me—"

She opened the door and walked in.

Bob sat at his desk in front of a huge window looking out onto the Capitol Building, a phone to his ear. Leigh stared at him. He looked up and lifted a finger indicating he'd be only a moment, looking all the world as if her appearance in his office wasn't a bit out of the ordinary. Disgust welled in her. It was as if nothing had ever happened. As if he were an ordinary decent human being instead of a contemptible piece of shit.

"Of course, Mr. Dole," he said meekly. "I'll get right on it. Thank you, sir. Good-bye."

The receptionist appeared behind Leigh's shoulder. "Congressman, I'm sorry. She just—"

"It's okay, Susie."

Deliberately, Leigh closed the door in the pretty blonde's face, wondering if she was Rebecca's successor.

Bob stood up and moved toward her, his face a mask of concern. "What can I do for you, Leigh?"

"Cut the crap," she said icily. "I have just one thing to say to you. I don't want you to ever come near me again. The only time I ever want to see your face is when I come to pick up Melissa and Aaron." Catching herself, she stopped. "No. Not even then. Just make yourself scarce when I come over. And remember this: If you *ever* touch me again, I'll have you arrested for assault and battery."

"Leigh." Bob put on an innocent face. "What are you talking about? Assault? Look, I don't know what happened the other night when I came over. I'd had one too many, and my memory is a little dim."

"Liar," Leigh said. "You know *exactly* what happened. And you should count yourself lucky I didn't call the cops on you then. Or better yet, the *Washington Post*." She had the satisfaction of seeing his eyes pop in genuine alarm. "What do you think *that* would've done to your pristine reputation on the Hill? You'd better take me seriously on this. There won't be any more warnings."

He moved toward her. "Come on, babe. I tell you, I was drunk! I didn't mean to hurt you." He reached out a hand to touch her bruised jaw.

She flinched. *"Don't!"*

Bob's hand fell to his side. "Okay. Just let me tell you why

I really came over Friday night." His brown eyes pleaded with her. "This kills me to admit it, babe, but I want you back. I'm ready to forgive you for what you did to me." He took a deep breath and went on, "And you have to forgive me, too. About Becky. I swear, she didn't mean a thing to me. You're the only woman I've ever loved. Come home, Leigh. The kids need you, and so do I. We'll be a real family this time."

Leigh stared at him, disgust rising in her throat like bile. "You revolt me," she said. "And you have for a long time. Even before Erik entered the picture."

She whirled around and left his office, walking past the mystified secretary. Knut was waiting in the reception room.

"I know you told me to wait outside, but I couldn't. I was afraid for you." His fingers brushed the dark bruise on her jaw. "Are you okay?"

She nodded. "A-okay."

"I still wish you'd let me take him apart!" His eyes blazed into hers.

"I took care of it," she said. "If he touches me again, I'll have his sorry ass in jail so fast, he won't know what hit him."

That evening when Knut picked her up at work, he didn't mention Bob again. Leigh knew he was still furious, but he understood she'd had to handle the situation herself. It was just another example of his sensitivity. Leigh gazed at his strong hands upon the steering wheel, feeling thankful that such a good man had entered her life.

When they arrived at her apartment, she took off her jacket and threw it on a chair. "I'm exhausted." She dropped to the sofa and stretched out her legs. "What do you want to do about dinner?"

"I'm not hungry. Are you?"

She looked at him. That was odd; usually, Knut couldn't wait to eat. "Not particularly," she said. Her stomach had been tied in knots ever since she'd seen Bob that morning.

"Good. We'll get something later. Meanwhile, I'll get you a drink. How about Scotch?"

Leigh closed her eyes. "Mmmm . . . sounds good."

It seemed like only a second later that Knut was at her side holding a glass of the amber-colored liquor. "Here. Drink this. It'll warm you up."

She sat up and took a sip. "Probably not a good idea on an empty stomach, is it?"

Knut's eyes were warm. "Just one won't hurt you. You've had a rough day."

After another sip, she placed the glass on the end table. "I think that's enough for now."

Knut's finger touched her bruised jaw gently. "Hurt much?"

She shook her head. "Just a little tender."

"The bastard. Is this why you left him? Did he beat you?"

"No. This was the first time he ever hit me. Knut—" Leigh adjusted herself on the sofa so she was facing him. "I think you should know the truth about my marriage. It wasn't entirely Bob's fault. True, I found out there was another woman . . . but that really had nothing to do with what I did. You see," she hesitated. How would he take this? "I was unfaithful, too. It wasn't something I planned. And it wasn't something sleazy. I loved him." Loved. She'd used the past tense. Why? Didn't she *still* love him? "Anyway, Bob has a lot of anger inside him."

"It doesn't matter what you did," Knut said. "He has no right to hit you. And if he ever does again, he'll have to answer to me." His hand squeezed hers. "Leigh, about this other man. Is he out of your life now?"

Leigh nodded. "Yes."

"It's the man in Norway, isn't it?"

"Yeah."

"Look, Leigh. I don't want to know what happened with him. But there's one thing I *do* know. He was a fool to let you go." His large hands moved to cradle her face. "But I'm glad he did." He leaned toward her and kissed her. Slowly and gently, but thoroughly. His mouth tasted of brandy and tobacco. The warmth of the liquor in her veins combined with the languorous fire his touch aroused in her, and she moaned softly when she felt his fingers unbuttoning her blouse. How was it possible she could feel this physical need for Knut when her heart was still bound to Erik?

She slid her hands under his sweater. "Oh, Knut . . . ," she murmured, kissing his jaw softly.

He covered her mouth with his own in another deep, insistent kiss. His hand slipped inside her blouse to cup the molded lace covering her right breast. Her fingernails dug into his shoulders as her desire intensified. Suddenly he wrenched away from her. She stared at him in surprise. He ran his hand through his rumpled hair and gazed back, his eyes slightly dilated behind his tortoiseshell glasses.

"I have to go," he said.

Dumbfounded, Leigh stared at him. What had she done?

"I'm sorry," he murmured. "I just have to think." He stood up and gazed down at her a moment, his face implacable. Leigh opened her mouth to speak, but before she could force out a strangled *why,* he turned and left her apartment.

Leigh heard the door close with a soft thud. She sat on the sofa stiffly, unable to comprehend what had just happened. Had she said something to offend him? Had she—oh, God— had she whispered Erik's name in the heat of the moment?

An hour later, Knut still hadn't returned, and Leigh realized he probably wouldn't. He might never come back. But why? She was still as puzzled as before. Her mind raced in circles. Why, *why*? Exhausted, mentally and physically, Leigh decided to take a hot bath and go to bed. Perhaps tomorrow she could think more clearly.

The knock came at the door just after she'd stepped out of the bath and drawn on her red satin kimono. Her heart jumped. She walked slowly to the foyer and looked through the peephole. It was Knut.

She opened the door but didn't speak. He was silent, too. They stared at each other. Finally, he said, "May I come in?"

When she nodded, he walked past her and then stood stiffly as if he didn't know what to do with himself. He took a deep breath. "I want you," he said quietly.

Leigh opened her mouth to respond sarcastically to that

statement, but something in his eyes stopped her. He went on, "But before we have any kind of physical relationship, I have to know you're not using me as a substitute for him."

Was she? Leigh wasn't sure how to answer. Perhaps in the beginning, when she'd first started seeing him, he'd reminded her of Erik. But now? She realized that until tonight she hadn't thought of Erik in weeks. Not like before. She remembered those empty nights she'd lain awake in bed, longing for him. But lately, her thoughts had been for Knut.

Leigh moved toward him. "Knut, I care for you. Maybe I even love you. But if you're asking for guarantees, I can't give you any. I've learned the hard way there is no such thing in a relationship." She stood a few inches away from him and gazed into his eyes. "As far as Erik is concerned . . . he's out of my life, and I've accepted that. Do you think you can?"

Slowly, Knut nodded. Leigh moved closer to him and, reaching up, took his glasses off, folded them, and put them onto the end table. Then, very slowly, she slid a hand up behind his neck and drew his head down to hers. His lips moved tentatively on hers, but slowly grew insistent and demanding. His hands slid down the satin fabric of her kimono to cup her buttocks. He groaned deep in his throat and dragged his mouth away from hers. Quickly, he untied the belt of her robe; it fell open to reveal her damp, nude body. *"Kristus!"* he whispered. *". . . Dromme kvinner . . .* You're a dream woman . . . too good to be believed."

"Believe it," Leigh whispered as they sank to the floor in front of the fireplace.

After their lovemaking, Leigh turned on her side to gaze at Knut's drowsing face in the flicker of the firelight. He was a beautiful man. Too good for her, really. Because even though she'd enjoyed the lovemaking, she felt as if she hadn't been able to give him all she could have. All he deserved. Somehow, despite her feelings for him, she hadn't been able to give him her heart. He had made love to her with warmth and gentleness . . . almost as if she were a fragile doll or the dream woman he'd called her. It had been nice, and even satisfying.

But with Erik, there had been fireworks. A tear glistened in the corner of her eye as she gazed at Knut. Her body still called out for Erik and the fireworks.

He moved suddenly in his sleep and reached out for her. "*Kjareste . . .*" he murmured.

A wave of pain washed over her. Right endearment, wrong voice. That had been Erik's special word for her. She didn't want to hear Knut call her sweetheart in Norwegian. But how could she stop him?

"I'm here," she whispered.

Slowly, his eyes opened, and he blinked sleepily. One hand moved tenderly up her shoulder. "I love you," he said. "Will you marry me?"

Melissa was finally going to meet Knut. She was coming into Georgetown for the weekend, and Leigh had planned a special dinner for the three of them. Ward had given her Friday afternoon off so she could get the apartment in shape and bake homemade bread. At half past five, everything was ready. The Queen Anne tables sparkled in the lamplight, and the scent of lemon polish mingled with the aroma of hickory-smoked ham and fresh bread from the kitchen. Mel and Knut were both due to arrive any second.

Leigh climbed the steps to the loft bedroom and pulled back the blue floral Laura Ashley draperies so she could look out onto M Street. Where were they? She wished she weren't so nervous. It was silly, this anxiety she felt. After all, surely Mel knew she wouldn't stay unattached forever. Yet, it would soon be obvious that there was more going on between her and Knut than an occasional date. Would she accept it? It would be so much simpler if she could tell Melissa they were going to get married. But right now, that was impossible.

Leigh had been stunned by Knut's proposal, but then she'd attributed it to his heightened state of emotion. Yet, the next morning, clearheaded from rich black coffee, he'd asked her again. Politely, but firmly, Leigh had refused. He was moving too fast. She wasn't ready for marriage again. There was a very good possibility she would never be. He hadn't pressed the issue. In fact, hadn't brought it up again. They'd gone on as before, except now he spent every weekend at her apartment. Many times, Leigh thought of asking him to move in, but she always stopped herself, unsure of such a big step. It was easier to float, just to let the decision slide.

Peering through the window, she saw Melissa ambling down the sidewalk. The brisk wind whipped her long blond hair around her face as she walked, one hand shoved deep into the pocket of her spring jacket and the other carrying an overnight case. Suddenly Leigh's throat tightened. Melissa seemed so confident, almost cocky, as she strode down the sidewalk, yet, there was also a sense of vulnerability about her. She was a child in a teen girl's body, and Leigh felt an overwhelming need to protect her. Things were progressing with her, but not at the speed Leigh had hoped for. Mel visited occasionally, and when she did, she chatted about school and friends, but kept a part of herself hidden behind a flippant, detached wall. Leigh knew better than to try to tear it down; this was Melissa's way of dealing with the hurt and sense of betrayal she still felt. But it didn't make it easy for Leigh when all she wanted to do was draw the teenager into her arms and hold her like she had when Mel was a little girl in need of comfort.

So when she met Melissa at the front door, Leigh had to force herself not to reach out and hug her. Instead, she summoned a big smile and opened the door wide. "Well, hi. I was starting to get worried."

Melissa threw her an odd look. "Why? I know how to get around."

"Well, I worry when you take the Metro. Never mind. I'm just being a mother." She led the way into the apartment and waited while Melissa shrugged out of her coat. After hanging it in the entrance closet, Leigh stepped into the living room and saw Melissa gazing around, a neutral expression on her pretty face. "I like what you've done to the apartment," she said. "Where's the new boyfriend?"

"I would hardly call him new. We've been seeing each other for over three months. Here, let me put your overnight bag in the guest room." When Leigh returned to the living room,

Melissa was standing at the window, staring out at the rock garden.

"So, what's this Knut Aabel like?" she asked.

"He's very nice. You'll like him." Leigh hesitated a second before going on. "He's Norwegian."

Mel turned from the window and looked at her, a speculative gleam in her eyes. "Oh? A friend of Erik's?"

Leigh sighed. "I really wish you wouldn't keep bringing him up. No, he doesn't know Erik. I met him on the flight to Norway. And he looked me up after he returned to Washington. He works for the Norwegian Embassy."

"How convenient for you," Mel said. "Now you can keep tabs on Erik."

"Melissa, let's try and make this a pleasant evening. Knut will be here any minute, and I know you want to make a good impression on him."

Melissa gave her hair a casual toss and said, "Where's the bathroom? I want to check my makeup."

Leigh directed her to the downstairs powder room. Melissa closed the door firmly in her face. With a sigh of exasperation, Leigh went into the kitchen to check on the ham. She hoped her daughter wouldn't be so surly with Knut.

But apparently, Melissa had made up her mind to be charming at dinner. Smiling sweetly, she asked Knut about his work and his hometown of Tromsø. She was delighted when she discovered he had a daughter about her age and suggested tentatively that perhaps they could be pen pals. Leigh held her breath, hoping Mel wouldn't mention her other Norwegian pen pal, Erik's brother. But with a cool look at her mother, Mel changed the subject to school and her cheerleading squad. "There's a big game tomorrow night. Why don't you and Mom come?" Leigh relaxed. Maybe her snide attitude earlier had been a defensive act.

But after dinner, Leigh's carefully planned evening fell apart. The three of them were in the kitchen cleaning up when the doorbell rang. Melissa threw down her dish towel. "Oh! That's Dillon." She hurried out of the kitchen. Leigh and Knut stared at each other.

"Who is Dillon?" Leigh whispered.

A moment later, Melissa stepped into the kitchen, her hand attached to the arm of a Billy Idol clone. "Mom, this is Dillon Ungar. He's the lead singer in a rock band."

Dillon Ungar was a tall lanky boy with platinum blond hair cut short and spiked, and he was dressed from head to toe in gleaming black leather. On his hands, he wore silver-studded leather gloves, and a silver cross dangled from one earlobe. Leigh had always imagined this situation. Now, she was living it. She felt faint.

"What's happening?" he said. And there it was. The upper lip curled in the trademark Idol smirk.

Finally, Leigh managed to speak. "Hello." But that was it. Nothing else came out. She watched her daughter drape herself all over the boy. Helplessly, she turned to Knut. He was methodically drying a skillet, his eyes captured by the scene in front of him.

"Well!" Melissa said brightly. "We have to go. Thanks for dinner, Mom. Don't wait up. I'll probably be in late."

Leigh found her voice. "Wait! Where're you going?"

"Oh. I have a date with Dillon. Didn't I mention it?"

"No, you didn't."

"Sorry. I thought I had."

"Mel, I thought we were going to spend the weekend together."

"We will! But I just happen to have a date tonight." Mel turned to look at Dillon. "Mom, can we discuss this when I get back. Tomorrow, okay?"

"Melissa . . ."

"We have to go. Nice meeting you, Knut. I'm sure I'll see you again. Ready, Dillon?"

He shrugged and Melissa led him out of the kitchen. A few seconds later, Leigh heard the front door slam. Incredulously, she turned and met Knut's amused eyes.

"It's not funny!" she wailed.

Immediately, he sobered. "You're right. It's not."

*   *   *

"Where the *hell* is she?"

Leigh moved restlessly against Knut's warm chest and glared at the grandfather clock in the corner. It was going on one in the morning, and Melissa still hadn't returned from her date. Knut scooped up the curls at the back of her head and planted a kiss on her neck.

"*Kjaereste*, don't worry. I'm sure she'll be home soon."

"I just don't understand how she could do this. She knew how much I was looking forward to this weekend with her." She turned around to gaze at him. "She's just trying to get back at me, isn't she? For everything I've done to screw up her life."

Knut pulled her back against him. "She's a teenager. It would be a rough time for her even if you and Bob hadn't broken up. Don't overreact. Believe me, Kristin put me through it, too, but now we're the best of friends. You and Melissa will be, too."

Leigh shook her head. "I just don't know what she sees in a boy like that."

Knut chuckled. "Think back. Remember some of your first boyfriends?"

An image of Mike Lawson came to mind. Dark auburn hair down to his shoulders, a Nehru jacket, love beads, and a psychedelic Volkswagen van. Leigh nodded, and a wry smile flickered on her lips. "Point taken."

Knut's warm breath tickled her ear. "I wish I could stay over tonight."

"Me, too. But we'll just have to wait until next weekend."

"Not next weekend. Remember, Aaron is coming over."

"Oh, yeah. Well, maybe you can come by one night next week." She turned in his arms and kissed him firmly on the lips. "Want some more wine?" He nodded, and she disentangled herself from his arms and scrambled to her feet. "I'm going to run to the bathroom, then I'll get it."

Leigh smiled as she washed her hands at the bathroom sink, thinking how good it was to see her home cluttered with Melissa's things. Like old times. Her eyes fell on the overflowing cosmetic bag on the toilet tank. God, did she really *use* all that stuff? Suddenly she stiffened. For a moment, she felt light-headed as her brain registered what her eyes saw. A sense of déjà vu swept over her as she reached for the box with the familiar photo of a sultry blonde with huge breasts.

She walked into the living room, the condom box in her hands. "Look what I found in Melissa's cosmetic bag."

"Is that what I think it is?" Knut asked.

Leigh's lips curled in disgust. "Yeah. Rough Riders, Bob's brand."

The doorbell rang. Still stunned with her discovery, Leigh went to answer it.

"Hi, Mom," Melissa said. "Did you have a nice evening? What's wrong? You look funny."

"Is this yours?"

Melissa's eyes dropped to the package in her mother's hand. "Yeah. So what?"

Knut appeared at Leigh's side. "I should get going. Give you and Melissa some time alone together." When she made no response, he went to the closet and brought out his coat. Then he kissed her lightly on the cheek. "I'll give you a call tomorrow. It was good to meet you, Melissa."

She smiled brightly at him. "Yeah. You're not going to forget the basketball game tomorrow night, are you?"

He glanced at Leigh. "Well, we'll see what your mother wants to do. Good night." His hand tightened on her shoulder, and leaning close, he whispered, "Calm down. At least she's smart enough to use protection." He went out the door, closing it gently behind him.

Leigh turned to Melissa. The girl shrugged out of her denim jacket and hung it in the closet. "So, what's your problem?" Without looking back, she sauntered into the living room and plopped onto the sofa.

Leigh followed. "These condoms are yours?"

Melissa rolled her eyes. "Yeah, so?"

Leigh's lips tightened. She sat down abruptly. "You mean, you're sleeping with that—that—"

"His name is Dillon. And yes, we have a good time to-gether. We have fun."

"Fun? Is that all it is to you?"

Melissa shrugged but didn't answer. A horrifying thought occurred to Leigh. "Melissa, your father told me you were dating a lot of different guys. You aren't—I mean—is Dillon the only—"

"Why don't you just say what you mean? Am I screwing them? Well, the answer is yes. That's what you do on dates, you know. I do every fine-looking guy who wants me."

Stunned, Leigh groped for words, but none came. God, this had to be a nightmare. But it wasn't. It was really happening. Melissa stared at her and then stood.

"Well, if you're done with your lecture, I'm going to bed."

Leigh found her voice. "Melissa, don't you care at all about your reputation?"

The look on Melissa's face was suddenly very old. "Not really," she said, and turned to go.

Leigh jumped up and grabbed her daughter's arm. "Mel, listen to me! You have to stop this self-destructive behavior. Now. Before you ruin your life."

She shook off Leigh's restraining hand. "You don't tell me what to do, Mother. After all, look at the example you set for me. You and Erik. If you can screw around, I can screw around. I'm going to bed. Good night."

26

Spring had come to Norway. In the green mountains of Telemark, flowers in a myriad of colors bloomed throughout the landscape; streams and brooks carved through bleak canyons and created a rushing melody from the thawed snows of winter. All through the great forests, woodland animals crept out of their sanctuaries to drink from the clear, cold waters.

Along the Norwegian coast, seabirds returned to their colonies on uninhabited islands. Puffins, kittiwakes, and sea eagles built their nests into the rocky ledges, presenting a breathtaking spectacle to the tourists on board coastal ferries.

In the countryside, fruit trees burst forth blossoms of pink and white, showering the earth with soft delicate petals.

As the sun lengthened the light in each day, a festive mood enveloped the cities. Heavy coats and furs were packed away, along with the cross-country skis and snowmobiles. Out came the kayaks and bicycles, the fishing equipment and hiking boots. Families everywhere swarmed to their country cabins for relaxing weekends of fishing, hiking, or just enjoying the warmth of the sun.

The Haukelands were no exception. On the first warm weekend in March, Arne had gone to their cabin in Ose to prepare it for the summer. Lately, Margit had been hinting to Erik that she wanted to get away for the weekend. He'd listened with half an ear. "We'll do it soon," he'd told her, and dismissed it. Finally, she'd come right out and asked if they could go to the cabin in Ose. His answer had been a vehement "No!" Had she forgotten so quickly he'd spent his last days with Kayleigh there? How could she even contemplate going there where his memories were still so fresh? Margit's face had clearly shown her pain, and he'd immediately felt guilty at hurting her. Yet, there was no way he could give in to her on this.

So when Bjørn showed up on Erik's lunch hour and offered the perfect solution to the problem, Erik had jumped at it. He'd been working at his new job at the shipbuilding company for a month. The work was strenuous, but he enjoyed it. Keeping busy with his hands helped to keep his mind off other, less pleasant things . . . like how he was wasting his life, something Margit and his mother never allowed him to forget. They still thought he was a fool for giving up his ambition to be a psychologist. Maybe he was. But right now, this kind of job was exactly what he needed.

Bjørn's appearance had surprised and pleased him. He didn't get to spend enough time with his older brother. They'd enjoyed a light lunch together, and that was when Bjørn made his suggestion. That evening, Erik had gone home to Margit in a good mood.

She was already preparing dinner when he walked into the

quiet apartment. Apparently, Gunny was napping. Erik sneaked up behind her and grabbed her around the waist. She gave a startled cry and turned in his arms.

"Erik! Are you trying to give me gray hair?"

He grinned. "Shut up and kiss me." Her arms crept around his neck as their lips met and clung for a long moment.

She drew away, her green eyes soft. "What was that for?"

"Does it have to be for anything?" Erik planted another kiss on the tip of her freckled nose. "What's for dinner?"

Margit smiled. "Your favorite. Gravlaks and *rommegrot*."

"Mmmm . . ." His hands slid down to her hips. He pulled her gently against him, feeling his penis stir at the touch of her womanly curves. "And what's for dessert?" he murmured against her neck.

"Erik!" Margit gave him a playful push. "Stop it, or you'll make me burn your supper."

"Okay. I'll be good." Erik wandered over to the refrigerator and pulled out a stalk of celery. He bit into one end. "Guess who I had lunch with today?"

"Who?" Margit stirred the sour cream porridge on top of the stove.

"Bjørn. He showed up at the shipyards. You'll never guess what he wants us to do."

"What's that?" She stared intently into the contents of the pot.

"Well, he and Anne-Lise are going to Stavanger over May seventeenth for the weekend. They're staying at her parents' cabin outside the city, and he has asked us to join them."

Margit stopped stirring. She turned to Erik and smiled. "Aren't they taking the girls?"

"No, Mother is watching them. And according to Bjørn, she's offered to watch Gunny, too, so we can go. What do you think?"

Margit's green eyes sparkled. "Sounds like fun. Does Anne-Lise know Bjørn has invited us?"

Erik shrugged. "I'm sure she does. I don't think he would've asked us without talking it over with her. So, do you want to do it?"

"Sure. We always have a good time with Bjørn and Anne-Lise. And you know Constitution Day is a tough holiday for me. You're trying to get my mind off Gunvor's death, aren't you?"

"It's not an easy holiday for either of us. I'll call Bjørn tomorrow and tell him the good news." Erik threw the stalk of celery into the garbage and came toward her, grinning. He felt lighthearted—and unusually horny. "Now, how about a sample of that dessert?"

Maybe it was spring. Or maybe he was finally getting over Kayleigh.

Bjørn's white Saab pulled into the gravel driveway of a rustic log cabin with a huge stone chimney. It was obvious to Margit's knowing eye that the weathered look of the building was a clever facade. Anne-Lise's family had plenty of money, and this little cabin in the hills of Stavanger showed evidence of it.

They had left Oslo the day before for the long drive to Stavanger, staying overnight at a charming hotel in the small town of Vegusdal. Stavanger, located on the Gand Fjord near the southwest coast, was an old city, some of it dating back 850 years. Besides ancient ruins and monuments, the city offered a variety of other entertainments. White sandy beaches fronted the Atlantic Ocean and offered sailing, swimming and deep-sea fishing for water-enthusiasts. In the city center, there were museums, botanical gardens, and Norway's best preserved medieval church, built in the twelfth century. As for nightlife, Stavanger was rampant with nightclubs, discos, and restaurants.

Anne-Lise's family cabin was situated in the hills outside Stavanger, not far from the Lyse Fjord, home of the famous Pulpit, a flat jutting rock that towered six hundred meters over the water. The spot was so breathtaking, it annually graced covers of countless travel books about Norway. Margit had never been there before, and she was looking forward to seeing if it lived up to its reputed majesty.

Everyone climbed out of Bjørn's car and stretched their

cramped muscles. It had been a long, tiring ride. Margit wondered why they hadn't taken a train or airplane. But that was
Bjørn! Had to be in control of everything. Only grudgingly
had he allowed Erik to help with the driving.

"Bjørn and I get first go at the hot tub," Anne-Lise said
now, breaking the tense silence she'd kept for most of the two-
day trip. Margit resisted a satisfied smile. *Not quite what you
had in mind for a romantic weekend, Anne-Lise? With me and
Erik along.*

"That hot tub is big enough for all four of us," Bjørn said.
"And I suggest we all go relax in it before dinner."

Margit's keen eyes caught the look of dismay on Anne-
Lise's face. She squeezed Erik's arm. "Oh, that sounds lovely.
Just lead us to our room, and I'll change into my swimsuit."

Anne-Lise unlocked the front door of the cabin and stood
back for them to enter. Margit looked around, impressed by
what she saw. The living room was sparsely decorated with
simple furniture, a deep tan sofa and several handcrafted
wooden rocking chairs. A multicolored braided rug lay upon
the gleaming knotty pine floors, and opposite a small kitchen
area, a flight of shining wood stairs led, presumably to the
sleeping quarters. Opposite the sofa, two full-length paned
windows flanked both sides of the rustic stone fireplace and
boasted a view of the redwood deck that held the hot tub, an
outdoor table, and several lounge chairs.

Margit peered beyond the deck to where Norway's south-
western mountains spanned the horizon in a hazy purple and
white mural. Closer to the cabin, the lush beauty of fruit trees
in blossom saturated the landscape. Margit had traveled a lot
in her homeland, but she still thought the West Country was
one of the most beautiful areas.

After changing into her sleek black-and-white-striped swimsuit, Margit stepped out onto the deck and saw Bjørn already
in the hot tub. She welcomed the moment alone with him, but
knew Erik would be along any second. He'd been changing
in the bathroom when she left. She tossed her towel onto a
lounge chair and plunged one slender foot into the bubbling
hot water.

Bjørn grinned. "Why are you wearing a swimsuit? We're all family here."

Margit's eyes scanned his glistening chest and moved downward. "You're not wearing anything?"

A devilish light twinkled in his eyes. "Get in and find out."

She smiled seductively and lowered herself into the hot tub. "Mmm . . . this is quite delicious . . ." The pulsating jets of water lifted her feet from the bottom of the tub, making it difficult to hold herself in one position. As Bjørn stared at her breasts, she felt a heated throb between her legs, but she wasn't sure if it was from the pulse of the water or the hungry look in his eyes. With a quick glance at the back door, she scooted over to him and ran one hand down his stomach. Just under his navel, she felt the sleek material of his swim trunks.

"You tease! You enticed me for nothing."

"You call *this* nothing?" His hand grabbed hers and pushed it against the stiff bulge pressing against the fabric of his trunks.

Margit drew in a sharp breath. "God, Bjørn! You like living dangerously!" But she couldn't stop herself from running her fingers down the length of his erection. Grinning, Bjørn thrust himself against her hand. "Bjørn! Stop it!" She snatched her hand away and slid over to the other side of the hot tub.

"You don't fool me," Bjørn said with a wolfish grin. "You love the danger as much as I do."

"Shut up. Here they come."

His voice lowered. "Meet me here at two o'clock." His eyes impaled her.

She glared at him and then smiled up at Erik as he came through the door. "Come in. The water feels lovely."

Erik stepped through the back door, and a moment later, Anne-Lise followed, her expression tense. They climbed into the hot tub. Bjørn drew Anne-Lise to his side and kept an arm around her. "I got something for you, honey," he whispered loud enough for Margit to hear. Gathering her to him, he kissed her long and hungrily. Margit felt the heat rise on her face. She knew Bjørn was just using his wife to relieve his pent-up desire . . . desire that she, Margit, had aroused, but still, it irritated her. In retaliation, she snuggled against Erik and casually slid a hand onto his flat, bare stomach. A fleeting vision of a foursome crossed her mind and was dismissed. Erik was too straight to go for it. Anne-Lise, too. But she wouldn't put anything past Bjørn. Wild, innovative Bjørn. Oh, the sex they'd shared in the last five years.

He drew away from his wife and spoke to Erik, "I asked Margit why she was wearing a swimsuit. Don't you think we should all be comfortable since we're staying here together?"

"Oh, Bjørn, don't be silly!" After that long kiss, Anne-Lise looked considerably more cheerful than before. Now, she actually laughed.

It wasn't until they'd climbed out of the hot tub that she brought up the subject of her moodiness. Erik and Bjørn had already gone upstairs, and Anne-Lise and Margit were sitting at the breakfast bar in their robes, drinking hot tea.

"I'm sorry if I've been surly since we left home." Anne-Lise met Margit's eyes squarely. "To be honest, I wasn't pleased when Bjørn told me he'd invited you two along. I was hoping for a romantic holiday . . . just the two of us."

"I thought as much," Margit said. "And you don't know how hard I tried to talk Erik out of accepting the invitation. But he just laughed. He said something like 'Those two have been married forever. Why do they need a romantic getaway?' I suppose I should've simply refused to come along. I'm sorry, Anne-Lise."

"No. It's not your fault. Not at all." Anne-Lise stared sadly into the bottom of her tea cup. "Bjørn was adamant about inviting you. He just doesn't want to be alone with me." When she looked up, her eyes swam with tears. "I think he's having an affair."

Jesus, woman, don't turn on the waterfall, Margit thought, and squirmed uneasily. Did Bjørn have any idea what she was putting up with down here? Besides, what did Anne-Lise have to feel so sad about? He'd given her plenty of attention in the hot tub. The idiot!

Margit forced a sympathetic expression. "Darling, why do you think such a thing? Didn't you notice how loving and attentive he was out there? See, already the mountain air is helping him to relax and forget all his worries back at the hospital." Margit reached over and clasped Anne-Lise's hand. "By the time we leave here Sunday morning, you two will feel like newlyweds."

"I hope you're right." Anne-Lise smiled weakly. She stood up. "I think I just heard the shower stop. Thanks for making me feel better, Margit. I'll see you at dinner."

Margit got up to pour herself another cup of tea. As she stirred a teaspoon of sugar into the amber liquid, a tiny smile came to her lips. Bjørn was right. She *did* enjoy this dangerous game. Two o'clock, he'd said. Should she? She felt a telltale tingle in the pit of her stomach.

How could she *not*?

Placing two fingers on Bjørn's half-opened lips, Margit smiled and eased down upon his engorged penis. The hot water bubbled around them, drowning his sharp intake of air. She gazed into his glazed eyes, barely discernible in the dim grayness of the early morning light, and took him inside her. His hands tightened on her waist. With the slightest of movements, he stroked her toward climax. It didn't take long. They were both ready. *Had* been ready before she'd slipped into the hot tub where he'd waited, fully erect with anticipation of their clandestine meeting.

Her hands dug into his shoulders as he brought her to an earth-shattering climax just before reaching his own. They clung to each other, shuddering. Afterwards, she eased herself away from him and without speaking a word, climbed out of the hot tub.

In the kitchen, she toweled off and then crept upstairs to her room. Moments later, her body damp from the tub and still tingling with the effects of Bjørn's lovemaking, she climbed into bed next to her sleeping husband.

"Aren't you feeling any better this morning, love?"

Erik bent over Margit with a solicitous frown. It was almost ten in the morning, and she was still in bed. Her answer was a soft groan. She flopped over on her stomach.

"Can I get something for you?" he asked.

"No," she mumbled. "Nothing helps when I get cramps like this."

Erik sat on the edge of the bed and massaged the small of her back. "Is it time for your period already? I thought you just had it a couple of weeks ago."

"Sometimes it comes early."

"How about if I get you a cup of tea?"

"No, sweetheart. Just let me sleep, okay?"

He kissed one bare shoulder. "Of course, darling. I'll be downstairs if you need me."

Margit stiffened. "But I thought you were going fishing."

"I'm not going anywhere with you feeling sick, love. I want to stay here and take care of you."

"Oh, Erik, I want you to go. It's not fair that you have to give up a day of fishing because I don't feel well." Margit turned over and looked at him.

"I'd much rather be with you than with a bunch of smelly cod."

He looked so earnest, she had to struggle not to laugh. Poor dumb Erik. "Darling, I *insist* you go fishing."

"I've made up my mind. I'm staying here with you."

Margit realized it was time for drastic action. "For God's sake, Erik! I'm not dying! I just have cramps. And I want to be *alone*! Can you get that through that thick skull of yours?" To emphasize her point, she grabbed a pillow and hurled it to the floor.

Erik stared at her thoughtfully. "I guess you've made that pretty clear." He started toward the door, then stopped and looked back. "Premenstrual syndrome. I did a paper on that at university once. But this is the first time I've seen a classic example."

"Erik . . ."

"Okay. I'm going. I'll try to bring back a good catch for dinner tonight. Hope you feel better soon . . ."

"I will," she said. "Go on, Erik, I'll be fine."

He went out and closed the door behind him. Margit relaxed. She'd give him a few minutes to be sure he was gone; then she'd get dressed. Bjørn would probably be back from dropping Anne-Lise off at the spa any minute now.

The sun passed behind a cloud, bringing a chill to the afternoon air. Margit sat up and drew on her heavy knit sweater. After a moment's search, she found her discarded panties and pulled them on, then adjusted her long floral print skirt so most of her legs were covered. She turned to look at Bjørn. He was asleep, his face mottled by the play of sun and shade through the leaves of the tree. She wondered why the cold hadn't awakened him. He was bare-chested, wearing only the jeans he'd pulled on after they'd made love for the second time. But the sudden crispness in the air didn't seem to bother him. Margit sighed.

What *was* it about the man? Compared to Erik, he was nothing. His hair was receding, and he was starting to develop a paunch from eating too many rich desserts. Yet, she found him irresistible. Always had. Even before she'd married Gunvor, she'd been strangely attracted to the eldest Haukeland boy. At that time, she'd called it a crush, never believing it could be more than that to him. As far as Bjørn was concerned, Margit Lovvig was simply a cute little neighbor who played with Erik and Dordei. Yet, today, she'd just spent three hours making love to him in the forest. And it had been extraordinary. Even better than that furtive coupling in the hot tub.

But now the position of the sun told her it was getting late. Erik might be coming back to the cabin at any time. Quickly, she nudged Bjørn's shoulder. "Hey, love! Wake up. We have get out of here."

He sat up, blinking. "Christ! What did you do to me? I feel like I couldn't lift a kitten."

Margit stood and adjusted her white peasant blouse so she was decently covered. "Don't blame it on me. It's not my fault you can't get enough."

Bjørn grinned. "Right. And I suppose it's also not your fault you're an enticing little witch?" He stood and reached toward her head. "You have apple blossoms in your hair." He plucked one out and let it fall to the ground. He kissed her softly. "You go on to the cabin. I have to go pick up Anne-Lise."

Her hands slid slowly down his warm chest. "Okay. We'll see each other next week, right?"

"You can count on it."

Margit took her time descending from the hill, following an overgrown path that led to the cabin. When she stepped in through the back door of the cabin, she saw Erik sitting at the kitchen table. He jumped up when he saw her, a worried scowl on his face. "Margit! Where the hell have you been? And where's Bjørn and Anne-Lise? I've been waiting here for over an hour."

Margit stared at him. Why was he acting so strangely? "The cramps went away, so I went for a walk. Why are you home so early?"

"That's not important. Margit, something has happened back home." He came to her and took her hands, a haggard look in his eyes.

Her stomach plunged, her blood running cold. "Oh, God! Not Gunny!"

Grimly, he nodded. "He's in hospital. Along with Inger-Lise."

Margit raced through the hospital doors with Bjørn and Anne-Lise close behind. At the emergency room desk, a young nurse referred them to the pediatric ward.

"You see, they are fine," Bjørn said to the two women in the elevator as it rose to the third floor. "They would never have taken them to Peds if they were still in danger."

Margit didn't respond. Her eyes were glued to the numbers at the top of the elevator doors. He *had* to be right. If she lost Gunny, she knew she would die. White-faced, Anne-Lise held onto Bjørn's arm. She hadn't spoken a word in hours.

The elevator doors slid open, and Margit came face-to-face with Grethe Haukeland. The woman looked twenty years older than she had on the morning they'd left Gunny at her house. Her skin was a papery gray, and her lovely white hair fell in unkempt strands around her face. She took one look at her son and melted into his arms, sobbing. Margit, in all the years she'd known Erik's mother, had never seen her lose her cool composure . . . until now. Margit stood stiffly, unable to find her voice as she stared at the aged woman in Bjørn's arms. Finally, it was Anne-Lise who spoke.

"Mother, how are the children?" Outwardly, her voice was quite calm, but Margit intuitively recognized the note of hysteria that lay just underneath. Because she felt it, too. *Why won't the old bat say something?* She continued to bawl into Bjørn's shirt front.

"Grethe, tell us!" Margit's command rang with authority, and slowly, Grethe pulled away from Bjørn to stare in wide-eyed anguish at her two daughters-in-law.

"It's over," she said clearly.

Margit's heart lurched, and Anne-Lise swayed on her feet.

"What do you mean, Mother?" Bjørn shook her brusquely.

Childlike, she looked up at him. "They'll be okay," she whispered. "Oh, Bjørn, I'm so sorry it happened."

Arne Haukeland appeared at their side and took his wife's arm. "Come and sit down, Grethe. You're distraught." After settling her on a sofa in the lounge, he returned. "Your mother is quite exhausted. I'm afraid this accident has just done her in."

"Father, will you just tell us how our children are?" Bjørn said.

"They're fine. Sleeping, now," Arne said. "Their stomachs were pumped, and they're showing no symptoms. The doctor wants to keep them overnight for observation, but he is sure they can be discharged tomorrow morning."

"I want to see my son," Margit said. "Where is he?"

"Room 316. He's sharing a room with Inger-Lise."

Bjørn looked at his father. "Tell us what happened."

"It wasn't your mother's fault, Bjørn. She put them down for a nap and then went to lie down. You know, she's been struggling with this cold lately. Hasn't been feeling in good form. The children simply got up and went into the bathroom to play doctor. I guess they saw her take some of the medicine for her cold and decided to do the same."

"But tablets!" said Bjørn. "Jesus, they taste so bad! Why would they eat them?"

"I don't think they did," Arne said. "The bottle was empty, but there were a few tablets scattered on the floor. I believe they flushed most of them down the toilet, but of course, we didn't want to take any chances."

"Did the lab results of their stomach contents come back yet?"

"Not that I know of." Arne's face was solemn. "Bjørn, please don't blame your mother. She's beside herself with guilt as it is."

Bjørn nodded. "I'll go talk to her."

Margit had heard enough. There seemed to be more concern for the old woman than there was for Gunny and Inger-Lise. She wished Erik had flown back with them, but he'd insisted on driving Bjørn's car back to Oslo. Why couldn't he have left it? She needed him here.

She glanced over at Grethe. Erik's mother sat stiffly, her hands in her lap, her eyes vacant. Feeling her gaze, she looked up at Margit, and her expression changed, became pleading. "I'm so sorry, Margit," she whispered.

Margit's lips tightened. She turned and walked down the hall toward Room 316.

27

A pediatric nurse pushed open the door of Room 316 and on rubber-soled shoes, moved over to the still form of Anne-Lise sitting near her daughter's bed. It was after midnight, and the only light in the room came from a tiny rectangle near the door. The nurse bent down near her and murmured a few words Margit couldn't make out.

Anne-Lise looked up blankly. "Oh. No, thank you. I'm fine. I just want to stay here with her."

The nurse nodded and made her way over to Margit, who

had been dozing in the large chair next to Gunny's bed for the last few hours.

"Mrs. Haukeland, why don't you go lie down in the empty room next door?"

Margit shook her head. "No, I don't want to sleep. In fact, I think I'll go out into the lounge for a cup of coffee." She stood up, wavering slightly from fatigue. After a moment, she moved toward the door and paused at the foot of Inger-Lise's bed. "Anne-Lise, would you like me to bring you some coffee?"

Anne-Lise smiled wearily. "No, thanks. I'll get some later."

Margit stepped into the hallway and walked slowly down to the lounge. She winced at the bright light in the room and waited for her eyes to adjust. When they did, she saw Grethe slouched in the corner of the sofa, dozing uneasily. Occasionally, she gave a twitch in her sleep as if she were reliving a nightmare. Margit stared at her a moment, indifferent to the woman's pain. She had no time or sympathy for her mother-in-law's guilt. Her own was enough for her to handle.

It wasn't Grethe Haukeland's fault that her son had almost died. It was her own. God was punishing her because she was having an affair with Bjørn. There was no doubt in her mind about that. She and Bjørn were being punished equally. Both of them had almost lost a child. For some obscure reason, they had been spared. Margit took that as a very serious warning. She knew it was time to face up to the way she'd been living.

She went to the coffee machine and inserted a coin. Behind her, she heard a footfall.

"Margit, are you all right?" It was Bjørn.

She looked over her shoulder, then turned back to reach for her coffee. "Yes." Carefully, she moved to a chair and sat down. Bjørn settled himself into another nearby.

"I just received the lab report. It seems there were only traces of the antihistamine in the children's stomachs. So, you see, they were never in any real danger."

Margit didn't react to the news, but just looked down into the strong black coffee in the Styrofoam cup.

"Margit?"

She looked up at Bjørn's concerned face. "It was all wrong," she said, glancing over at his sleeping mother. Her voice lowered. "It was because of us, you know."

"Margit, you're still in shock. You just need to get some sleep."

"I don't want to sleep," she said. "Bjørn, if Gunny had died, I would've killed myself." Her voice was flat and emotionless. His hand reached out to cover hers. She flinched and jerked away. "It's over. I'm going to try to make amends. Be a good wife to Erik." Her eyes met his. "And you must do the same for Anne-Lise. Please, don't ever approach me again."

"Honey . . . I need you."

Margit shook her head. "No, you don't. It's just a habit. And we must break it. Bjørn, I'm begging you. Let me go."

He stared at her a long moment. "If that's really what you want, I have no choice. But Margit, I think once you're over the shock, you'll change your mind. We're addicted to each other. You know it."

Margit placed her nearly full coffee cup on the end table nearby and stood up. "No, we're not, Bjørn. We're addicted to the danger." And quickly, she left the lounge.

On the Fourth of July, a Canadian cold front swept into the Washington area, bringing a welcome relief from the string of stifling, sultry days that had been holding residents hostage to their air conditioners. It was after midnight. Leigh and Knut lay in bed under a satin comforter she'd pulled out of the closet because of the cool snap. Outside the window, firecrackers popped intermittently, and occasionally the whistle of a cherry bomb shattered the night from a few streets away. Raucous shouts and noisy laughter erupted in the street, and a few minutes ago, a scuffle outside their window had disturbed them. Obviously, some of Georgetown's inhabitants had no intention of halting their merrymaking until the wee hours.

"Do you think they'll ever stop partying?" Leigh murmured, and turned onto her stomach.

Knut lay on his back, hands folded beneath his head. He stared up at the dancing pattern of leafy tree branches illuminated on the ceiling by streetlamps. "Eventually."

Leigh groaned and buried her face in the pillow. She'd been so sleepy after they'd made love, but just as she'd drifted off, there had been a loud crack outside the bedroom window, and all thought of sleep had vanished.

Knut turned on his side and gazed at her. "Can't sleep?"

Leigh laughed into her pillow. "Knut, you are the most astute man I've ever met."

He grinned and slid a hand onto her shoulder. "I do have my good qualities, don't I?" He was silent for a moment. Then, "Leigh, tonight at the concert, you were so quiet. Rather distant, I thought. Was it something I did?"

Leigh turned over to face him. "No, of course not. I just have some things on my mind."

"Anything I can help you with?"

With a finger, she traced the line of his jaw. He was such a good man. Too bad she didn't deserve him. "Not really. It's just the kids. I have to work it out myself."

How easily the lies came to her lips. And she hated herself for it. But how could she tell him that Erik had been on her mind as they'd sat on the Capitol lawn listening to the National Symphony Orchestra. And when the fireworks had exploded behind the Washington Monument, how could she say she'd been reliving last year's Fourth when he'd been there on the mall with her and her family?

Since Leigh had begun the relationship with Knut, Erik had faded to a dim memory. But tonight, he'd returned in startling clarity. And with him, melancholy. She'd thought she was over him, finally. But now she knew that wasn't true, and she wondered if she ever would be.

What was he doing now? Was he happy with Margit? At least she loved him. That was one small piece of comfort to her. She wouldn't be lying in bed next to him thinking of another man. Leigh didn't want to do that to Knut, but it was impossible to control her thoughts . . . and the aching emptiness she still felt inside.

There was a rustle of movement at her side. "Perhaps since we can't sleep, we should get up and have a drink."

"I have a better idea." Leigh slid over and clutched him to her. Knut deserved more than she was giving him. If she tried harder, she could push Erik out of her mind. She began to nuzzle the hollow of his throat.

He chuckled and ran a hand over the smooth skin of her back. "*Kristus*, Leigh, I'm not Superman, you know."

"I think you're pretty super," she murmured, kissing his chest. "I don't want you to do anything. Just lie back and let me take care of you." In one swift movement, she rolled over on top of him and began sliding down his body, leaving a trail of wet kisses behind her.

"Temptress," he said huskily, closing his eyes.

Suddenly the phone at the bedside shrilled. Leigh stiffened and then scrambled over to her side of the bed. Unless it was a wrong number, a phone call this late meant trouble.

"Hello?" Her heart lurched as she recognized Bob's voice.

"Leigh, can you get over to the house right away? It's Melissa."

"What's happened?"

His voice hardened. "Are you coming over or not? I need you."

"If this is some kind of trick, Bob—"

"Damn it, Leigh. She came home hysterical a while ago, and now she's locked herself into her room. Won't talk to anyone. Maybe you can do something."

"Okay. I'll be right over." She hung up the phone and looked at Knut. "There's something wrong with Melissa. I'm going over there."

Knut threw back the comforter. "I'll come with you."

"You don't have to."

But he was already pulling on his pants. His face wore a determined look. "After what he did to you, I'm not about to let you go over there without me."

Bob's face was haggard when he opened the door, but as soon as he saw Knut standing behind her, it became hostile.

"What's he doing here?"

"Guarding me from *you*." Leigh brushed past him and into the house. "She's still in her room?"

"Yeah."

Leigh ran up the stairs. There was no response when she knocked on Melissa's door. "Melissa, please. Let me in. I just want to talk."

After a long silence, she heard Melissa's voice. It was muffled as if she'd buried her face deep into a pillow. "Go away."

"I won't do that, so you might as well let me in."

It was silent in the room, but Leigh knew her daughter was listening. She went on, "Mel, I don't know what happened tonight. But I *do* know everything is much worse if you keep it inside." Leigh sank down on the carpeted hallway in front of her door. "You know that day in Rehoboth? When it all came out about Erik and me? I thought my heart was breaking, especially when I saw your face. I'll never forget how betrayed you looked. It was the worst day of my life, and until then, I didn't know what pain was. Is that how you feel now? Like it hurts so badly you can't breathe?"

She waited. And finally, she heard it. A small voice. "Yes."

"But that day, Mel, I wasn't alone. I had someone to share the pain with me. And I know you don't want to hear this, but if Erik hadn't been there, I don't know what I would've done. Do you understand what I'm saying? While the pain is bad, it's so much worse when you have to bear it alone." There was no movement inside the room. Only silence. "Mel?" Leigh slumped against the door. It wasn't working. What else could she say?

There was a soft click, and Leigh moved away from the door. Slowly, it opened. Leigh stood up and stared at her daughter. Mel's blond hair hung wet and stringy around her mascara-stained face. Her blue eyes wore a haunted look. She turned and threw herself back onto her bed. Leigh stepped into the room and carefully sat down beside her.

"Are you ready to talk about what happened?"

Melissa had turned her face away. "I don't think you're going to understand."

"I'll try."

A long sigh escaped her lips, and finally, she turned onto her back. "I feel . . . really dirty."

Leigh met her daughter's eyes steadily. She'd been afraid it was going to be something like this, and in her mind, she'd already prepared a speech. "Mel, we all make mistakes. But half the battle is learning from them before it's too late."

Melissa shook her head. "You *don't* understand. It's already too late, Mom. I thought I knew what I was doing." The tears welled in her eyes again. "I was so stupid."

Leigh gathered Melissa into her arms and allowed her to cry. "Baby, it's going to be okay," she said, stroking her damp hair.

After a few moments, Melissa's sobbing softened. Finally, she pulled away. She stared down at the geometric pattern on her bedspread and traced it with a fingernail.

"I went out with Larry Noyle tonight," she said. "We were making out in the backseat of his car . . . and . . . he . . . tried to . . ." She looked up at Leigh, her eyes wild. "Mom, I told him I didn't want to do it, but he wouldn't listen. He just—" She shook her head. "He . . . tried to—"

Leigh blinked, feeling the blood draining from her face. "Oh, my God! Melissa, did he . . . *rape* you?"

She shook her head wildly, fresh tears streaming down her face. "I bit him. Bit him hard, and he let me go. But it was so scary, Mom. He ripped my blouse. And tried to—tried to—" She closed her eyes, shuddering. "I got out of the car and ran. I found a Seven-Eleven and called Andrea to come pick me up." She collapsed against her pillow sobbing. "I can't go back to school. If I see him, I'm going to be sick."

Leigh's mind spun. She remembered Mel's derisive voice on the night she'd found her box of condoms. *I do every fine-looking guy who wants me.* "Honey . . ." She stroked her tangled blond hair. "You're telling me the truth? He really didn't rape you?"

She shook her head, still hiding her face against the pillow. "He would've, though. I'd never been out with a guy like that. He was different from all the others. He wasn't going to take no for an answer."

Leigh bit her lip, hesitating before taking the plunge. "Melissa, what *about* those other guys? If you didn't want anything to happen with this one, why were you making out with him in the backseat?" When she didn't answer, Leigh went on. "Your school isn't that big. Don't you think word might have gotten around . . . about the other guys?"

Melissa looked up at her mother, her face white. "There were no other guys, Mom."

Leigh stared at her blankly. "What are you talking about? There was that Billy Idol character, and God knows how many others. You told me yourself."

"I lied," she said softly. "I wanted to get back at you . . . for leaving us. For breaking up with Dad. I thought you'd blame yourself for my sleeping around. I guess I just wanted to hurt you, like you hurt me when you went off with Erik."

"Jesus, Melissa," Leigh said, close to tears herself. "You didn't hurt me nearly as much as you hurt yourself."

An abrupt knock came at Melissa's door. Still in shock, Leigh stood up and opened it. She found herself face-to-face with Mark. It was the first time she'd seen her eldest son since the day she'd returned from Norway. His brooding face didn't change expression when he saw her; he simply pushed past her and went to his sister.

He bent over her prostrate body. "Mellie, are you okay?"

Her eyes focused on him, then decisively, she turned on her side away from him. Mark stared at her a moment, then straightened and turned to his mother, eyes accusing. "What the hell are you doing here? You'll just make things worse."

Helplessly, Leigh gazed back. Twenty-one years ago, she'd given birth to this sardonically handsome young man, but at the moment, she felt as if she were looking at a complete stranger. They'd been so close a year ago. Not a day had gone by without some kind of affectionate exchange between them. But that had all changed. Now, he looked at her with revulsion, and it was almost more than Leigh could bear. His hatred was tangible, like a poisonous reptile writhing between them.

When she spoke, her voice was tentative, and she hated herself for her meekness. "I came here to help."

"The only way you can help her is to stay out of her life," Mark said coldly. "She doesn't need you. None of us do. Why don't you just go back to Norway and leave us alone."

Like a flash, Melissa sprang up on the bed. "Stop it, Mark. Don't talk to her like that." Her tear-streaked face wore a desperate look. "Maybe you don't need her, but I do, okay?"

Mark stared at her silently.

In a softer tone, she went on, "Don't you think it's time we all tried to put our lives back together? Mark, no matter what she's done . . . she's still our mother, isn't she?"

Mark didn't answer. His eyes slid from Melissa to Leigh, then slowly, he turned and walked out of the room. Leigh's breath escaped her lungs in a soft sigh. She hadn't realized she was holding it.

"I'm sorry, Mom," Melissa said. "Mark and I have really been rotten to you. I haven't liked myself much since all that happened last summer. I guess I haven't been very grown-up about it." She slid off the bed and moved over to her dressing table where she started rearranging her array of perfume bottles. "I tried to put myself in your place. You know, about the way you felt about Erik. But I just couldn't imagine being you . . . and not loving Dad anymore." She looked up at her mother. "I know he's probably not very romantic . . . and sometimes, he didn't treat you very nice. But you loved him once, didn't you? And I guess I just don't understand how you could just stop loving him."

Because he stopped loving me first, perhaps? But she couldn't tell her daughter that. "I don't understand it myself," she said quietly.

Melissa picked up a perfume bottle and stared intently at the label. "I'm not ever going to get married . . ." Her voice was very soft. "Men are *scum*."

"Oh, Melissa . . ." Leigh took her daughter into her arms. Melissa began to weep softly, and Leigh could only rock the girl in her arms as her own tears streamed down her face.

28

The door to the chalet opened and Margit joined Erik on the deck overlooking the Norwegian Sea.

"Finally!" She plopped down into a lounge chair, drawing her sweater closer around her. "He's asleep. I thought he'd *never* go down."

Erik chuckled. "He's not used to sunshine around the clock."

It was 11:15 P.M., yet the midnight sun hovered just above the darkened silhouette of the mountainous islands off the coast, casting a golden-reddish light over the sea. In another forty-five minutes, it would nearly disappear behind the islands, but its glow would not. After only a few minutes of enchanted twilight, the sun would rise again to shine high in the sky for another day. From the middle of May through the end of July, the scenario would be repeated, until finally, night would come to northern Norway once again.

Erik loved Hammerfest, the northernmost city in the world. Although it had all the conveniences of modern living, it seemed almost untouched by human hands. Despite the usual tourist traps, hotels, and restaurants, the city in Finnmark had never lost its wild beauty and old-world charm. Here, Erik felt as if he were at the top of the world, which he was, literally. Only a few miles up the coast was North Cape, a barren promontory that dropped 307 vertical meters into the Arctic Ocean—land's end.

Erik was glad Margit had talked him into spending a week here. They'd dipped into her savings and booked the trip to Hammerfest on June 22, arriving just in time for the Midsummer Night festivities on the 23rd. All across Norway, the traditional bonfires had been lighted. Legend held that the flames warded off the trolls and witches who congregated on the cliffs to dance and feast on this shortest night of the year. For children, it was a night of scary stories and magic; for adults, it was a night for love. Thirteen years ago on Midsummer Night, Erik had lost his virginity to a pretty nineteen-year-old back-packer from Australia, and from that year on, the holiday always made him amorous.

As Margit settled beside him on the deck, he reached over and squeezed her hand. Bonfires still flickered over the countryside and would continue to burn throughout the short night. Gunny had enjoyed himself that evening at the celebration in the village, in spite of, or perhaps *because* of the hair-raising stories that had kept him awake until a few minutes ago. Erik supposed parents all over Norway were having trouble getting their little ones to sleep tonight.

Margit looked over at him. "You know what I was just thinking about?"

"What?"

"That other Midsummer Night we spent here. Remember? It was the first year I was married to Gunvor. You brought some girl up with you. I can't remember her name—"

"I do. Ingrid Jakobsen. Cute little blonde."

Margit threw him a sharp look. "You certainly have a good memory! All I remember about her is that she was always polishing her nails." She gazed out toward the sun-kissed sea. "We had a good time, didn't we? Who would've thought back then you and I would be here now . . . a couple."

"Yeah. Life is strange, isn't it?"

"Erik?" Margit's voice was soft. "What do you think you'd be doing now if we hadn't been married?"

A vision of Kayleigh flashed briefly across his mind. Resolutely, he pushed it away. "I've never really thought about it."

"Have you ever regretted doing it?" she asked.

There was a long silence before he answered. Then, "I try never to regret anything. There's no point to it." Abruptly, he stood up and pulled her to her feet. "I'm happy with you, Margit. You can be sure of that." His hands tugged on the lapels of her knit cardigan. He pulled her to him for a kiss, then kept an arm around her as he guided her to the door of the chalet. "Let's go to bed."

* * *

Through half-closed eyes, Margit watched Erik undress. She lay naked under the summer covers. The rising sun cast a golden light into the room, bathing Erik's bare chest in its glow. Finally, nude, he stood before her. In one swift movement, he drew back the covers and slid into bed. Margit reached out to draw his body to hers. Without speaking, he kissed her, his tongue exploring the inner contours of her mouth. Lightly, she ran her fingers through the golden hairs on his chest. He dragged his mouth away from hers and murmured her name. Slowly, he slid down her firm body until his lips were even with her pert breasts. His tongue circled her nipple. She shuddered.

"How do you do this to me?" he whispered. "I never thought I could ever feel this way about you. . . ." His penis was stiff against her thigh. He moved his lips down her flat stomach. Tiny delicious kisses. Soft animal sounds came from her throat. Her thighs parted, an open invitation to his sensitive mouth and tongue.

A moment later, Margit moved spasmodically and cried out in a frenzy of desire, "Erik! Please—"

"Now?" he asked. He entered her slowly. Her fingernails dug into the tender skin of his back. He closed his eyes and began to move. Peak after peak, they climbed, upward from one plane of sensation to another. Until finally, they reached the summit together.

When the storm was over, Margit opened her eyes and gazed into Erik's. They were warm and blue, and filled with such deep tenderness it was almost a physical pain for her to look at him. He grimaced with a last shudder of orgasmic pleasure and then slowly withdrew. Rolling over on his side, he pulled her to him and slid a hand down her slender back.

"Darling . . . that was the best ever."

She smiled and kissed the hollow of his throat. It *had* been good. In fact, the sex had been getting better and better. Especially since she'd quit seeing Bjørn. Perhaps it was only a matter of time before she really did fall in love with Erik. After all, what was *not* to fall in love with? He was tall, blond, gorgeous, and kindhearted. A perfect husband. Wonderful father. Intelligent, caring, sensitive. An exceptionally good lover—maybe even better than Bjørn. What more could a girl want?

Yet, Margit *did* want more. She hated to admit it, even to herself, but she missed the danger and excitement of an illicit affair. And she knew Bjørn did, too. Still, she'd made a pact with herself, and had no intention of breaking it. She was determined to make a go of her marriage with Erik.

Her lips lifted to kiss his chin. He pulled her up so her face was even with his. He kissed her softly on the lips. When he pulled away, his eyes gazed into hers intently.

"Margit," he said. "I'm falling in love with you."

At Leigh's suggestion, Melissa moved into the spare room at Leigh's apartment for the rest of the summer. The incident with the near-date rape had really scared the teenager, but it had also brought her and Leigh closer together. It was wonderful having her around, even though she spent most of her time in the spare room, reading or listening to music. At Leigh's suggestion, Melissa joined a tennis club down the street. It didn't take her long to make some new girlfriends there, and then, she was never home, but out shopping at the mall, going to movies, or hanging out at the local pizza place on the corner. Leigh was relieved. It seemed like she'd come through a scary situation without any permanent scars. Except that there were no boys in the picture. Still, Leigh didn't think that was an altogether bad thing. A little break from the stressful world of dating would probably be good for her.

It was a hot, humid Saturday in August, and Leigh was curled in the window seat, working on a charcoal. The apartment was quiet except for the music of Mozart's Symphony no. 41 that played softly from the compact disc player. Melissa had gone off with a group of girlfriends to Georgetown Mall. They couldn't afford anything there, but had fun pretending.

Leigh placed her drawing board down onto the window seat and went into the kitchen for iced tea. Brushing her limp curls away from her damp forehead, she opened the refrigerator door. The blast of cool air hit her hot skin like a balmy wave of water. The unseasonable cool snap of the Fourth had given way to the typical Mid-Atlantic heat and humidity, and even though the air conditioner ran constantly, she couldn't seem to get comfortable. *Premenopausal symptoms?* she wondered. The mere thought of it depressed her. No matter what anyone said, menopause seemed synonymous with the death of her womanhood. And she wasn't ready for that.

Back in the living room, Leigh took a long sip of the lemon-spiked iced tea and gazed down at her charcoal drawing. The sketch was of a mother and daughter sunning themselves on a flat rock next to a rushing brook. She hoped Ward would like it enough to display it at the gallery. Working there had given her the incentive to try to market more of her own art. Already, two of her watercolors had sold.

The doorbell pealed out over the music. Leigh looked at her watch. It was too early for Knut, who was coming over later to barbecue steaks on the patio. She placed the iced tea glass on a coaster, went to the door, and looked through the peephole. Her heart jumped. It was Mark! She took a deep breath, trying to calm her suddenly racing pulse. She didn't feel up to a fight. And what else could he want, unless he was here to see Melissa? She plastered on a rigid smile and opened the door. "Hi, Mark."

He walked in, a noncommittal expression on his handsome young face. "Is Mel around?" he asked, glancing into the living room.

"No. She went to the mall with some friends." Leigh held the door open, expecting him to turn and leave.

Instead, he stood with his hands in his pockets, his eyes refusing to meet hers. "Oh."

Leigh waited a second, and then plunged in. "Want some iced tea? It's already made. With lemon the way you like it."

He shrugged. "Yeah. Why not?"

For a second, she wondered if her ears were playing tricks on her, but when he still didn't turn for the door, she realized he was really going to stay. "Go have a seat in the living room. I'll get the tea."

When she returned to the living room, he was sitting at the window seat studying her charcoal. She gazed at her son, feeling an unidentifiable emotion gnawing at her—almost a hunger. A need for his love that was so great, it made her feel dizzy. Her eyes dwelled upon him, moving over his strong, straight nose, his slightly stubbled triangular chin, his glossy dark brown hair that tumbled casually onto his forehead. How many times in the past had she watched him study her work in just this way? The years fell away, and for a moment, he was a loving, affectionate ten-year-old again. Her firstborn. In his adoring eyes, she could do no wrong. But he'd grown up and realized his mother was fallible.

He looked up and their eyes met. Mark's face reddened. "Nice," he said, motioning to the charcoal.

"Thanks." Leigh crossed the room toward him. "Here's your tea."

"Thank you," he said stiffly. He took a sip of the drink. A long tense silence filled the room. Finally, he spoke, "So, you're still busy with your art?"

Leigh sat down on the end of the white sofa, facing him. "Yeah. I'm mostly doing charcoals or watercolors to sell at the gallery. I haven't been commissioned to do any more illustrations for a while. But I like it like this. No pressure, you know. No deadlines."

"Uh-huh." Mark turned to look out the window. "Nice place. Nice little backyard."

"Yeah, except it's too darn hot to go outside lately."

"Sure is. Oh, God . . ." His expression changed and he stood up. "I left something outside your door."

He disappeared into the foyer. Leigh followed behind, curious. A moment later, he stepped back into the foyer with a large cardboard box. He looked at her with a rather strange expression. "I brought something for Melissa," he said. "I hope you don't mind."

He opened the box and, with gentle hands, drew out a small calico kitten. It squirmed in his hands and meowed plaintively, struggling to get away.

"Oh, Mark . . ." Instinctively, Leigh reached for it. He handed it over.

"It's for Melissa," he said quickly, following her as she carried the kitten into the living room. "Vicki found her at the shelter. There were two of them, and she took one. She couldn't bear to leave the other one behind."

"I can see why. She's adorable!" Its tiny claws dug into the skin of her hand. "Ouch! You don't have to scratch me, cutie." She let it down, expecting it to run off under the sofa. But the kitten surprised her by sitting on her haunches and licking her paws with a tiny pink tongue. After she'd finished grooming herself, she turned up a pair of green eyes to Leigh as if to say, "Okay, I'm no longer contaminated by your touch."

Leigh laughed. "She's beautiful!"

"It's for Melissa," he said again, and squatted near the cat, sticking out a finger in front of her eyes. The kitten made a halfhearted bat at it and then yawned daintily.

"Uh . . . there's a little problem with that, Mark," Leigh said. "And I think you know what it is." When he didn't answer, she went on, "Your father's allergy. And Melissa intends to move back home when school starts."

Mark stood at the window, staring out. "I thought maybe you'd keep the cat here for her. You know, when she comes to visit. She's always wanted a cat."

Leigh watched his stiff back. A smile came to her lips. It wasn't only Melissa who'd wanted a cat. Mark knew how much Leigh loved them. Once, when she'd stopped over at Vicki's house, he'd noticed how taken she'd been with her cat. He'd commented on it later, wishing he'd be allowed to get her one for her birthday. But it was impossible. Bob claimed cat hair made him sneeze.

Mark didn't stay much longer. At the door, he looked uncomfortable again, and his eyes centered on a point somewhere off Leigh's left cheek. "I hope Mel likes the cat," he said, and opened the door. "Tell her I brought it for her."

"Mark . . . ," she murmured as he started out the door. He looked back. "Will you stop by again?" When he didn't answer right away, she added, "To see the cat, I mean."

He seemed to think about it for a moment. Then, "Yeah. I'll drop by now and then. To see Mel *and* the cat."

"Okay." Leigh tried to sound offhand, like an uninvolved bystander.

"See you." Without another backward glance, he loped down the stoop to the sidewalk.

After she closed the door behind him, Leigh walked back into the living room and saw the kitten curled into a fluffy ball on the window seat. Lightly, she stroked her long multi-hued fur. It was a moment before she realized she was crying.

29

The December night was clear and cold. Erik parked the Volkswagen in his father's driveway and stepped out to pull back the front seat for Gunny. "I'm taking Gunny to see the lights, Margit," he said as she exited the car on the other side. "Want to come to the hill?"

Margit smiled at him over the top of the car. "No, darling. I've seen them countless times, and I'm freezing. You go ahead, but don't be long. We don't want Gunny to catch a cold."

Hand in hand, Erik and his son climbed the small hill behind the house where he grew up. It had been one of his favorite play areas, especially when he and his brothers played war games. The hill had been the major strategic point of battle. At the top, the man and little boy faced northward, where bright lights shimmered on the horizon in hues of white, green, and sometimes blue. The northern lights. It wasn't often they were seen this far south, but on exceptionally cold, clear nights, they were an exciting spectacle. Erik and Gunny stood watching for a few moments as the lights danced across the sky sometimes changing shapes while they watched.

"The lights are pretty," Gunny said, a delighted smile on his face. "Like Christmas lights!"

Erik smiled down at his son and tugged his knit hat down

firmly over his ears. He squatted in front of him. "Did you ever hear the story of how the northern lights were born? My mother used to tell me the legend when I was a little boy."

Gunny shook his head. "Tell me, Father."

Erik smiled at the sound of Gunny calling him father. "A long time ago in the far north, there was a young maiden named Torill who was very beautiful, but the most unusual thing about her was her long golden hair."

"Like Mommy's?"

Erik smiled. "Sort of. But this maiden's hair was so bright and shining, it literally blinded the eyes of her many suitors. You see, an evil troll had cast a spell upon her because she wouldn't marry him. It saddened her that her hair blinded the men who wooed her, so she covered it with a long black hooded cape. One day a handsome young man named Olav arrived to court her, and she fell immediately in love with him. He asked for her hand in marriage and she accepted. The night before the wedding, they were out walking on the dark fells when a wolf bounded out of the darkness and snatched her cape away from her. Her golden hair tumbled down around her shoulders, and the polar night was suddenly dazzled by a bright light. Olav tried to shield his eyes, but it was too late. He would never see again."

"Did it hurt, Father?"

"Oh, I'm certain it did. Anyway, Torill was so upset because of the pain she'd caused her lover that she ran away to the North Cape, and there, she chopped off all her beautiful hair and tossed it into the Arctic Ocean. And two miracles happened. Olav got his eyesight back, and he and Torill lived happily ever after."

"What was the second miracle, Father?"

Erik grinned. "Well, when Torill threw her golden hair into the ocean, something magical happened. Since that day, on cold clear winter nights, the bright lights from her golden hair still dance in the heavens to the north. The northern lights. And you know what else your grandmother told me?"

Gunny shook his head soberly.

"She said when you watch the northern lights, if you wish

hard enough, whatever you desire will come true."

Gunny's face brightened. "I'll wish for a new train set for Christmas! Do you think my wish will come true?"

"I think it might."

"Did all your wishes come true?"

For a brief instant, Erik thought of Kayleigh. Then he shook his head and stared out at the lights. "Not all of them. But you see, you have to save your most important wishes for the northern lights. You can't expect every little wish you have to come true."

"Well, a train set is my most important wish," Gunny said firmly.

Erik laughed. "It won't be long before you find out if it comes true, son. In just a few hours."

"Are we going to take some *rommegrot* out to the *nissen*?" Gunny asked.

On Christmas Eve in Norway, it was a popular tradition for children to place a bowl of porridge in the barn for the good-luck elf who lived there. For city or suburban dwellers, a garage or even a front porch would do as a replacement for the barn.

"Sure," Erik said. "Right after dinner."

"Can we go in now? I'm hungry."

"Yes, go on. I'll be just a moment."

Gunny ran down the hill to the Haukeland house. Erik watched him until he was safely inside and then turned again to stare pensively at the performance of the lights across the sky.

Kayleigh, I wish you would return to me.

The thought was out before he realized he'd formulated it. As if to brush away an annoying insect, Erik shook his head and spoke aloud, "No! I'm in love with my wife. I don't need Kayleigh anymore. I don't want her."

He turned and made his way down the hill.

The Haukeland's Christmas Eve party was in full progress when Erik entered the house. He found the women busy in the kitchen, putting together the traditional holiday foods. The men were busy, too. *Skaling* each other with their shot glasses of aquavit around the Christmas tree. They greeted him garrulously when he stepped into the room, and a moment later, he found a stein of beer in one hand and a shot glass of aquavit in the other. But some of the cheer had gone out of Christmas for him. The image of Kayleigh lingered in his mind. Just when he was beginning to think he was over her, she'd come back to haunt him with dreams of what might have been. For a moment, Erik felt her presence so strongly it was all he could do not to turn around and scan the room for her. Was she thinking of him? Or was she so enmeshed in her new life she'd completely forgotten him?

Grethe announced dinner. Erik tossed down the rest of his beer and followed the others out of the room.

By some stroke of ill luck, Margit found herself seated next to Bjørn at the dinner table. All evening, she'd been purposely staying out of his way because she didn't trust her dangerous emotions. His eyes had been following her every move. How on earth was it possible no one else seemed to notice? It had been seven long months since she'd ended their affair, yet, it was obvious to her tonight that their ardor hadn't cooled. And she was finding it increasingly difficult to remain strong. So far, she'd resisted the temptation to resume their relationship simply by looking at her healthy young son and being grateful he was still alive. But how much longer could it last? Especially when a mere smile from Bjørn made her knees weak. Having him at the dinner table next to her was almost her undoing.

While she sat there smiling politely and nibbling *gravlaks*, Bjørn, who'd been hitting the aquavit bottle at a fairly liberal rate, had his practiced medical hand up her dress. No one even noticed. They were used to his American habit of using only one hand to eat; it was one he'd picked up during his years of medical school at Pope University. At first, she'd pushed his hand away but when it stubbornly returned, she gave up, reasoning the only way to stop him would be to cause a scene. That, she would never do.

Across the table, Erik smiled at his wife. She was looking radiant tonight. He hoped it was because she had good news to share with him. She'd visited her gynecologist yesterday, but when he'd asked about it, she'd shrugged and told him it could wait. He guessed she was waiting for Christmas to arrive before she told him. What a great gift that would be. A new daughter or son. This time, he'd be there to share the birth with her. He glanced at her again and was startled to see a dark flush on her cheekbones.

"Margit, are you feeling all right?" he asked.

She stared at him blankly for a second and then nodded. "Yes, sweetheart, just a bit overheated."

"Perhaps you should step outside for some air."

"No, I'll be fine." She threw him a teasing smile. "Don't hover so!"

Everyone laughed. Dordei, sitting next to Erik, leaned closer and whispered, "I just have to admit I was wrong about you and Margit. I didn't think you could be happy with her. But it's so obvious now you're mad about each other."

Erik smiled at his sister. "Well, I had my doubts about our marriage, too. But I'm glad I was wrong."

"Me, too."

From the head of the table, Arne's voice boomed out. "Erik! How long have you and Margit been married now?"

Erik chewed thoughtfully on a piece of mutton. "We celebrate our first anniversary next month."

Margit smiled dreamily at him across the table. "Doesn't time fly?" Her eyes appeared glassy. Erik wondered if she'd had a bit too much to drink.

"So, when are you going to make us grandparents again?" Arne asked bluntly.

Erik shrugged. "You're asking the wrong person."

All eyes turned to Margit. For a moment, Erik thought she was having a seizure. Her eyes were strangely unfocused, and for a few seconds, she seemed to shudder in her chair. Suddenly she became aware she was the focus of attention. Her face turned crimson. She covered her mouth with a hand and stood up rather unsteadily.

"I think I'm going to be sick," she murmured.

As she left the room, she cast a baleful glare at Bjørn. Erik felt the amused gazes of everyone upon him. He grinned back at them and shrugged.

"There's your answer," Arne said.

Erik stood up. "Excuse me. I'd better go check on her."

Erik tapped on the door of the bathroom. "Margit, are you okay?"

He heard the sound of running water. Then, "Yes, Erik. The heat just got to me." Her voice was impatient.

Still, he wasn't convinced. He waited a moment. "You're sure?"

The bathroom door swung open. Margit glared at him. "Damn it, Erik. I said I'm fine. Must you treat me like a child?"

Erik reached out and grasped her hands, gazing at her intently. "Margit, are you pregnant?"

Her mouth dropped open. "Where did you get such an absurd idea?"

"Absurd? Correct me if I'm wrong, but I thought we were planning on having a baby?"

"Yes, we talked about it, but I've never given you any reason to believe I'm pregnant now."

"But you went to your doctor yesterday!"

She looked at him oddly. "Yes. I went to see him because I haven't conceived. After the holidays, he wants to conduct a battery of tests. On you, too, if he can't find anything wrong with me."

"Well, why didn't you tell me?" Erik said. "You were being so secretive I thought you had good news."

Margit sighed. "I didn't want to ruin your holiday. I thought we'd discuss it afterwards. It's no big deal, really. Dr. Sjaastad suspects it's some kind of glandular problem."

Erik took her into his arms. "Oh, love, don't keep things from me. Don't you know I want to share everything with you? Even if it isn't good."

"Hey, you two lovebirds!" Mags appeared in the hallway.

"Come on, the children are ready to open their gifts."

Erik guided Margit toward the living room. As they met Mags, he gave her a concerned smile. "Feeling better, sis?"

She nodded, but her face was grim.

An hour later, all the gifts had been opened, and Grethe brought out coffee and dessert. By this time, Bjørn was obviously and irrevocably drunk. Erik didn't remember ever seeing him like this. He lurched around the family room to the disapproving glares of Anne-Lise and his mother, once nearly falling into the Christmas tree. Shortly after that, he tried to maneuver his wife under the doorway where the mistletoe hung, but she deftly moved out of his grasp. He turned to Margit standing nearby. Before she could guess his intentions, he pushed her against the door frame and drunkenly bent down and ground his mouth into hers. With raised eyebrows, Erik rose from his chair to rescue Margit, but before he could move, she ripped away from him. Her hand lashed out against his ruddy cheek with a resounding slap. There was a dead silence as everyone in the room turned to look at Margit and Bjørn. Erik stood up.

"I think it's time we get going."

As Johnny Mathis' "Have Yourself a Merry Little Christmas" flowed from the stereo speakers, Leigh looked around at all her close friends and said a silent prayer of thanks. How perfect this Christmas was turning out to be. Deanna had come down from New York, Ward and Egan were here, and so were the kids. Even Mark had turned up, Vicki in tow. And, of course, there was Knut. Dear sweet Knut.

This year was so different from last Christmas. On Christmas Eve last year, she'd been thrashing in a fevered delirium inside a small stone cottage on a snow-covered mountain. Thinking back, she could almost smell the scent of blue spruce, a scent she would always associate with Norway. And then, so vividly that she drew in a sharp breath, she saw Erik dressed in a red Norwegian sweater, his cheeks ruddy from the frigid air, his blond hair tousled by the wind. The thought of him brought a sudden wave of pain spearing through her.

It was followed by anger. She'd thought the memory of Erik had lost its power to hurt her. But obviously, she was wrong.

Abruptly, she stood and made her way to the kitchen, ostensibly to bring out more food. A moment later, Deanna followed her in and sat down at the table in front of the shuttered window. "Damn! It's getting warm in there."

"Yeah. Knut always has that fire blazing." Leigh opened the back door. A blast of cold air swept into the room.

"Oooh. That feels better." Deanna watched Leigh wrap a slice of prosciutto around a chunk of honeydew. "I really like Knut. Where do you *find* these great men?"

Leigh shrugged. "Just lucky, I guess."

"Damn right." Deanna got up and sidled over to snatch a slice of prosciutto from the tray. She popped it into her mouth. "You *do* realize he's crazy about you?"

"Uh-huh."

"And you?"

Leigh looked up at her. "I like him . . . a lot. In fact, you could say I love him . . ." Her voice trailed off.

"But?"

"But nothing. I *do* love him."

Deanna stared at her for a moment. "So, is it wedding bells?"

Leigh shook her head. "I'm not ready to get married again. But I've been thinking about asking him to move in."

"I'm surprised he hasn't already."

"Let's just say I'm playing it cautiously this time." Leigh assembled the last hors d'oeuvre and placed the rest of the melon into the refrigerator.

"Have you heard from Erik?"

Leigh froze. Slowly, she turned back to Deanna. "No, of course not."

"Jesus!" Deanna said. "His name still has the power to turn your face white."

Leigh grabbed a dishcloth and briskly wiped down the counter. "It's just that I was thinking about him tonight. About last Christmas. How different tonight is from last year."

"Yeah." Deanna's face was rueful. "It wasn't a great Christmas for either one of us, was it? You were stuck in a cabin in Norway with pneumonia, and I was recovering from a double mastectomy."

"I guess we have a lot to be thankful for this year, don't we?" Leigh said softly.

Deanna threw an arm around her shoulder and grinned. "You betcha. I have brand-new reconstructed breasts, and you have Knut. Stick with him, Leigh. He's a good man."

"I know."

Deanna shivered. "Shit! It's colder than a witch's tit in here. Come on, let's go in and celebrate."

Leigh laughed as Deanna disappeared through the swinging door. Still smiling, she closed the back door, grabbed the silver tray, and followed her.

Knut walked over to the television set and turned it off in the middle of the Mormon Tabernacle Choir's rendition of "Bring a Torch, Jeanette Isabella." It was five minutes after one in the morning.

"Want a nightcap?" he asked.

Leigh had kicked off her shoes and was relaxing on the sofa with Rosie curled up on her stomach. She yawned. "Yeah, a little brandy would be nice."

Deanna had already gone off to bed in the spare room just after the last of the guests departed. Leigh knew she should do the same thing. There were no little kids to get up at the crack of dawn on Christmas morning, but she had a turkey to get into the oven so they could eat at a reasonable hour. Mel, Mark, and Aaron were coming over for Christmas dinner. It would be like a real family with Knut and Deanna here.

When Knut arrived with the drinks, Leigh sat up to make room for him on the sofa. Rosie gave her an irritated look and jumped off to scamper out of the room. "How are you feeling?" Leigh asked as she took her drink from him. "I've noticed your cough isn't so bad tonight."

Knut took a sip of his drink. "*Ja,* maybe I'm finally starting to shake this cold."

The week before, Knut had missed a day of work because

of a nasty cold. When Leigh checked on him after work, it had taken her about two seconds to coax him into coming back with her to her apartment. Luckily, it had been a Friday evening, so she'd had the entire weekend to nurse him back to health in time for the Christmas party.

"You're staying tonight, aren't you?"

He glanced toward the guest room. "I don't know. Should I?"

Leigh laughed. "Knut! It's Deanna, for God's sake. You can see she's not exactly the most conservative person in the world."

He smiled. "That, she's not. Well, if you want me to stay . . ."

Leigh leaned toward him and kissed him lightly on the lips. "What do you think?"

"Okay, you've talked me into it." He rummaged into his pocket and brought out his pipe. "Just a little smoke, and we'll go to bed, *ja*?"

"Knut, what do you say to making our arrangement permanent?"

Knut paused in lighting his pipe and raised his eyebrows. Leigh, feeling a sudden shyness come over her, focused on the way the pipe dangled between his lips. Finally, he spoke, "Are you proposing to me?"

Leigh gulped. "Not exactly. I'm proposing you move in with me."

Knut grinned. "You mean . . . live in sin? *Kristus*, Leigh, I'm shocked! And I thought you were such a proper lady."

Leigh punched him gently. "Come on, Knut. I'm serious!"

"I'm serious, too." He took the pipe out of his mouth and bent toward her to kiss her gently. He drew away and gazed into her eyes. "And I want you to know there's no other woman in the world I'd rather live in sin with. When would you like me to bring my things over?"

"How about the day after Christmas?"

"Then the day after Christmas, it will be." He kissed her again, more hungrily this time. Afterwards, he dropped his pipe to the end table. "To hell with the smoke. Come on, let's go to bed."

On an evening in January, Knut came home from work wearing a bigger grin than usual. Leigh, who'd left the gallery an hour earlier, was putting a roast into the oven for dinner. He silently crept up behind her and grabbed her around the waist, kissing her lustily on the neck.

"Quit trying to startle me," Leigh said, smiling. "Rosie heard you at the door and scampered out to meet you."

Knut sighed. "Cats aren't supposed to do things like that."

"She thinks she's a dog." Leigh turned in his arms and kissed him. "Mmm . . . that was nice. Let's do it again."

"You'll get no refusal from me." Their lips clung together for a long moment. Knut pulled away first, an expectant smile on his face.

"Why are you grinning like the Cheshire cat?" Leigh asked, knowing something was up.

"How do you feel about a little holiday in February?"

"It sounds wonderful. What do you have in mind? Hawaii . . . the Caribbean?"

"Well, actually, I was thinking of going to a high altitude. Maybe someplace that can give me some relief from my allergies." In the last month, Knut had been suffering from an extraordinary amount of coughing and wheezing.

"Skiing in Colorado, right?" She thought of the cute teal ski-bib and matching parka she'd seen at Ski Chalet the other day. This weekend, she'd get Melissa to go shopping with her.

"Skiing, *ja.* But not Colorado. And *we* won't be doing any skiing. I was thinking more of France. Albertville, to be exact."

"Albertville?" Leigh's eyes flashed with excitement. "Knut, do you mean it? You *are* talking about the Winter Olympics, aren't you?"

Grinning, he pulled two airline tickets from his jacket. "For you, madame."

"Oh, Knut!" She threw her arms around him. "Oh, you

don't know what you've done for me! I've always dreamed of going to the Winter Olympics."

"I know." Knut's voice was muffled against her hair. "You told me, remember? When we watched the U.S. Figure Skating Championships on TV. Do you think you'll have any problem getting off from work?"

"Are you kidding? With Ward?"

The phone interrupted them. Leigh reached for it. "Knut, would you look and see if I turned the oven on? You got me so excited, I can't remember—Hello? Oh, hi, Mel. How's it going? I'm fine. You aren't going to believe what's happened. Knut and I are going to France for the Winter Olympics."

There was a small pause at the other end of the line. Then, Melissa spoke quietly, "That's great, Mom. Uh . . . maybe I shouldn't tell you this, but . . . well, I think you should be prepared—"

"What?" Leigh's eyebrows furrowed.

"Well, when I got home from school, I found a letter from Mags waiting for me. He's made the Norwegian ski-jumping team for the Olympics. It's possible you might run into Erik there."

Leigh felt the blood drain from her face.

30

Leigh shivered as a frigid wind from the north blew into the stadium in Albertville. She snuggled closer to Knut, amazed that the cold didn't appear to be bothering him. He looked so Scandinavian in his heavy overcoat and the Russian fur hat pulled down snugly over his ears. Despite the blue fox jacket she wore and Knut's Christmas present, a matching imitation fur hat, Leigh was slowly growing numb. They'd been here at the opening ceremonies for two hours now, and the French were putting on a breathtaking show.

This was just the beginning of two weeks of exciting events. Leigh had so many favorites, it was hard to decide which ones to attend. She had a feeling they would be spending most of their time at the ski-jumping events. That was fine with her, as long as they could watch the figure skating in the evenings. She also hoped they'd be able to take in some of the Alpine skiing. What could be more thrilling than watching those skiers hurtling down the mountain at breakneck speed while the sound of Swiss cowbells reverberated through the crisp cold air?

Yet, Knut's heart belonged to one group of men—the ones who flew through the air as gracefully as any bird—the ski jumpers. Leigh was surprised to learn he'd done a little jumping back in Norway. But when he was eighteen, he'd taken a bad fall during a gusty wind and injured a knee badly enough to need surgery. That had been the end of ski-jumping for him. He admitted it had been one of the great disappointments of his life.

Knut unscrewed the cap from a thermos of coffee and poured some of the steaming brew into a plastic cup. He gave it to Leigh. "I wish I'd thought to put some aquavit in it. That would keep us warm. But then, you don't like our national firewater, do you?"

Leigh took a sip of the hot coffee, relishing the warmth of the cup between her gloved hands. "Mmm . . . this is perfect . . . even without the aquavit. God, my fingers are numb!"

Knut turned to her. "Here. Put the coffee down, and take off your gloves." He stripped off his gloves and took her hands between his, rubbing them briskly. "Better?" he asked after a moment.

Leigh nodded. "But you'd better get your gloves back on before you get frostbite."

"The only thing wrong with my hands is this damn swelling." Knut held one out to her. "It's been like this for several days now. Could it be the altitude?" The knuckles and joints on his right hand did look swollen, but Leigh had never heard of high altitude causing it.

"Did it ever happen to you in Tromsø?" she asked. After all, the area he came from was mountainous.

He shook his head. "Well, if it doesn't go down by the time

we get home, I'll have it checked out." He slipped his glove back on.

Leigh looked at him closely. "You know, even your face looks a little puffy. Do you think it could be something you ate? My mother is allergic to shellfish, and I can't eat fresh pineapple without having something like an asthma attack."

"No, I don't think so. Oh, look! The athletes are coming in."

A thrill of excitement coursed through her as she saw the flag of Greece coming toward them. By tradition, Greece was always the first country to march into the stadium even though the actual number of Greek athletes in the Winter Olympics was nominal. Leigh scanned the long line of athletes, and her heartbeat accelerated.

Erik's brother would be in there somewhere. In fact, Erik himself could be here. Her eyes swept the huge stadium. Over on the left, she saw a few Norwegian flags waving in the crowd. Was it possible? Still, she didn't ask to borrow Knut's binoculars. Maybe she didn't really want to know. She hadn't mentioned to Knut that she knew one of Norway's participants in the ski jumping. It would just bring up difficult questions. Ones she still didn't feel comfortable answering. No, it was better just to leave it alone.

"You should get one of those," Leigh said to him, pointing to the Norwegian flags.

"I will," he said with a short laugh. "During the ski jumping. I want to be prepared when Norway wins the gold medal."

France's athletes passed by, decked out in red, white, and blue. A tumultuous cheer shook the stadium as the partisan crowd greeted their countrymen.

Other countries passed by at a leisurely pace, or so it seemed to Leigh. A reunited Germany paraded by, sending an emotional reaction sweeping through the crowd. For the first time since 1938, East and West would perform under the same flag.

South Korea. Tiny Luxembourg. The Netherlands. Leigh's heart jolted as she glimpsed the familiar red flag with the blue bars. And finally, there they were in front of her. The Norwegians wearing royal blue parkas and red knit hats. Leigh scanned their faces, but it was impossible to pick out Mags from among them. Knut gazed through the binoculars.

"See anyone you recognize?" Leigh asked lightly.

He turned to smile at her, his face shining with pride. "Here. You look for a while."

Her hands trembled as she lifted the glasses to her eyes and began to move them over the waving athletes from Norway. It would almost be a relief if he weren't there. Perhaps then she could quit fantasizing about Erik being nearby. But two rows from the back of the group, she focused the binoculars on one young man. His hat was pulled down low over his ears, but it couldn't hide the long blond hair that fell from the back of his neck onto his shoulders. And his walk was uncannily similar to Erik's.

Leigh felt faint. That was Mags Haukeland. She knew it. And there was one other thing she knew with certainty. Because every fiber in her body was screaming it out.

Erik was somewhere in this stadium.

The next day dawned sunny and windless, a perfect day for ski jumping. Knut was beside himself with excitement; Leigh could barely get him to eat his breakfast before going out to the park where the ski jump would be held. He didn't notice that her own hand trembled on her fork as she scooped up a bite of omelette. But there was another emotion mingled with her anticipation of the event. Fear. Fear of seeing Erik—or worse, not seeing him.

Mags was just about to take the lift up to the hill. He turned to Erik, his face pale. "Well, this is it. The moment I've been waiting for all these years."

Erik reached out and clasped his hand. "You'll do it, Mags. You're going to be great."

"Damn! I feel like I'm going to upchuck!"

"Just nerves. By the time you sit on that bar up there, you'll be fine." Erik gave his younger brother a brisk hug. "I want to be the first to congratulate you on your medal win after that second jump, okay?"

Mags grinned nervously. "You got it." His brow furrowed and he ran his hand through his blond locks. "Dirk jumps right in front of me. Do you think that's good for me or not?"

"Of course," Erik said firmly. "Then you'll know exactly what it will take to beat him. You'd better go. See you down the hill, brother." Erik turned and made his way back to where Margit had secured seats at the bottom of the landing area.

"There he is!" Knut said. "The Austrian I was telling you about. Onfrol Dirk. Watch this. The man has feathers instead of skin."

At the end of the ramp, the Austrian got off a powerful jump, rising high in the air, his entire body nearly parallel to his skis. It looked like it was going to be a perfect jump—until the gust of wind assaulted him. A cry of concern rose from the crowd as his skis wobbled in the air. Suddenly the jumper was out of control, his arms flailing about helplessly as he tried to regain his balance. Just as quickly as he'd sailed into the air, he dropped and skidded down the hill on his back, finally coming to a violent stop against the high fence at the side of the course. Medics and officials swarmed around the fallen man as the horrified eyes of thousands watched in stunned silence. Moments later, he was carried away from the course on a stretcher.

Leigh grasped Knut's arm. "What happened to him?"

"My guess is a gust of wind threw him off. It's unfortunate, but it happens. I should know."

"Well, will they postpone the rest of the jumps?"

Knut glanced over at the wind indicator at the top of the starting gate. It turned lazily. He shook his head. "No. Look, someone is on the bar now."

A disembodied female voice rang out over the PA. "Number Twenty-three, representing Norway, Magnus Haukeland." She repeated the announcement in French.

Leigh caught her breath. She squinted at the small figure in red at the top of the ramp. Knut had the binoculars, and there was no way she could ask for them. He'd been waiting all day to see a Norwegian jump. Mags skied down the run-in and sailed into the air flawlessly. He glided 275 feet down the hill before settling to the ground with a perfect Telemark landing. The crowd broke into cheers. Knut stood, frantically waving the Norwegian flag he'd bought that morning. Leigh was on her feet, too, clutching Knut in excitement. "He's got it, he's got it, Knut!"

And she was right. With that beautiful jump, Mags had put himself into the number-one position.

Knut squeezed her, smiling broadly. "*Ja*, but don't forget, there's at least twenty-five more jumpers. And this is still only the first jump. But *englebarn* . . . Norway has at least the bronze. I'm sure of it!"

Leigh watched as the red-suited jumper skated to the fence to shake hands with spectators. "Can I have the binoculars?" she asked. Knut handed them over. She focused them on Mags and the people around him. After a few seconds, she sighed and dropped them. It was no use. They were just too far away to see clearly. Even Mags was unidentifiable at that distance.

"When we come back for the ninety-meter, I want to try to get seats farther down the hill," she said to Knut. "Maybe down near the bottom."

"Okay," he said and turned to kiss her. "*Kristus*, Leigh! If Norway could win the gold medal today, I'd be the happiest man in the world."

"Me, too," Leigh said. "That Magnus Haukeland is really something, isn't he?" She glanced back toward where he'd been, but he had already melted into the crowd.

Leigh watched Knut make his way back to their seats with two Styrofoam bowls of steaming beef stew. For fear of missing anything, they'd been reluctant to leave the ski-jump area to have lunch in one of the many nearby restaurants. But so far, there had been no more activity at the top of the hill. Knut settled down beside her and handed her one of the bowls. "Bon appétit."

Leigh gazed down at the thick beef-and-vegetable mixture. "It smells delicious, but I hope you aren't expecting me to eat it with my fingers."

Knut chuckled and reached into the pocket of his parka to draw out two cellophane-wrapped plastic spoons. "I know this is rugged, but I'm not a barbarian."

"Like your ancestors?" Leigh grinned, tearing open the package.

"I beg your pardon!" Knut pretended to be affronted. "Not all of the Vikings were murderous savages. Some of them were peace-loving family men. Why, except for one or two raids a year, they spent all their time at home."

"Of course." Leigh took a bite of the savory stew. "Those history books are just notorious for exaggeration, aren't they?" She dabbed a paper napkin at her lips and turned to Knut. "I'm kind of confused about something. It's the distance that counts in the ski jumping, right? So, where do the style points come in?"

"You see that structure over there by the hill? The one with the windows?" Knut jabbed the end of his spoon across the ski-jumping course. "Five judges sit at each window and score the jumper for style points. Basically, that means how beautiful the flight is. Things like parallel skis, good aerodynamic form—good Telemark landing. The style points are combined with jump distance for a total score."

"So, do you remember what Magnus Haukeland's style points were?" Leigh asked, carefully using his real name instead of the shortened nickname.

"It's right there on the scoreboard. Fifty-two. Quite good marks. Even if his distance isn't as great in this next jump, if he can maintain good style points, he can probably take the gold. Of course, he must have decent distance. There's just no need for him to hit the K-point."

"K-point?"

"That's the spot where the slope flattens out. It can be quite dangerous for a jumper to land that far down the hill. It's like jumping out of a four-story building onto a flat ground. But I've seen Pael Myklebust from Finland do it several times."

"Do you think he'll do it this afternoon?"

Knut shrugged. "It's possible. But I hope he doesn't, for Norway's sake."

Leigh hoped he wouldn't, either. In the last few hours, it had become very important to her for Mags to win his gold medal. She remembered so vividly sitting next to the cheerful seventeen-year-old at a holiday dinner while he told her of his Olympic dreams. Of course, now he was eighteen, and one of the youngest competitors in the ski-jumping competition. How proud Erik would be of his younger brother if he brought home the gold. Then again, knowing Erik, he would be proud of him anyway, no matter how he fared. Suddenly, Leigh wished with all her heart she could be with Erik to watch his brother fly down that hill.

She placed the bowl of stew down on the seat next to her and picked up the binoculars. Scanning the crowd, she concentrated on any area where she saw a red-and-blue flag. *Oh, Erik . . . where are you?*

The PA system crackled. "We are now ready to begin the second jump of the seventy-meter ski-jumping competition. Our first jumper, Number Fifty-one, from The Netherlands . . ."

Leigh gave the binoculars back to Knut and looked toward the hill.

31

Through dark-shaded sunglasses, Margit gazed up at the hill as a blue-suited competitor skied down the run-in. He landed safely, and she yawned. Would this competition *never* end? She glanced over at Anne-Lise and Dordei, both of whom wore enthralled expressions on their faces. Margit sighed. From the time her father had first taken her to Holmenkollen to watch the ski jumping, she'd been bored to tears, and she still was. Each jumper looked alike—except of course, when one of them took a tumble like that Austrian. That always perked things up, but it didn't happen often enough. Not that she wanted anyone to get hurt. But it certainly made for more exciting viewing.

She turned to Erik. "When is Mags going to jump?"

He threw her an exasperated look. "Christ, Margit! You'd think this was the first competition you've ever been to. Mags came in first, so he'll jump last. You know that."

Margit's chin lifted defiantly. "Well, I don't pay attention to those stupid rules. Why is it everyone thinks that just because I'm Norwegian, I was born with skis attached to my feet?"

Next to Erik, Bjørn leaned forward and grinned. "So that's why Erik always has those deep gouge marks on his legs."

Margit bit her lip and looked away. The needling bastard! She could cheerfully strangle Bjørn at the moment. His snide little remarks were grating on her nerves. She knew it was his way of punishing her for ending their affair. But damn it, he wasn't the only one who was suffering withdrawal pains.

At her side, Erik leaned forward, a pair of binoculars glued to his eyes. "That's Myklebust up there on the bar. I hope he doesn't pull off a miracle like he did at Lahti last year." He was referring to the jump at the World Cup stop in Finland when the ski-jumping champion had landed beyond the K-point and brought home the gold.

"I just wish he'd get on with it," Margit said sulkily.

Erik's lips tightened. She was being a royal pain in the ass today. *And of all days!* His stomach churned with nerves because of Mags's upcoming jump. If Margit hated being here so much, why didn't she just go back to the hotel? For that matter, why didn't she just go home? She'd done nothing but bitch since they'd arrived.

Myklebust began his run down the ramp, and Erik leaned forward intently, forgetting about Margit and her bad attitude. He didn't intentionally wish the Finn a bad jump, but he did hope it wouldn't be so good Mags couldn't beat it. Myklebust landed a fair distance down the hill, but his technique was somewhat off, and Erik was sure his style points wouldn't be high. He was right. The judges awarded him only forty-one points for style. Erik breathed easier. With Myklebust's mediocre jump, a gold medal for Norway had become a real possibility. There were only three jumpers at the top of the hill. A Canadian, an Austrian, and Mags.

The two foreigners had good but not spectacular jumps. Then finally, Mags was sitting on the bar.

Erik barely drew in a breath as he watched his brother's red-suited figure poised at the top of the run-in. A sudden hush encompassed the crowd around them as Mags pushed off.

His eyes glued to his younger brother, Erik rose to his feet as Mags reached the end of the ramp and jumped. Like a paper airplane, Mags floated effortlessly through the air. "Christ," Erik murmured. "He's picked up a head wind."

Mags landed with finesse near the K-point, and squatting down, allowed the skis to take him up the hill, where he turned to gaze back at the scoreboard. No one else in the crowd had to look at the score. Mags Haukeland had the longest jump of the day on the seventy-meter hill and, equally important, high style points from the judges.

As the score flashed on the board, the Haukelands grabbed each other, laughing and hugging in delirium. All around them, the cheers of the crowd resounded, and everywhere, Norwegian flags had materialized and were waving wildly. Erik pulled away from Bjørn's grip and made his way down to the fence that separated the skiers from the crowd.

When he reached Mags, he found him swamped by the other skiers on the Norwegian team. Finally, Mags managed to pull himself away from their grip and skied over to Erik. A wide grin stretched from ear to ear, but Erik didn't miss the glimmer of happy tears in his brother's blue eyes. Over the fence, Erik grabbed his younger brother and hugged him for all he was worth. A mini-camera moved in close to record the celebration.

"Magnus," a voice said nearby. "Can we get an interview for Euro-Sports?"

Mags pulled away and grinned at the sports commentator. "Sure," he said, and grabbed Erik's arm as he started to move away. "This is my brother, Erik. I want him with me."

Erik grinned. His baby brother was already acting like the star he'd just become.

*   *   *

In the hotel bar, Leigh sank into a plush dove-gray chair and sighed. Only a quarter past four, and she was exhausted. But it was a good fatigue. Mags's medal win had made her day. She couldn't have felt prouder if it had been Mark or Melissa who'd won the Olympic gold medal. And she knew Knut felt the same. He sat across from her, smoking contentedly on his pipe and wearing a grin that under other circumstances, she might have thought was punch-drunk. Yet, she knew her own face held the same expression. If only she could've been able to offer Mags her congratulations. Instead, she had to pretend he was just an anonymous Norwegian. She wondered why she was doing it. Why not come clean with Knut? Confess everything about the Haukelands. Knut was a reasonable man. He'd never judged her before. Why should he now?

Leigh leaned across the table toward him. "Knut—"

"Look!" His eyes focused on the TV behind her right shoulder. "They're talking about the seventy-meter jump."

Leigh turned around in her chair and gazed at the color television set mounted above the bar. On the screen, a British commentator was, indeed, speaking about the seventy-meter competition. "Here's a replay of Magnus Haukeland's winning jump on the seventy-meter hill, recorded earlier this afternoon."

For the first time, Leigh saw Mags up close as he sat on the bar preparing to make his jump. His hands moved up to adjust his goggles, and then he was perfectly still, waiting for the signal to go. He was off, moving smoothly down the run-in, and then like an eagle, he soared into the air, his body perfectly parallel to his skis. Lightly, with deceptive ease, he settled onto the snow in a textbook Telemark landing.

"Christ, that's beautiful!" Knut said, his voice soft with respect.

The picture on the television screen dissolved, replaced by two blond men smiling uneasily into the camera. Leigh's heart lurched, and from a great distance, she heard another commentator's voice.

"I'm here with the gold medal winner of the seventy-meter

ski-jumping competition, Magnus Haukeland, and his brother, Erik. Magnus, when you were flying through the air on that second jump, did you know you had the gold medal?"

The camera drew in on a close-up of Mags. "Well, I knew it was a good jump. I felt that immediately, but I didn't know for sure until I turned and saw the signal at the hundred-twelve-meter mark."

"You're the youngest Norwegian ever to win a gold medal in the seventy-meter ski jump. How does that make you feel?"

Mags grinned. "Great! It's been my dream for many years."

"I hear you brought a fan club with you from Norway. Here's one of them. Your brother, Erik. Does that help your confidence when you have relatives here to cheer you on?"

"Sure, it does. When they're here watching, you definitely don't want to make any mistakes. I'm especially grateful Erik is here. He's been a great source of inspiration and encouragement to me through the years."

Leigh's eyes were frozen to the screen—to the face that had been alive in her dreams ever since she'd left him in Norway. She drank in the sharp lines of Erik's high cheekbones, the deep blue of his eyes. He smiled into the camera, and her heart jumped. How many times had that smile been reserved for her? She leaned closer, trying to hear his voice over the droning conversation in the bar.

"We're thrilled—all of us are," Erik said. "My parents couldn't be here to watch Mags win his medal, but I know they're watching at home. I think right now, we're probably the proudest family in Norway."

The camera panned back to Mags. The commentator shook his hand and wished him best of luck on the ninety-meter hill scheduled for the next day. The scene switched back to the other anchor, who began to talk about the upcoming hockey game between Russia and the USA. Slowly, Leigh turned back to Knut. Her fingers trembled as she reached out for her cup of hot tea.

Knut still wore his pleased grin. "Who would've thought an eighteen-year-old from Norway would come in and take the gold medal like that? *Kristus*! I don't think anyone had ever heard of him before today!"

I had, Leigh thought. She took a sip of the tea. It was tasteless.

Knut went on, "I can't wait to go to the medal presentation tonight. Maybe we can get up close. I'd sure like to congratulate that young man."

Leigh's tea cup clattered to the table and abruptly, she stood up. "Excuse me," she said. "I'm going to the ladies' room."

Inside the ladies' room, Leigh moved slowly to an elegant boudoir chair in front of a lighted mirror. Her legs felt stiff and awkward as she sat. She placed her purse on the counter and then met her reflection in the mirror. Her color was pale, her eyes huge and frightened.

It was decision time. As much as she wanted to see Erik again, craved to see him, she knew she couldn't risk it. Her life was good now with Knut. She loved him, maybe not in the way she loved Erik, but it was a pure and true love, and she had no desire to hurt him. If she went to this medal presentation and came face-to-face with Erik, she didn't know if she could be strong enough. Just seeing him on television a few moments ago was enough to make every nerve in her body cry out for him. No, she wouldn't go. Knut could go to the presentation by himself. Trembling, Leigh stood up and rummaged in her purse for a comb.

"For us, Knut . . . ," she whispered and briskly ran the comb through her hair.

Leigh overslept the next morning, and Knut was already dressed and ready to go downstairs for breakfast when she finally dragged herself up.

"Damn! What time is it?" She ran her fingers through her rumpled hair.

"Almost eight-thirty," he said, scanning the day's events in the local paper.

Leigh looked over at him. "How was last night?"

"Great." He smiled at her. "But I missed you. How's your head?"

"So far, so good," she muttered, and swung her legs over the side of the bed. She'd faked a headache to get out of going to the awards ceremony with him. But it had turned into reality as she watched Mags accept his gold medal on television. "I'm going to hit the shower."

After her shower, she felt almost human again. She stepped out of the bathroom wearing a silk kimono and a soft peach towel wrapped around her head. Knut was staring out the window. He turned when he heard her. "Oh. You look luscious."

Leigh smiled, thinking he must truly love her if he thought she looked good now. She studied him. "Knut, you're all flushed. Like you've been jogging or something."

Knut tugged at the collar of his heavy cable-knit sweater. "It *is* a bit warm in here, isn't it?"

Concerned, Leigh moved closer. "Do you have a fever? Your eyes are glittering." She touched his forehead. "Knut! You're burning up!"

"No, I'm not!" He grabbed her hand and held it between his. "You're imagining things. And my eyes are glittering because I'm excited about the ninety-meter jump. I want to see Norway win another medal."

Unconvinced, Leigh stared at him. Knut sighed and pulled her into his arms. "Stop worrying. I feel fine." He kissed her forehead and then gently pushed her away. "Now, go get your makeup on. I'm going down to the restaurant to secure us a table. Meet me down there when you're ready. And don't take too long. I have a surprise for you."

Thirty-five minutes later, Leigh stepped out of the elevator and headed toward the entrance of the hotel's restaurant. The attractive young woman at the hostess desk smiled at her. "One for breakfast, madam?"

Leigh scanned the room for Knut. "Thanks, but I see my party—" He was seated at a table near the window and appeared to be in an animated conversation with someone across from him. Leigh couldn't see who it was because her view was obscured by a potted plant. So typical of Knut. He made friends everywhere he went. Smiling, she threaded her way between the other diners toward his table. When she reached it, her smile froze as her eyes fixed upon Knut's companion.

It was Mags Haukeland.

As if in slow motion, Leigh turned to escape, but before she could move away, Knut looked up and saw her. Mags followed his gaze, and a light of recognition blazed in his blue eyes. His expression changed to puzzlement as he glanced back at Knut.

Knut smiled. "Here she is now. Didn't I tell you she would be the most beautiful woman in the room? Leigh! Here's my surprise!"

Trembling, Leigh sat down in the chair Knut pulled out for her. She felt light-headed, and her stomach churned with anxiety.

"I'd like you to meet Magnus Haukeland, the ski jumper who won the gold medal yesterday."

Leigh smiled weakly at Mags, who nodded and peered speculatively at her.

"I met him at the medal presentations last night," Knut said. "And invited him to join us for breakfast."

The waiter arrived and filled Leigh's coffee cup. She waited until he moved around the table to refill Mags's cup before speaking. "You should've prepared me, Knut. I would've taken more care with my appearance."

"You look great," Mags said. "Knut tells me you had a headache last night. I hope you're feeling better."

Leigh looked at him, and for the first time, their eyes met. She felt a momentary wave of relief. He wasn't going to say anything. Intuitively, he'd realized she didn't want Knut to know they'd met before. "Thank you. Some Tylenol and an early night took care of it. Congratulations on your medal. I guess Knut told you we were rooting for you."

Mags grinned. "Oh, *ja*. It's wonderful to know we Norwegians have some American support."

"Now, wait a minute," Knut said. "I haven't given up my Norwegian citizenship just because I live in the States." He gave a short laugh that suddenly turned into a cough. He rummaged in his pocket and pulled out a handkerchief. A moment later, he drew it away from his mouth, the spasm under control. But his face wore a grimace of pain.

Leigh leaned toward him. "Knut, are you okay?"

His hand tugged at the neck of his sweater. "*Ja*," he said. "Just a little twinge in my chest. I think I pulled something with this damn cough. Ah, here's our food. Leigh, I ordered your usual. Swiss cheese omelette and bacon."

Leigh sat silently, nibbling at her omelette as Knut and Mags discussed ski jumping, her mind a jumble of disconnected thoughts. What would Mags tell Erik? And if he learned she was here in Albertville, what would he do? Nothing, most likely. After all, he'd left her in Norway without even a good-bye. What made her think everything would be different here? Their situation hadn't changed, except that Erik was probably married, and she and Knut were as good as husband and wife. Somehow, she had to convince Mags not to tell Erik he'd seen her. But how to get him alone?

The breakfast dishes were cleared away, and the waiter refilled their coffee cups. "Well, of course, I'm going to do my best on the ninety-meter," Mags said. "But the seventy seems to be my strong suit. Then, there's the ninety-meter team jump. I think we can pull out another medal there."

"Excuse me," Knut said abruptly, and stood. "You two finish your coffee. I'll be right back."

Leigh's eyes followed him as he headed toward the men's rest room. He didn't look well.

"Kayleigh?"

Her heart lurched at Mags's use of her real name. She looked back at him.

"I'm sorry if my presence caused you to be uncomfortable."

"It's not your fault, Mags." His nickname slipped out easily. "It's just that Knut doesn't know—"

"About you and Erik?" he said quietly.

Her eyes flashed up to him. "You know?"

He nodded. "Erik told me. He loved you very much, you know."

Leigh blinked back sudden tears. "I know he's here," she said softly. "Is Margit with him?"

"*Ja*, she's here. Kayleigh, look, Erik has changed since he married Margit. He's morose and distant these days. I don't think he's happy with her."

Leigh shook her head and, with her napkin, began to jerkily dab at a coffee stain on the linen tablecloth. "I'm sorry to hear that. After the way he left me, I thought—oh, forget it." She looked up at him. "Mags, don't tell him you saw me. It won't do any of us any good."

"Here comes Knut," Mags said.

"Oh, sorry about that!" Knut sat back down. "A bit of indigestion, I'm afraid."

"Are you sure you feel like going to the competition?" Leigh asked.

"Wouldn't miss it," Knut said, taking a sip of ice water.

Mags looked at his crimson Swatch watch. "I've got to get going myself. The coach wants us there by ten-thirty."

Knut leaned toward him. "Need a ride? We've rented a car for the week."

"No, thanks." Mags grinned. "A few young ladies on the Canadian Alpine team are giving me a lift."

Leigh looked him straight in the eye. "It was great meeting you, Magnus. Good luck on the jump today." *Please don't tell Erik.*

His expression was noncommittal. He smiled, shook their hands, and sauntered out of the restaurant, the picture of a confident young Olympic athlete.

A few minutes later, Knut and Leigh made their way into the lobby of the hotel. "Why don't you wait for me here?" he said. "I'll go up and get the binoculars and our coats."

When fifteen minutes passed and Knut still hadn't returned to the lobby, Leigh entered the elevator to go up and find out what was keeping him. She stepped out into the hallway and saw that their door was open. What on earth was he doing?

"Knut?" She strode through the door. The room was empty. She moved over toward the open bathroom door. "Knut?" She stopped short. "*Oh, my God!*"

Knut lay on the bathroom floor, his hands clawing helplessly at his chest. Strangled gurgling sounds came from his throat; his face was a gruesome shade of blue. Leigh whirled around and stumbled toward the phone on the bedside table. "Oh, dear God, please *answer!*" Her voice rose. "Yes! This is—oh Jesus, what room am I in?" Then, she saw the room number on the phone. "Room 714. I need an ambulance. My husband has had a heart attack. Please hurry—" She dropped the phone and ran back into the bathroom to Knut.

32

Erik saw Mags beckon to him from the ski-lift area. He waved back and threaded his way through the crowd toward him. Masses had turned out for the ninety-meter jump, and it was next to impossible to walk anywhere without a struggle. Finally, Erik reached his brother's side.

"Christ! What took you so long to get here?" Mags said. "I haven't much time."

"Traffic," Erik said. "Margit told me you called while I was in the shower. What's up?"

"Something big. You'll think it is, anyway." Mags paused and made sure he had Erik's full attention. "Kayleigh's here in Albertville."

Erik drew in a sharp breath. For a moment, he couldn't speak. Mags's words echoed in his brain. "Kayleigh? Here?" His voice was ragged.

Impatiently, Mags glanced over his shoulder at the top of the hill. "Yes. Look, I don't have time to explain. She's here. I had breakfast with her this morning." He reached into his parka and pulled out a white slip of paper. "Here's the address and phone number of the hotel where she's staying."

Hand trembling, Erik reached out to take it. Mags moved toward the ski lift, but then he stopped and turned back. "Oh, and Erik? She has a man with her. A Norwegian who works at the embassy in Washington, D.C. I don't think she's married to him, but they look pretty close, if you know what I mean."

Through dazed eyes, Erik watched Mags's figure grow

smaller. His brain was still trying to assimilate the earth-shattering information he'd just received. Kayleigh, here in the same city? How was it possible he hadn't known? Had she been here in the crowd when Mags made his spectacular jump yesterday? Was she here now?

Erik's eyes swept the faces around him. How would he ever find her? He looked down at the paper in his hand. Thank God, Mags had had the foresight to write the address down. His little brother had known how important Kayleigh was to him. Erik decided to find the public phones and call her hotel—just in case she was still there. What would he say?

He had no idea. He just knew he had to see her again. Would she agree to meet with him? He just had to make up for the way he'd left her. What a fool he'd been to listen to Margit.

Margit. What about her? She was his wife now. Only recently, he'd managed to convince himself he was in love with her. But now, after just hearing Kayleigh's name, he knew it wasn't true. Christ! He didn't want to hurt Margit, but he loved Kayleigh. Had never stopped loving her. He knew he *had* to see her again . . . at any cost. Even if it destroyed his marriage.

Erik dropped the coin into the pay phone and quickly punched out the numbers. After the first ring, he heard a click and then a female voice. "Bonjour. Hotel Chamonde."

Erik was silent. Mags had forgotten to write down a room number. "Do you speak English?"

"Of course, monsieur. May I help you?"

"I need to reach someone who's staying in your hotel, but I'm afraid I don't have her room number. Can you check your log for Kayleigh, or perhaps Leigh Fallon?"

"Could you spell the last name, please?"

Erik did and waited. A moment later, the voice chirped in his ear. "I'm sorry, monsieur. We have no one by that name listed."

"Merci." He hung up the phone and turned, staring blankly ahead of him. Of course. If she were with a man, they would be sharing the same room under his name. A tide of burning jealousy ripped through him. A Norwegian, Mags had said.

He remembered that she'd met a Norwegian on the flight from New York to Oslo. Could it possibly be the same one?

But what had he expected? A woman as wonderful as Kayleigh wouldn't be alone for long. Intellectually, he knew that. Knew that he should be happy she'd found someone, yet, it was different when he was confronted with the reality of it.

Erik made his way back to where Margit was sitting, his emotions still reeling. It was almost time for the competition to begin. He would simply have to wait until after the first jump to corner Mags and find out the man's name. Meanwhile, he would keep looking. Kayleigh just might be here in the crowd somewhere. And just maybe he'd be lucky enough to find her.

Knut Aabel. The name *did* sound familiar. Erik was sure it was the same name on the business card he'd ripped up. So, he'd been right to be jealous. As he dropped the coin into the pay phone, he felt a sudden wave of insecurity wash over him. What if Kayleigh had no desire to hear from him? Suppose she was really in love with this guy? No! That was one thing he had no doubt about. Kayleigh loved him. That had never changed.

The hotel operator answered the phone and he asked her to ring Knut Aabel's room. It rang ten times before the operator came back on the line. "I'm sorry, monsieur. No one is picking up. Perhaps you can try again later."

Frustrated, Erik hung up. There was only one thing to do. He'd go to the hotel and wait for her to show up. She'd have to, sooner or later.

The phone was ringing as Leigh unlocked the door to the hotel room. She rushed over to answer it, but it was too late. Whoever it was had already hung up. Well, if it had been the hospital, they'd call back. The doctor had assured her that Knut was going to be okay. Her worst fears had been allayed when she'd learned it hadn't been a heart attack at all, but a lung abscess. A chest tube had been inserted to drain out the infectious material, and they had started Knut on antibiotics.

With a tired sigh, Leigh sat down in the wing-back chair near the window. She was physically and mentally exhausted. How she wished she could take the time out to relax in a tub of hot water. But now she had to get busy and start packing. On the recommendation of a nurse on Knut's floor, she'd decided to move to a hotel closer to the hospital. The taxi ride back had taken almost thirty-five minutes, and the traffic had been horrible. The friendly nurse, whose husband owned a small hotel only three blocks from the hospital, told her there had been a cancellation that morning for a single room.

As she folded Knut's sweaters and shirts and placed them into his suitcase, she felt a wave of euphoria rush over her. Thank God, it hadn't been a heart attack. When she'd found him struggling for breath on the bathroom floor, she'd thought he was dying. Fortunately, there had been a doctor in the dining room who'd been called up to help. He'd stayed with Knut until the ambulance arrived.

Leigh took a last look around the hotel room to make sure she hadn't forgotten anything. Too bad, she thought. This was such a nice place. And poor Knut. He'd missed the ninety-meter ski jump today. She wondered how Mags had fared. Her brow furrowed at the thought of Mags. She'd forgotten all about seeing him this morning. By now, he'd probably told Erik she was here. Would he try and find her? It didn't really matter, because once she left this hotel, she'd be untraceable.

She took the elevator down to the lobby and made her way to the front desk, where she returned the key and paid the bill. In the underground garage, she unlocked the door of the Renault rental car. Her plan was to drive it back to the airport and then get a taxi to her new hotel. With Knut in the hospital, there would be no need for a rental car. She drove out into the sunlight and stopped to wait for the traffic to clear. A taxi slowed, flashing its right blinker and turned into the hotel entrance. After it passed, Leigh pulled out and continued past the hotel toward the airport.

The taxi pulled to a stop in front of the hotel. Erik paid the driver and hurried into the building. A pretty young woman looked up from the desk and smiled brightly. "Bonjour, monsieur."

"Bonjour. I'd like to leave a message for one of your guests. A Mrs. Aabel. Room 714."

Her smile faded. "Oh, I'm sorry, monsieur. You just missed her. She checked out only a moment before."

Erik felt as if his heart had stopped beating. "Any forwarding address?" he asked, knowing what her answer would be.

"Oh, *oui!*" she smiled, happy to help. "Here it is. 621 M Street. Washington, D.C. in America. Does that help you?"

Crestfallen, Erik stared down at the ledger, automatically memorizing Leigh's address. "I'm afraid it doesn't. Are you sure she wasn't moving to another hotel here in the city?"

"I'm sorry, monsieur. I really couldn't say. I would think it's highly unlikely. We get very few complaints here. Besides, it would be nearly impossible to find a vacancy now."

"*Merci.*" Erik turned away, his shoulders slumped in defeat. Still, he took some small comfort in knowing that Leigh's Washington address was burned into his brain for future reference. Just in case he didn't find her here.

Margit lay stiffly in the queen-size bed next to Erik and stared bitterly up at the dark ceiling. He was turned away from her, lying as close to the edge of the bed as possible. It was as if he were afraid he'd accidently brush up against her. She just couldn't understand it. It reminded her of the early days of their marriage when he'd seemed to dislike her so intensely.

Earlier, she'd attempted to make love to him, but he'd brushed her off, insisting he was exhausted from the day's activities. *What activities?* she wondered. She'd barely seen him. He'd left her in the stands with Bjørn and Dordei and disappeared before Mags's jump. Later, he'd returned for a few minutes only to leave again on some evasive errand. After Mags's second jump, which had been amazingly unspectacular, Margit had waited around with Anne-Lise and Dordei while the men searched for Erik. A half hour later, they'd returned with a disappointed Mags, but no Erik. Finally, he'd shown up, breathless and irritable.

Back in their hotel room, he'd evaded her questions with abrupt replies and brooding silence, finally growling out, "Christ, Margit. I just needed some time alone. Can't you give me some space?"

"Of course," she said icily. With that, she'd turned and slammed out of the room.

After a drink in the hotel bar, she'd returned to the room and found Erik in bed. In the bathroom, she stripped off her clothes and slid into a sexy new negligee.

"Erik?" she whispered as she slipped into bed. When he didn't answer, she slid over against his nude body, one hand playfully caressing his sinewy bicep. Her lips nibbled the back of his neck, just under his silky blond hair. No response. "Erik?" Her hand found its way to his chest and traveled down the mat of springy hair that narrowed to his pubic bone. Margit's breathing quickened. She felt the warm wetness between her legs, and for a moment, she felt as she always had with Bjørn. Hungry with desire. Her hand closed upon his penis. She drew away in revulsion. He was limp, flaccid.

"Erik. What is wrong with you?" Her voice was harsh with frustration. Except for that first time in Greece, Erik had never had any kind of impotence problem. In fact, usually he became instantly hard just at a certain look in her eye or at the inflection of her voice. Every time she'd felt the need for sex, he'd been ready. Until tonight . . .

"I'm tired, Margit," he said. "It's been a long day." He turned on his stomach, as if to protect himself from her advances.

That was a half hour ago. Since then, Margit had been lying here, sleepless. Frustration boiled inside her like a volcano of molten lava. How much longer before she erupted into an explosion of hot fury? Uncaring if she disturbed Erik, she rolled over onto her side with a spasmodic jerk. In his sleep, he turned. She felt his hand slide onto her hip. *What the hell?* She turned to face him. He reached for her. Then, distinctly, he said one word. "Kayleigh . . ."

Margit stiffened. In the half-light from the bathroom, she saw the smile on his sleeping face, and in that moment, she hated him. So, it was still that American bitch. What *was* it about that woman that obsessed him so? Viciously, she threw back the covers and climbed out of bed. For months now, she'd been faithful to her husband, even gave up Bjørn for him, and all the time, he was still hot for a middle-aged American whore.

Her face set grimly, Margit walked over to the desk and picked up the phone. "Room 326, please."

Bjørn answered on the first ring. "Yes?"

"It's me," she said quietly. "Make an excuse not to go to the Nordic-Combined tomorrow. When everyone leaves, I'll meet you in your room." Without waiting for an answer, she hung up.

Turning back toward the bed, she cast a scornful glance at her sleeping husband and muttered, "Fuck you, Erik."

The next morning when Margit informed him she wasn't going to the Nordic-Combined, Erik barely reacted. "Okay," he said and continued shaving. Through the long night, Margit's anger hadn't cooled, and now with his indifferent attitude, it blazed even more intensely.

"Surely there's something better to do than go watch that damn ski jumping," she snarled. "And there's nothing more boring on earth than watching cross-country skiing."

Erik pursed his lips as he stroked the razor under his chin in quick, practiced motions. His eyes didn't move from the mirror. "That's fine with me, Margit. Do what you want."

"Oh, I will," Margit said. "I'll find something to do." *Or someone.*

Actually, Erik was relieved that she wasn't going today. After the morning ski jumping, they would be leaving for the second half of the Nordic-Combined featuring the cross-country ten-kilometer relay. He didn't want to be burdened by Margit's presence . . . because he intended to look for Kayleigh.

After he finished shaving, Erik got dressed and then glanced over at Margit. With a pair of burgundy glasses perched on her nose, she looked like an attractive but haughty librarian as she sat at the table in front of the window, riffling through a fashion magazine. Erik wished he had something to say to her. Since yesterday, all the old feelings had returned. The ones of being trapped in a loveless marriage. How had he been able to deceive himself all these months—actually believing he had fallen in love with his wife?

Since discovering Kayleigh was in Albertville, his thoughts and emotions were in turmoil, but he'd come to an obvious conclusion. One he didn't like. Kayleigh had changed hotels because she didn't want him to find her. Mags had told him how he'd met Knut Aabel at the medal ceremony, and Kayleigh hadn't been with him. Mags was sure his presence had been a shock to her at breakfast the next morning. When he'd described the way the color had drained from her face, Erik had felt a lurch in his chest. Without a doubt, he knew she'd reacted that way because she still loved him, and seeing Mags had been like confronting a ghost from the past. But then why, if she loved him, had she changed hotels, thereby erasing any hope of him finding her in a city full of sports spectators?

Yet, he *would* find her. He was determined to. And when he did? What then? Erik hadn't thought past that. He just knew one thing. When he finally did find Kayleigh again—this time, he'd never let her go.

33

Erik met Mags downstairs in the lobby. Except for the team competition in ski jumping, the Olympics were over for Mags. After his initial disappointment at finishing fourth in the ninety-meter jump, Mags had finally realized that winning only one gold medal was not a bad thing. Besides, there might yet be another medal in store for him in next week's team jump.

They'd been waiting for five minutes when Anne-Lise and Dordei arrived.

"Where're the men?" Erik asked.

Anne-Lise shrugged. "It seems both of them have better things to do today."

"What? Better than the Nordic-Combined?" Mags said. "Who is she?"

Anne-Lise smiled uneasily, and Dordei rolled her eyes to the ceiling. "I'm afraid Hakon has a frightful headache this morning," she said. "He got looped in the bar last night. I guess he'll stay in bed all day."

"And Bjørn insists on going over to watch that afternoon hockey game between Norway and Canada," Anne-Lise said.

Erik lifted an eyebrow. "I hadn't realized he was a hockey buff."

"Nor did I. But he seems to be throwing around surprises these days." A stony glint blazed in her eyes. Erik wondered if they'd had a tiff.

"Well, shall we get going?" he said.

"What about Margit?" Dordei asked.

"It seems Margit is becoming bored with our national sport. She'll probably go out and do some shopping. Actually, I don't know what she's up to, but we're probably better off without her whining." He threw an arm around Mags. "Come on. Let's go watch Norway win another medal today."

"How does *this* feel?" Margit gazed into the dark pools of Bjørn's eyes and slowly lowered her nude body down onto his erect penis. "Ahhh . . ." She eased down, stopping tantalizingly before his full length was enveloped inside her. She smiled. "Mmmm? Do you like this?"

His answer was a tortured groan.

"Did you miss me, Bjørn? Did you miss fucking me?" She slid down another inch. He thrust upward, and she drew away. "Uh-uh. No cheating. Answer me, Bjørn. Did you miss it?"

"You know I did . . . ," Bjørn said hoarsely.

"Say it. Say the words." With her vaginal muscles, she tightened her hold.

"Christ, Margit. You're driving me crazy."

"Say it, Bjørn."

"I missed fucking you, damn it!" Reaching up, he clamped

his hands upon her buttocks and pulled her down, ramming his engorged shaft into her. She bit her lip as she moved sensuously on top of him, her eyes closed. "Witch," he whispered, his hands spreading out over her tempting pink-tinged nipples. In one swift movement, he rolled her over onto her back. "Now, my sweet, I'm going to fuck the living daylights out of you."

"Go for it," she whispered.

"We have a bottle of wine in my room." Margit's toe moved slowly up Bjørn's hairy calf. She smiled and burrowed her face into the hollow of his throat, greedily licking up trails of salty sweat. "Shall I go get it?"

"Mmmm . . . in a moment. I just want you here like this for a little while longer." He lifted a strand of gold-red hair to his lips. "How did I do without you for so long?"

"I don't know. I was wondering that myself." Margit looked up at him and giggled. "I mean, I don't know how I did without *you*."

Bjørn's mouth twitched. "Vixen! I know what you meant." A finger trailed down her neck onto the swell of her breast. "So, what made you change your mind?"

Margit pulled away from him and sat up on the bed. Her tangled hair fell over her face, hiding her expression. "Your brother, the bastard!"

Amused, Bjørn propped himself up with an elbow. "What has he done now?"

"It's Kayleigh again. Last night, he called out her name in his sleep. And I'm sick of playing second string to her."

In a flash, Bjørn scrambled up and roughly drew her around to face him. "So, is that what I'm playing to *you*? Second string?"

She stared at him. "No! Of course not. Bjørn, you know how I've always felt about you. It's just that I'm his wife! And he shouldn't be longing for someone else."

Bjørn relaxed his hold on her shoulders. "That's my Margit. You can't stand it if you aren't number one with everyone."

He slid back down on the bed, pulling her with him. "Kiss me. Then I'll let you get that wine."

Her mouth opened pliantly beneath his, and she felt her blood stir again. Why couldn't she get enough of this man? Would it be the same if she were married to him? Somehow, she didn't think so. Reluctantly, she pulled away. "Let me go. It won't take but a minute." She sat on the edge of the bed and looked around. "Do you have something I can slip on to run across the hall?"

Bjørn grinned. "Sure. There's my shirt on the floor. Of course, the way you ripped it off me, it might not be in one piece."

Margit grabbed the pillow from the bed and tossed it at him. A moment later, she stood before him wearing his light blue broadcloth shirt. "How do I look?"

"Fetching. But if I were you, I'd button it up."

Margit laughed and quickly fastened the buttons. "I'll be right back. Don't go anywhere." She was still smiling when she opened his door and glanced into the empty hall. She scurried across the corridor and unlocked her door. It took only a moment to find the wine bottle in the bottom of her suitcase. She'd bought it for a romantic evening with Erik, but romance didn't seem to be on his mind these days. Not with her, at any rate.

She crossed the hall and reached Bjørn's door. But when her hand went to turn the knob, it refused to budge. "Damn!" she muttered. It must have locked automatically on the way out. Just as she started to knock, a door down the hall opened, and Hakon stepped out from his room.

Margit froze. Hakon stared. A slow grin spread over his face, and he moved toward her. Margit's mind whirled as she tried to think of an innocent reason she'd be entering Bjørn's room, half-naked, with a bottle of wine in her hand. But the expression on Hakon's face told her there was no need for an explanation.

He moved up next to her. "Nice shirt," he said softly, his blue eyes sweeping over her body insolently. "Bjørn has good taste, doesn't he?"

Margit didn't answer.

Hakon's smile widened. "Why, Margit, I don't believe I've ever seen you at such a loss for words. Don't worry. Your secret is safe with me." He paused and rubbed his chin thoughtfully. "But you know, if I *do* keep quiet, I suppose I'll be doing a disservice to my wife. After all, she's quite fond of Erik. If she knew you were—how shall I put it?—cuckolding her brother . . . with her *other* brother . . . well, you see what I'm getting at . . ."

Margit's eyes bored into the gold-plated number on Bjørn's door. "Hakon, just say whatever it is you're trying to say."

His hand reached out and a finger traced the deep vee opening of her shirt. Margit shuddered and pulled away. "Ah, don't be like that, Margit," Hakon said. "Why should Bjørn be the only one to savor your charms? Surely you and I can make a little arrangement, and then perhaps I'll forget everything I've seen this afternoon."

Margit stared at him. He smiled lazily, and his eyes moved to her lips. In repulsed fascination, she watched the tip of his tongue snake out to lick at his upper lip. A wave of sickness engulfed her. Quickly, she reached up and grabbed the hand that still stroked the skin above her shirt. She gave it a sharp twist. "You pig!" She threw his hand away from her as if it were contaminated. "I'd rather sleep with a cockroach! Now, why don't you get the hell away from me."

Hakon's face reddened, and his mouth curled. "You're some snotty bitch! What makes you think I won't go to Erik and tell him his wife is screwing his brother?"

Margit looked him straight in the eye. "Because you're a cowardly prick, that's why. And as long as you think you're holding something over me, you'll keep trying to get me into your bed. But it's not going to work, Hakon. I may be an adulteress, but I'm not a whore. Now, if you'll excuse me . . ." She rapped sharply on Bjørn's door and turned back to Hakon. "I'd get out of here if I were you. Unless you don't mind getting your ass kicked by Bjørn . . ."

Without another word, Hakon turned and walked away. Rubbing his eyes, Bjørn opened the door, and Margit slipped inside, slamming it behind her. She looked up at Bjørn.

"Did you hear that?"

"What?" He shook his head groggily. "Sorry, love, I must've dropped off." He looked at her closer. "Christ, Margit! You're white as snow! What is it?"

Margit took a deep tremulous breath. "Hakon knows about us."

"He won't say anything," Bjørn said firmly when Margit described what had happened out in the hall. "Not after I have a word with him. I feel like breaking his goddamn neck. Coming on to you like that."

"That's nothing new." Margit took a sip of white wine. "He's been doing that ever since Dordei first brought him around. This is just the first time he's ever attempted blackmail."

"Don't waste your time worrying about him. He knows if he tells Erik, I'll come gunning for him." Bjørn tossed off the last of his wine. "What time is it?"

Margit looked at her wristwatch. "Half two. Why? Do you have an appointment?"

"As a matter-of-fact . . ." He took the glass of wine from her hands and placed it on the bedside table. Grinning, he pushed her down onto the bed.

"I got it!" Erik flashed a grin at Anne-Lise as he took his seat beside her. "It's going to be a great photo. I snapped it just as Svelland touched Jakobsen for the relay."

They were sitting in the stands just beyond the stone bridge that had been designated the midway point of the ten-kilometer race. Norway was in a close second to the Russian Unified Team, but their strongest cross-country skier, Sigbørn Syse, would take over for the last leg of the competition. Erik was convinced he'd be the key to a Norwegian victory.

He glanced around. "Where's Mags and Dordei?"

"They went over to the food stand for some hot chocolate," Anne-Lise huddled in her fur coat against the brisk wind. She glanced over at Erik. Should she tell him her suspicions now that they were alone?

But how? How could she come right out and tell him she thought Margit was having an affair with Bjørn? Several times in the past year, that idea had crossed her mind—usually at the Haukelands', when she'd spied them laughing together over something silly, or exchanging a meaningful glance across the room. But she'd always dismissed it. It was just her imagination. After all, Margit was her sister-in-law. What kind of woman would betray her husband with his own brother? And yet, the thought kept returning.

Last night, there had been the phone call. It was late, some-time after midnight. She'd awakened to hear Bjørn answer it. It hadn't taken long, and when he hung up, she'd sleepily asked about it. "Wrong number," he'd replied, and rolled over onto his side away from her. She'd thought no more about it until this morning when she'd discovered Margit wasn't going along to the Nordic-Combined. A cold chill had entered her heart when Erik made that announcement. Coincidental with Bjørn's sudden interest in hockey?

Again, she wrestled with the decision to tell Erik. But how could she? She had no proof, just her intuition. And that wasn't enough reason to ruin Erik's marriage. She glanced over at him. He was scanning the crowd with his binoculars.

"Who are you looking for?" she asked.

He dropped the binoculars and gave her an odd glance. "You wouldn't understand if I told you."

"What does that mean?"

He just shook his head. "Oh, here comes Mags and Dordei with your hot chocolate. Look, I'm going to take a walk. I'll be back in a while."

Erik made his way from the stands and milled through the spectators along the course. Surely Kayleigh was here some-where. Even so, the chances of finding her were slim. Too many people and too large an area to search. Once, he thought he saw her. A slim ash-blond woman dressed in red skiwear. But when he circled around to catch a glimpse of her face, he saw she was a college-age girl. He walked for over an hour, just sweeping the faces of everyone around him. But it was no use. If she was here in this crowd somewhere, he wasn't going to find her.

When he returned to his seat in the stands, Anne-Lise saw the bleak look on his face, and she wondered what had happened. Had he somehow discovered about Margit and Bjørn? She wanted to ask, but fear of his answer kept her silent.

Leigh tied the last of the string around a wrapped oil painting and smiled at the elderly blue-haired patron across from her desk. "I'm so glad you decided on the Hadley Adair," she said. "He's going to be the talk of New York next season."

With a flourish, the woman signed her charge slip and pushed it back to Leigh. She smiled sweetly. "Yes, I do think you're right. He's a very talented young artist."

Leigh carried the painting to the front door of the gallery and handed it over to the woman with a smile. "Thank you, Mrs. Carleton, you have a nice evening."

After she closed the door behind her, Leigh locked it and switched over the tiny gold plaque that read CLOSED. She breathed a sigh of relief and began to turn off the lights. Ward had left hours ago to attend a meeting in New York, and she'd been working alone in the gallery. As luck would have it, it had been a busy afternoon. She was eager to get home to a quiet dinner with Knut.

Since their return from France, they'd grown even closer than before. The antibiotics had done the job, and Knut had recovered quickly from the lung abscess. When he'd gone back to the doctor for a chest X-ray at the end of March, the abscess had healed completely. The frightening episode was in the past, and now she and Knut were enjoying each other more than ever.

Sometimes, Leigh couldn't believe they had been together for over a year. For the first time in their relationship, she really began to think of it as permanent. The other night as she lay in bed next to him, she'd surprised herself by thinking of marriage. If he asked her again . . . would she consider it?

She thought perhaps she would. And strangely enough, Albertville would be the reason for it.

It was as if she'd closed an emotional door that day when she'd checked out of the Chamonde Hotel, having made the decision to walk away from Erik. Now, for the first time, she believed she *was* free of him. He no longer had the power to haunt her.

Leigh stepped into the back room to get her jacket. She was just about to get her purse from Ward's desk when she heard a knock at the front door. "Oh, hell." She hated it when a patron insisted on coming in even though the gallery was closed. It happened all the time. Just because they had money, they felt they were owed special privileges. Trouble was, they usually got them.

She returned to the gallery and peered through the window. It was Knut. Smiling, she hurried to the door. What was he doing here? She thought he'd be waiting at home.

"Hi, darling. What brings you here?" She closed the door behind him and locked it, then turned and reached up to kiss him. His hands clutched her shoulders tightly. With difficulty, she pulled away. "Wow! What did I do to deserve that reception?" She looked up at him, and for the first time, noticed the odd expression on his face. "Knut? What's wrong?"

His face was devoid of color, and his eyes wore an eerie look. "Is there anything to drink around here?" he asked in a subdued voice.

"I think Ward has a bottle of Chivas in the back. Knut, did you have bad news from home?"

He shook his head. "How about if we have a drink first?"

"Okay. I'll get it."

She found the bottle in the bottom of Ward's desk and pulled out a wineglass from the cabinet where the supplies were kept. Her hands trembled slightly as she splashed whisky into the glass. She didn't know what Knut had to tell her, but obviously, it was going to be something she didn't want to hear. When she walked back into the gallery, he was standing at the window staring out at the bright spring afternoon.

"Here."

As he turned to take the glass, his eyes met hers. She re-coiled from the stark agony she saw there. "Knut, please tell me what's wrong?"

He lifted the glass to his lips and drained it. "You'd better sit down." He waited until she sank onto a soft leather sofa. Still standing, he began to turn his wineglass in his hands. Leigh's eyes followed the motion hypnotically. Her hands clutched her skirt.

Knut cleared his throat. "I didn't tell you this before, be-cause I hoped it would all come to nothing. But now, it's obvious that—" His voice caught raggedly, and he turned away, unable to face her.

"Honey—" Leigh moved to get up.

"No," he said quickly. "Please stay where you are. If you come and touch me, I won't be able to go on. I'm trying very hard not to fall apart on you."

Leigh felt the blood drain from her face. Oh, God, he was leaving her! And just when she'd finally realized how much she loved him. She tried to speak, but suddenly, she felt as if she were choking. The pain was worse than she ever thought it would be.

But when he finally spoke, she realized she hadn't begun to understand the depth of pain. And with all her heart, she wished her instinct had been correct. "Leigh, they found a spot on my lungs when I went in for that X-ray after we came back from France." His voice was remote, as if he were talking about someone else.

Leigh shook her head. "No, Knut. You told me you were fine. The antibiotics cleared up the abscess. It was gone, you said."

"Yes. The abscess was gone." He turned around to face her. "But there was another spot. I went in for a biopsy. It's cancer, Leigh."

Leigh's fingernails dug into her thighs. Panic swept over her as the meaning of that one word sank into her brain. But then she thought of Deanna. Deanna, who'd undergone a dou-ble mastectomy, who was now still alive and well in New York. Writing novels. Living a full life. Cancer didn't have to be a death sentence, did it? Quickly, she got up and went to him. "There's surgery, Knut. Chemotherapy."

Shaking his head, he met her eyes. "Come and sit down." He led her back to the sofa and sat with her, holding her hand. "I have a form of lung cancer called small cell anaplastic carcinoma. According to the oncologist, it's the most aggressive type, and it spreads rapidly."

Leigh squeezed his hand. "But surely they discovered it early! You've had no symptoms."

Knut gazed at her solemnly. "I *did* have symptoms. Coughing, chest pain. Swollen joints, remember? But with this particular type of cancer, even when it's discovered early, only three percent survive for five years or more. And in my case . . . it's already spread. It's all through my body, Leigh."

A silent moment ticked by. Outside, the anguished wail of a siren swelled above the city traffic. It was the same sound her heart was making inside her body. Slowly, she pulled her hand away from his and stood. She moved over to the window.

Out there, everything was just as it had been a half hour before. Shoppers sauntered down the sidewalks, swinging their purchases in glossy bags from trendy boutiques. Businessmen hurried along in their dapper three-piece suits in an attempt to beat the onslaught of rush-hour traffic. Impatient automobile horns beeped. Vendors on the sidewalks continued to sell their pretzels, popcorn and hotdogs. Nothing had changed in Georgetown—except that Knut was dying.

With an effort, Leigh tried to compose her expression before she turned to face him. Her voice came out hoarse. "What about chemotherapy? Radiation? Isn't there something they can do?"

Knut rested his elbows on his knees and stared down at the mauve Oriental rug. "My doctor has suggested adjuvant chemotherapy where three or four agents are combined for treatment. He's been very blunt with me. I will be violently ill, my resistance to infection will be dangerously low, and, of course, my hair will fall out." He looked up at her, face stark. "With that, there's no evidence to suggest that my survival time will be any longer. And even if a remission is reached, it will be but a reprieve. Two or three years at most."

"And if you do nothing?" Leigh's voice was a whisper.

His eyes dropped back to the rug. "Three months . . . more or less."

Leigh whirled away. "No! I can't believe this!"

Knut crossed the room and took her into his arms. She clung to his light spring jacket, her body trembling. This couldn't be happening! He didn't try to console her with words, for there weren't any in either of their languages to make the pain any less. Instead, he just held her close. After a long moment, she drew away slightly.

"What are you going to do?" she asked, her voice cracking because of the huge lump in her throat.

"I haven't decided."

As she leaned against him with her face plastered against his solid chest, it was impossible to believe that a virulent disease was eating away at him, taking him from her. "You can't take too long," she said.

"I know."

His voice was a pleasant rumble in her ear. Oh, God, how could this be happening? She drew away and reached up to touch his face. Lovingly, her fingers traced the bones of his cheeks, the laugh lines around his blue eyes, his warm smooth lips. "You don't look sick," she whispered. "Could it be a mistake? A mixed-up chest X-ray?"

Gently, he took her hand away from his cheek and kissed it. "It's no mistake, Leigh."

Her hands dropped to his waist. She leaned her forehead against his chest, wishing she could find the strength to cry. But she was too eaten with fear, still too full of shock to do anything but hold him close.

34

That evening there was no more discussion of the calamity that had befallen them. It was only in the middle of the night when they were in bed that the full horror of the situation sank upon them. Leigh had awakened from a nightmare of ghostly faces and bottomless pits, and for a moment she lay frozen, wondering where she was. Next to her, Knut turned restlessly in his sleep and moaned softly. He reached for her. She took him into her arms, rocking him back and forth as he shuddered against her in unabashed fear. Slow tears tracked down her face as she tried to give him the comfort he so desperately sought.

"It's going to be okay, Knut," she whispered. "I'll be with you through this. No matter what happens, you won't be alone."

Erik sat at a traffic light, hypnotized by the swish of the windshield wipers against the glass. Because of the darkness of the day, his headlights were on, casting a dim, lonely glow onto the slick blackness of the street. A horn honked behind him, and startled, he glanced up to see the light had changed. He eased out the clutch and moved through the intersection.

It was a rainy morning in late May, with thick gray clouds scudding in from the North Atlantic. The night before, there had been gale warnings out along the coast, and today, throughout the city, the spring storm had left reminders of its violent visit. Broken branches and other debris littered the streets, and many areas of Oslo were impassable because of flooding from streams and rivers.

Again, Erik wondered why Dr. Oien had asked specifically to see him alone this morning. Surely he knew Margit would want to be included when he was told the results of his tests. After all, this concerned their future.

With a baby, please God, maybe that future wouldn't look

so bleak. Reality had returned as soon as they'd arrived back in Norway. His determination to find Kayleigh had been nothing more than wishful bravado. He'd realized that as the airliner sped down the runway and lifted into the skies. Kayleigh had made sure he wouldn't find her. That meant only one thing. She was happy with her new life. Once Erik realized that, he knew his only choice was to continue to make a go of the marriage with Margit. And a baby just might make that more tolerable.

After they'd arrived back in Oslo, Margit had received a phone call from her gynecologist concerning the fertility tests she'd undergone after Christmas.

"I'm fine," Margit had told him. "Nothing wrong with my reproductive system. Dr. Wassmo has suggested you see a urologist, unless you want to just keep trying for a few more months."

"No. I'll go in for the tests."

He hoped that if he and Margit could share something as special as the birth of a son or daughter, their marriage would be strengthened. Maybe he could even fool himself again. Pretend he was in love with her. Just as he had after Gunny's hospitalization.

Erik made a left-hand turn into the parking lot of a new office building. The rain drummed against the windshield, falling harder now. He reached into the backseat of the Volkswagen and drew out a large black umbrella. Opening the door to get out, he was overcome with a feeling of foreboding as black and heavy as the leaden skies.

Dr. Oien, a slight bald man with wire-rimmed glasses, sat at his desk, looking over a collection of scattered papers. With a glance up at Erik, he motioned for him to take a seat and then cleared his throat. His thick white fingers reached for a yellow folder. "Ah . . . yes, Mr. Haukeland. Just a moment, and I'll be right with you." He pushed his glasses up on his squat nose and opened up the folder.

Erik glanced at his watch. How long was this going to take? He needed to get over to the university to talk to Dr. Stalsett, his counselor. After returning from France, he'd made the decision to start work on his thesis again. The year of hard labor had been good for him, but now it was time think about a secure future for his family. Margit was thrilled about that, of course.

While Dr. Oien perused the contents of the folder, Erik glanced around his office. Just as in Bjørn's, there were the usual diplomas and certificates on the walls, heavy medical books laden with dust on a shelf in the corner, and a wilting plant on the physician's desk. To the right of the desk hung a thin curtain that surrounded an examination table. Suppressing a yawn, Erik glanced up at the ceiling. His eyes widened at the sight of a full-page color centerfold of a nude beauty taped to the ceiling above the examination table. So, that's what the guys concentrated on during vasectomies. Somehow, he didn't think even a buxom blonde could take his mind off what was happening down below his waist.

The thought of a vasectomy brought to mind something he'd been meaning to discuss with Margit. What form of birth control would they use after she had the baby? As much as the thought filled him with dread, he had to admit vasectomy would be the right choice. His eyes scanned the blonde again.

How about a date, love? Maybe this time next year?

Dr. Oien cleared his throat and looked up. "Mr. Haukeland, you had mumps as a child."

Erik answered blankly, "I had most of the childhood diseases. I suppose mumps was one of them."

The doctor dropped his chin onto folded hands and stared at him. "According to your records, you were thirteen. Are you aware that mumps can cause sterility?"

"I guess I've heard that. Doctor, are you telling me Margit can't get pregnant because I had the mumps?"

His expression softened. "Son, your sperm count is extremely low. I'm sorry, but it's practically impossible for your wife to become pregnant. It was the mumps, you see. Apparently, you suffered an inflammation of the testicles at that time, and the result is—technically, you're sterile."

Erik felt as if he couldn't breathe. This was the last thing he'd expected to hear. All these years, he'd dreamed of being a father, but from the time he was thirteen—

He stiffened, and his eyes drilled into Dr. Oien's. "But it's impossible! You see, I *have* a son. Gunny was born four years ago. Perhaps there's been a mistake in the laboratory test."

Dr. Oien's face reddened as he looked down at Erik's records. "I'm aware you have a son. That's why I asked you here alone. To prevent embarrassment." He opened the desk drawer and pulled out a roll of mints. "Have one? No?" The doctor popped a mint into his mouth. "No, Mr. Haukeland. The tests were run several times. And the results always come out the same." His eyes finally met Erik's. "To put it bluntly, you've been sterile since puberty. Perhaps you should go home and talk to your wife. There is no way you could have fathered a son four years ago."

Leigh awoke early. For a moment, she lay in bed stiffly, wondering why she felt such a heavy weight pressing down upon her. When the last cobwebs of sleep dissipated and she remembered about Knut, a sledgehammer stab of pain slammed through her body. She turned on her side toward him. He was awake and staring at her, his face streaked with tears.

"Oh, Knut . . ." Her hand reached out to touch the wetness on his cheeks.

He covered her hand with his and slowly moved it to his lips. "I'm sorry," he said softly. "I suppose I'm not being very courageous. I should be strong for you."

Leigh slid over to him and buried her face in the hollow of his throat. "Just don't accept it, Knut," she said. "Please fight. I can't bear it if you give up."

He was silent. His hand moved slowly over the skin of her back. Finally, he spoke. "Last night. About what you said. I appreciate your offer, and I love you for it, but I'm not going to hold you to it. I would never ask someone—especially someone I love—to go through that."

Leigh pulled away and stared at him. "You didn't ask! Knut, I love you. I can't run away from this, and I won't! We *will* go through it together, no matter what happens."

His fingers caressed her jaw. "What did I do to deserve you?"

What did you do to deserve cancer? She didn't say it aloud, but suddenly, the question hovered in both their minds. He was only forty-six. Of course, he was a smoker, but not a heavy one. Leigh's father had put away two packs a day for the last fifty years, and he was still healthy at seventy-one. Anyway, cancer was indiscriminate, striking infants and children as well as the elderly. There was simply no reasoning to it. Just a game of chance. It reminded Leigh of Shirley Jackson's "The Lottery." This time, Knut had been the one to get the slip of paper with a black dot.

"Leigh . . ." Knut drew her close and rested his chin on the top of her head. "If I chose not to have the chemo, and I deteriorated to a point where—well, you know—where I can't . . ." He trailed off, and then blurted out, "where I'm no longer human, do you think you could help me die?"

Leigh stiffened. "What do you mean?" It was a stall. She knew what he meant.

"Help me commit suicide."

"Knut, please . . . let's not talk about that now. You still have chemotherapy as an option. You haven't ruled it out, have you?"

He was silent for a long moment. Then, "I haven't made a firm decision."

"We could go to New York," Leigh said. "Deanna had her surgery at Sloan-Kettering. Or we could go to Johns Hopkins in Baltimore. We don't even have to do that. Howard University, right here in D.C., has a cancer center. Knut, I *know* you can fight this thing!"

He kissed the top of her head. She felt her heart sink. Why was she so sure he'd already given up?

"I think I should write Kristin today and tell her," he said. "Don't you think that would be better than telling her on the phone?"

"Yes," Leigh murmured, and made a move to get out of bed. Knut's arms tightened around her.

"No, don't go." His hands moved down her body. "You

know, I don't feel sick yet. In fact . . ." He smiled. "There are parts of me that feel quite healthy."

Leigh pulled away. "Oh, Knut . . . I don't think we should. . . ."

"Why not? Don't you want to?" When she didn't answer, he went on. "There will come a time when we won't be able to make love, Leigh. But for now, I need you." He stared into her eyes solemnly. His voice dropped lower. "When I'm inside you, I feel safe. And I need that right now."

Leigh blinked back tears and leaned down to kiss him. His hands slid the straps of her nightgown from her shoulders, and gently, he pushed her back on the bed. "No matter what happens, I'll always be grateful you came into my life when you did," he said. Then his mouth clamped on to hers, and for a few exquisite moments, she stopped thinking about the cancer cells running amok in his body.

For two weeks, Leigh and Knut went on with their life as if it hadn't been destroyed by the deadly report of an X-ray film. By an unspoken pact, they didn't discuss his illness. Leigh wanted to give him time to make a decision about the chemotherapy, and she realized it was something he had to do by himself. As much as she prayed he'd go for the chemo and at least try to save himself, she knew it would do no good at all to plead with him. This was a decision he'd have to be at peace with, and she had no right to try to influence him in any way.

They took two weeks off from work just to be together, spending long lazy afternoons strolling the mall or gazing at the spring explosion of cherry blossoms on the trees surrounding the Tidal Basin. Occasionally, they would pack a picnic basket and spread a blanket below a huge weeping willow near the reflecting pond of the Lincoln Memorial. There, they'd sit back and watch the parade of people go by.

Their long leisurely strolls through the mall became very important to them, but Leigh worried about his draining strength. Was it her imagination, or was he already growing weaker? At her insistence, they rested often on park benches along the grassy paths. Knut drank in his surroundings as if he were filling his memory banks with the essence of Washington. One sunny afternoon, they found themselves at the threshold of the Vietnam Memorial. Leigh silently tugged on Knut's hand to change direction. This was something he definitely didn't need right now. But Knut stopped and stared at the statue of the three Vietnam veterans standing in bedraggled companionship. He squeezed her hand. "I'd like to walk through. Do you mind?"

She did mind, but didn't try to dissuade him. Even on the best of days, she found the Vietnam Memorial a difficult place to visit. Still, she followed behind him as he walked along the black wall etched with the names of the dead. Here and there, clumps of dried flowers lay on the ground, forlorn remnants of grief from wives, parents, and children. The ones left behind. Knut stopped at a point about halfway along the wall. Leigh caught up with him and took his hand. There, in the grass in front of the wall, stood an unopened bottle of Coors beer with a red bow attached to it. Up until this moment, Leigh had managed to keep her tremulous emotions under control, but this incongruous sight caused her to break. Her eyes blurred with tears.

Knut placed his arm around her. A sudden gust of wind blew a blizzard of cherry blossoms around them, and one lodged in Leigh's hair. Knut plucked it out and brought it up to his nose to smell its perfume. Then, for the first time in almost two weeks, he brought up the subject that had been weighing on their minds.

"At least, I've had forty-six good years. Not like these poor guys. Mere children, some of them."

Leigh stared at him. "You sound like you've made a decision."

He took her hand, and they walked toward the end of the wall. When they exited, he led her to a park bench just outside the memorial. For a long moment, they sat silently, holding hands. For Knut's sake, Leigh tried to compose her face into a semblance of serenity, but inside, her brain shrieked an alarm. She knew what he was going to say, and she didn't want to hear it.

In a quiet, even voice, he began, "Back when Sigurd and I were first married, I watched my mother die of ovarian cancer. There had been months of chemotherapy where she was so ill she couldn't keep anything down for days at a time. It was horrible to watch, but I kept telling myself the treatments were helping her to get better. Finally, she went into a remission that lasted ten months. But then she got sick again. There was more chemotherapy, more nausea. Her hair fell out again. After four months of chemo, a scan showed that the cancer had spread. We decided to take her home to die." A jogger ran by, a male in superlative physical condition. Knut's eyes followed him. "That's what she wanted. But she didn't die right away. Instead, she was tortured by pain. They gave her morphine for it. It helped a little, but in the process, it caused severe constipation. Her stomach swelled like a basketball." He closed his eyes and shook his head. Leigh squeezed his fingers, but didn't speak. "Christ! Can you imagine how she felt? Plugged up like a helium balloon ready to burst? Shriveled like an old raisin? She was a wasted shadow of her former self. That's when I realized the emaciated human in that bed was no longer my mother. She had died long before her body did."

When he didn't speak again, Leigh realized he'd said all he had to say. And she knew what it meant. Still, she couldn't bring herself to believe it.

Knut turned to look at her. "Yesterday, I received an answer from Kristin. She wants me to come home. Sigurd added a note to her letter. She agrees it would be the best thing."

Leigh bit her lower lip. "You'll go to Norway to have chemo?"

"No." Knut's eyes dropped. "I'm going back home to die."

An airliner passed behind the Washington Monument to make its descent into National Airport. The planes come too close to the monument, Leigh thought as she watched it. Someday there was going to be another horrible air disaster in the nation's capital. A toddler ran by the bench, shrieking and laughing, followed closely by a bearded man dressed in casual slacks and an Izod shirt of bright yellow. *Capitol Hill lawyer,* Leigh guessed. *Or maybe a congressman. Probably married to an attractive business woman, one who'd taken a month off to have the baby, all the time conducting her affairs by phone* . . .

Vaguely, she realized Knut was talking again. She tried to focus on what he was saying, but the numbness that had set in when he'd told her of his decision melted away to be replaced by anger. *Why?* she wanted to scream at him. *How can you give up like this? Don't you want to live?* But when she opened her mouth to blurt out these questions, the words died on her lips. It was the look in his eyes. Not an expression of defeat or resignation. Just the sure steadfast expression of a man who'd made a decision and was at peace with it. Her heart dropped. There would be no more discussion about it. He knew what he wanted to do.

"I've been reading Elisabeth Kubler-Ross's books. It's all about making peace with yourself before you die. Taking care of all the unfinished business. That's why I need to go back to Norway. I left a lot of unfinished business there."

"I'll go with you," she said. Then a disturbing thought occurred to her. Maybe he didn't want her there. After all, some of that unfinished business surely had to do with his ex-wife. "That is—unless you don't want me to."

A tender look crossed Knut's face. His hand tightened on hers. "You have your job here, your kids. I can't ask you to drop everything and come watch me die."

Leigh winced. Did he have to be so blunt?

Knut noticed and said, "Better get used to it. I'm beginning to face up to what's going to happen. You must, too. Especially if you really intend to come to Norway with me."

"I do," Leigh said. "I'll talk to Ward about a leave of absence. I can probably find someone to sublet the apartment. I'm sure Ward will take Rosie. And as far as my kids are concerned, I know they'll understand when I tell them why I'm going." Her hand lifted to touch his chiseled cheekbone. Was it her imagination, or was he already beginning to lose weight? "Knut, you're one of the most important things in my life. And if you really want me to be with you when . . ." She couldn't say it.

"When I die? Say it, Leigh." His eyes implored her.

"When you die." It was a whisper.

He gathered her into his arms. From the green lawn of the mall, a blur of orange whizzed toward them. The Frisbee landed with a clatter at the foot of the park bench.

Knut released her and reached down to scoop up the flying disk. He stood up and threw it back to the group of teenage boys in the middle of the green lawn.

"Thanks, mister," one of them called out.

Knut waved at him and returned to the park bench. "That felt good. We should get one of those things."

Leigh nodded and attempted to smile. "We'll stop by Woolworth's on our way home."

35

By the middle of May, all the arrangements had been made for the trip to Norway. They were to leave in mid-June, just after Mel's graduation from high school. With stunned faces, the children had listened to Leigh's explanation about Knut's condition. Melissa had burst into tears and run from the room. In the months since Christmas, she'd grown close to Knut. For the first time in her life, she had a father figure who really seemed to see her when he looked at her. To listen when she spoke. And now, he was to be taken from her? Aaron and Mark were just as upset, but showed it in other ways. Mark had withdrawn into himself, and Aaron's anger had come out in temper tantrums and blatant disobedience. Leigh was surprised the news of Knut's terminal illness had had such an impact on them. How ironic that just as they'd grown to love their mother's companion, he was to be taken from them.

It was a Saturday afternoon, and the apartment was quiet. Knut had gone off on his own to Rock Creek Park. More and more lately, he'd been doing that. As if he needed the time alone. *To do what? Make deals with God? Or come to terms with the inevitable?* That, Leigh hadn't accepted. And she didn't know if she ever would.

She was curled up on the sofa, sketching in her pad. Lately, she hadn't been able to draw anything but somber landscapes and people with hollow eyes. She felt empty of everything but pain. The doorbell rang three times before she heard it. She got up to answer it, and for a moment, stood staring at Deanna's face without a flicker of recognition. Before she could speak, Deanna took her into her arms.

The dam inside her broke, and once again she allowed her pain to escape, even though she knew it would be back. She sobbed into her friend's comforting shoulder, much as Deanna had done more than a year ago in her New York penthouse. When there were no more tears left to cry, Leigh straightened and looked at Deanna. Her friend's face was haggard, her eyes wet.

"It's so fucking unfair," Deanna said.

Leigh turned and walked into the living room. She grabbed a tissue from the end table and blew her nose. "How did you find out?"

Deanna sat down upon the sofa. "Melissa called me. The poor kid was so distraught, she could barely talk. Goddamn it, Leigh, why didn't you tell me? You shouldn't have to go through this alone."

Leigh shook her head. "Dee, I didn't want to remind you about your cancer. It's bad enough having had it once. You've got to worry about it showing up again. And . . . there's not going to be a happy ending here. Not with Knut."

Deanna's eyes darkened. "Mel said there's no hope. That's true?"

"Not as long as he refuses chemotherapy. God, Dee, he's so stubborn. I can't convince him not to give up." She dropped to the sofa next to her friend, a new hope flickering through her. Perhaps Deanna would help her convince Knut to change his mind.

Deanna was silent for a long moment. When she finally

spoke, Leigh had never seen her so serious. "He must know he's going to die. He feels it. Leigh, you can't win against a certainty like that. And if you can't accept that, you're going to be worse off than he is."

Leigh jumped up. "Damn it! I'm so sick of hearing that. There are people out there who have *survived* cancer. You're one of them. Deanna, you can convince him not to give up hope. Just tell him what happened to you."

Deanna looked at her sadly. "I can't, Leigh. Don't you understand? He has *already* given up hope. Mel told me he's going back to Norway to die. And you're going with him." She grabbed Leigh's hand and pulled her back down to the sofa. "Don't do it, Leigh. Not unless you're willing to let him go. Because if you go to be with him at the end, he needs someone who can do that. It won't help him if you keep hanging on."

"How can I not?" Leigh cried. "I love him."

Deanna's eyes were solemn. "I know you do. And that's why you're going to have to let him go."

Erik canceled his meeting with Dr. Stalsett at the university. There was no way he could concentrate on his studies while Dr. Oien's shocking revelation thrummed in his mind. It *had* to be a mistake. Gunny was his son. Wasn't he? If he wasn't— if Gunvor was the father—that meant Erik had married Margit for nothing. Their entire marriage was a sham. Of course, it was anyway, but now with this disturbing news, what little meaning it had held for him was gone.

Kayleigh. Oh, dear God, Kayleigh. That day in the hospital, he could've gone to her. Told her how much he loved her. That he wanted to go back to America with her. But for Margit's arrival, he would've done exactly that.

Of course, he couldn't blame Margit. From the very beginning, she'd believed the child she was carrying was Gunvor's. If it weren't for the blood test when Gunny had been ill with hepatitis, no one would ever have known of the blood incompatibility. But Bjørn had figured it out.

Bjørn. Could it be possible he'd made a mistake? Erik decided to drive over to his office. It was almost lunchtime. He hoped he'd be able to catch his brother before he left.

Cranky children and harried mothers filled the waiting room in Bjørn's office. The blond receptionist was only slightly less disheveled; she looked up and smiled wearily when she recognized Erik. She was an unusually attractive woman, and not for the first time, Erik wondered why she was working in a dead-end job as a medical receptionist. Amazing how Bjørn always managed to surround himself with glamorous women. He couldn't imagine his brother offering employment to a woman who couldn't qualify for the Miss Norway title.

"Hello, Erik," she said. "What brings you here today?"

"Hi, Britta. I have something to discuss with my brother." Erik looked around. "What's going on here today? I thought he'd be ready to leave for lunch."

The woman sighed. "He was called out to examine a premie just before ten and didn't get back until a few moments ago. Meanwhile, we have a backlog of patients here. But if it's important, I can ask him to see you after the patient he's with now."

Erik glanced over at the morose face of a young mother holding a screaming infant in her arms. He grimaced at the din the child was making. "No. I'll wait until he has a break. This is his early day, isn't it?"

"Yes. As soon as he finishes here, he has some free time until he has to make hospital rounds at three o'clock."

"Thanks." Erik took a seat in the corner as far away from the wailing baby as he could get. Every female eye in the room bored into him. Ignoring them, he leaned forward to take a magazine from the table in front of him. It was about kids. Babies. "Christ," he muttered in English and threw it back down.

It was almost two o'clock when the last mother led a big-eyed sulky little girl out of Bjørn's examination room. Britta looked at Erik and smiled. "I'll tell him you're here."

A moment later, Bjørn walked into the waiting room, wearing a welcoming grin. "Erik. What are you doing here?"

Erik stood up. "I need to talk to you."

A curious look appeared in Bjørn's eyes. "Okay. Sure. Come on in my office."

Erik sat down in a plush chair as Bjørn settled himself unceremoniously on the edge of his desk. He peered at his younger brother. "What's up?"

Erik didn't know what to say. What was he doing here anyway? What did he really expect to find out?

"Erik?"

Bjørn's concerned voice brought him back to the reason he'd come. He *had* to find out for sure. "It's about Gunny," Erik said. "You were the one who discovered Gunvor couldn't be his father, right? Were the blood tests really conclusive? Or was it possible a mistake was made?"

Bjørn stared at him. Abruptly, he stood and walked over to the window. The rain drummed against the windows, slanting diagonally across the angry skies. "What's this about, Erik? Why are you so concerned now?"

"I have my reasons." There was no way he was going to get into his medical problems with Bjørn. "I just need to know if a mistake could've been made."

Bjørn moved briskly to his desk and pushed a button on his intercom. "Britta, can you please bring me Gunvor Haukeland's records?"

"Of course, doctor."

He looked back at Erik. "It should be only a moment."

The two brothers were silent while they waited for Britta. Erik sat quietly in his chair and stared at a poster of Bert and Ernie from *Sesame Street* while Bjørn gazed out the window at the rain.

Britta walked in, smiled at Erik, and handed Bjørn a blue folder. He waited until she left before opening it. His eyes flicked over it. "Here it is." He placed the opened folder on the desk in front of Erik. "My notes. You see here that Gunny's blood type is AB positive, and here, I've recorded Margit's blood type. B positive." His index finger dropped to the next line. "And here, finally, is Gunvor's. O negative. It's a medically known fact that B and O cannot produce a child with AB blood."

Erik stared at the file for a long moment. Finally, he spoke, "Is it possible there's a mistake in Gunvor or Margit's blood type?"

Bjørn shook his head. "No. We did another type and cross-match on Margit as soon as I saw these results. It came out the same. And as far as Gunvor is concerned, his medical records list this blood type three separate times. When he had an appendectomy at seventeen, when he joined the service at twenty-two, and when he and Margit were married at twenty-four. Not to mention his birth certificate that has the same type listed. There's no mistake, Erik. Gunvor Lovvig was definitely *not* Gunny's father. Now, do you mind telling me what this is all about?"

"Then who *is* his father?" Erik said quietly.

Bjørn's eyes bulged. "What kind of question is that? You are."

Erik stared up at his brother. "That's where you're wrong, Bjørn. According to my urologist, I can't get a woman pregnant. I've been sterile since I had the mumps at thirteen. So, if I'm not the father, and Gunvor wasn't the father, that leaves only one other alternative. Sweet, innocent Margit was screwing around with someone while she was supposedly happily married to Gunvor."

It had been eighteen months ago that Leigh had first made this trip across the North Atlantic to Norway. How different it had been then. At that time, she'd been filled with a mixture of anticipation and worry at the thought of seeing Erik again. Now, she felt a sick fear in the pit of her stomach. It had been there since that day in early April when Knut had walked into the gallery and given her the chilling news about his terminal illness.

On that other flight, he'd been sitting next to her, as he was now. But then he'd been cheerful and healthy, drinking aquavit and entertaining her with anecdotes of his native country. Now, he was sleeping uneasily, his head lolling against the soft leather seat. His lean face was drawn and shadowed. It pained Leigh to look at him. The vitality was draining out of

him as surely as if a huge leeching machine had been attached
to draw out his diseased blood.

Since Knut had made his decision to forgo treatment, Leigh
had found herself getting unreasonably angry at little things.
She knew her anger was the result of the helplessness she felt
at Knut's decision. In order to relieve the frustration, she realized she should direct that anger at him, but couldn't bring
herself to let him know how she really felt. She'd promised
to be there for him no matter what decision he made, and that,
she was determined to do. Even if she had to watch him give
up. Watch him die.

After they passed through customs, Leigh reached down to
grab her luggage. She'd managed to get by with only one
suitcase and an overnight bag. It had been difficult to pack
when she didn't know how long she'd be here. Knut was still
in fairly good health. At his last appointment with the oncologist, he'd been warned his condition would deteriorate rapidly once the decline began. Yet, death wouldn't necessarily
come quickly. Theoretically, he could remain in a pain-racked,
bedridden state for months.

That was the thing Knut feared most. Living a life that no
longer had any meaning. With just a few words, Leigh knew
she could quell his fear. "I'll help you die." That's what he
wanted to hear. But she simply couldn't say it. As much as
she loved him, she didn't think she could help him commit
suicide. It went against everything she'd been taught about the
sanctity of life.

"You don't need to carry that," Knut said. He took her overnight bag from her. "I have a porter to help us."

"Far!" A girlish voice called out from across the gate separating the customs area from the main terminal.

Knut's head shot up. "Kristin," he said softly. Then his eyes
found her in the crowd waiting for the arriving passengers.
"Kristin!" He grabbed Leigh's hand, and they started forward.

A sandy-haired teenager waited for them at the gate. As
soon as they passed through, she was in her father's arms,

tears rolling down her face. "Oh, Father, I'm so glad you're home."

After a moment, Knut pulled away from his daughter and spoke in Norwegian. The girl took off a pair of wire-rimmed glasses and cleaned them with the tail of her cotton shirt. With a tremulous smile, she murmured something in their common language. But her smile did nothing to dispel the tragic look in her eyes.

Knut put an arm around Leigh and spoke in English, "Krissy, this is Leigh."

Kristin put her glasses back on and eyed her up and down. She smiled and enveloped Leigh in a warm hug. "You've been good to my father," she said in lilting English. "And I thank you for that."

Leigh blinked back tears as the ever-present lump in her throat tightened. It was amazing. From the beginning, Knut had kept nothing from his daughter about his terminal illness. And here she was, watching her father return to his native country to die. So brave and accepting. Why couldn't *she* feel like that? It would be so much easier.

The girl stepped away from Leigh and turned to her father. "Is there anything I can help you carry?" She spoke English for Leigh's benefit.

"No." Knut nodded to the porter at his side. "I believe this gentleman is taking care of everything."

Leigh gazed at Kristin. She looked younger than her sixteen years. Or maybe that was because she was so used to American teenagers and their obsessive desire to look older. Kristin wore her sun-streaked brown hair long and straight, reminiscent of the sixties, and her lightly freckled face was devoid of make-up. Her green eyes sparkled with lively intelligence, and Leigh had the feeling that if it weren't such a sober occasion, a cascade of laughter would bubble from her wide, friendly mouth.

"Well, are we ready?" Kristin said. "We have a house rented for you. It's just down the street from us. Rather small, but we thought you'd make do."

She led them down a large crowded promenade and stopped

a few feet away from a deserted domestic flight lounge. With an apologetic glance at Leigh, she turned to Knut. "*Mor* didn't wish to intrude upon our reunion, so she waited here for us. There she is, in the corner near the window."

Knut glanced into the lounge and turned to Leigh. She saw the haggard look on his face. Her heart skipped a beat. He still loved her. It was written all over him.

"Do you mind if I have a moment alone with her?" he asked softly.

Leigh took a deep breath and smiled. "Of course not. Kristin, is there someplace you and I can go for a soft drink?"

"Sure," she said with a smile that looked uncannily like Knut's.

Knut stared at Leigh long and hard. "Thank you," he whispered. He turned to meet his ex-wife.

36

"Hello." Leigh extended a tentative hand to Knut's ex-wife. "It's nice to meet you."

Sigurd Aabel gave her a sharp scrutiny and apparently approved of what she saw. She grasped Leigh's hand warmly. "Kristin tells me she feels like she knows you from Knut's letters." She paused a moment. "I hope you don't mind I'm here. Kris asked me to come with her. And—" She glanced quickly at Knut, who was watching them closely. "Well, to be perfectly honest, I do still care a lot for my ex-husband. I hope you can understand that."

Leigh found herself squeezing Sigurd's hand reassuringly. "I do," she said softly. Funny thing. She *did* understand, and she felt absolutely no threat from Sigurd's obvious affection for her ex-husband. But would it be the same if Knut were a healthy man? If he had more than a few months to live?

"You can see we had quite a storm here last night," Sigurd said as she drove expertly through the wet Oslo streets. "It looks as if the rain is here to stay."

Appropriate weather for Knut's homecoming, Leigh thought. It was as if all of Norway were in mourning. From the back seat of Sigurd's gray Volvo, Leigh studied Knut's ex-wife. Sigurd wasn't exactly plain, but she didn't have the kind of beauty she'd imagined Knut's ex-wife would have. Perhaps because her chestnut hair had liberal streaks of gray running through it, she seemed older than she was, mid-forties if she was Knut's age. Her eyes, a clear shade of aquamarine, were easily her most attractive feature. The only thing that marred them was a slight shadow of sadness. *Put there by the knowledge of Knut's impending death?*

As soon as this thought went through her mind, Sigurd shocked her. She turned to Knut in the passenger seat and said, "I have everything ready in the house. IV hook-up. Hospital bed. Everything you'll need for when you can no longer get around normally."

Knut nodded. "Thank you."

Leigh drew in a sharp breath. Sigurd had sounded so matter-of-fact. Almost cold. How could she do it? Then Leigh remembered she was a nurse. Perhaps her bluntness was the result of the mandatory distance her profession demanded. Yet, she was talking about a man she once loved! Maybe *still* loved.

Nevertheless, Leigh felt reassured that they would be staying near Sigurd and Kristin. With her medical knowledge, Sigurd would be a great help in caring for Knut. As much as she loved him, Leigh dreaded the nursing care expected of her.

The Volvo pulled into a tiny driveway at the side of a small white house on Kjelsasveien Gate. Sigurd glanced apologetically back at Leigh and spoke, "I know it's terribly small, but rental housing is becoming very difficult to find here in town. We were quite lucky to get this, actually. Old *Fru* Ostby lived here for over fifty years. She died recently and her son decided to rent until his daughter marries next spring. Then he'll give her the house as a wedding gift."

Next spring. No danger of Knut being alive then. Suddenly Leigh was overcome with a bone-clenching anger. Why were they all just accepting it? Where was the fight in these people?

Especially Knut! How could he have accepted his prognosis so quickly? Well, *she* wasn't ready to accept it!

"I guess we'll just have to find another place when she's ready to get married," Leigh said firmly. Defiantly.

Sigurd threw her an odd look. Knut turned and reached over the front seat for her hand. His face was warm, his eyes sad. "That's my Leigh. Always the optimist."

"She *should* be optimistic, *Far*," Kristin spoke up. She smiled at Leigh gratefully. "I am. There's always room for hope, isn't there?"

"As long as you realize there's a difference between hope and wishful thinking, Kris," her mother said gently. She opened the car door. "Shall we go in?"

Sigurd had prepared the house for them with what Leigh was to learn would be her usual efficiency. The heavy living room furniture smelled faintly of lemon oil, and fresh flowers had been placed in every room. Even the cupboards in the old-fashioned kitchen were stocked with staples. In one small bedroom, there was an antique dresser and a matching double bed covered with a delicate embroidered quilt in Norwegian red, white and blue. It was a cozy room reminiscent of the Scandinavian countryside, and Leigh found it charming. But when she looked into the second bedroom down the hall, the sight that met her eyes chilled her to the bone.

It was a stark hospital bed, crisply made and waiting. At its side, stood an IV pole with a plastic bag of clear fluid hanging from it. In a corner behind the IV setup crouched a heavy green tank labeled OXYGEN and the paraphernalia that went with it. On the other side of the bed was a metal table holding a box of tissues and an emesis basin. The door below the drawer was open, and in it, Leigh saw a bedpan resting on a box of plastic bed liners. She remembered using them when she was in the hospital after giving birth. They were to protect the sheets from leaking blood. But with Knut, they would be used for the incontinence he was sure to have in his last days.

The horror of the situation flooded upon her. Until this moment, she hadn't really thought about the reality of what lay ahead. Dear God, how could she watch Knut be reduced to the helplessness of an infant?

She felt a presence behind her and turned to face Sigurd. Her lovely aquamarine eyes searched Leigh's face. Sigurd reached out and clasped Leigh's hand. "You really *do* love him, don't you? I'm glad. Knut deserves someone who can give love unselfishly. That was something I was never able to do."

Leigh found herself wanting to open up to this woman. "I'm so scared," she whispered. "I don't know if I'm strong enough to go through this with him."

"But you will," Sigurd said. "All of us have reserves of strength stored up inside. And when we most need them, they will be there. We're going to get through this together. The four of us. That is, if you truly don't mind our being around?"

"You and Kristin are Knut's family. How could I mind?"

Sigurd smiled. "That's good. We'll all make sure Knut has a peaceful and dignified death."

Leigh stared at her. "Why are you so ready to give up on him? Perhaps if all of us convince him to have chemotherapy, we can extend his life."

The only change in her expression was a softening in her eyes. "Leigh, I've worked oncology for many years now. I know how slim the chances are for someone with an advanced case of lung cancer and metastasis, even with chemotherapy. And I can look in someone's eyes and know when they've accepted their impending death. That look is in Knut's. You don't see it, and Kristin doesn't either. But it's there. And it will be much easier on both of you when you accept it. It will be easier for Knut, too."

Leigh snatched her hand away. "I *can't* accept it, don't you see? Knut is a young man. He has so much to live for. Why can't he at least *try?*" She whirled away and faced the bed. It lay before her like a malevolent creature. Just waiting for Knut. "God, I hate him because he won't try!"

"Your anger is good," Sigurd said. "Don't try to hide it from him. And don't try to make him hang on to hope that is non-existent. Most important, don't hide your feelings from him.

He needs you to be open with him. He'll want to talk about death and how it will feel. Don't discourage this. It will be difficult, of course, but if he isn't allowed to express his feelings, it will impede a peaceful death."

Leigh stood rigidly, unable to speak. Who was this woman? Knut's ex-wife or some kind of programmed computer? Leigh found herself hating her. When she turned around a moment later, the room was empty.

Erik took a bite of lamb stew and chewed it thoughtfully, staring at Margit across the table. She was unusually pretty tonight in her new bright red sweater. Her hair was different, too. Pulled back on the sides and falling to her shoulders in shimmering red-gold waves. So angelic-looking. Was it possible she'd been sleeping around on Gunvor? Bjørn had tried to convince him it couldn't be true. But how to explain Gunny's parentage?

He didn't want to think about it. Not now. Anyway, Bjørn had a point. He'd suggested Dr. Oien might have made a mistake. Perhaps his lab had screwed up with the results of his tests. Bjørn had given him the name of a urologist, a colleague at his hospital. Why not give Margit the benefit of doubt and go for a second opinion?

Erik didn't want to believe Gunny wasn't his. He looked over at the red-haired little boy who was shoveling the stew into his mouth with a chunky hand. Gunny saw Erik's glance, and his lips parted in a huge messy grin.

"Father, will you show me the fountain on Saturday?"

Erik looked at him blankly. Margit sighed. "Have you forgotten already? We're spending the day with your family at *Frognerparken*."

"Oh. I *had* forgotten. Sure, Gunny, I'll show you the fountain."

Erik frowned and looked down at his stew. His appetite had really vanished now. Since Kayleigh's visit almost two years ago, he'd tried to avoid Frogner Park because of the bittersweet memories the place aroused in him. Especially Vigeland's Sculpture Park. As if it were yesterday, he remembered that blustery morning they'd spent in the nearly deserted park, exchanging warm kisses in the falling snow.

He dragged his thoughts back to Gunny. It hurt like hell to think the little guy wasn't really his son. Of course, nothing could change his love for the boy. But the truth could damn well destroy what little feeling he had left for his mother. Had she known from the beginning? Had she purposely destroyed his future with Kayleigh?

His head throbbed at the thoughts racing through his brain. Who was the man? A married lover? Or just another one-night stand? After all, it had happened with him. Why not someone else? And then, there was the other possibility. That Dr. Oien had been wrong, and Gunny really *was* his son.

Tomorrow, he would make that call to the urologist. One way or another, soon, he'd know the truth.

Anne-Lise reached over and touched Erik's arm. "Look at Gunny and Inger-Lise."

Erik followed her glance to the children sitting on the grass nearby. Gunny was up on his knees, meticulously threading wildflowers into the little girl's white-blond curls. Erik chuckled. "What do you think that means? Will he be a lover or simply a hairdresser?"

Anne-Lise grinned. "Well, if he's anything like his father, I'd say he *definitely* won't be a hairdresser."

Erik frowned.

"That wasn't meant as an insult, you know."

He looked over at her and smiled. "I know. It wasn't that. I just have a lot on my mind."

He stretched out on the blanket and gazed up at the clear blue sky. It was a balmy day in June, one that was too rare this far north. The temperature, in the mid-seventies, would've been considered a heat wave if it weren't for a light playful breeze that rippled in from the south.

The entire Haukeland family had already picnicked on a smorgasbord spread and were now either relaxing in the shade of the fir trees or walking off their hearty appetites nearby in Vigeland's Sculpture Park. Erik had chosen to stay behind

with Anne-Lise, his parents, and the children. He just couldn't
bring himself to face the sculpture park. There were too many
memories.

Erik felt a small hand tug at the sleeve of his cotton shirt.
"Father, you promised to take me to see the fountain."

He groaned and propped himself on an elbow to gaze into
Gunny's earnest face. "Just let me rest awhile, Gun. When
your mother gets back, we'll go."

Appeased, the little boy wandered back to Inger-Lise. Anne-
Lise looked over at Erik. "It seems Bjørn and Margit have
something important to discuss. They've been gone for almost
a half hour." An amused light glimmered in her blue eyes.

"Mmmm?" Erik dropped back to the blanket and closed his
eyes. The picnic lunch had made him sleepy.

"I wonder if it has anything to do with a certain birthday
coming up next week?"

Erik opened one eye and grinned. "What have you heard,
Anne-Lise? I don't want some silly surprise party."

Anne-Lise laughed. "I'm not saying a thing." She turned
over on her stomach and propped her chin on her hand.

Erik contemplated her for a moment. He'd noticed a sparkle
to her lately; she looked younger and more attractive than she
had a year ago. Bjørn was a damn lucky man to have a wife
like Anne-Lise. She was so open and unassuming. Fresh. For
a long time, he'd thought Margit was that way. But now, every
time he looked at his wife, he saw a slyness he'd never noticed
before. Or was it his imagination? He'd know for sure in a
few weeks. His appointment with the new urologist was scheduled for next Thursday. As soon as the tests results came in,
he would know the truth about Margit.

"You really look happy, Anne-Lise," he said. "There's quite
a difference in you since we were in France."

"Yes, I guess you could say I've done some growing up
since then. There were a lot of things running through my
mind about Bjørn. You wouldn't believe some of the stuff I
was imagining." She laughed and then eyed him thoughtfully
before going on. "I'm so ashamed of myself now. For a while,
I actually believed Bjørn was having an affair with Margit."

Erik propped his head on his hand and looked at her. "Are you serious?"

Anne-Lise nodded. "I hate to admit it, but I really did think that."

"What did you have to base it on?"

"That's just it. Nothing. It was just a feeling. But now I know I was being paranoid. When we got back home, Bjørn and I had it out. I discovered he was feeling neglected because of the time I spent at work, so he retaliated by putting in more time at the hospital and neglecting *me*. It was one of those vicious circles. Since we cleared the air about it, he's been so much more loving and attentive. And I've been making sure I have more time for him. Erik, don't make that mistake with Margit. Be sure to plan time together, away from Gunny. It makes such a difference in a marriage."

Erik sat up. "Did you ask Bjørn about him and Margit?"

"Of course. I was very angry, and I hurled the accusation at him."

"And what did he say?"

"He denied it, of course."

"Do you believe him?" Erik asked quietly.

Anne-Lise looked at him. "Come on, Erik, don't look like that. I told you, I was imagining all kinds of things about Bjørn. And yes! I *do* believe him. He's been wonderful to me lately. I was a fool to be suspicious of him."

"Yes, I suppose you're right. It's ludicrous to think of him and Margit together." Erik dropped back down to the blanket and closed his eyes. "They've known each other since she was a girl. She's like a little sister to him."

Yet, he couldn't quite dismiss the sudden image in his mind of Bjørn and Margit—in bed together.

"We can talk here," Bjørn said after they'd been walking silently for several minutes inside the huge black-and-white granite slabs of Vigeland's Labyrinth.

Margit turned to face him. "I don't think this is a very good idea. What if Erik comes looking for me?"

"This won't take long," Bjørn said grimly. "And it's important."

"Well, what is it?"

"Erik came to my office on Thursday and dropped a bombshell in my lap. You know those tests he took to determine his sperm count? Well, apparently, he hasn't got many of those little buggers swimming around in those stallion balls of his. He's sterile!"

Margit stared at him. "Why did he tell you instead of me? He hasn't mentioned a word of it."

Bjørn gripped her shoulders. "My dear little addle-brained redhead, I don't think you understand what I'm saying. He's sterile because of a childhood disease. Mumps. Remember it? It balloons out your cheeks and makes you look like a little chipmunk."

"So, what of it?" Margit gave an exasperated sigh. "Bjørn, would you get to the point?"

"Think, darling. He was an adolescent when he had the mumps. That means he's been sterile since then. No babymaking powers. Yet, you turned up pregnant with Gunny. And we proved Gunvor couldn't be the father because of his blood type."

Margit felt the blood drain from her face. "So, that means—"

Bjørn nodded. "Bingo. You're looking at Papa. Unless you had yet another man on the side."

"Oh, God." Her eyes focused blankly on the labyrinth wall. Then she looked back at Bjørn. "What did you tell him? Christ, Bjørn, you didn't tell him we were sleeping together?"

"Of course not. I've bought us some time. I convinced him to go to another urologist for more tests. That will give us a few weeks, at least."

Panic curled in her stomach. "But then what will we do? Bjørn, if he finds out you're Gunny's father and I made him marry me, he'll be furious! He'll never understand I sincerely believed he was the father."

Bjørn grimaced. "Oh, come on, Margit! We both knew from

the start Gunny could've been mine. But we decided you should marry Erik to cover up our affair."

"*You* decided," Margit reminded him. "You were dead-set against him going off with that American woman. And you used me to keep him here."

Bjørn's voice was cold. "I don't remember you protesting too loudly about it at the time, my sweet."

"Perhaps I didn't. But let me tell you one thing, smart boy. *I* was the one who got rid of that bitch. Your little plan almost backfired. When I went to that hospital in Ose, I had to do some fast talking to convince Erik to marry me. He wanted to see her again. And if he had, I don't think he'd be here now. But I took care of it. I convinced him to write her one of his gushy good-bye notes. Then I said I'd take it to her." Margit smiled. "But I didn't. I tore it into little pieces. So, you can thank *me* for making sure she wouldn't turn up again. I've been on the ball the entire time. You're the one who seems to be screwing up these days. What are you going to do about this?"

Bjørn's face was grim. "Don't worry. I have it covered. The urologist he's seeing next week is a friend. And he owes me a favor or two. I don't think I'll have any problem convincing him to make sure Erik's test results show plenty of little swimmers."

Margit's lips tightened. "You'd better, Bjørn. Because if you don't, it's our skin. And brother or not, I don't think Erik will stop at anything to come after you."

37

Margit and Bjørn's voices drifted away. Hakon realized they were moving toward the exit of the labyrinth. His ears still rang from what he'd just heard. What a stroke of luck it had been when he'd lost them in the maze. When he first saw them enter Vigeland's granite slabs, he'd tried to follow behind, hoping he'd be able to pick up some useful information, but only a few seconds later, he'd lost them in the confusing twists and turns of the place. After searching for a few minutes longer, he'd given up and stopped to light a cigarette. That was when he'd heard their voices from just over the slab he was leaning against. Motionless, barely breathing, he'd listened, a slow grin spreading across his face as their words sank in.

So, little Gunny is Bjørn's son. Since discovering Margit and Bjørn's tête-à-tête in France, he'd been relishing their little secret, wondering exactly what he could do with it.

He still remembered the look on Margit's face when he'd propositioned her. She'd gazed upon him like he was some kind of primordial creature that had just climbed out of a slime pool. No woman had *ever* looked at him like that before. Margit was going to be sorry she had. With this little gift of information, he was going to bring that snobbish redhead down into the muck where she belonged. And Bjørn with her.

Hakon grinned as he left the labyrinth. He knew just how he was going to do it.

As Margit exited the labyrinth with Bjørn, she idly glanced over at a group of people walking past on the sidewalk. There was something very familiar about one woman, a tall, attractive blonde dressed in a lavender-paisley muslin skirt and a linen blouse. She walked beside an older man who moved tentatively as if he were out of practice at walking. Two others, an older woman and a teenage girl, completed the group. For a moment, Margit had no idea why the blond woman looked so familiar. Then it hit her with the impact of an icy plunge into a fjord.

Kayleigh! Erik's American woman. Margit stopped and stared. What on earth was she doing back in Norway? Looking for Erik? If so, Margit would have to make damn sure she didn't find him.

"Come on," Bjørn said. "Why are you stopping?"

She almost told him about Kayleigh, but then changed her mind. He might let it slip to Erik. "Why don't you go on ahead, Bjørn. I need to be alone for a few minutes."

"I'll see you later." He turned and headed for the exit.

Margit followed Kayleigh and her friends. She wasn't sure how to approach her. Perhaps if she followed long enough, she'd find a chance to get the American woman alone. But after a few moments of trailing the group, Margit realized Kayleigh was sticking to the frail-looking man like glue. Who was he, anyway? Too young to be her father. Her husband? But why would she bring him to Norway, especially if she were planning to look up Erik? And who were the other two? The dark-haired older woman reached the shade of a blue spruce tree and turned around to the others as if to ask if the spot was agreeable to them. Margit watched as Kayleigh and the teenager spread a quilt onto the ground. The man stretched out upon it while the women unpacked a picnic basket. Margit decided she couldn't wait any longer to approach her. Let the others think what they would.

Kayleigh didn't see her until she spoke.

"Hello, Kayleigh. What brings you back to Norway?"

The American woman looked up, and Margit was pleased to see her face whiten with shock. Slowly, she stood and faced her. The other woman and the teenager paused in what they were doing to stare at her curiously. Margit felt the eyes of the man upon her, too. Kayleigh finally spoke, "It's Margit, right?"

Margit bristled at her false tone. The American woman knew damn well who she was. She watched as Kayleigh's hazel eyes searched the area behind her. Looking for Erik, she supposed. Thank God he hadn't been with her in the sculpture park, or surely he would've seen her, too. And if he had? What would be happening right now?

"Oh, so you *do* remember me? I wasn't sure."

Kayleigh looked around at the others. "Oh, yes. I met Margit on my first visit here. Margit, I'd like you to meet some very good friends of mine. This is Sigurd and Knut Aabel and their daughter, Kristin."

Sigurd, the older woman, smiled warmly at Margit and spoke in English, "Won't you join us for *lunsj*? We have plenty of food."

"No, thank you. I've already eaten." So, they were Norwegian. But how were they connected with Kayleigh? Her gaze returned to the American woman. "Actually, I'd love to have a word with you in private. If your friends could spare you for just a moment."

"Of course," Sigurd said. "But hurry back, Leigh, if you want some food. Kris is at an age where she eats like a hungry wolf."

As they walked away, Margit heard the teenager protest at her mother's affectionate dig. Silently, they headed back toward the entrance of the labyrinth. Margit realized Kayleigh wasn't about to initiate the conversation. With irritation, she noticed the American woman's color had returned, along with her composure. Margit felt an irresistible urge to shake it up again.

"So, did you come back to Norway to see Erik?"

Kayleigh stared at her. "No. Of course not!"

Margit eyed her coolly. "I hope that's true. Because he hasn't the slightest interest in seeing you again." She didn't miss the wounded look that flared in Kayleigh's eyes, and decided to press her advantage. "As a matter of fact, he's told me many times how much he regrets the relationship he had with you."

"He told you about us?" Kayleigh's voice was soft with shock.

"*Ja*, he told me everything. All about your sleazy affair in America. *His* words, by the way. Let's see, how did he put it? Something about 'middle-aged American ass.' "

"I don't believe you." Anger flared in Leigh's hazel eyes, and Margit congratulated herself. She'd obliterate every ounce of feeling this woman had for her husband if it was the last thing she ever did. "Erik would never have been so vulgar."

Margit met her shocked gaze calmly. "But Kayleigh, you didn't really know Erik, did you? You couldn't have. The only thing you two ever had in common was a hot bed. Oh, at first, he believed he was in love with you. But after we married, he realized how shallow your relationship was. And now he hates you for seducing him."

"I seduced *him*?" Kayleigh's face had gone bloodless. She didn't speak for a moment, then, she said softly, "I never realized you were such a vicious bitch."

Margit held back a delighted laugh. Oh, this was going too well. She sighed and casually examined the end of her long braid. "I am trying to save you from yourself. I know you must be here searching for Erik. And I simply want to spare you the humiliation of confronting him. These words coming from him would hurt much more, don't you think?"

"What I *think* is that you must not be very sure of yourself or your marriage if you're going to all this trouble to warn me to stay away from Erik." Kayleigh said. Her face was still white, but her eyes glittered with anger. It didn't matter. Margit was finished with her. She had a feeling their little conversation had been very effective.

"That's what you would like to believe, isn't it?" She smiled and touched the American woman on the shoulder. "Anyway, I must go. Erik is over in the park with our son. You should see him. He's growing so big, and looks just like his father. Erik is so proud of him. But then, he's such a wonderful daddy. We just couldn't be happier, the three of us. Nice seeing you again."

With a satisfied smile, Margit turned and walked away from Kayleigh. When she passed her friends, she smiled and waved. "Nice meeting you. Take good care of Kayleigh. She's a sweetheart!"

Trembling, Leigh walked back to where the Aabels were waiting. Not only was she devastated by Margit's cruel words, she was stunned by the difference in the Norwegian woman's personality. When she'd met her the first time, Margit had been friendly and outgoing. Nothing in her manner had hinted at the viciousness she'd just displayed. The attack had been so sudden. What hatred must have festered in her these last two years. But why? Because of the things Erik had told her? He must've told her. How else would she have known? That hurt the most. Knowing Erik had shared with her the intimate details of their relationship. "Middle-aged American ass." Could he have really said that? He *had* said some pretty vile things in the past when he'd been angry. Even if he hadn't said it in those words, wasn't it possible he'd implied as much to Margit? Perhaps it was true. Maybe this was how he thought of her now after he'd gained some perspective. Middle-aged American ass.

Leigh blinked back tears. She'd finally found the strength to bury her feelings for Erik in the back of her heart, but now, to think he might not have ever loved her at all—it hurt more than she ever thought possible.

By the time she reached the quilt they'd spread out on the ground, Leigh had managed to compose her face into what she hoped was an expression of serenity. Knut smiled and reached a hand up to her. "Ah, good. You're back. Sigurd just brought out the gravlaks."

Leigh looked over at the delicate pink salmon flecked with dill and other spices. A wave of queasiness rushed over her. "I don't feel like anything just now."

Knut's hand tightened on hers. He peered at her closely. "What's wrong?"

Leigh shook her head. "Nothing. I guess the sun is getting to me."

Kristin grinned. "What sun? You're in the shade."

"Kris!" Sigurd reprimanded. "Mind your manners!"

"So, who is this Margit?" Knut asked.

Leigh rubbed her forehead where a headache was beginning to throb. "Oh, she's someone I met on my first visit here. A family friend of . . . someone I used to know." She didn't look at Knut, but she knew what he was thinking. Strange. Not once had he ever asked her about Erik. It was as if he didn't want to know.

"Kayleigh," he said.

Leigh stiffened.

"That's what she called you. It's such a beautiful name. I can't understand why you don't like it."

Abruptly, Leigh stood. "I have to get some air."

She walked aimlessly, her mind echoing with Margit's caustic words. *Why does it hurt so badly?* she wondered. It had been over with Erik long ago. *It shouldn't hurt this bad.*

She found herself at the Fountain of Life. As she stared up at the worn faces of the elderly men straining to carry the weight of the fountain, her eyes misted with tears. It had been a mistake to come this way. The sharp memory of being at this very spot with Erik pierced her. Had that been a lie? That day . . . the look of love in his eyes. Had it all been a lie?

She heard Norwegian voices on the other side of the fountain. Abruptly, she turned away and retraced her steps. She didn't want anyone to see the tears streaking down her face.

"Here we are, Gunny. The Fountain of Life!"

Erik hoisted the little boy onto his shoulders. Gunny clapped his hands and laughed.

"Go closer, Father. I want to feel the spray!"

"No way, little one," Erik laughed. "Your mother will kill us."

"Walk around it then. I want to see it all."

Erik strolled around the fountain. Out of the corner of his eye, he caught a glimpse of a slim blond woman in a lavender-paisley skirt making her way down the steps. His stomach contracted. How like Kayleigh she looked. Even moved like her.

Bitterly, he shook his head and turned back to the fountain. He had to stop this nonsense! Was he going to live his entire life seeing Kayleigh's ghost in every attractive blond woman he passed?

"Gunny, I've taken you to the fountain as I promised. Are you quite happy now?"

"Yes, Father. Now can we go to the Labyrinth?"

"All right. But only for a few moments."

Erik walked on. The sight of the blond woman had cast a pall over his day. His lips tightened.

I'm glad you're happy, son. Enjoy it. Because happiness is fleeting.

It was Monday morning, two days after their picnic at Frogner Park. Erik was just about to get into his Volkswagen when he found the first note under the wiper blade. It was unsigned and scrawled clumsily with a green marker. And it asked the same question he'd been asking himself for the last week.

Who was Margit sleeping with the year Gunvor died? (Besides you?)

No one, not even Knut or Sigurd, realized the outing in Frogner Park would be his last. That night he began to cough and his temperature shot up to 102. Sigurd guessed it was a cold, but it wasn't to be taken lightly. With his lowered resistance, it could easily turn into pneumonia. She called in a doctor, who immediately prescribed a precautionary decongestant. Even though he was terribly ill, Knut continued to sleep in the big bed with Leigh. She held him closely as violent episodes of coughing racked his wasting body, thinking if only she could keep him in this bed with her, instead of surrendering him to the one in that other horrible room, she could stop him from dying.

After a few days, his temperature returned to normal, and the coughing eased. Yet, he remained weak and lethargic. Leigh made frequent trips to the library to keep him in reading material. She was becoming quite familiar with the streetcar system of Oslo, and more and more, she enjoyed her time away from the depressing little house on Kjelsaveien Gate. It made her feel guilty when she found herself gazing at the sights of Oslo instead of thinking of Knut. But then, she knew he would be happy she wasn't spending all her time worrying about him, and conversely, that made her feel even more guilty. After a few hours away from him, she would step off the streetcar at the corner of Storoveien and Kjelsaveien and walk down the street to their house. As she approached, her stride would slow until it felt like she was barely moving at all. By the time she reached the door, her heart would be as heavy as the load of books she carried in a bag.

For the first few weeks in the house, the two of them had enjoyed nightly strolls in the neighborhood. But this stopped after he caught the cold, and since then, he hadn't felt like trying it. Still, Leigh continued to encourage him to walk again. She thought if she could just get him to take a walk with her, she might be able to delay what was going to happen. But Knut always pleaded fatigue. And each time he said it, Leigh's heart sank a little lower.

Every night at nine o'clock, Leigh poured him a glass of aquavit, and after he drank it, she helped him to his feet and led him to bed. Their bed. And in her mind, she could hear her own voice screaming out defiance to the hospital bed in the other room.

"No. You can't have him yet. Not yet!"

38

Erik had no idea who had left the note. Or why. But it did serve to increase the likelihood that Dr. Oien was right and Gunny wasn't his son. It sounded like whoever had placed it under his windshield wiper had inside information. But who could it be? Someone in the family? Someone in Gunvor's family perhaps? Or—could it be Margit's lover? He would certainly have reason to benefit if their marriage crumbled.

Still, Erik wasn't about to condemn her on the evidence of one anonymous note. He'd wait and see how his tests turned out with this other doctor Bjørn had recommended. If the results came back showing he did have enough live sperm to impregnate Margit, the whole thing could be dropped.

That was before he received the second note, scrawled in the same green marker.

Ask Britta about Bjørn's extra apartment.

In the pleasant sun-filled hospital dining hall, Leigh sat across from a uniform-clad Sigurd and watched her stir sugar into a mug of coffee. Leigh took a sip of weak iced tea and glanced through a window that overlooked a small courtyard. Several robed patients were gathered there to enjoy the warmth of the summer sun. How depressing to be in a hospital on a beautiful day like this! She thought of Knut back at the house with

Kristin. Inside watching television or reading like he did now all the time. It had been weeks since he'd been outside.

Leigh wished Sigurd had been able to take her lunch break away from the hospital. She felt the need to get away from all this sickness, to go to a place where people were healthy. Where life was normal. Some place like a mall or an amusement park where she could see smiles instead of sadness, laughter instead of tears.

"Leigh! Didn't you hear what I said?"

Leigh jerked her attention back to Sigurd. "No, I'm sorry. What?"

"I asked you if he seemed any different today?"

"No. The same as usual."

Sigurd didn't need to ask. Every night after work, she came by the house to check on him. Leigh was always happy to see her. Just having her there, even for a short time, relieved some of the pressure. Knut was becoming increasingly dependent upon Leigh, and because he hated it, he was sometimes brusque and impatient. It hurt Leigh when he growled at her, yet, she understood why he did it. But knowing why didn't make it hurt any less.

Raising the mug to her lips, Sigurd cast an assessing look at Leigh. She took a sip and then spoke, "It's not going to be long before he'll have to move into the other room."

Her stomach lurched. "No. It's not time. He still manages to get around the house by himself." Her hand trembled as she brushed back a stray lock of hair. "In fact, lately, I think he's been feeling better. He isn't coughing as much."

Sigurd eyed her solemnly. "When are you going to stop fooling yourself, Leigh? Even Kristin has finally accepted reality."

Something snapped inside Leigh. It was impossible to hold back her anger. "You mean she's given up, just like you and Knut. Well, I can't do that! And I don't understand how you can either. You say you love him, and you know what, I believe that. I don't think you ever *stopped* loving him. And I think he loves you, too. That doesn't bother me. In fact, I think it's pretty damn wonderful. I don't know what went wrong with your marriage, but I think it's a shame two people who love each other as much as you do wasted so many years. But you know what's even more shameful than that? It's shameful that a man we both love is wasting away right in front of our eyes every day, and we're not doing a damn thing to stop it." Leigh ended her tirade with a long shuddering breath.

Sigurd reached across the table and took her hand. "There is nothing we can do, Leigh. We can only let him go."

Leigh snatched her hand away and stood up, her eyes burning. "Well, there's something I can do. I'm going back to the house right now, and I'm going to *demand* that Knut start chemotherapy immediately."

Instead of taking the streetcar to Bygdoy Peninsula, where she'd intended to tour the Viking ship museum, Leigh caught the one heading back toward the house on Kjelsaveien. She walked in the front door and slammed it behind her. Startled, Kristin looked up from the TV.

"Leigh! What are you doing back so soon? You were supposed to take the whole afternoon."

Leigh stared at Knut's daughter. "I changed my mind. Where's Knut?"

"Sleeping. He was very tired after lunch."

Leigh strode restlessly to the window and glanced out at the quiet street. She couldn't wake him. It would have to wait. But she was determined to convince him to try chemo.

"What is it?" Kristin said softly. "What has happened?"

Leigh turned to look at Kristin's earnest young face. A wave of tenderness swept over her. She moved over to the sofa and sat beside the girl. "Kris . . ." Her hand lifted to sweep away a strand of sandy hair from the girl's smooth forehead. "Have you given up on him?"

Kristin's green eyes dropped to her lap, and her hands twisted the cotton fabric of her blue shorts. Leigh stared at her long blond lashes through her wire-rimmed glasses as they blinked quickly to hold back tears. Kristin didn't speak. Leigh reached over and squeezed her fine-boned hand.

"It's okay," she whispered. "You don't have to answer."

Her silence had answered for her.

Kristin left a short while later. And still Knut slept on. Finally, at four o'clock, Leigh heard him moving about the room. She went to his door. He stood on unsteady feet, clumsily tying the belt of his robe. The only sound in the room was his raspy breathing, a result of the congestion he'd developed lately while sleeping. He looked up and saw her. A haggard smile crossed his face.

"Hello, *englebarn*. Did you have a nice afternoon?"

"It was fine," she said. "Knut, I want to talk. When you're ready, I'll be in the living room."

The urgency in her voice must have been obvious. A moment later, he shuffled into the room and dropped onto the sofa. A shaft of fear coursed through Leigh's body at his weakness. It grew worse every day. Even more reason to go on with what she had to say.

Leigh sat down in a chair opposite the sofa. He wore an expectant look as if he knew she was about to say something he didn't want to hear. She plunged in. "I want you to have chemotherapy."

When he didn't react, she went on as if the speed of her delivery would be enough to convince him to change his mind. "You have to try it, not just for yourself, but for all of us who love you. For Kristin and Sigurd. And me. Knut, you can't just give up and die. With chemo, you might be able to prolong your life. And isn't a few months better than nothing at all? And who knows? It might even cure you. It *has* happened, Knut. I've read about it. And if it doesn't work, we can try something else. We can go to Mexico and you can try laetrile. People have done that, and they've survived. And another thing. Just the other day, I was reading a book about Steve McQueen. He had lung cancer, too. They had him on this new treatment . . . coffee enemas, a raw food diet. Some kind of therapy with vitamin C. And yes, he died, but it wasn't from the cancer. When they opened him up in surgery, the tumors practically fell out. They had stopped growing. The cancer didn't kill Steve McQueen, Knut. It was the blood-clotting drug they gave him as a precaution against internal bleeding.

A clot formed and went to his heart. But Knut, the treatment was killing the cancer! Don't you see, there are things we can try, instead of just waiting for you to die. If the laetrile or the diet doesn't work, we'll find something else!" Finally, she ran out of breath and stopped, waiting for some kind of reaction.

Thoughtfully, he gazed in her direction and then slowly nodded. "*Ja.* If the laetrile or the diet doesn't work, we can join one of those religions. You know, the ones that tell you all disease is in the mind. Perhaps transcendental meditation will make the cancer go away. But if *that* doesn't work, perhaps we can fly to Haiti and have a witch doctor perform voodoo on the cancer. And, of course, there's always garlic I can tie around my neck. . . ."

Leigh stared at him. The moment of triumph she'd experienced at the beginning of his reply drained away. Was there nothing she could say that would make the slightest dent in his martyrlike armor? She jumped up from her chair.

"You're nothing but a coward, Knut Aabel!" Angry tears spilled down her face. "You're *afraid* to fight for your life, aren't you? Why don't you just admit it?" She strode to the window and looked out at the quiet street where normal people were going about their normal lives. It had clouded up and the first drops of summer rain splattered against the glass. She whirled to face him again. "You know something? I don't know of *anyone* in your situation who wouldn't at least *try* to fight this disease. Look at Deanna! Did she give up when they told her she had cancer? Hell, no! She had the surgery, she had radiation treatments. And look at her now! Churning out one book after another. She's *cured*, Knut, because she *didn't give up*! My God! Even Bob wouldn't give up if this had happened to him. And we both know what a wimp he is. Why are you giving up? *Why?*"

Knut shook his head, but didn't answer for a moment. Finally, in a soft controlled voice, he spoke, "In Norse mythology, there's a story about three goddesses who spin the threads of life for the mortals below. No one knows how long their thread will be. You either get a nice long one or you may get a short one. My thread is running out, Leigh. I know it, and

I accept it. That's what you must do, as well. You must accept it. If you can't do it for yourself, do it for me." He held out his hand to her in a silent plea.

Leigh had never seen a more vulnerable look on a human face. She moved to him and gathered him into her arms. "I love you, Knut," she sobbed. "I don't want you to die." As she held him, she was aware of the sharpness of his bones through his thin pajamas. So much weight loss in so few weeks. Already, with his gaunt cheekbones and the dark shadows under his eyes, he bore only a fleeting resemblance to the man she'd known back in Georgetown. *He's dying*. The thought ran through her mind and for the first time since she'd received the bad news, she really believed it. Slowly, she pulled away from him and with the back of her hand, wiped the tears away.

"I'll go start dinner."

After that episode, she should have been prepared for what was to come that night, but when it happened, it was like being hit in the stomach with a cannonball.

It was just after nine o'clock, and she was assisting Knut on his walk to the bedroom. They'd just reached the threshold when he stopped and placed one trembling hand on the door frame. He shook his bowed head and said one word.

"No."

He looked up at her slowly, and in his eyes Leigh saw the torment of a ravaged soul. She bit her lower lip and then wordlessly took his arm and led him down the hallway to that other bedroom where the hospital bed waited. Still silent, she pulled back the covers. When he was in bed, she tucked the blanket around him and bent down to kiss him on the forehead. His eyes had already closed, but his hand squeezed hers weakly. Quietly, she moved away from him and left the room.

In the kitchen, she went to the phone and dialed Sigurd's number. She spoke to her for a moment in a calm measured voice. After she hung up, she moved to the stove and put on a kettle for tea. Sigurd would probably like a cup after she was finished hooking up Knut's IV.

While waiting for the water to boil, Leigh wandered restlessly around the small house, but avoided the hallway that led to the bedrooms. In the living room, she stopped in front of a print on the wall above the fireplace. Although she'd noticed it before, she'd never really paid much attention to it. Now, she studied it as if it were suddenly important she burn it into her memory. It was of a group of people in a room that contained a half-obscured bed and a chair facing away from the viewer, preventing the occupant from being seen. In the foreground, a woman sat with her head bowed, her hands clasped and another woman stood behind her, an expression of despair on her white oval face. Leigh's eyes dropped to the title at the bottom of the print. A chill swept through her body and settled in the pit of her stomach.

The painting was by Edvard Munch and it was titled *Chamber of Death*.

Britta Gjerde lived in a small flat near Oslo University, not far from where Erik had lived before he married Margit. Nostalgic memories of his college days surrounded him as he walked along the quiet street along the campus. Life had been so simple then. "So fucking uncomplicated," he whispered to himself. Not like now.

With each step, Erik grew angrier with himself for following up on this anonymous tip. What could Bjørn's extra flat possibly have to do with Margit? Yet, if he didn't believe there was a connection, he wouldn't be on his way to see Britta.

He'd gone in for the tests with the new urologist yesterday, so within a few days, a week at the most, that question would be answered. As for the rest—well, perhaps there wouldn't be a need for other questions. Meanwhile, like an ass, he was chasing around town because of some sly bastard who enjoyed leaving cryptic notes on car windows. If he had any brains at all, he'd turn around right now and go home.

But he didn't.

He knocked at the door of Britta's flat, and she opened it immediately, smiling. "Hello, Erik. I'm so glad you called before coming over. I had intended to spend the afternoon in my sweats. I looked frightful."

She looked anything but frightful right now, dressed in tight jeans and a sexy white eyelet top. Her long blond hair, usually kept in a neat chignon at the office, fell around her shoulders in a silky curtain. Erik noticed all of this in a detached sort of way. He wasn't oblivious to the sexual signals Britta sent out in his direction; he simply wasn't interested. Kayleigh had done that. With her, sex had become more than just a physical meshing of bodies, something almost spiritual. He knew now he could never go back to the old days of casual sex. Not even if he and Margit—

What was he thinking about? Divorce? No way. Not if he was assured Gunny was his son. But if not? For the first time, Erik thought about what would happen if the second tests came back the same as the first. He'd be free of Margit. Really free.

"Would you like something to drink?" Britta asked. "A Coca-Cola or perhaps some coffee?"

"A cup of coffee sounds good," Erik said, and then wished he hadn't. Why not just ask her the stupid question and get the hell out? But he didn't know how to bring it up.

Britta returned to the small living room with two cups of steaming coffee. "Milk or sugar?"

"No. Just black."

"Ah, like a true Norseman." She handed him his coffee and sat down on the edge of the sofa. "Well, how was your birthday party? Were you surprised?"

Erik looked up at her, puzzled. "About what? And how did you know Tuesday was my birthday?"

"Margit told me about the surprise party she and Bjørn were cooking up for you. Did it work? Were you surprised?"

I am now, Erik thought. "No one had a party for me. Margit baked a cake, and we celebrated with a quiet evening at home. What's this about Bjørn and Margit planning a surprise party?"

"Oh, yes," Britta said. "Margit told me on the phone she had to talk to Bjørn about your birthday party. And she made it sound very hush-hush."

"When was this?"

She looked thoughtful. "Let's see—it was at least a month ago. Oh, I know! It was the day you came to the office to see Bjørn. She called after Bjørn left for the hospital, saying she was returning his call about the surprise party. Oh, well, I guess the plans fell through. Too bad. I love surprises, don't you?"

"It depends," Erik said. His mind turned over this bit of information. The whole thing sounded odd. So, Bjørn had called Margit at the day-care center just after Erik had left his office that stormy day. For what? A surprise party that had never come off? Thinking of Bjørn reminded him why he was here at Britta's flat. He decided to take the plunge. "Britta, what do you know about Bjørn's extra flat?"

A wary look crossed her face. "Bjørn doesn't have an extra flat."

But she said it too fast, and Erik knew she was lying. "Why are you protecting him?" he asked.

Abruptly, she placed her coffee mug on the end table and stood, her face reddening. "He's my boss. What am I supposed to do?" She moved over to the hearth and touched a small figurine of a Scottish terrier.

"Just tell me about the extra flat, Britta."

For a moment, she looked panicked; then gradually, her face calmed. She sighed. "I don't know much. About six years ago, he gave me a key and asked me if I could be discreet. He said he sometimes 'uses' a friend's flat. He didn't say what for, and I didn't ask. But of course, I guessed. I keep the key in my desk, and when he needs it, he takes it. No questions asked."

"You believe he has a mistress." It was a statement.

Britta shrugged. "I don't know of any other reason he would use someone's flat."

"Do you know when he usually takes the key?"

"Sometimes at lunchtime. Not every day, of course. Once or twice a week. And when I'm not here, he can come in and take it at any time. I don't keep my desk locked."

"Why did he give you a key? Why risk letting you in on his secret?"

She blushed. "He . . . hoped I'd join him there sometime. And I might have done so, except I knew there would be three of us. I don't get into that kind of thing."

Erik's mouth dropped open. "I can't believe it. Bjørn?"

She stared at him steadily. "How well do you know your brother?"

He stood and paced the room, his hands tunneling through his hair. He stopped and stared at her. "Could you find out who rents the flat? Who his friend is?"

"How?" Britta asked.

"You could follow him."

The panicked look returned to her face. "Oh, no, Erik. I couldn't do that. He's my boss!"

Erik strode to her. "Look, I'm not asking you to hang around and see who shows up. Simply get the name of the renter from the post." His blue eyes were compelling, and he knew it. "Please, Britta. I need your help."

She swayed toward him. "Oh, God," she whispered. "I must be crazy, but okay. I'll do it."

Her lips were just a few tantalizing inches away. Erik squeezed her shoulders briefly and smiled. "Thank you." He moved away from her. "You'll give me a call as soon as you know something, right?"

Britta's face clearly showed her disappointment, yet she managed a seductive smile. "Of course, Erik. You can count on me."

"Thanks." He moved toward the door. "I have to get going. Margit is expecting me home early this afternoon."

When Erik reached the sidewalk outside her flat, he took a deep breath and stared across the street at the campus lawn. Students taking summer courses were gathered in the cool shade of pines, studying for exams or trying to arrange an evening's date. Doing the kind of things college students did all over the world every day, year in and year out. But Erik saw none of this.

An image emerged in his mind, taking shape like a child's puzzle. The pieces were beginning to fit together, but the picture was one he didn't want to see.

39

Leigh hated the print of Munch's *Chamber of Death*, but still, it mesmerized her. One afternoon in late July, she almost took it down. That was the day Knut couldn't get up to go to the bathroom. He'd called to her and asked for a bedpan, his face burning with humiliation. Equally embarrassed, Leigh gave it to him, then left the room so he could have privacy. A few minutes later, he'd summoned her back in to take it away. His eyes had refused to meet hers. Instead, he'd stared up at the IV bottle.

"This is just the beginning," he'd whispered.

Leigh knew what he meant. Soon, he'd be too weak to get on the bedpan by himself. And then it would only be a matter of time before he'd be so incontinent he wouldn't have time to get on it at all. She tried to shake the ominous thoughts from her mind. There was still time before that happened. Wasn't there?

It was at that point when she'd almost taken the print off the wall. In fact, her hands were on the frame, ready to remove it. But she stopped. No. It wouldn't do any good. It would still be there, even if it were hidden away in a closet. The *Chamber of Death* wasn't just a vision in the mind of a long-dead artist. It was a reality, and it was in the tiny house on Kjelsasveien. After this realization, the painting became a comfort to her. She wasn't alone. Others had gone through this situation before.

Knut was moody for the rest of the day, more so after each session with the bedpan or urinal. When Leigh brought in his lunch, chicken broth, and toast with a cup of hot tea, he gave her a black stare and refused it.

Leigh tried to smile. "Oh, come on, darling. You need to eat to keep your strength up."

The remark had been made lightly, thoughtlessly. She wasn't prepared for his reaction. With all the strength he had left in his frail body, he sat up in bed, his face a gray wash of fury, and with one bony hand, he reached over and wrenched out his IV needle. Dark blood gushed from his open vein and trickled down his arm, spilling onto the white sheet.

"Knut!" Leigh dropped the tray on the bureau and rushed over to him.

"No!" His roar was that of a weakened, but enraged lion. "I don't want your fucking food! I don't want this fucking IV! I just want you to let me die! Do you hear me, Leigh? *Let me fucking die!"*

Leigh began to cry. "Your arm, Knut. Let me help—"

"No. Go! Just get out of here, and leave me the hell alone!"

"But Knut—"

"Please! I can't stand to see the pity on your face, Leigh." Tears streamed down his gaunt face. "Just go away. For a little while. Let me be alone."

With fists clenched helplessly, she stared at him. When she could no longer bear to look at his anguished face, she whirled and ran out of the room. Her fingers trembled as she dialed Sigurd at work.

"I'll be right over," Sigurd said crisply.

When she walked in the door a half hour later, Leigh had never been so glad to see another person in her life. Sigurd went immediately to Knut's room and shut the door. An hour passed. Leigh was sitting numbly at the table when Sigurd walked into the kitchen and put on a pot of coffee. A few minutes later, she placed a cup of the steaming brew in front of Leigh.

"Drink this," she said. "I've put a bit of aquavit in it for your nerves."

Automatically, Leigh lifted it to her lips, forgetting she'd vowed to never drink aquavit again. But it tasted good, and almost immediately she felt the calm begin to flow throughout her body.

The two women sat silently at the table and drank their laced coffee. Finally, Sigurd spoke, "The IV's back in. I've given him a sedative, but before he fell asleep, he asked me to tell you he's sorry. He loves you very much, and he didn't mean to hurt you. He'll tell you himself tomorrow, but he wanted you to know right now."

"I've never seen him like that," Leigh said.

"An independent man finds it very difficult to be helpless. And even though he's dying, he still has his pride. You are the woman he loves. A woman he was sexually involved with. It's only natural he doesn't want you to empty his bedpans and change his soiled sheets. He finds it humiliating."

"But he shouldn't!"

"He does." Sigurd took another sip of her coffee. "I think—" She looked Leigh in the eye. "—it's time we hire round-the-clock nurses for him."

They gazed at one another. Then slowly, Leigh nodded.

Erik heard nothing from Britta in the next two weeks. He decided she'd changed her mind about helping after all. And now, it seemed as if he'd reached a dead end. Unless he could find the person leaving the notes. Then another thought occurred to him. Perhaps he'd already found her. If Britta knew Margit and Bjørn were having an affair, maybe this was her way of discreetly informing the cuckolded husband. Obviously, she was interested in pursuing more than a friendly relationship with him. And if he were to find out his wife was unfaithful, Britta would be waiting on the sidelines to console him. But then, if that were the case, why not just come right out and tell him about Bjørn and Margit? Why the game of leaving mysterious notes on car windows? Erik didn't know what to think anymore.

Life with Margit had become more and more strained. He tried his best to carry on normally, but every time he looked at her now, he saw a stranger. She was no longer the sweet, quiet girl he'd grown up with, nor was she the forlorn young widow who'd struggled bravely to raise her young son in the face of adversity. This Margit, he didn't know at all any more. She had become a temptress, a siren. Even her reddish hair glowed with hidden sultry lights that beckoned to be disheveled by masculine fingers. From the beginning, her prowess in bed had surprised him. It had seemed so alien to her demure personality. But then he'd believed she was in love with him. That he excited her so much she happily discarded all inhibitions. Now, he wondered if the bedtime Margit wasn't perhaps the real Margit. Had Bjørn been her teacher all these years?

Erik had to know. Why hadn't Britta called? And another thing. The results of the tests he'd taken over two weeks ago still weren't in. He didn't know what was causing the delay. When he called the urologist's office for information, the receptionist had been evasive. But she'd assured him the doctor would call as soon as he had something to report.

That had been two days ago. Erik decided to try again, and this time, he would ask to speak to Dr. Borgen personally. It didn't work. The receptionist informed him that the doctor was with a patient, but she would have him return his call as soon as possible. Erik slammed down the phone. Before he could remove his hand, it rang.

"Yes?"

Her voice was smooth as honey. "Erik, it's me, Britta. I have the information you want."

His name was Egil Karlsefne, and he rented a small flat on Wilhelms Gate near Bislet Stadium. Near also to the childcare center where Margit worked, Erik thought ruefully. The flat was just a few streets away from the hospital where Karlsefne worked as a resident—the same hospital where Bjørn was on staff. Erik figured it was approximately halfway between the child care center and the hospital. Conveniently close enough for a one-hour lunch break.

As Erik had expected, there was no answer to his knock at the door. It was hard to imagine Margit arriving at this place for a rendezvous with Bjørn. Perhaps because it was so sleazy, and that was one word that, even now, he couldn't associate with his wife. Seductive, yes, but not sleazy. Still, he half-admitted to himself he'd gone to the flat on the chance he would catch her in the act. What would he have done if he'd seen her come out of the building, her face flushed by the excitement of recent lovemaking, her clothes rumpled and hastily donned?

He went on to the hospital. At the information desk, an attractive young receptionist told him Dr. Karlsefne was on duty in the emergency room, and would probably be unavailable for the rest of the day. Erik thanked her and turned to make his way to the emergency room.

Although it was only ten in the morning, the waiting room was filled with a conglomeration of ailing people. With a resigned expression on his face, Erik stepped over to the nurse at the triage desk.

"I need to speak to Dr. Karlsefne when he has a free moment."

The woman looked up at him and ran a nervous hand through her graying hair. "A free moment? I don't think he remembers what that is. But I'll give him your message."

The emergency room activity didn't slow down until nearly noon. Erik had almost given up on ever seeing the young resident when a figure appeared at his side.

"You wanted to see me?"

Erik looked up into the boyish face of a man with a punkish Kevin Bacon haircut, dressed in a white jacket over green surgical scrubs. His hazel eyes assessed Erik and then glimmered with recognition. "Hey, aren't you Bjørn's brother? I think we've met before."

Erik didn't remember him, but then he'd met so many of Bjørn's colleagues at various functions. He felt a vague stirring of apprehension. Suppose this guy was so loyal to Bjørn that he wouldn't volunteer any information? "Yes, I'm Erik. Listen, I know you're busy. I just wondered if I could ask you a couple of questions."

Egil Karlsefne plopped down on a chair with a relaxed grin. "Sure. What do you need to know?"

"Well, I'm aware you lend your flat to Bjørn occasionally. Has he ever told you why he uses it?"

Egil laughed. "Christ! Of course, he has never come out and said anything, but I can make a few guesses. The practice is not that uncommon around here. And a lot of us residents won't turn down an opportunity to make a few extra krone, if you know what I mean."

When it looked as if the resident had said all he would, Erik withdrew his wallet from his jeans and pulled out a fifty-krone bill. "I think I know what you mean. Will this help?"

Egil took the bill and slipped it into the pocket of his jacket. "I don't know who the woman is. I've never seen her. But one thing I do know. She's a redhead."

Erik's heart gave a lurch. "How do you know that?"

"Doctor!" The nurse from the triage desk appeared at his side. "Sorry, but you're needed back in emergency."

Egil stood up. "She left a hairbrush there last week, and it's full of long reddish-blond hair. I have to get back to work." He extended his hand. "Hey, if I can help out again, let me know."

Erik watched the young resident disappear back into the mysterious interior of the emergency room. So, Bjørn's mistress was a redhead. One more piece of the puzzle complete. But was it enough to see the entire picture? In his heart, Erik felt as if he already knew the answer. Margit and Bjørn were having an affair. Anne-Lise had suspected it back in France. And thinking back upon it, he remembered that day when Margit and Bjørn had stayed behind when everyone else went to the Nordic-Combined. A perfect opportunity for a tryst.

Erik stood. No, he didn't need to wait for the test results. He would confront her . . . tonight.

The phone was ringing when he entered their flat late that afternoon. Margit and Gunny weren't home from the child-care center yet. He dropped his lunch box on the counter and grabbed the phone. It was the receptionist at Dr. Borgen's office. His test results were in. Could he stop by the office tomorrow afternoon at four-thirty to talk to the doctor?

Erik hung up. Slowly, he moved to the kitchen window that overlooked the parking lot. Okay. One more day. He'd give it until then. Until he knew what the tests results were. As if there were any doubt . . .

He had trouble sleeping that night. Earlier, Margit had turned to him, pressing her breasts against him in the dark, sliding her cool, slim hands over his chest and abdomen. "Make love to me, Erik," she'd whispered. And he had turned away. Coldly and without explanation. He couldn't bring himself to touch her. Not now. Not until he knew. It had been several weeks now since they'd made love, and he knew she was mystified. But he felt no qualms. He didn't want her, couldn't bear the thought of touching her.

Tomorrow would almost be a relief. When he found out he was definitely sterile, it would give him the opportunity to end this sham he'd been living for the past twenty months. It would mean losing Gunny, of course, and the thought killed him. Yet, there was no way he could go through the rest of his life living with Margit and her lies. Not even for Gunny.

He thought of Kayleigh. Dare he return to the States? What about the man Mags had seen her with in France? Suppose she'd married him? He couldn't deal with that right now. First things first. Tomorrow. He had to get through tomorrow.

40

Erik stepped out of the medical center into the late afternoon sunlight, blinking against the glare. For a moment, he stood still because he couldn't remember where he'd parked. Only twenty minutes ago, he'd entered the building, prepared, or so he'd thought, for what Dr. Borgen had to tell him. It seemed like hours. Even days. How could so much change in a matter of minutes? He could still hear the urologist's words.

"You're perfectly healthy, Erik. Normal sperm count. No abnormalities of any kind. I think if you just give it time, you and your wife will be able to conceive."

His brain spun. Could it be true? Had it all been a mistake? Everything . . . starting with the results of Dr. Oien's tests. But then, what about all the evidence he'd compiled about Margit and Bjørn? Too many coincidences. And . . . here was something that had to be considered. Dr. Borgen was a close friend of Bjørn's, and God knows that doctors stuck together. Could Bjørn have "encouraged" Borgen to come up with the new test results? Christ, he didn't want to believe that! But so many things had come to light in the last weeks. Things he never would've believed his brother was capable of. Knowing all this, how could he *not* suspect these new results?

But then—what if the test results were true? That meant he really *was* Gunny's father. His heart spasmed as he thought of the little blond boy with the laughing blue eyes. His son. Oh, Christ, he wanted to believe that with all his heart. And now, on the heels of that thought, he felt a deep, enveloping shame. How readily he'd been about to give up all claim to Gunny in exchange for a life with the woman he loved. What kind of man did that make him?

He needed to believe those results. Needed to believe that Margit hadn't been playing him for a fool all along. Wasn't it possible that there was an explanation for everything he'd learned about Bjørn? After all, there were plenty of redheads in Oslo. That didn't mean Margit was the one he was sleeping with. Yet . . . the notes. What about the notes?

He shook his head. No answer for that. Another thought hit him, and his face grew warm. Wasn't it true that deep down inside he'd hoped his suspicions would be proved correct? So he would have an excuse to end his marriage to Margit. That was the most vile thing of all. To wish his son away so he could leave his wife. Only once before had Erik felt like such a scoundrel. On the night he'd told Kayleigh about his one night stand with Margit.

There was only one thing to do. He had to confront Margit. Show her the notes. Ask her flat-out. He would know if she lying. Wouldn't he? Something would give her away.

Right now, he wanted—needed—to get home to his son. Hold the boy in his arms and feel his warmth, breathe in his little boy scent. It was the only thing that would make the doubts go away.

On the way home, he stopped at a toy store and bought an elaborate fire truck for Gunny. Little enough to assuage his guilty conscience. If anything ever could.

When he pulled into the parking lot, he was pleased to see Margit's Saab already there. Good. It was time to find out the truth, once and for all.

He was just about to insert his key in the lock of their flat when he remembered he'd left Gunny's gift in the boot of the car. Shaking his head in disgust, he turned to go back to the parking lot.

As he bounded down the outside stairs to the ground, he saw a figure bending over the windshield of his car. Erik's eyes narrowed. There was something very familiar about the man's stance. He broke into a run.

"What the fuck are you doing?"

Hakon's head snapped up and his eyes darkened in fear when he saw Erik. His hand reached for the note he'd just placed under the windshield wiper, but Erik beat him to it. Roughly, he pushed Hakon away from the Volkswagen and grabbed the slip of paper. Out of the corner of his eye, he saw his brother-in-law start to slink away.

"You take one more step," Erik said grimly, "and you're going to be looking for your balls up your asshole." He unfolded the note and stared down at the green printing.

Ask your brother if his blood type matches Gunny's.

Erik's eyes stabbed into Hakon. The man quaked with fear. Erik grinned, but there was nothing warm in it. He walked over to Hakon and threw an arm around his shoulder, crushing his bone in a steel-banded bear hug. "What do you say, Hakon? Let's you and I go have a couple of beers. One brother-in-law to another."

Hakon smiled weakly. "Some other time perhaps . . ." Erik's grip on his arm tightened. "On second thought, now is as good a time as any."

"I thought you'd see it my way," Erik said.

*   *   *

Leigh opened the door to Sigurd's knock. Dully, she stared at her, too tired to even feel relief at her arrival. Sigurd grabbed her arm and searched her face, concern mirrored in her eyes.

"You aren't sleeping," she said.

"I can't. When I try, I have nightmares."

Sigurd dropped her purse on the floor and headed for the kitchen. "I'll put on some tea." Over her shoulder, she went on. "Is the nurse with Knut?"

Leigh nodded, but when she realized Sigurd wasn't looking at her, she followed her into the kitchen. "Yes, she's in there." She sat at the heavy pine table. "I think it's going to be over soon. Knut hasn't responded to anything in five days now."

Sigurd put the kettle on the stove and then sat opposite her. She looked at Leigh sadly. "That's not necessarily true. He could go on like this for months, you know. It happens."

Horrified, Leigh gazed at Knut's ex-wife. "You're not serious?"

She nodded. "I *did* warn you about this."

"Yes, but—oh, God, he looks so awful. And the pain! If he doesn't get the morphine every few hours, he's in agony."

Sigurd had no answer. They sat silently, both of them lost in their own thoughts. The shrill whistle of the tea kettle broke the silence. Sigurd got up to pour the water into cups. She brought two steaming mugs to the table and sat again. Without speaking, she stirred sugar into her tea and then folded her hands together and studied Leigh.

"Has Knut asked you to help him die?"

Leigh's stomach lurched. "He brought it up once. Or maybe it was a couple of times. I don't know. . . ." Wearily, she ran her fingers through her rumpled hair. "I told him I couldn't do it, and he dropped it."

Sigurd's voice was quiet. "Do you think it's right for a person to be forced to live when he's suffering? When he *wants* to die?"

"Of course not! But I can't help him. It's murder!"

"That's what some people will say. Others prefer to call it euthanasia."

"I don't care." Leigh shook her head. "It boils down to the same thing. Killing. And I can't do it."

They finished their tea in silence. Sigurd stood up. "Why don't you go lie down? I'll check on Knut."

Leigh nodded. She would try to sleep. If only the nightmares would let her.

Erik's mouth tightened as he left the pay phone in the bar. There was no doubt in his mind everything Hakon had told him was true. It all made sense. Finally.

His life was a sham. His marriage. His son. His brother. All a sham. And it had started years ago when Gunvor was still alive. Margit and Bjørn had been sleeping together while Gunvor was away on the North Sea. And Bjørn, not Erik, had fathered Gunny. Because Erik was sterile. With a smile of satisfaction, Hakon had repeated Bjørn and Margit's hurried conversation in the labyrinth. Yes, even his test results were a sham.

Erik climbed into his car and sat a moment, knowing he was too angry to drive immediately. Beside him, Hakon huddled, his face the shade of gray putty. Erik knew he was probably thinking about the upcoming confrontation with Bjørn. Unlike Hakon, Erik was looking forward to it. He would never forgive them for this. And it wasn't because of the affair or the deceptions. It was for a far more personal reason. If not for Bjørn and Margit, he would be in America today with Kayleigh. Almost two years out of his life had been wasted on an unfaithful wife and a child who, much as he loved him, wasn't his own. Those years he could never get back.

And Kayleigh? Was she gone forever, too?

He turned to Hakon and smiled. "Ready for the showdown?"

When the doorbell rang, Margit looked at her watch and smiled. She had a hunch it was Erik. He must have forgotten his key. Or else his hands were full of goodies for her. It would be just like him to come home with champagne and flowers to celebrate his reassurance of virility. Just as Bjørn had promised, his doctor-friend had changed the results of Erik's test. Now, she and Erik could get their marriage back on track. Of course, considering he really *was* sterile, there wouldn't be any babies in the future for them, but that was something they'd simply have to accept. Just one of those things. Actually, it was fine with her. Another baby would give her more stretch marks.

Margit still wore her grin when she opened the door. It faded. "What are you doing here?"

Bjørn walked into the apartment. "I was hoping *you* could tell me. Erik isn't home yet?"

Bewildered, Margit stared at him. "No. Is he supposed to be?"

His face was tense. "I just got a call from him. He told me he had to meet with me here. Said it was urgent."

Margit's heart gave a lurch. "What do you think?"

"How the hell do I know what to think?" Bjørn said. "I need a drink."

He strode to the liquor cabinet and mixed a gin and tonic. As he lifted it to his lips, the door opened. Bjørn and Margit looked up to see a grim-faced Erik.

"Where's Gunny?" he asked tersely.

Margit trembled at the cold look in his eyes. "He's taking his nap. Why?"

When Erik didn't answer, Margit summoned a smile to her lips and moved toward him. "What's wrong, darling? What did the doctor say?" Her hands slid up his shirtfront as she stood on tiptoe to give him a kiss. His lips were like ice. She drew away, her heart slamming in her chest.

He stared at her a moment, imagining his two hands slipping around her elegant throat, his thumbs settling over her fragile windpipe, then squeezing—

So, this is what it's like. To feel hatred—hatred so potent it makes you want to kill. His eyes slid to Bjørn. "He said," Erik said slowly, "that my sperm count is practically nonexistent."

The blood drained from Margit's face; Bjørn's flooded with color. "But there must be a mistake," he growled.

Erik smiled grimly. "The only mistake was the one you made in France, dear brother. In being so careless while you were screwing my wife." He glanced back at the front door. "You can come on in now, Hakon."

"Oh, God!" Margit looked as if she were going to faint.

Hakon walked into the room, wearing a look of fright mingled with satisfaction. He stole a quick glance at Bjørn and then fastened his gaze on Margit. His slight smile turned into a gloat.

"I told him everything," he said. "About that day in Albertville. And about the conversation I overheard between you and Bjørn in the labyrinth. Oh, you didn't know about that, did you? Yeah, I heard it all. How you two set him up from the beginning." He was obviously starting to enjoy himself. "Margit, you married Erik so it would be a good cover for your affair with Bjørn. And you, Bjørn, when you found out Erik couldn't be Gunny's father, you forged the test results." Hakon turned to Erik. "Oh, and did I tell you it was Bjørn who first came up with the idea of Margit marrying you?" He shrugged. "Who knows why, maybe Anne-Lise was getting suspicious. But when Bjørn discovered Gunny's blood type was incompatible with Gunvor's and Margit admitted the two of you had slept together, he decided to put this plan in motion."

"Now, just a minute!" Bjørn cut in. A vein throbbed in his forehead.

The possibility of a stroke entered Erik's mind. He was mildly surprised when he found he didn't care. "Shut up, Bjørn," he said, and nodded for Hakon to go on.

"And Margit, you accused Bjørn of being determined to get that American woman out of Erik's life. I wonder why she was such a threat. Was it because he was afraid Erik would go back to America with her? And then the two of you would have no reason to see each other at social functions."

Bjørn glowered at his brother-in-law. "You little cocksucker."

Suddenly Margit threw herself at Erik. "Darling, you have to believe me! He's a liar! He's saying all these awful things about me because I won't sleep with him." Her arms clung to his neck. Erik was reminded of a black widow spider spinning the deadly web around her prey. How had he never seen this in her before? "Erik, sweetheart, I love you! I would never do such evil things. This is all a fantasy in Hakon's sick mind."

Erik unhooked her arms from his neck and stepped back. "It was all a lie, wasn't it, Margit?" he said quietly, staring into her white face. "Even that night I spent with you after Gunvor died. You didn't love him. Even then, you were screwing my brother."

"That's not the worst of it, Erik," Hakon interrupted, a triumphant smile on his handsome face. "There was something else she said that day in the labyrinth. About the American woman, Kayleigh."

For the first time since he'd entered the apartment, Erik lost his composure. His body grew rigid. "What about her?" He could barely hear his own voice over the sudden drumming of his blood in his ears.

Margit took a step toward him. "Hakon, no!" Her voice came out in a ragged whisper.

Ignoring her, Hakon turned to Erik. "Do you remember a note you wrote to Kayleigh back in that hospital in Ose?"

Erik's hands clenched into fists. "Yes."

"She never received it. Why not ask Margit why?"

Slowly, Erik turned to her. He felt a red-hot curtain of rage falling before his eyes. "You didn't give it to her." His voice was deceptively soft.

Her face was sheet-white, her lips a slash of red where she'd bitten them. She didn't speak. There was no need. Her guilt was written all over her.

For a blinding moment, Erik imagined wrapping his fingers into the silky strands of her golden-red hair, pulling at her scalp, exposing her elegant neck to the glittering sharpness of a hunting knife. Slicing into her flesh, spilling her warm blood much like his Viking ancestors would've done centuries before. He trembled with fury; hatred raged through his veins, poisoning.

He took a step forward. She shrank back. But somewhere

in the deep recesses of his mind, he held onto his sanity. He moved past her to the bar where a glittering array of decanters stood filled with liquors of jeweled amber. In one violent movement, he swept them over the edge where they crashed to the hardwood floor, splintering into fragments of glass and bleeding liquid. Erik stared down at the mess, his chest heaving as he fought to control himself. Margit, Bjørn and Hakon stood stone-still.

Erik looked up, first at Margit, then at Bjørn. When he spoke, his voice was soft with contempt. "I loved her. But I don't expect either one of you to understand that."

"Mummy, what's wrong?"

Gunny stood at the door of the living room, rubbing his eyes sleepily. He yawned and looked over to see the broken liquor decanters. "Oh! Who made the mess?" His eyes caught Erik and he grinned. "Father!" On short stocky legs, he ran over to Erik and threw his arms around his knees. "Pick me up!"

Erik's hands gently touched Gunny's gold-red curls. He bent over and scooped the little boy into his arms. Gunny hugged him tightly, snuggling against him. Tears welled in Erik's eyes as his arms tightened about him. Over his head, he gazed at Margit and Bjørn.

"You've hurt *me*," he said softly. "But my God, have you thought about what you've done to him?"

For a long moment, he held the little boy close while the others stared at him, speechless. Heart aching, he turned his face into Gunny's sleep-warmed neck and breathed in his sweet scent. Then, with a challenging look at Margit and Bjørn, he turned and strode out of the room. When he reached Gunny's room, he settled the boy on his bed and sat on the edge next to him. For a long moment, he gazed down at Gunny's heart-shaped face, stroking his damp hair.

"What's wrong, Father?" Gunny's saucer-like blue eyes stared back at him. "You told Mummy you were hurt. Is that why you're crying?"

Erik blinked hard, his throat clogged with emotion. "Yes, Gunny," he said, his voice a ragged whisper. "I am hurt, but it's inside where you can't see it. I'm hurt because I have to go away. I don't know for how long, but it won't be forever. I'll come back and visit you. That's a promise."

Confusion clouded Gunny's eyes. "Is Mummy leaving, too?"

Erik shook his head. "No, son. Your mother will always be with you. But I . . . we won't be living together any more."

"Why not?" He seemed only mildly curious.

Erik closed his eyes. Christ, how to explain something like this to a four-year-old? Nothing to do but muddle through it. "It's just that . . . sometimes adults find themselves growing apart from each other. And they realize they will be happier if they don't live together anymore. That's how it is with me and your mother."

Gunny studied him solemnly. "You don't like Mummy any more?"

"Oh, Gunny." Erik stroked his head. "It's so much more complicated than that. I wish I knew the right words to make you understand."

Gunny chewed his bottom lip, a question in his eyes. "Do you still like me?" he asked in a soft, vulnerable voice.

That's when Erik lost it. He gathered the little boy into his arms and buried his face into his silky hair, tears streaming down his face. "Gunny, *yes*! I more than like you, I love you with all my heart. And that will never change. You've got to believe that, son."

Gunny clung to him, and for a long moment, Erik rocked the boy in his arms, struggling to compose himself. And suddenly it hit him. He could not, in good conscience, walk away from this little boy. Whatever happened, he *vowed* he would do whatever possible to stay in some capacity in Gunny's life. Even if it meant only occasional visits. And if Margit was cruel enough to object to that, he'd fight her. Take her to court if he had to. Gunny might not be the son of his flesh, but he would always be the son of his heart.

"*Unnskyld, Fru* Aabel. He is asking for you."

Blankly, Leigh looked up at the middle-aged nurse standing

in the doorway to the living room. What had she said? Her brain refused to function these days. How long had it been since the night Knut had surrendered himself to his hospital bed? Her unrealistic hopes of a recovery had dwindled away in the days that followed. How many days? Fourteen? Twenty? A month?

She'd finally accepted the reality. Knut was dying. But God, how long was it going to take? She couldn't remember the last time he'd been aware of her or the last time he'd spoken to her. It was just as he'd warned her when he'd told her of his mother. Inside that frail skeletal body, his heart still beat, still forced the cancer-ridden blood through tired veins, but the Knut she'd known was gone. What was left was only a spent shell.

"*Fru* Aabel, did you hear me?"

Leigh focused upon the nurse again. "I'm sorry. What did you say?" The poor woman! She was so confused. Not knowing which Mrs. Aabel was which. Sigurd was in and out so much it was entirely possible the nurse thought *she* was Knut's wife. Leigh had never volunteered the information that she and Knut had never actually married. What did it matter now, anyway? Her pain could be no deeper if she were his wife.

"*Herr* Aabel is asking for you."

The words finally sank in. On unsteady legs, Leigh stood and moved toward the nurse. "Are you sure?" she whispered. In her heart, she'd believed he'd never awaken again.

The nurse nodded. "You should hurry. I do not think he will be lucid for long."

A soft light glowed on the nightstand next to Knut's bed. Leigh approached him slowly, her heart thudding. She was afraid. Afraid of the way he would look, the things he would say. But when she finally reached the aluminum rails at the bedside, she saw it was already too late. He'd lapsed back into unconsciousness. A long shuddering sigh escaped her as she stared down at the man who used to be Knut. The pallid skin on his face had stretched into a death mask that molded to the brittle bones of his skull. Murky gray patches circled once laughing eyes that were now closed in comatose sleep. Purple-veined lines snaked over paper-thin eyelids and, at the corner of his dry caked lips, a thin stream of spittle trailed down his chin and onto the collar of his red-striped pajama top. Under the covers, a hard ball poked up from his midsection, testimony to the chronic constipation he suffered from the overuse of painkillers. "Oh, Knut . . . ," she said softly, and reached out to touch the bony hand that lay limply at his side.

His eyes opened. It was the only part of Knut she really recognized. Those lovely gray-blue eyes. He tried to smile at her, but it was more a grimace. His hand tightened into a fist as a wave of agony twisted his face.

Leigh bent over him. "Do you need another shot? I'll get the nurse."

"No!" From somewhere, he gathered the strength to clasp her hand.

"What is it, Knut?" Leigh cried out, near tears. "What can I do?"

Tears welled in his eyes. He summoned a deep breath, and his voice came out in a rasping plea. "Leigh, please . . . help me."

And she knew what he meant. No more shots or drugs. Just peace. He wanted her to give him peace. With those haunted eyes begging her, she said the only thing she could.

"Yes, Knut. I will. I promise."

41

Sigurd was the only one in the world that could help her with what she knew she had to do. But would she? It was after 11:00 P.M., and Sigurd was in with Knut now. She'd taken a leave of absence from her job at the hospital to share the nursing duties with *Fru* Flagstad. They'd worked out an arrangement for Sigurd to take the night shift so she could be home with Kristin during the day.

Shortly after Knut's brief lucid period, the teenager had arrived to visit with him as she did every afternoon. When she discovered he'd come out of the coma for a short time, she was heartbroken to have missed it. In spite of her mother's loving support, Kristin was having a difficult time dealing with her father's impending death. She'd left in tears at nine o'clock. Sigurd had been with him ever since.

Listlessly, Leigh got up from the sofa and moved into the kitchen to put on a pot of tea. Sigurd would be needing it soon. And she wouldn't be the only one. Caffeine wouldn't be a strong drug, not like aquavit or a good shot of whiskey, but maybe it would give her the courage she needed to say what she had to. But how? How could one say such a thing? That you wanted help with committing a crime. With . . . *Say it, Leigh. Murder.*

Because there was no other way to put it. Knut was asking her to commit murder. Pure and simple. Oh, sure. There were fancy names for it. Euthanasia. Ending the suffering. Putting out of misery. But it still boiled down to killing, didn't it, even if it had the word *mercy* tacked in front? Yet, Leigh knew she had to do it.

She thought back to the short, idyllic year they'd had together. That was something she'd been doing a lot lately. Scenes of their life together kept passing in front of her eyes. Knut had been the balm that had soothed the pain of her breakup with Erik. He'd been there for her during the troubled times with Mark, through Melissa's angst-filled moments. And he'd been there to protect her from Bob's hostility and futile attempts to win her back. He'd been a strong and stable presence in her chaotic life. A lifeline. Now, finally, it was her turn to be *his* lifeline, even if that line led only to death. But she couldn't do it alone. She would need Sigurd's help.

Just as she poured the steaming tea into dainty china cups, Sigurd walked into the room, moving silently on her soft-soled nurse's shoes. She slumped into a chair at the pine table and stared down at the burnished wood, her forehead resting against the heel of her hand. Without speaking, Leigh brought the cups of tea to the table and sat down opposite the Norwegian woman. Sigurd reached out for the sugar bowl and wearily pulled it toward her. After dropping two teaspoons of sugar into the tea, she stirred it slowly and then looked up at Leigh. Dark shadows rimmed her beautiful aquamarine eyes. Leigh realized she looked ten years older than she had on the day they'd arrived. How much had she *herself* aged since that day? She knew she *felt* ancient.

Sigurd took a sip of her tea and a hint of a smile touched her lips. *"Takk,"* she said. *"Det god."*

She was exhausted, Leigh knew. It was only when she was really tired that she lapsed into Norwegian. Maybe it wouldn't be a good time to bring this up. But then she thought of the agony on Knut's poor shrunken face, and knew it could wait no longer. Sigurd would understand, and she'd know what to do. After all, hadn't she mentioned it once before? She tried to recall the gist of the conversation, but all she could remember was the horror of the idea, and how she simply didn't want anything to do with it. That seemed like a million years ago when it had seemed so wrong to help a man die. Now— dear God—it seemed like the *only* right thing to do.

Leigh couldn't sit still. She jumped up and went to the refrigerator on the pretense of looking for something to eat. But it didn't fool Sigurd; neither of them had had an appetite for days. Leigh slammed the refrigerator door and whirled around.

"We have to help Knut die."

Sigurd looked up from her tea. She didn't speak.

Leigh moved back to the table. "Sigurd, please try and understand. He *wants* this. He begged me today. To help him." Desperately she clutched the other woman's arm. "We both know what he means. I can't bear to see him go on like this."

For a long moment, Sigurd didn't speak. Leigh held her breath, prepared for anything. Accusations, shocked reprimands, horror at her unspeakably monstrous suggestion. Sigurd moved suddenly, covering Leigh's grasping hand with her own. Her eyes were huge and somber. "It won't be much longer, Leigh. I promise you that."

Leigh's heart sank. What was she saying? No? Was she refusing to help her ex-husband? But how could she? She still loved him; Leigh knew that. It was obvious she and Knut had never lost the love they'd felt for one another. How could she sit there and refuse to help him die?

"You don't understand, Sigurd," Leigh said. "I *promised* him we would help him. Tomorrow. As soon as you can . . . surely you know how we can do it. Drugs. The right combination that will just let him drift into sleep. Sigurd, *please*—dear God, he needs us! This is the last thing he wanted. To lie in there like a helpless animal. But at least an animal would be put out of his misery!"

"Leigh . . ." Her voice was very soft. Her eyes drilled into Leigh's. "You have to trust me to do what is right. Okay?"

Leigh stared at her. Moments ticked by. Finally, her eyes dropped. "Okay. I'll trust you because I know you love him as much as I do."

Sigurd blinked quickly and looked down into her tea. But she couldn't hide the tears shimmering in her pale eyelashes. "*Ja*, I do love him. He was my first love. I met him at a ski-jumping meet outside of Tromsø. When I saw him sail into the air, I felt like my heart was sailing right along with him. We were married three months later." She stood and took her tea cup to the sink. When she turned around, the tears were gone and her face wore a curious anger. "I made the biggest mistake of my life when I returned to Norway and left Knut in America. I was a fool, and I knew it almost immediately. But I was too stubborn to admit my mistake. Anyway, I'm glad he found you. At least, I know he was happy in the last two years of his life."

Leigh's eyes blurred. She stood and crossed the small room to Sigurd. At first, the Norwegian woman's body was rigid, but as Leigh wrapped her arms around her, the tension eased away. They held each other tightly, allowing their love for the same man to flow over in the sweet agony of tears.

Leigh dreamed she was at the bottom of the ocean. She wore no tank suit, no life support system, yet, she breathed easily. A playful dolphin swam around her, knifing through the clear turquoise water, occasionally bumping against her as if to challenge her to a game of tag. Sunlight speared into the shal-

low depths, illuminating the hundreds of species of brightly
colored fish that cavorted in and out of the coral reef. She
followed the dolphin, somehow knowing it would lead her to
something she wanted desperately. The silhouette of a man
loomed in front of her, and as she grew closer, she saw it was
Knut. A perfect, whole Knut, ruddy with health. She opened
her mouth to speak, but nothing came out. His hand reached
toward her, beckoning. When she finally drew close to him,
she felt his fingers brush her cheek. He smiled and nodded.
Then he pointed back behind her in the direction she'd come.
A soft gentle push and she was floating away from him. "No!"
she tried to scream, but no sound came out. She wanted to
stay with him. But he shook his head, his eyes warm, but
determined. And again, he pointed. She turned away to look
behind her, but saw nothing except sunlit blue-green water.
When she turned back, Knut was gone. Once again, she moved
along the ocean floor. And now, ahead of her, another figure
waited. Beckoning her.

It was Erik.

She sat up in bed, heart pounding. For a moment, she looked
around the shadowy bedroom, sure Erik was there. It had been
so real, so clear. A soft tap came at the door. Leigh clutched
at the cotton of her nightgown as terror washed over her.

"It's me. Sigurd. May I come in?"

"Of course." Her heart bumped unsteadily as she looked
over at the alarm clock on the bedside table—4:18 A.M.
Why—? The door opened and Sigurd walked in, her shoes
whispering across the hardwood floor. Leigh ran her hands
anxiously through her disheveled hair. "What is it?"

Sigurd sat down on the edge of the bed. Her strong work-
worn hands reached out to clasp Leigh's. "It's time," she said,
her voice just above a whisper. "Do you want to be with him?"

Leigh's heart pounded and a dull ache spread through her
stomach. She nodded and threw back the covers. With trembling hands, she drew on her robe.

Sigurd was already back at Knut's bedside when Leigh
stepped into the room. With a growing dread, she moved
closer, her eyes sweeping the monitor measuring his vital

signs. It was erratic, bouncing all over the place like an old Atari game gone amok. Even as she moved to the bed, his blood pressure was falling at a terrifying rate.

"Knut?" She took his dry, waxy hand and leaned over him.

His eyes were half-open, but the glaze they wore told her he wasn't seeing anything in this world any longer She blinked back tears and swept a lock of his thin, brown hair away from his ghost-white forehead.

"Oh, Knut . . . I love you."

Across the bed, she felt Sigurd's eyes upon her, lovely aquamarine eyes shimmering with tears as she held his other hand. How very odd this all was. His ex-wife and his lover in the room together, sharing the intimate moment of his death. But it felt so right. As incongruous as it seemed, it was beautiful.

"*Ja*," Sigurd murmured, lapsing into Norwegian as she stroked his skeletal jaw.

Leigh had no idea what she was saying to her ex-husband, but one thing was clear. Her voice was full of love.

Knut's vacant expression didn't change, but Leigh hoped and prayed he could hear them and know he wasn't alone. Sigurd had told her days before that hearing was the last of the five senses to go, and that a dying person should always leave this world with the voices of their loved ones ushering them on.

Poor Kristin. She should've been here with her father in his last moments. But there apparently hadn't been time to call her. It wouldn't be until later that she'd realize the true reason Sigurd hadn't telephoned their daughter.

A harsh rattle came from Knut's throat. He shuddered. Leigh's eyes flew to Sigurd's. She was gazing at the monitor, her plain face blank, eyes haunted. Leigh followed her gaze and saw the flat line next to the respiration indicator. Yet, his heart beat on. The monitor beeped once, twice, three times, then it, too, became a flat line.

Slowly, Sigurd turned the switch off and the monotone hum stopped. She brushed her hand over Knut's eyes, closing them. Her eyes met Leigh's. "It was an easy death," she whispered.

"The last thing he heard were words of love. We should all be so lucky."

Leigh looked down at Knut, hoping to see an expression of peace in his ravaged face, but he didn't really look much different than he had in the last few weeks. Lucky? No. Sigurd was wrong there. No one who'd gone through the last four months of hell that Knut had could be called lucky.

"Would you mind if I have a moment alone with him?" Sigurd asked, her voice tentative.

Leigh shook her head. "Of course not." One last time, she brushed his hair back from his forehead, then turned to go.

A few minutes later, Sigurd joined her in the living room. "I've called the medical examiner." She sat down on the sofa opposite Leigh.

"I can't believe it's over," Leigh whispered. An expression of wonder crossed her face. "And I didn't have to do anything, did I? Isn't it weird? Just when I faced the fact I had to . . . help him . . ." Her voice trailed away.

There was something in Sigurd's eyes. It flickered for only a second and then disappeared. Leigh stared at her. Sigurd looked away, toward the window where the first misty light of dawn had appeared.

And Leigh knew the truth. That was why Sigurd hadn't called Kristin. If there was an investigation, she didn't want her daughter involved. At the moment their eyes had met, an unspoken understanding had passed between them. Sigurd stood.

"The medical examiner should be here soon. I'll put on a pot of coffee."

"Sigurd?"

"Yes?"

"There won't be a problem, will there? I mean—with the authorities? You'll be okay?"

She looked back, her eyes soft with gratitude. "I'll be fine. All of us will be fine."

Leigh's eyes followed her as she left the room, closing the door softly behind her. Sigurd was a brave woman. It was no wonder Knut had loved her so deeply.

Knut. After Sigurd left the room, her tears began again, washing down her face in a slow, but cleansing river. Different tears than all the others she'd cried in the last months. Because with the sorrow she felt for Knut's death, she felt another emotion, one she'd never expected to feel. It was relief.

He was finally at peace.

As Erik inserted the key into the flat's lock, he heard the phone ringing. Good. Margit had kept her word and was staying away while he packed his belongings. He strode over to the wall phone in the kitchen.

"Haukeland residence. Erik speaking." Not for much longer, he thought wryly. In less than an hour, there would no longer be an Erik Haukeland at this address.

"Hello?" Erik said again. But whoever it was had hung up. He put the phone back into its cradle, a grim smile on his lips. It was probably Bjørn, calling for Margit. Was he wondering if Erik was back to stay?

"You can have her, Bjørn," Erik muttered as he made his way to the bedroom. "You two were made for each other."

In the bedroom, he drew out the large Samsonite suitcase from the closet. All he wanted were his clothes and his books. Margit could have everything else. A few days ago, he'd moved in with an old college friend. The arrangement was strictly temporary. Because within a few days, he planned to leave for America. Not forever. Just for long enough to find out whether he had a future with Kayleigh. He placed the last of his books in a box and closed the lid of the suitcase. There was one last thing he had to do.

The call to Directory Assistance in the USA went through immediately. His voice trembled slightly as he read Leigh's address to the operator in Washington, D.C. A moment later, he had her phone number. A strange voice answered on the third ring.

"She's out of the country," the voice said. "I'm supposed to refer any calls to Deanna Harper in New York. You want the number?"

Erik scribbled down Deanna's number and hung up the

phone, his mind whirling. Maybe he wouldn't be going to America after all. Where had Kayleigh gone? There was only one way to find out. He dialed Deanna Harper's number.

The phone picked up, and Erik heard Deanna's nasal Brooklyn accent as if she were next door. He spoke quickly, hoping she wouldn't hang up. "This is Erik Haukeland, calling from Norway. You have to help me get in touch with Kayleigh. It's imperative that I talk to her."

There was a short, stunned silence. Then, "Well, god*damn*! Erik Haukeland. Listen, sweetie, you're calling the wrong part of the world. She—shit. She'll probably kick my ass if I tell you, but what the hell! I like you, Erik, in spite of the way you fucked her over. And she sure as hell loves you. Look, I'll tell you where she is, but before you go flying off the handle, you have to listen to the circumstances."

Erik's hand tightened upon the receiver as she talked. He grabbed the notepad and scribbled on it. When Deanna finished, he cleared his suddenly husky voice. "*Ja*, I understand. Thank you, Deanna. I'll never forget this. *Ja*, I'll tell her. Good-bye."

For a moment, he stood stiffly, his hand clutching the phone. Still in a state of shock, he tore the page from the notebook and stared down at the name and address Deanna had given him. Kayleigh was here. In Oslo. Just across the city. And had been here for almost three months. How was it he hadn't known? Hadn't sensed it? Suddenly, he remembered the day at Frogner Park. The blond woman hurrying down the steps from the fountain. Dear God, could it have been—?

Somewhere in the back of his brain, he heard the front door open. The musky scent of Margit's perfume preceded her into the room. He folded the slip of paper and tucked it into the pocket of his jeans. He turned to her, his body rigid.

"You told me you wouldn't be here," he said.

The paleness of her face made her freckles stand out like lighted beacons. She bit her lip nervously. "I know. But I had to come. I have to talk to you."

"The only thing we have to talk about is Gunny," Erik said

shortly. "You're not going to stand in the way of my visitations, are you?"

"Of course not, Erik. He loves you. He believes you're his father."

"Fine." Erik brushed past her to get his things from the bedroom.

She followed and stood in the doorway. "I don't expect you to forgive me. I know the things I did were wrong. But Erik, you must believe I really didn't think you loved her. I thought your infatuation would pass, that we could make our marriage work."

"Yeah? And did you also think fucking Bjørn was going to help our marriage? Oh hell, Margit!" Erik turned away and grabbed his suitcase. "This was exactly why I didn't want you here. Don't you understand? There's nothing left for us to say to each other."

"But there is!" Margit protested. "Erik, remember when Gunny was in hospital for taking those pills? I broke it off with Bjørn then. And I began to fall in love with you. Don't you remember? We were happy then."

"We were?" Erik said, his lips twisted in a sneer. "And that's why you crawled back into his bed when we were in France?"

Margit flushed angrily. "I crawled back into Bjørn's bed because your mind was on that American slut of yours!"

Erik stared at her and then spoke very softly, "Get out of my way."

She did. But as he reached the front door of the flat, she spoke again. "Like I said before, I don't expect you to forgive *me*. But Bjørn is another matter. He's your brother, Erik. And he's miserable. Please go talk to him."

Erik paused at the door, his jaw tightening. "I can't do it, Margit," he said. "Not now. God help me, I don't know if I can ever forgive him." For the last time, he went through the door of Margit's flat, closing it firmly behind him.

42

Leigh hung up the phone and turned to look into Sigurd's questioning eyes. "He's there."

"So. You're going?"

Leigh nodded and turned to the knapsack on the bed. She rolled up a heavy cardigan and stuffed it in with her change of clothing. The nights were getting cool. "I can't really explain this, Sigurd," she said. "It's like something is calling me back there. It was just a traumatic period of my life and—"

"I understand," Sigurd said. "You feel a need to confront the past."

Leigh zipped up the knapsack and sat on the edge of the bed. She shook her head. "I don't know. I just have to go back."

Sigurd was silent for a moment. Then, "If you really want to confront the past, shouldn't you meet with Erik?"

Leigh's heart jumped. "No." Her fingers twisted in the cord of the knapsack. "I don't ever want to see him again. That's why I had to make sure he was in Oslo."

A cool breeze drifted in through the opened window of the bedroom. Sigurd stood and wandered over to stare out into the afternoon sunshine. "I feel very honored you felt close enough to share your story about Erik. Now, I hope you won't be offended if I give you some advice. I think you should see him. It's obvious you still love him. No, don't interrupt me, I *know* you loved Knut. But even so, you've never stopped loving Erik."

"Sigurd, I—"

She held up her hand. "Please, Leigh, let me finish. You're not being disloyal to Knut by being in love with Erik. You loved Knut with everything you had, but that had nothing to do with your love for Erik. Knut is gone. You're here in Norway. Erik is here. And from everything you've told me, I believe it's very possible he still loves you. Why not see him? What could it hurt?"

Leigh shook her head. "But what if he *doesn't* love me? What if Margit was telling the truth in the park that day? I don't know if I can bear seeing him and hearing him admit that to me."

"One thing you're not, Leigh, is a coward. You've proved that during this ordeal with Knut. How can you go back to America without seeing Erik? Without knowing for sure how he feels?"

Leigh stood up and grabbed the knapsack. "My train leaves in an hour. We should get going."

Sigurd stared at her a moment, then shrugged. "As you wish."

It was the second time a train had swept her through the fertile valleys of Setesdal, but this time, instead of a thick carpet of snow, the ground was covered with emerald grass and lush green forests in a kaleidoscope of changing scenery. Glasslike blue lakes and picturesque farms dotted the landscape along with grazing cows and flocks of sheep tended by white-blond shepherd boys. Through the train windows, she caught thrilling glimpses of sheer gray cliffs and deep, blue-green fjords fed by vertical waterfalls. It looked just as Erik had told her it would in summer.

Why, *really*, was she going back to Byglandsfjord? What did she think she'd find there? Peace? An answer to her confused feelings? Balm for her grief at the loss of Knut?

She didn't know. It was just like she'd tried to explain to Sigurd. Something was calling her back. And she knew she couldn't leave Norway without seeing the cabin one more time. Perhaps it *was* time to confront the past.

Or more realistically, maybe it was time to say good-bye to it.

Sigurd turned right onto Kjelsasveien. As she neared the tiny house where Knut had died, her foot automatically went to the brake pedal and her left hand to the blinker. With a start, she clenched the steering wheel and pressed on the accelerator. She wondered if she'd ever break the habit. Would she ever be able to go by this house again without thinking of him? She was a nurse. Over the years, she'd seen hundreds of patients die. She'd thought she'd been prepared for Knut's death, too, but that wasn't true. Perhaps it was a little naive to believe one could ever be prepared for the loss of a loved one.

A yellow Volkswagen was parked in front of her house. She pulled into the driveway and turned off the ignition. A man stood up from the front porch step and came toward her. He was tall and blond.

Sigurd knew exactly who he was.

Leigh parked the rented Saab on the steep incline behind the cabin and pulled on the parking brake. She opened the door and stepped out. Except for the lack of pristine snow nestling around it, the cabin looked exactly as it had on that December evening almost two years ago. A cool mountain breeze rippled through her hair. She pulled her sweater more snugly around her, glad she'd decided to wear jeans, thick socks, and hiking boots. There was a definite nip in the air. The silence of the mountain wrapped around her. She heard only the sound of the wind rustling through the pines and the tranquil song of birds in the trees.

The late summer air was fragrant with the scent of pine needles that crunched under her feet as she climbed the hill overlooking the fjord. When she reached the top, a soft sigh escaped her as she took in the awesome sight. Far below, the deep, green waters of the Byglandsfjord glimmered in the afternoon sunlight. She remembered Erik's words, about how beautiful the fjord was in summer. At the time, she was sure she'd never be here to see it. Yet, here she was. But under such strange circumstances. If Knut hadn't been struck with cancer, if he had never walked into the art gallery, if she hadn't allowed herself to love him—

She blinked quickly. No crying. She'd cried enough. She turned back to the cabin. The key would probably be under the doormat, just as it had been that night. As she walked around to the front door, she wondered why she was doing this to herself. Was she being a masochist? Opening up old wounds, and for what purpose? To purge herself of what? Guilt? Love?

She stared down at the key. No one was around. They'd never know she'd trespassed. Her hand reached for the key. A moment later, she was inside, gazing at the familiar surroundings. There was the fireplace she'd sat in front of, drinking aquavit to relieve her hacking cough. And there, in the kitchen area was the water pump, the one that had frozen during the blizzard.

Her gaze centered on the bed, still covered with the same homemade country quilt. On that bed, she'd waited alone for Erik to come to her, and when he hadn't, she'd gone to him. And on that bed, he'd taken her into his arms, to warm her during the chilling spells caused by the pneumonia. Slowly, she walked into the tiny bedroom.

Ah, *this* bed held memories. She sat down on the edge of it, her hand moving softly across the embroidered linen. Yes, in this bed, she'd been brought to the heights of passion by an intense and angry Erik. And it was also in this bed that he'd tortured her with a cold sponge bath to bring down her raging fever. A sad smile came to her lips. It hadn't been easy for him. She could still see the agony in his eyes as he'd pressed the wet sponge to her naked skin.

Suddenly, in that moment, she knew.

Margit had lied. Erik would *never* have defiled what they'd had together with those ugly words. How could she have let her insecurity allow her to believe that for a moment?

Still, it didn't matter anymore. It was all in the past. Leigh could believe that now. Finally. Obviously, Margit loved Erik a great deal, otherwise she wouldn't have felt so threatened. Leigh just hoped he was happy.

She had a lot to thank him for. He'd awakened a dormant part of her, one Bob had never bothered to explore. He'd brought love into her life, an emotional crazy high that rivaled the best of roller-coaster rides, and inadvertently, he'd brought another kind of love to her, the quiet and comforting love of

Knut. If it hadn't been for her love of Erik, she would never have met Knut.

There was, yet, another gift Erik had brought her. Independence. If not for Erik, how long would she have stayed married to Bob, existing in an unhappy relationship, too afraid to reach for a new life? And when she'd finally gathered the courage to do just that, she'd learned she *could* live without a man. That she could make it on her own. Because of Erik, she had no fear of the life ahead of her. She would go back to Washington, back to her Georgetown apartment, and her job at the art gallery. Perhaps someday, she would own her own gallery. Or perhaps she would concentrate on her art. It wasn't impossible she might have a New York showing someday.

She supposed she *had* returned to this isolated cabin in the mountains of Aust-Agder to say goodbye to Norway—and the past. She stood and went to the door. Her eyes lingered on the tiny room as she stood in the doorway.

"Good-bye, Erik," she whispered.

Outside, she placed the key under the mat and stepped down from the porch. There was one other place she had to say good-bye to before the long drive back to Kristiansand.

Erik's heart pounded as he maneuvered the rented Fiat up the winding mountain road. Only a few more minutes now. She *had* to be there. That woman, Sigurd Aabel, had been positive Kayleigh had gone to Byglandsfjord. *Please, God, she has to be right.*

How long had it been since he'd last seen her? Almost two years. God, it seemed like forever. It seemed like yesterday. What would he say? How could he convince her of his love? Would he find the right words?

His throat felt as if an iron claw had tightened around it. What if no words would come? And if they did, what would he do if she rejected him?

He rounded the last curve and the cabin came into sight. Suddenly he found it difficult to breathe. There was no car parked there. But how else could she have come up the moun-

ain? Dear God, could she have come and gone already? He
didn't waste time pulling the car around the back, but parked
at the side of the cabin and put on the brake. In four huge
strides, he reached the porch and tried the door. Locked. An
icicle of fear prickled down his back as he swept the mat away
and stared down at the key, his eyes blurring with tears of
disappointment.

She wasn't here.

Still, he had to make sure. His hands shook so badly he
dropped the key as he tried to fit it into the lock. Cursing, he
grabbed it and tried again. This time, his hand worked and the
door creaked open. He walked in, knowing deep in his heart
he would find the place empty. His eyes scanned the room.
Nothing out of place. It was all just the way his mother had
left it on their last holiday here. What had he expected?

He walked into the small bedroom. Everything was immaculate. He sat down heavily on the bed. Now, what? He closed
his eyes, and suddenly she was there, beside him. He felt her
presence, smelled her scent. But when he opened his eyes, he
was still alone.

He wanted to scream out his pain, pummel the walls, kick
and fight and plead for her to come back. But he did nothing.
It wasn't over. He would go to America. Find her. Convince
her they belonged together. He would swallow his disappointment. He'd so wanted to see her again, right now. To feel her
in his arms, taste her lips. But that could wait. It would happen.

Back out at the car, he hesitated, and then, on impulse,
strode around the side of the cabin. He stopped, frozen in his
tracks, and stared at the blue Saab.

His heart began to race.

The roar of the waterfall drowned out all other sound. Reiardsfossen. Leigh stood near the precipitous cliff and gazed at the
breathtaking sight in front of her. The froth of white water
surged from the top of the smooth gray rock, knifing down in
a sheer drop for hundreds of feet into the narrow gorge below.
She thought of the first time Erik had brought her here. They'd

both been so full of pain then. She tried to remember the way she'd felt that day, but it seemed like a hundred years ago.

Today, there was no pain; even the memories of Erik no longer hurt. There was only peace here now, and this was the way she'd remember Reiardsfossen. Not for the tragedy of Reiard and his lovely Anne who'd died here. Not for Erik and their impossible love for each other. But for the peace she felt now and the acceptance of events in her life she had no control over.

She looked down at the sterling silver ring on her finger, at the initials of *E* and *K* entwined. The symbolic thing to do, of course, would be to throw it off into the gorge below. But she knew she wouldn't do it. Couldn't make herself do it.

There was no sound or movement to alert her of another presence behind her, but she felt it all the same. Erik had taught her to move slowly so as not to startle the wildlife in the area. She thought of the fox that had crept up behind them last time. Almost imperceptibly, she turned her head and out of the corner of her eye, she saw the form of a man. A hunter probably. She turned to call out a greeting.

The breath left her body in one startled gasp. Erik's blue eyes drilled into her. His face wore a strange expression, a mixture of elation, fear and longing. He stood stiffly, unable to move. Leigh was frozen, too.

Thoughts raced through her mind, one after the other. But only one of them mattered. *I still love him. It can't work between us, but I can't stop loving him.*

Still, she could say nothing. A century went by before Erik finally moved. He walked toward her. It was the signal Leigh needed to unlock the muscles of her body. She took a step forward to meet him. His face changed. Became vulnerable. Tears sparkled in his eyes. Inches away, he stopped.

When he spoke, his voice was husky, almost a croak. "Kayleigh . . ."

She moved. And his arms closed around her.

The late afternoon shadows lengthened inside the cabin, making it difficult for Erik to see Kayleigh clearly across the room.

For hours, they'd talked. Poured everything out to each other. Her time with Knut, Margit's deception, their near meeting in France. They'd said everything except what was really important. Neither of them had broached the subject of their feelings for each other.

It was as if they were suddenly shy teenagers. Strangers. Now that the moment was at hand, Erik found he was afraid to ask her if they could start again. For the first time in his life, he feared rejection. He didn't know if he could stand it if she refused him. So, he said nothing.

A silence had finally fallen between them. Leigh glanced nervously around the room and then looked down at her wristwatch. "God! Look at the time. I don't want to have to drive down this mountain in the dark." She stood.

Erik's heart jumped. She couldn't leave! He stared at her. His mouth opened but nothing came out. She stood stiffly, making no move toward the door. Or toward him. Since that first embrace out by the waterfall, they hadn't touched. And every second she'd spent here in the cabin with him, he'd had to consciously force himself not to go near her. He was afraid of losing control, pushing things too fast and forever losing the chance to bring her back into his life. And now, she was leaving, and if he didn't do something or say something, he would lose her.

Leigh cleared her throat. "I'm glad you were here today. I was always sorry we hadn't said good-bye before."

Good-bye. She was saying good-bye. Why couldn't he move? Where was his voice? Jesus Christ, what was wrong with him? He was frozen, like a statue, like one of goddamn Vigeland's sculptures.

"Well . . ." Something caught in Leigh's throat. She swallowed hard. He thought he saw a glimmer of tears in her eyes. "I have to go." She turned and went to the door.

Suddenly Erik's paralysis disappeared. In the second it took her to open the front door, he was there and with one hand, he slammed it closed. Her hazel eyes gazed up at him, wide and questioning. Erik stared down at her. Yes, there were tears there. His eyes devoured her, lingering softly on her parted lips, caressing her lovely breasts as they rose and fell with her taut breathing. They stared at each other, their eyes speaking what words could not. But Erik knew it wasn't enough to make her stay.

"I love you," he said.

Her eyes flickered, but still, she didn't speak.

"I've never stopped loving you," he went on. "And I think, God, I *hope* you still love me. Because I'm following you back to America, and I'll haunt your every step. I'll never give up until I make you love me again, Kayleigh. I swear it. And please, I don't want to hear your objections about the age difference, or about how your children detest me." His voice was low, urgent. "I don't give a *damn* about any of your objections. I just know I can't live without you, Kayleigh. And I won't any longer."

"Erik . . ." She reached out to touch his jaw, her hand trembling. Her mouth lifted toward his.

It was enough for Erik. He grabbed her shoulders and his mouth clamped down on hers, his tongue searching her familiar sweetness. Like a parched desert wanderer he drank in her goodness, the essence of her that had been missing from his life for so long. There was no longer any doubt in his mind. She still loved him.

Reluctantly, he dragged his mouth away from hers and swept her into his arms. He gently placed her on the bed and then covered her body with his own, careful not to put his full weight upon her. In her glazed eyes, he saw the desire shimmering there, and he remembered she'd looked the same way that wintry day they'd first made love. But now, it was so different. They were both free, or would be very soon.

"You'll stay tonight?" he whispered.

Her tongue moistened her kiss-smudged lips. The memory of her dream returned to her—the ocean depths, Knut's warm blue eyes, his gentle push propelling her back to Erik's waiting arms. Slowly, she nodded. "I'll stay with you forever, Erik. Here. America. Anywhere in the world."

His sigh of relief was audible. He slumped against her and then rolled over on his side, pulling her with him. His hands wrapped around her and gathered her close, stroking his face against her silky hair. He closed his eyes, inhaling her sweet fragrance. The desire to make love to her hadn't ebbed; his body called out for her, for this woman who'd changed his life, the only woman he'd ever loved. But the lovemaking could wait. They had many, many more afternoons of long, slow loving. The rest of their lives. For now, it was enough to just hold her close.